His Gaze Brought Out
the Devil in the Angel . . .

He was awake. Watching her.

A part of her tried to look away, but he beckoned, and she was magnetically drawn to him. His gaze held her suspended, breathless. Time passed. She didn't know how much. Then, slowly, very slowly he lifted the cover from his body, inviting her to join him. To lie next to him. To touch him. Feel the heady warmth of his bare body pressed against hers. To hold. To enfold.

Rachel's trembling fingers reached for the set of ribbons that trapped her in the nightgown.

Jake knew he was either dreaming or hallucinating.

She wanted him as much as he wanted her; he could see it in her eyes . . .

CAPTIVE ANGEL

ELAINE CRAWFORD

DIAMOND BOOKS, NEW YORK

This book is a Diamond original edition, and has never
been previously published.

CAPTIVE ANGEL

A Diamond Book / published by arrangement with
the author

PRINTING HISTORY
Diamond edition / September 1992

ISBN: 1-55773-766-5

Diamond Books are published by The Berkley Publishing Group,
200 Madison Avenue, New York, New York 10016.
The name "DIAMOND" and its logo are trademarks
belonging to Charter Communications, Inc.

PRINTED IN THE UNITED STATES OF AMERICA

10   9   8   7   6   5   4   3   2   1

THIS BOOK IS DEDICATED TO

BYRON CRAWFORD, my husband, who always believes in me whether I deserve it or not.

DON STANSBURY, my first Creative Writing teacher, for his encouragement and gentle instruction.

DEBBY BAILEY (DEBORAH JAMES), SALLY LAITY, JEANNIE LEVIG, and SUE RICH, constant friends and unfailing critics.

ROB COHEN, my agent, and MELINDA METZ, my editor, for making this publication possible.

Thank you.

⦅ chapter 1 ⦆

April, 1853

FIRE *engulfed the ship. She dodged through the burning debris. Flames licked all about her, up the masts, along the rigging. Tatters of blazing sails flailed in the wind. The ship was doomed, yet fiery arrows still pierced the night sky, arcing from the evil dragon ship of the Vikings. One struck her skirt, pinning it to the deck, setting it ablaze. Fire chased up toward her face. Her frantic fingers ripped the dress from her body, baring agonizingly white flesh that shouted its nakedness against the flaring reds and yellows.*

She ran for the railing. Climbed on top. Looked down, into a black swirling pool. *Jumped back to the deck, and whirled around.* What to do? *Burn, be sucked into the bottomless ocean, or die at the hands of the Viking plunderers . . . after they . . . ?*

The direful ship banged alongside, and Norse pirates swung aboard on great long ropes, crashing down, one after another in their armor-clad vests and horned helmets. Then she saw him. *He hit the deck with the grace of a pouncing panther. He stood head and shoulders above the rest, his body bulging with muscled strength. A burning bush from out of hell covered the lower half of his face, while his glittering emerald gaze darted about, looking, searching.*

Then, he found her. He smiled, a slow, menacing leer, his gaze sliding down her starkly bare form.

Her feet finally reacted to the racing of her panicked

1

pulse. She sprinted for the rail. It shrank from her. Farther and farther.

The Viking's footsteps pounded. Closer.

Straining, stretching, she reached for the rail.

An immense hand gripped her arm. Jerked her back.

"Miss Chambers. Wake up."

Rachel Chambers's eyes flew open to see Mr. Dorset's pudgy hand squeezing her arm. She gasped and sprang to her feet. A volume of *The Viking Lore of Eric the Red* slid from her lap and hit the floor with a bang. "Oh, dear." She reached down and swept it up.

"Don't worry about it. It's been tossed around for years," replied the balding storekeeper. His roll of a face dimpled with a grin. "Sorry to wake you, but Jake Stone's here. Come on out and meet your intended."

Rachel Chambers's heart tripped over itself, then began to thud with such force her ears rang. "I'm sorry, Mr. Dorset, what did you say?"

"He's here. Jake's finally here."

"I see." She hoped the proprietor didn't detect the quaver in her voice. "Where is he?"

"Out front, in the store."

"Thank you." She clasped her hands together to still their trembling. "Tell Mr. Stone I'll be out shortly."

Rachel stared after Homer Dorset, the chubby merchant who, without complaint, had kept her small stove burning and fed her during the worst days of her illness. As he shut the door behind him, the room closed in around her—this drafty, cluttered storeroom in far-off Oregon where she'd spent the past two weeks recovering from malaria . . . these last two weeks alone awaiting the incredibly tardy stranger.

And now he'd finally come. She should be thrilled to leave this dingy room. But, to marry a complete stranger? A knot lodged in her throat. She must, she had no choice.

Rachel reached up to tighten the pins securing her

honey-colored hair, but her hands did more damage than good to her chignon. Turning to fetch her mirror off a crate, she caught her black grosgrain skirt on a splinter. "Oh, my," she moaned as her fear-numbed fingers worked to dislodge the fabric.

Why couldn't he have come yesterday when she'd worn her blue gabardine? It didn't make her look so sickly. Maybe she had time to change. No, she'd said she'd be right out.

She picked up the looking glass framed in an elegant swirl of silver. The face that stared back at her was a ravaged shadow of what it had been five months ago. The delicate contours were now sharpened by hollows, and her eyes seemed to dominate her face. She certainly didn't look like her mother's "little porcelain doll" now. Rachel brushed a finger across her cheek, so thin and drawn, then touched the dark circles under her eyes.

Mr. Stone was out there waiting. How could she greet her husband-to-be looking like this?

She peered more intently into her reflection. A sickly yellow tinged the feature she had always considered her best, her almost transparent silvery-blue eyes. Sighing, she flipped the mirror over and placed it once again on the wooden box.

With the scantest resolve, she relaxed her face into a placid expression and turned toward the door.

What if he refuses to marry me? she thought. But who knows, maybe my illness is a blessing in disguise. He could be old and ugly. Her gaze darted to the book lying on the crate. Or worse, a barbarian. And he wants me no matter what. She looked toward the rear exit. She could escape. But to where? To what? It's marry him or return to prison.

"Well, what's keeping her?" A very masculine voice rumbled from the other room. The mellow timbre instilled her with courage. With a trembly hand, she opened the door.

The men stood with their backs to her. The stranger, whose coarsely woven gray shirt stretched across the widest shoulders she'd ever seen, towered above the portly merchant. Staring at the giant, Rachel felt even smaller than her five feet three inches and far more emaciated.

"She's probably just splashin' on some perfume or some such foolishness." The one wispy curl on Mr. Dorset's bald pate bobbed as he chuckled. "Speaking of foolishness, did you know Bone and Leland Cooter signed up for wives, too?"

"Bone and Cooter?" The big man dipped his blond head in Mr. Dorset's direction. "I've never known those two yahoos to have more'n two nickels to rub together. Where'd they come up with enough cash money to send for wives?"

"My guess is McLean."

"McLean? Kyle McLean?"

"Yeah. He's been comin' up from Oregon City real regular. He's even set up an office over at the hotel. And Charley Bone and Leland has come in to see him ever' time."

"Come in?" The high shine of Mr. Stone's freshly polished boots caught the window light as he stepped closer. "From where?"

"If you hadn't been over to the coast loadin' loggin' schooners, you'd know. Them two good-for-nothin's has homesteaded that stretch just north of you. You know, the land betwixt you and McLean's holdin's. And now that they got wives, they'll be able to file on twice the land."

"I see." Muscles bunched across Mr. Stone's beamlike shoulders. "And you think McLean's planning to log it off?"

"More'n likely. A tinker come through here the other day. Said a bunch of homesteaders up on the Columbia has quit their places and left 'em to McLean's crew to log off."

"What about the land recorder? Didn't Harvey Best have something to say about that?"

"That citified dandy? I don't see him goin' against a big-time operator like McLean. Fact is, the last time he come through to record claims, he and Mr. McLean had supper together."

"That so?" Mr. Stone jammed his hands in his pockets, and Rachel couldn't help staring at the way the denim strained across his lean hips. "When's Best coming through next? I'll be needing to record my wife's section when he gets here. It *is* still there waiting for me, isn't it?"

"Oh, sure. Harvey's not that dumb. He's comin' by again next month. When he does, I'll get word to you."

"Thanks. What's keeping that woman?"

Rachel swallowed hard. "Gentlemen?"

The men swung to face her, and she froze. In contrast to Mr. Stone's pleasantly rich voice, a startling red beard hid the lower half of his face, and his flaxen mane wandered across his forehead, covering most of the rest. But most unnerving was the fiercely massive chest. Her knees wobbled, threatening to collapse. *He was the man from her dream.* She clutched at a nearby barrel, steadying herself, and touched her cheek to check for fever; surely she was hallucinating. But her face felt dead-cold. And still he stood there, this living, breathing presence that wholly dominated the room.

His hazel eyes returned her stare with their own shocked expression. "You're joking. Where's the *real* one?"

"Now, Jake," Mr. Dorset cajoled. "She's been sickly. Fatten her up, and she'll flesh out real fine."

Mr. Stone cocked a golden brow. "You're not serious."

"I'd bet the store on it. Her hair? Now, you'll like that. It's the color o'honey and hangs down clear past her bu—uh—past here." Mr. Dorset ran a finger across the back of his thigh as his small round eyes darted her way.

Rachel was caught with her mouth open in mute protest.

Quickly he continued. "Besides, like I said, you're gonna have to take what you get. You're two weeks late. If you'd been here when the women first come, you could've had your pick same as everyone else."

Mr. Stone shifted his immense frame. "And I told you, I would've been here if I could. But when that chain broke, and that log rolled over me, I was too stove up to even get on a horse, let alone ride all the way in from the coast."

"Gentlemen," Rachel intervened, hoping to put an end to the tactless haggling. "It seems that Mr. Stone wishes to be released from his bargain. I'm sure there's no law that says he must marry me."

Mr. Stone's golden-green gaze moved to her. "I'll take care of this, lady."

"Jake, I think you're missing the point here." The storekeeper grabbed him by the arm and pulled him toward the door. "Miss Chambers, would you excuse us? Jake and me's gonna walk outside a minute."

Rachel watched them until Mr. Dorset closed the front door after them. Please God, she pleaded, wishing she could hear what the storekeeper was saying. Please, don't let him convince that Norse giant to marry me. But if he doesn't, her better sense warned, you'll be sent back to St. Louis. Fear drizzled down her spine. To prison.

No, Mr. Dorset wouldn't do that. He was too nice a man. He'd simply find her another husband. Noticing her hands were clenched, Rachel unfurled them and refolded them more lightly. She had to appear unruffled when the men returned.

A moment later, they did—sporting grins so exuberant Rachel's stomach crimped in another attack of anxiety. For a certainty, the storekeeper had told Mr. Stone that she'd been jailed on the shameful charge of prostitution.

"I guess I acted a little hasty," the man said with enthusiasm, his bright smile counteracting some of his fierce bearing. "Like Homer says, a deal's a deal."

Rachel made no comment. What could she say? After all, he was the only one with a choice. Her knuckles grew white as her grip tightened again.

"Fine." The proprietor's tiny blue eyes sparkled as if he'd just finalized a very profitable sale. "Come on over here, you two. We need to fill out the marriage form."

Mr. Dorset, assuming his roll as justice of the peace, stepped behind the counter and withdrew a certificate. Mr. Stone went to stand before him, but Rachel's legs would not move. Couldn't.

"Jake, what's your full name?" Mr. Dorset asked as he dipped a quill into an inkwell.

"I don't see any reason for that. You know who I am."

"Jake. I need your whole name, or it won't be legal."

The man placed huge, weather-bronzed hands on the display case. "Are you trying to tell me, if I don't give you my full name, I can't get married?"

"That's right," Homer answered. "Now, what is it?"

Pulled by curiosity, Rachel stepped up to the counter.

The big man gritted his straight white teeth. He took a deep breath. "Jacob Obadiah . . . Cherubim . . . Stone. And if you tell a single soul, your scruffy hide's mine."

The plump man's lips twitched as he scrawled the name. "I think that's a fine name. 'Specially Cherubim."

"I mean it, Homer."

"All right, all right. Just joshin'." A grin escaped when Mr. Dorset turned to Rachel. "And what's your name?"

She hesitated. If she didn't give her full name, there would be no marriage to the Oregon Viking.

"What's the matter? Are you ashamed of yours, too?"

Looking down at her, Mr. Stone's autumn eyes softened.

Rachel's tension eased slightly. Just how evil could a person named Cherubim be? She felt the corners of her own mouth tickle. "No, my name is Rachel Elizabeth Chambers."

"Well, now, we're finally getting somewhere. Jake, where were you born?"

"Northwest Territory, along a trap line on the Minnesota River."

"That's in Minnesota, ain't it?"

"Reckon so." Mr. Stone's firm lips spread in a smile, disclosing straight white teeth. "Unless they moved it."

"And where were you born, Miss Chambers?"

"Illinois. Peoria, Illinois."

"Ah, yes," the storekeeper said with a remembering nod. "Lovely town. Passed through there once."

"Thank you. We're proud of it."

The front door opened, capturing everyone's attention.

"Just in time, Sam," Mr. Dorset said to a burly man wearing a heavy blacksmith's apron.

"Time for what?" asked the man with a face permanently flushed by years of exposure to fiery heat.

"Jake's here to marry the last of the women from St. Louis, and I need you to be the witness."

"Congratulations!" Sam slapped Mr. Stone on the back with a soot-smudged hand. "Better keep a close eye on her, though. Hank Reins brung his big gray in to be shod this mornin' madder'n a gut-shot bear. *His* bride's run off."

Mr. Dorset leaned across the counter. "Is that right?"

"Yeah. She found his poke and took that, too."

"He picked that redhead, didn't he?"

"Yeah, the *bosomy* one," Sam said, rolling his eyes as Mr. Stone's narrowed.

"Figured she'd be trouble," the storekeeper said. "She wasn't a'tall like our Miss Chambers. Miss Chambers has been a real lady the whole time she's been here."

"Thank you, Mr. Dorset. And of course, I fully intend to honor my vows," she said staunchly, though her quivering insides belied the determined tone.

"Well, let's get started," Mr. Dorset said. "Jake, take Rachel's hand. Do you take this woman . . ."

The man's huge hand enveloped hers, triggering a poignant memory from her childhood. She saw herself strolling along the boardwalk hand in hand with her father. Her papa had been so kind, so giving. A true gentleman. He should've lived to walk her down the aisle. But then, there was no aisle. Rachel glanced about, and a sigh escaped. No church, no guests. Only me and three strangers standing among the barrels and sacks in a dry-goods store.

"Rachel . . . Miss Chambers," Homer Dorset called, pulling her attention back to him.

"What? I'm sorry. What did you say?"

"Do you promise to love, honor, and obey, for better or worse, for richer or poorer, in sickness or in health, forsaking all others till death do you part?"

God help her. "Yes."

"Then, I now pronounce you man and wife. Jake, you can kiss your bride now."

Jacob Stone turned to Rachel and bent down from his great height. His eyes drew her to him in an uncommonly intimate invitation.

Rachel's heart careened crazily. A wave of heat rushed up to her cheeks.

"Go on," Mr. Dorset urged. "Kiss her."

The big man glanced at the storekeeper, then at the blacksmith. His mouth dropped into a lopsided grin, then he gently brushed her lips with his.

His wiry beard tickled, but the tender caress held the promise of other, more interesting, kisses. A soft tingle lingered.

"Now that we got that taken care of," the storekeeper said, "Jake, you still got some accounts to settle."

"What do you mean?"

"Well, there's the little matter of Mrs. Stone's room and board for the last two weeks. Comes to four dollars. Then there's her trunks. She come with five. Griffin said it cost extra to ship that many. Comes to twenty dollars."

"*Five trunks?* How many dresses does the woman need?"

"Only one trunk contains my clothing, Mr. Stone," Rachel interjected crisply. "The other trunks are full of housekeeping items. China—linens—blankets—medicines. I'm sure you'll find them well worth the shipping charge."

"That's different," he drawled as he dug into his pocket for several coins he then tossed onto the counter.

"Oh, I forgot," Mr. Dorset said as he scooped up the money. "And there's a fifty-cent fee for my services."

Mr. Stone flipped two more coins into the fleshy palm.

"And while Sam's here, I'd get him to help me with them trunks if I was you. Some of 'em look purty hefty."

"Sure, be glad to," the blacksmith said.

Rachel rushed ahead to gather up her necessaries. She

placed them in one chest, then moved to another and lifted out a dove-gray bonnet decorated with pink satin roses, then a pair of matching gloves . . . all the time feeling Mr. Stone's eyes on her. Securing the last latch, she stepped aside to make way for the men.

They carried the first trunk out to the wagon, and Rachel followed as far as the front door where she stopped to put on her accessories. But her gaze continued on. Jake Stone's muscles corded and bulged, stretching the weave of his homespun shirt as he hoisted a chest heavily laden with kitchenware onto the buckboard. Seeing them flexed sent the curl of a tremor through her, but, strangely, it was caused not so much by fear as by the thought of seeing his chest bared, of running her hands over the hard smoothness. . . .

Suddenly embarrassed, Rachel looked away. How could she possibly allow her mind to run so wild? But then, she'd heard more talk in the past few months about private moments than any decent lady would normally hear in ten lifetimes. She could still hear the prostitutes' throaty chuckles, the words spoken in rushed whispers. She didn't glance Mr. Stone's way again until he'd loaded the last trunk.

He turned toward her with a confident, expecting grin—a grin that left no doubt what he had planned for *her very near future*. "Time to go."

Time to go. She forced a smile as the icy tendrils of fear gripped again. She'd known she was coming to Oregon to marry a stranger when she sailed here with her more worldly companions. So, why on earth hadn't she had the good sense to ask the kind of questions that would help her now? And here she was, preparing to ride off into the wilderness with this giant. For all she knew, he was every bit as barbaric as the pirate of her nightmare.

Time to go. The words continued to echo, encircling her, trapping her. With all the stiff-backed bravado she could muster, Rachel strode down the steps to Jake Stone.

He placed commanding hands about her waist and lifted

her up to the platform with no more effort than an average man might expend on a sack of feathers. Then he swung up beside her. The bench springs sank with his weight, tilting the seat. Before she could catch herself, Rachel fell against him. Though separated by layers of heavy fabric, contact with the solid strength of his body sent a jolt through her. She bolted upright and scooted to a respectable distance, abashed more by her intense awareness of his masculinity than her clumsiness.

Mr. Stone glanced at her and flashed a grin. Had he felt it, too?

"Excuse me," she finally remembered to say.

At last he turned away. "Thanks, Homer." Then, gathering up the set of doubles, he flicked them across the two big chestnuts' backs. The wagon jerked, then started to roll down the empty street in the direction of the wharf.

They'd passed a two-storied white hotel that faced a couple of small steep-roofed houses when Mr. Stone turned and nodded to someone. He blocked Rachel's view, and she couldn't see who'd caught his attention.

"McLean." His greeting held the ring of a challenge.

Oh, yes, Rachel remembered, the lumberman he and Mr. Dorset had discussed earlier. She looked up to see if her new husband's expression revealed any hostility. But he exposed no hint of an emotion behind that blasted beard.

They rode past the livery barn and a cluster of sawmill buildings as they headed for the raft waiting to ferry them across the Willamette River. The only sign of life was at the mill pond where two men stood on floating logs and, with long poles, guided timber toward a chute.

Rachel gazed back at Independence, the rustic village nestled along the swiftly flowing river, and waved good-bye to Mr. Dorset, the only person she knew in the hamlet. He'd been the one person she'd seen during the long fortnight she'd lain in his back room, the only one who'd come to administer the quinine when she burned with fever.

Turning forward again, Rachel looked across the river,

then on to the rut-lined road that disappeared into a dense,
dark forest of evergreens. Sitting in the shadow of Jacob
Stone, she felt panic gnarl within again.

She flicked a wary glance up at her new husband. What
did he have waiting for her at the other end of that road?

⟨⟨ chapter 2 ⟩⟩

JACOB Stone drove the team and wagon onto a crude raft hooked to a rope suspended over the river. Then a skinny kid poled them across water greener than the cedars and hemlock that crowded the edge. The dark-haired boy grinned the whole time as if he had a delicious secret. And whenever he passed Rachel, he stole glances.

She chose to ignore his rude behavior. She already had more to deal with than she knew how to handle.

Reaching shore, the wagon bounced up the bank, and they left the exasperating boy behind. Then she and Mr. Stone began their journey down the weather-ravaged trail in a silence that bewildered her. Rachel had assumed her new husband would be full of questions or, at least, would want to tell her about his homestead and his dreams for the future. But, she mused, maybe he felt as awkward as she. Then she noted the totally relaxed manner in which he held the reins. Obviously, he didn't even know how to be nervous. Well, if he wasn't the least bit curious, she most definitely was.

"Mr. Stone—"

"Call me Jake." He glanced down at her. "Everyone does."

"Thank you. And, of course, you may call me Rachel," she added, attempting a gracious smile, as the straining horses hauled them up a small hill. "Mr. Dorset mentioned you had a homestead. How much farther is it?"

"'Bout fifteen miles."

Fifteen miles from the nearest town? Oh, my God, she

cried silently. "My, that is a ways." Her voice sounded high, thin. "But, of course, you have neighbors nearby."

"Yeah. The Jenningses live on up another mile or so."

"That far?" she croaked.

"Close enough to run my stock over to whenever I'm going to be gone a spell."

She knew the answer to her next question—Mr. Dorset had told her—but she had to ask. "Do you live there alone?"

The weight of one of his oversized hands dropped onto her leg as his brows gave a lively quirk. "Not any more."

His hand had claimed her thigh! She almost jumped from the wagon. She clutched the seat edge.

Her face must have mirrored her shock. He chuckled. A sure sign of his evil intent. Then, to her amazement, he removed his hand and returned his attention to the road.

Rachel turned away, her breath coming much too fast and hard. She tried to concentrate on the trees and the almost impenetrable tangle of thorny undergrowth crowding the road while the hammering pulse at her temples subsided. Perhaps fifteen miles wasn't far enough. How could she possibly steel herself for the night to come in that short a time? But, somehow, between now and when they reached his farm she simply *had* to find the words to tell him about herself.

Yet, how could she speak to a stranger about such a delicate matter? But she had to. Or else tonight she could very well be facing the fearsome violator of her nightmare.

Oh, Papa, Papa. How do I say it?

Just tell him the plain unvarnished truth, she could almost hear her father drawl in that gentle, eternally weary voice. Being the only doctor in Peoria, he'd had more than his share of telling patients hard truths.

But what if Mr. Stone didn't believe her? No one else had. Yet, how could he not? After all, how could a *virgin be a prostitute*?

Rachel shot a fleeting glance at him sitting there so impregnable. . . . But where to start? Perhaps from when

Papa had decided they'd take Mama to New Mexico. Poor Papa. He'd been so desperate. He wouldn't believe it was already too late for a dry climate to help Mama's consumption. As it turned out, she hadn't even survived the boat trip just to St. Louis. Poor Mama. And Papa, having to bury her in a lonely churchyard so far from home.

St. Louis. An icy cringe shot through her at the mere thought. She never wanted to see that place again. The hotel room. Her papa lying there for days, never eating, tears seeping from beneath his lashes. The depth of his grief ripped at her heart.

Then finally he did get up. He dressed with care and went out to secure passage back to Peoria.

But he didn't come back till the middle of the night. And when he did, he was so drunk she couldn't understand a word he said. The next day was a repeat of the first, and the next. It was as if he'd died with her mother and some stranger had taken his place. She begged him to take her home, but he said there were too many memories. And the reason for going on to Santa Fe was gone, dead, buried.

But what about me, Papa? Couldn't you see I needed you, too? A sigh escaped.

Suddenly remembering that she sat beside Mr. Stone, Rachel looked up to see if he'd noticed. But apparently he was lost in his own reverie. Probably reliving some past conquest, she surmised, her apprehension returning. She wondered if the victim of his musing was man or beast . . . or some hapless woman.

Breathing in the fresh, pine-scented air, she pulled her thoughts back to her father, and felt a prick of guilt for her selfishness. He now lay beside his wife where he needed to be. But to die in a saloon? Struck down by a stray bullet? What a wholly unworthy end to such a noble life.

After seeing to his burial, Rachel's only desire had been to return to her friends in Peoria. She'd bought a ticket for a steamboat leaving the next morning. The trunks were all packed. If only she hadn't answered the knock on the door. If only . . .

The bangs had been loud, jarring. Rachel remembered being startled but not afraid.

A garishly attired girl waited, out of breath, purple satin straining against her sparse bosom. "The doc's gotta come! Quick!"

"I'm sorry, he can't. You see—"

The girl's long nails dug into Rachel's arm. "He has to! I think Annie's dying. *Please.*"

The girl seemed so desperate, her eyes so frightened, and the freckled nose so innocent, that Rachel spoke without any thought of the consequences. "Where is this Annie? Maybe I can help. I've assisted my father for years."

"No. I need the doc. Tell him. I know he'll come."

"I'm sorry. But you see, he's"—the words dug into Rachel's throat "—passed away."

"Can't be. He was at O'Reilly's just the other night. Doc Chambers, from Peoria. Please, she's real bad."

"I'm sorry. But I'll bring his bag and do what I can."

The skinny girl looked close to tears. "Oh, all right. But hurry, I already been gone too long. Went to Doc Hurd's first, but he was gone."

Rachel followed the girl down an alley and into the faintly lit back room of a saloon. Through a cracked door, she heard an out-of-tune piano clanging out a lively melody amid slurred singing and bursts of laughter, and the stench of whiskey and stale tobacco caused her nose to curl. What in the world had possessed her to come?

The girl seized her arm. "Come on. Up the stairs."

Steep steps led up to a long dark hall with doors on either side. Passing the first room, Rachel heard the rapid squeaking of bedsprings.

A giggling won.an shrieked, and a man howled raucously.

Rachel flushed and scurried past.

Ahead of her, the girl rushed to a door across the hall and opened it. "In here." She pulled Rachel into a cramped cell-like room.

Rachel stepped across a heap of scarlet taffeta and disarrayed undergarments to reach the bed. From a nearby oil lamp, light shafted across the still face of a grotesquely battered woman. Blood was everywhere, across the pillow, the sheets. It matted her dark hair and had soaked a bandage wadded at the side of her head.

Hot bile rose in Rachel's throat. "My God."

"Please. Do somethin'," the girl croaked in a whisper. "She's gonna die."

Rachel lifted the unconscious woman's wrist. After a moment of searching, she discovered a faintly tapping pulse.

"Is she gonna die?"

She looked dead already, Rachel thought while watching the nearly imperceptible rise and fall of the woman's chest. "I'll do what I can." She lowered the covers to the woman's waist and found her unclothed. Again, dried blood splayed across pale skin discolored by large bruises, but no cuts. Apparently, all the blood originated from the head wound.

Rachel turned to the girl. "What's your name?"

"Joy Ann." Her eyes were wide with fear.

"That's lovely," she said, hoping to convey a sense of calmness. "Would you please fetch some clean rags?"

The girl quickly returned with several lengths of sheeting and Rachel sat down next to the woman. "Bring the lamp closer," she ordered as she lifted off the soaked dressing. A flood of blood surged forth, covering her hand and the lace trim of her sleeve. Drops oozed down onto the buff-yellow of her percale skirt. "Quick! A bandage!"

"Shoulda been me," Joy Ann moaned as she shoved a strip into Rachel's free hand. "He wanted me, but Annie took my place. Said she knowed how to handle him."

Rachel swiped away the blood until she found the source. A swath had been sliced down the side of the woman's head. Rachel gasped. *The ear was gone.*

Feeling light-headed, Rachel pressed the folded material

against the gaping wound and breathed deeply until her vision cleared. "Whoever did this should be hanged."

"Orletta's gone for the police. She'll be back soon."

"The only hope I have of saving your friend is to cauterize the wound."

"Oh, no."

"I'll need you to hold the lamp. Can you do that?"

"I'll try," she whined faintly. "But, hurry." Joy Ann held the light fairly steady as Rachel worked. Her freckles stood out even more as she paled, but she didn't turn away.

Afterward, while they washed the woman and changed her linens, Rachel felt their ministrations served only to ease Joy Ann's suffering. Not once had the woman moved or made a sound, and Rachel was now sure she never would.

Tucking the blankets on the other side of the bed, Rachel looked across to the girl. "Who did this?"

"It's best you stay out of it, ma'am. They's real bad men. 'Sides, like I said, Orletta's gone for the law."

"Good. This evil man must be brought to justice. Is he still here?"

"No, he lit out. No tellin' where he went. He come in off the Missouri. He's one o' them scalp hunters."

"Oh, my!" A chill coursed down Rachel's spine. "Do you know his name?"

"Catlin. Crow Dog Catlin." Joy Ann stared vacantly a moment and shuddered before touching Rachel's sleeve. "Miss Chambers, better take that dress off and get the blood out."

"Don't worry about it."

"But it's such a fine dress. Please. I feel bad already, askin' you to come into this awful place. I'll take it downstairs and put it to soak in the washtub."

"Thank you, but I must be going now."

"You're not gonna leave yet, are you?" Joy Ann's saucer-wide eyes swung to the dying woman on the bed.

Rachel couldn't refuse her plea. "I'll stay for a while longer. But, no matter what, I must leave by dawn. I'm traveling to Peoria first thing in the morning."

Joy Ann's face brightened. "Bless you. Now give me that dress. I'll have it clean and ready by then, iffin I have to iron it dry."

Rachel smiled. "Very well. Do you have something I could put on till then?"

Joy Ann reached into a trunk against the wall. "Here, wear this." She tossed a black silk wrapper trimmed with feathers to Rachel. "Turn around, and I'll unbutton you."

After Joy Ann left, Rachel donned the slinky dressing gown reeking of cheap perfume, then leaned back in the chair and closed her eyes, hoping for a little rest before morn.

But no more than a few minutes passed before the walls vibrated with the thundering of heavy-booted men charging up the stairs. Doors banged. Men shouted. A woman screamed.

Rachel jumped to her feet and looked wildly about her. *What's happening?*

The door crashed open. A man clad in a navy blue uniform burst in. "This is the room," he shouted over his shoulder, then grabbed Rachel and pulled her with him to the bed. He looked down at the woman. "She looks real bad."

"She's dying. And, sir, I'll thank you to unhand me." Rachel tried to wrench her arm free, but his grip tightened.

Another policeman, towing a scantily clad blonde, came to the door.

Rachel's captor placed fingers at the side of Annie's neck for a moment, then turned to the other officer. "She's dead. Haul the rest of these louse-ridden whores down to the jail. It's time we cleaned house."

"I'll have you know," said the blonde whose celestial features seemed out of place, *"I do not have lice."*

"And I'm *not* a—a soiled dove," Rachel said with force. "I'm merely here to help this poor woman."

"And I'm the king of England." The policeman snorted, and shoved her toward the man at the door.

The next morning, at a trial that lasted no more than two minutes, the judge didn't believe her, either. And at the prison, the warden refused her request to send a missive to her friends back home.

She was placed in a tiny cell and left alone to contemplate her *sinful* ways, a Bible her only comfort—until that fateful day two months later, the day when the guard brought her to the warden's office and she was given the opportunity to go to Oregon to marry a homesteader.

Rachel was taken to a room holding six other women who were also to be released. And to her surprise, Joy Ann was one of them. She'd been arrested a week after Rachel. For a fleeting moment hope surged forth. Joy Ann could corroborate her story, clear her of the ignominious charges.

But, as before, no one was interested in anything a couple of "fallen" women had to say.

But thank goodness, Mr. Griffin, the agent from Oregon, had been considerate enough to let the women collect their property. Knowing the value of the housekeeping items and especially her father's medical supplies, he had even paid the storage fee on the trunks at Rachel's hotel.

The trip down the Mississippi and the voyage to Panama had been relatively pleasant. Orletta, Joy Ann's worldly friend, had kept Rachel safe from the amorous advances of the sailors. But then the journey had turned grim. To reach the Pacific Ocean, they were forced to trek across the isthmus through muggy, bug-infested jungle. Then, after boarding a second ship, it wasn't two days before Joy Ann came down with malaria. A few days later, Belle, another of the women, contracted it, and Rachel spent most of the voyage north to Oregon nursing them back to health. Then, just three days before reaching the mouth of the Columbia, she, too, came down with the dreaded fever.

When they finally arrived, the others met and married their awaiting grooms, while Rachel was deposited in the back room of the store to recover and wait for the one man still missing, Jake Stone.

And now, here she was, riding deep into the wilderness with a frontiersman so massively built he took up most of the seat. She peeked from beneath her bonnet at the man whom, this very afternoon, she'd given the right to do with her body as he wished. She closed her eyes, trying to shut out the ominous possibilities. She grasped at the remembrance of his tender kiss after the wedding. Let that be the real him, she prayed. But then she recalled the gleam that had been in his eyes when he'd come back from talking with Mr. Dorset, and her mind shot to her nightmare and the instant the dangerous pirate had ravaged her with his mauling leer. Had the dream portended her fate?

Eluding her thoughts, she peered up at the intensely blue afternoon sky. It was denuded of even the wisp of a cloud . . . as starkly naked as she'd been when the unstoppable Norse god had sighted her. With a wavering hand, she checked the buttons at her throat.

You silly goose! Rachel yanked her attention to the trees. Her gaze followed them to tips waving above so high they seemed to brush the very heavens. Then, at the side of the road, she counted the fern sprigs unfurling in their first stretch of spring. She absolutely refused to allow herself to fall victim to any more fantasies.

Though larger than most, Mr. Stone was merely a man, and, like the others who had ventured to Oregon, he was following the simple, honest life of a homesteader. If he were a more daring sort, he'd be chasing after gold in California. Who knows, he might even have family here—a whole passel of brothers and sisters. Yes, that's a far more plausible picture. Far more likely.

She'd set her mind to rest once and for all. She tipped her face to see clearly past the bill of her bonnet. "Mr. Stone?"

He jumped slightly, then turned to her. "Jake."

"Uh—yes. You mentioned that you were born in the wilderness. Has your family since moved here to Oregon?"

His eyes found the road again. "I don't have a family. My ma died when I was two, and my pa was killed when I was about nine or ten."

"Oh, I'm so sorry. I feel for your loss. I, too, was orphaned recently."

A smile tilted one side of his mouth, and he snorted.

A rush of anger stiffened her illness-weakened limbs. She inhaled deeply then spoke with emphasis. "I'm not in the habit of lying."

"Whatever you say." He shrugged in a provoking manner.

Rachel pressed her lips tightly together to prevent an angry retort and took another calming breath. "Now, getting back to your family, do you have any brothers or sisters?"

"Nope."

"Your father never remarried?"

"Not so's you'd notice."

What kind of answer is that? she thought, unwilling to accept the evasion. "Forgive me, but I don't understand."

"There weren't any white women roaming the mountains in those days. The trappers would maybe keep a squaw for a time, but nothing permanent. Fact is, Pa got himself killed fighting over one with a Frenchy. And she wasn't even that pretty. But they were so drunk neither of 'em noticed."

Drunk? Fighting? And over a heathen woman at that. "Oh, my. And you, just a child. Alone to fend for yourself in the wilderness."

"Naw. The others sort of passed me around. Taught me everything I know about hunting and trapping. Ol' Farnsby even taught me how to read and how to talk without saying *ain't* and such. Said it'd come in handy someday, and he was right. Civilization just keeps crowding in."

They'd been driving along this rolling forest road for at least two hours, and they hadn't seen even one other human being. *And he calls this civilization?*

"That's the road to Amos Colfax's place." Mr. Stone nodded toward a set of dirt tracks that curved out of view behind a stand of spruce. "He bought a bride out of St. Louis, too." A chuckle rumbled up from his barrel of a chest. "You can bet he's got his hands full about now."

"Why is that, Mr.—uh—Jake?" Rachel wondered if he considered all brides a handful or just the tainted ones.

"Amos is a widower with three grown boys. And when Griffin went east for wives, we thought he'd be bringing back hardworking farm women. I *know* Amos wasn't expecting what he got." Turning toward her, he smiled and winked.

Feeling heat rise to her cheeks, she looked down and pretended to straighten her gloves.

"Amos isn't the sort to want to share his new bride with his sons," Jake continued. "He's got a lot of white-man ideas that way. And with her being the sort she is, bet he's having to beat his young bucks off with a stick."

White-man ideas? What kind of wild man was he? If she jumped down right now, maybe she could reach the Colfax farm before he could turn the wagon around and catch her. Maybe Orletta was there, or even Joy Ann. Rachel edged to the side and looked down. But it seemed a mile to the ground. And, besides, as weak as the malaria had rendered her, did she really think she could outrun this . . . Odin? She sighed and swallowed back a tear. "How much farther to your farm?" she managed.

"About another hour." He peered down at her, his eyes narrowing. "A lot of hard work ahead," he mumbled before turning back to guide the horses around a mudhole. "I've spent most of my life free, hunting and trapping. And I've scouted some for the wagon trains. Always made enough to buy anything I needed. But I'm past thirty now. Time for a family. A man needs sons to carry on his name."

That's the only reason he wants a wife? Well, what else did she expect from a man who would marry any strange woman sent to him?

Rachel could think of no ladylike response, and they lapsed into silence again, leaving her to stare into the shadows as they crested another hill. Her only comfort came from the chirping of a few hardy sparrows and the occasional squirrel that scampered across the road.

Rachel guessed they were nearing Mr. Stone's homestead when he guided the wagon team off the road and onto tracks that cut through a patch of prickly berry vines, before threading again into the protection of the evergreens. Her increased tension added to the chill of the rapidly dropping temperature. Under normal circumstances she would have asked him to stop so she could fetch her shawl.

Just as her teeth began to chatter, the wagon broke out of the firs. And for the first time, Rachel fully viewed the sweeping grandeur of the distant mountains to the north and east of them. The slant of late afternoon light turned to amber the gracefully sloped snow-draped peaks that rose up magically behind fir-covered hills. In comparison to the rolling plains of Illinois, the majesty of the Cascade Range seemed larger than life.

Just like Jake.

They drove down a slope into a lovely meadow sprinkled with the first yellows, oranges, and purples of spring. Several old oaks stood sentinel, their crusty limbs outstretched. On a small rise at the far end of the clearing clustered a barn, a log cabin, and two sheds. Behind the cabin stood a new outhouse, its unweathered timber gleaming gold in the late afternoon sun.

The white-stockinged geldings quickened their gait, and Rachel's heartbeat joined the race. After two months locked in a cell and three more aboard ship, she was finally at a place she could call home.

Undaunted by the crudeness of the structures, she envisioned a multitude of improvements that could make the place more habitable. With the mountains in the background and the lush pine-scented forest framing the April-green valley, it was beautiful beyond anything she could have imagined. She suddenly had no doubt. She could make a good life for herself here. She would be strong. After all, she was her mother's daughter—even to the end, her mother had never lost the joy of discovering fresh delights.

A new strength flowed into her as they drove across the meadow and up the knoll. Squaring her frail shoulders, she leaned slightly forward in her eagerness to reach her new home. To feel the ground beneath her feet.

Yes, she would make a success of this new chance. She would be a good wife and, God willing, a loving mother.

She turned to Mr. Stone . . . and her newfound courage dribbled away. *First she had to get through tonight.*

((chapter 3))

JAKE pulled the team to a halt, then bounded off the buckboard and came around to Rachel's side. "Think you can handle supper while I bring in your trunks?" His huge hands enveloped her waist, and he swung her down so fast her skirts soared up behind her.

Hastily she stopped their revealing flight and turned toward the log cabin. "Certainly." A porch supported by posts of stripped limbs triggered a picture of her sitting there, nuzzling a baby on a balmy summer's eve.

I'm really married, she thought.

In the past, marriage had always seemed a distant dream, for another time, after her father no longer needed her to care for her mother . . . and after her unladylike passion for medical knowledge had been sated.

"You *can* cook, can't you?" Jake passed her with a steamer trunk balanced on his shoulder.

"Here, let me." Rachel rushed toward the split-wood door and opened it. "And, yes," she added as he breezed by.

"Where do you want this dang thing?"

Looking around the room, Rachel's gaze grappled onto a bearskin rug, replete with a teeth-baring head and lethal claws, lying between a stone fireplace and two rocking chairs. Startled by the savagery, she took a backward step and bumped into something coarse, hairy. She whirled around to find a great buffalo coat hanging on a rack of elk horns.

"Don't worry, it's dead." Rachel couldn't miss the

amusement in his drawl. "Lady, where do you want this?"

"Oh, I'm sorry. Let's see." She glanced around. A homemade table with chairs sat in the middle of the planked floor. At the other end, an obviously new cook stove stood on shiny black legs. Then she saw the door to another room, the bedroom, she was sure. Staring at it, she froze.

"I take it you want it over there by the door," Jake said as he walked across the room and eased down the chest.

Again Rachel's gaze followed the fluidness of his movements, supple muscles straining against his shirt.

Turning, he caught her staring. "What's the matter?"

"I—uh—need wood."

Wagging his head, he grunted. "It's out on the porch."

By the time Jake finished unloading her trunks, Rachel had a fire roaring in the stove. Closing the firebox door, she turned and found him watching her. Nervously, she reached up and tucked an errant strand within her amber coils. "What would you like for supper?"

"Whatever you can find," he said, still staring.

She could hardly think. "Where do you keep the meat?"

"Out in the smokehouse." His gaze mellowed. "And the vegetables are in the cellar. Come on, I'll show you."

After pointing Rachel in the right direction, Jake strode to the team of sturdy Soffolks he'd won from a greenhorn at Fort Vancouver the year before. The larger, Sparky, swung its head toward Jake and whinnied.

"Hold your horses, I'm coming." Catching the animal's thick leather collar, he led the team and wagon to the side of the barn and unhitched them. He then followed the animals inside and let them into their quarters.

In another stall, Jake's prized black stallion perked its ears and nickered through rubbery lips.

"How ya doin', Prince? You know how I've been promising you a filly? Well, now that I've got mine, you're next. Well, maybe mine isn't quite a filly," he said, grabbing a hayfork. "More like a frisky switch-tailed mare."

She wasn't what he'd expected, that was sure. A saloon

girl. He should've known it would turn out like this. But that's what he got for thinking real life could be like some romantic play. Well, he could still build a future on the sons she'd give him. And, who knew, even if she wasn't capable of taking on her share of the load, maybe in time she'd take an interest in the farm.

Who was he kidding? Whores liked towns, saloons, fancy dresses and such. What was it that whore in Astoria said? "Only a stupid horse or a *decent* woman would work themselves to death for a man."

One thing was certain, though. He'd be keeping his eye on her. She wasn't taking off like Reins's woman did. At least not till she'd had a baby or two. And in the meantime— His mouth lazed into a grin. "We'll make do."

His lusty musing was suddenly replaced by a picture of the staunchly stiff lady in somber black who'd ridden next to him all afternoon. "Naw," he said, shaking his head. "She's just putting on airs. That'll all change once we get in bed tonight." Burying the pitchfork into a pile of fodder, he scooped up a load and filled the stud's manger.

While the stallion took a mouthful, Jake ran a hand along the shiny coat of the animal's neck and wondered if his new bride's skin would feel as silken.

Ginger, his brown-spotted cow, stretched her neck over the top rail and beckoned with a long, low moo.

Reminded of his chores, he finished feeding and watering the animals, then grabbed the milking stool and a pail. "Move over, old girl," he murmured in a soothing voice as he wedged himself into Ginger's stall and placed the bucket beneath her. Sitting down, he leaned his cheek against her warm flank and took hold of two teats.

"Hoped I wouldn't have to do this any more," he said, squeezing down until the first squirt *ping*'d into the metal pail. "But I guess I've got a racehorse instead of a workhorse. Well, at least she didn't act like a stranger to the stove. If I can get her to do the cooking and washing, I guess I can just keep on doing the rest. She'll be making up for it in bed."

Jake's thoughts shifted to Griffin. Why had their agent brought back convicted prostitutes instead of the kind of women he'd been sent east for? The answer came almost before Jake formed the question—the same reason no one else came to Oregon any more—gold fever. Nowadays, anyone adventurous enough to come west went to California. So, Griffin'd had no choice but to scrape the bottom of the barrel. And a wife who could come down with another bout of malaria at any moment was the bottom of the bottom.

The cow kicked a hind leg and leaned into Jake.

"Whoa, there, Ginger," he said, shoving her away. To calm her, he began to sing in a smooth mellow voice:

> Oh, don't you remember sweet Betsey from Pike,
> Who cross'd the big mountains with her lover Ike,
> With two yoke of cattle, a large yellow dog,
> A tall Shanghai rooster and one spotted hog.
>
> One evening quite early they camped on the Platte,
> 'Twas near by the road on a green shady flat,
> Where Betsey, sore-footed, lay down to repose—
> With wonder Ike gazed on that Pike County rose.

Jake chuckled as he recalled another Betsey. She'd lain down to repose, too, with every young buck on the wagon train. And not just along the Platte, either. It was by the Snake River at the fork in the trail that she came to him. After a week of parlaying with the Shoshone, he'd ridden into camp late, and was down washing up when he heard her whisper his name. What was it she said? Yeah. She wanted to see what it felt like to lie with a man *big* as a tree.

A twinge of guilt tugged at Jake, even now, after four years. He shouldn't have done it. Her ma and pa were good people. It took a long time before he could look either of the Redmans square in the eye after that. He wondered if they knew about the way their daughter had carried on. Probably did. They didn't seem none too put out when she ran off to California with the Thurman brothers.

The last time he was up their way, they'd looked happy and fit—a dang sight better than when they'd first headed up Oregon City way for their homestead, all hollow-eyed and dragging.

Jake shifted his hands to the other two teats. Maybe Homer's right, he thought. It never did take these pioneer women any time at all before they were all filled out and starched up again. Who knows? Once the yellow's gone from Rachel's eyes and there's more'n just bones inside her skin, his little bride might turn out right pretty—even if she wasn't any bigger'n a spindly fawn.

"Yeah. Probably so." Jake's hands stopped working, and the corners of his mouth curled into a grin. And besides, she looked like she might be fun. He really liked the way she'd sneaked peeks at him all afternoon.

Ginger swung her head around and peered at him with large liquid brown eyes.

Milking her again, he lifted his voice in song:

One evening quite early they camped on the Platte,
'Twas near by the road on a green shady flat,
Where *Rachel,* all golden, lay down to repose—
With wonder *Jake* gazed on that *jailhouse . . . rose.*

By the time Jake sauntered through the cabin door once more, the aroma of biscuits filled the air.

"Here," he said and handed Rachel the pail of milk.

Jake drew a chair out from the table and sat down. He propped a booted foot across his opposite knee and leaned back to watch the way her skirts swayed about her whenever she moved. She was looking better all the time.

Rachel sensed the bore of his stare as she checked the potatoes for tenderness. Her cheeks flamed. While flipping the venison steaks sizzling in the skillet, she began to feel as if she were being stripped of her clothing . . . piece by flimsy piece. Becoming rattled, she swung around. "Better wash up. Supper's almost done."

"Wash?" His mouth slid into a lopsided grin. "Sure."

Rachel watched him go outside with relief, however temporary his departure. While he was gone, she set the table with his dented tin plates and cups and utensils that looked fashioned by the local blacksmith. These would have to do for tonight, but tomorrow she would definitely unpack her own things. She might be living in some remote backwoods cabin, but she had no intention of lowering any standards she didn't absolutely have to.

While she rummaged below the counter, Jake returned and took his seat at the table again.

She turned around. "Where's your cheesecloth?" she said, trying to ignore the golden flecks dancing roguishly in his eyes. "I need to strain the cream off the milk."

"Don't have one. Just ladle it off, best I can."

"I see. Well, that'll have to do for now. I'll find one in my things tomorrow." *Tomorrow.* Her throat tightened as her gaze darted to the bedroom door. Before tomorrow, there was . . . *tonight.*

"If I was you, I'd just stir the cream back in. You could use the extra."

It took a moment for his meaning to overtake her panic. Then ignoring his implication, Rachel placed the food on the table as quickly as possible. Over dinner she'd coax him into a conversation—ease the tension enough to tell him about herself before it was too late.

She sat down across from him.

After they filled their plates, she waited for him to say grace, but, heathen that he was, he just started eating. "Mr. Stone—"

He glanced up. "Jake," he corrected.

"Yes. Jake." She forced a smile. "This is such a lovely little valley. You're to be congratulated on your choice. Might I ask what your plans are for the land?"

"Meat tastes kinda queer," he said, swallowing a chunk. "Does it taste bad?"

"No, it's fine, just different."

"Maybe it's the black pepper. I used some of mine."

"Yeah, that's probably it. All I have is salt."

From the manner in which he shoveled in his food, Rachel knew he either really appreciated her cooking or was exceptionally hungry. She was obviously the only one at the table anxious about the immediate future. She tried again. "What crops do you plan to raise?"

He peered up from his food with unconcealed reluctance. "Thought I'd put in pears and apples. Sublette Simpkins sold me some saplings. But it'll take a few years before they bring in any cash, so I'll do some logging in the meantime. I seeded barley and rye to winter the stock. And from the look of you, I'll have to put in the garden, too."

She noted the skeptical cock of a brow. "I'm sure if you explain what needs to be done, I could do it."

"I knew it," he mumbled past a mouthful, then swallowed. "I could tell by those soft hands. You've never even held a hoe, have you?"

"No, but I'm willing to learn. I want to make this a good place to live, the same as you do."

"Sure," he said lamely, then returned to his supper.

"I'm sure that together we could make a fine home here to raise those sons you want." She breathed deeply, trying to inflate her sinking resolve. "Speaking of sons—"

Jake looked up. Rachel now had his full attention.

"There's something I need to discuss with you—not discuss, exactly—tell you. I'm not what you think I am."

"You're sure not what I expected." His mouth dropped into a suggestive grin. "But, we'll make do."

Rachel's cheeks burned hot again. She chose to ignore his last innuendo. "I know I look a sight, but in a few weeks I'll regain my weight, and, I assure you, I'll look much healthier."

He pointed his fork at her untouched plate. "Not if you don't start eating."

Rachel speared a potato wedge and put it in her mouth.

"That's better," Jake said, returning to his own meal.

After choking down the bite, she gamely repeated, "I'm not what you think. I'm not a—a—fallen woman."

"A what?" He looked up in surprise.

"You know, a woman who sells her favors to . . . men."

"You mean a saloon girl?"

"Yes, exactly. I'm not one. It was all a mistake. I was imprisoned, that's true. But it was a mistake."

"You said that already."

"I was just at that house of ill repute to help an injured woman as an act of charity. I was mistaken for one of them merely because I was there. And no matter how I tried to explain, no one would listen."

"Look, if you want to pretend you're not a whore, it's fine with me. Tell folks whatever you want." He forked some carrots into his mouth.

"No, you don't understand. I'm really *not* what you think. I'm not . . . experienced in the . . ."

"You mean?"

"I—I've never been with a . . . man."

He looked so stunned, Rachel thought maybe he had something caught in his throat. Then his eyes flared. "Son of a bitch!" He lurched up, his chair toppling with a crash to the floor. *"Are you telling me you don't know how to do . . . ? You're nothing but a sickly . . . ?"* He loomed over her like a wall.

Shrinking back in her seat, she snatched at his last phrase. "I'm not sick any more. I'm almost well."

His narrow-eyed glare tore into her. He opened his mouth as if to speak, then rammed the heel of his boot into the fallen chair, sending it skittering across the floor. He turned and stalked out the door, slamming it with such force the windows rattled.

Jake charged to the barn, making one swerving detour to deal a savage kick to the shovel-end of the plow lying next to the doorway. Metal won out over his leather boot, and he limped away. But he didn't care. At least for the moment, the pain took his mind off how badly he'd been swindled by Griffin and Dorset.

He stood in the middle of the building in a fighting stance, his sledgehammer-sized fists clenched at his sides. He wanted to bellow his outrage loud enough to be heard three hills away. But he couldn't let the woman inside overhear his frustration and fury at being hoodwinked.

Griffin may have hightailed it upriver, but Homer hadn't. That fat little runt would pay. Not only would he make Dorset take her back and return his money, Jake vowed never to trade with the hornswoggler again—even if it meant going downriver to Salem every time he needed something.

Jake's anger subsided slightly, but he was still so riled, he grabbed the bull rake and started mucking out stalls. While raking around Sparky, he rambled aloud, a habit he'd picked up during the solitary winters he'd spent trapping. "Homer knew all along she wasn't a saloon girl. If I'd paid closer attention, he wouldn't have flimflammed me like he did. Telling me she's a whore in one breath, and a lady in the next. Raise your foot, Sparky." Jake reached down for the animal's furry white fetlock and raked beneath. "Homer knew, all right. Just wanted to get rid of her 'fore she comes down with the fever again and shakes to death."

Then Jake remembered the look on Rachel's face when he'd stormed at her—that same wide-eyed look a fawn gets when it's scared. He paused a moment, stopped by a tug of guilt. "I shouldn't have yelled. It's not her fault."

Jake started working again. "Soon as I get the garden in, I'll take her back to Independence. She'll understand. Being so spindly, she's just not strong enough for frontier life. And, hell, there's such a shortage of womenfolk, I'm sure Homer'll be able to find her another husband. A town man who can afford to hire a maid. And one who can afford to keep a supply of quinine on hand." Yeah, he thought, she'll be fine. He'd go in and tell her just as soon as he finished the stalls. The way he'd scared her, she'd probably be glad to leave.

He stopped dead. "But that means I can't bed her before I take her back."

Feeling more morose than ever, Jake lit a lantern in the dimming dusk, then, eyes averted, he went into the stallion's stall. He knew Prince hadn't understood his previous bragging words, but still he hesitated to face the spirited stud.

While he raked, the horse's gaze followed him until, foolishly unnerved, he blurted out, "All right. So neither of us is going to have any fun tonight."

Stunned and profoundly confused, Rachel sat without moving for a long time, expecting Jake to return. When he didn't, she rose and crossed to the window to search the area between the house and the barn. She then scanned the wagon tracks across the meadow from whence they'd come, but still couldn't find him. He must be in the barn, she thought. The doors stood open, but in the dimming shades of dusk, no light penetrated the interior. What was he thinking? Planning? What would he do about her? To her?

After a time, a light sparked in the barn, then grew. Well, at least he was in there and planned to stay a while.

Rachel turned from the window to face a room that had darkened while she'd watched out the pane. Remembering an oil lamp sitting on the shelf beside the stove, she headed in that direction. She lit it and carried it to the table.

Left uneaten, her food had grown cold. Unappetizing as it looked, she sat down and forced herself to take several bites. She couldn't afford to lose any more weight.

Why is he so angry? she thought, her fork poised between bites. Didn't men always prefer to marry virgins? I know he's not pleased because I look so unhealthy right now. Yet, he did accept me this way. . . . *But only because he thought I was a tart?*

She stared into space a moment, then placed a bite of venison in her mouth. She grimaced. Wild tasting! She must remember to soak it before she cooked any more of his uncivilized meat. Tonight she'd had no choice. There'd been nothing in the smokehouse but a fresh-killed deer and some other unrecognizable varmint. Mother had always said that without a woman's influence, men were quite barbaric. And since Mr. Stone had spent the better part of his life in the wilderness, she was sure he'd been deprived of proper female upbringing. Rachel scooped in a couple of carrot rounds and absently began to chew. But, with a little patience, a little gentle persuasion, she was sure he'd see the advantage of a faithful wife and a cozy home.

His faithful wife. An intriguing picture of Jake's muscles rippling across his very manly shoulders invaded her thoughts again, and Rachel wondered if he'd look as magnificent with his shirt off as her Viking.

"Oh, dear." Rachel placed cooling hands to her cheeks. Such wanton thoughts she'd been having today.

When she could choke down no more food, she got up and looked out the window again. The interior of the barn still glowed. She stoked up the fire in the stove to heat dishwater. Never let it be said that she was untidy.

While cleaning the kitchen, Rachel repeatedly glanced out the window above the drain board. She told herself not to, but her eyes simply would not obey. After putting away the last dish, she checked the barn once more. The light within still burned.

She knew she should retire, but the very thought of undressing and climbing into his bed melted her into a quivering pond of panic. Instead, she decided to put her time to good use. But first she wanted warmth and light. She flamed another lamp on the mantel beside a stack of dog-eared books, then tossed an armload of wood into the fireplace. That accomplished, she attacked the shelves above the stove. This kitchen would be in proper order before morning or her name wasn't Rachel Chambers.

Her heart snagged. "Rachel Stone," she corrected in a whisper. Stone. The name epitomized her rock-hard husband, but on her it hung heavy, dragging her down with its weight.

* * *

Finished with the hated stable chore, Jake reached for the lantern. Midway, he halted. "Jumping Jehosephat! What am I thinking about? I can't get rid of the woman till I file on my other parcel of acres." He slammed a fist into the post. The lantern bumped against it and light danced crazily throughout the hollows of the barn.

"Homer! You bastard! You knew I couldn't bring her back. Well, *I will*," he railed with such intensity his temples drummed.

"Calm down, Stone. The plan will still work." Jake knew he'd just have to keep his new bride a little longer. Just until Harvey Best came through Independence again.

Prince whinnied and stamped a foot.

"You're laughing at me, aren't you?" Jake growled. "Don't think I can keep her here for weeks without bedding her, do you? Well, I have to, or I'll be stuck with her."

Jake reached for the lamp again. Puckering his lips to extinguish it, he hesitated. He looked out the doors toward the cabin now flooded with light, and his thoughts returned to earlier, when he'd watched her softly rounded little bottom tip up as she bent to look into the oven. She'd turned back toward him with her cheeks all rosy from the heat, and that's when he'd seen the promise of her delicate beauty. And when she told him to go wash up, her sweeping stare had flashed with more spirit than he'd thought her capable of.

His loins began to tempt him. He expelled a long sigh. Maybe he'd better stay in the barn a while longer.

"Prince." He strode toward the black stallion. "I've been neglecting you. Time I gave you a good brushing."

Within a couple of hours, the kitchen was hers. Rachel had emptied the contents of two trunks, stacking her own kitchenware and linens within easy reach. A pink tablecloth now covered the rough-grained table, and two needlepoint pillows decked the seats of the oak rocking chairs. Pleased but exhausted, she plopped down in one of the rockers and surveyed her efforts. Already the split-log interior felt more comfortable, less barren. Later, with curtains to frame the windows and cupboards, and some matching cushions on the dining chairs, it would look quite homey.

She stretched tall and looked out the window for what seemed like the thousandth time. "I'm being ridiculous," she decided. "I must go to bed." She stood up and blew out the first lamp. Taking the second, she purposefully strode to that door she'd avoided all evening.

She opened it . . . to the pungent scent of cedar. Unlike the front room, the bedroom walls were lined with milled boards of the fragrant wood. Very nice, but odd. Rachel had not expected this kind of refinement.

Mr. Dorset had probably told him that cedar would keep the moths away from his woolens. So instead of building a chest like any normal person, her giant had built a whole room. At the thought, her lips lilted into a full smile.

A huge bed of sturdy beams stood before her, and spread over the top lay a quilt of silky furs. Stepping close, she caressed a meltingly luxurious pelt. Pure heaven.

Suddenly, Rachel couldn't wait to climb into bed.

The rogue ship rammed hers, its lethal spiked rods piercing the hull, gouging and ripping. The mangled timbers of her clipper screeched and moaned. She ran to the rail and looked down. A thundering rush of water poured through the gaping breech, the roar echoing through the bowels of the vessel. Frantic, she looked up—into the wicked yellow eyes of the dragon head. It hurled laughter at her. Then, suddenly, from out of its fanged mouth a holocaust spewed like the fiery breath of Satan.

Instantly her dress, black as death, exploded into flames. Buttons! My God, the dress had hundreds of buttons! Her fingers flew to her throat. She reached for the first. But it crumbled to powder in her hand! She glanced down and found that all the buttons and her clothing had disintegrated. All that remained was a ring of ash at her feet. She stood naked before the sneering eyes of the dragon demon.

Then she saw him. *Like a god, he leapt from his ship to hers. With naught but a loincloth covering his bronzed savagery, he soared across the midnight depths toward her.*
Run!
But her feet wouldn't move. Heaven help her, she couldn't lift a toe.
He landed before her in a cunning crouch, his keen hunter's eyes tracking her every hill, her every valley as, slowly, he uncoiled before her.
She counted his every sculptured muscle honed to perfection, from those trailing up his narrow torso to the mammoth-sized ones bulging in his chest and shoulders. His arms, commanding, pulled her to him as he captured her. His hard flesh burned hot against her nakedness, scorching her. She could hear the sizzle. She didn't care. She wanted to feel more of the enrapturing heat. Her hands rode up to his stalwart neck and clasped onto him. She melted closer, pouring across him like molten lava. His heart pounded hard against hers. With hers. Becoming one.
Her gaze drifted up from the swell of his chest to . . . the bared leering teeth of the fire-snorting dragon head.
She screamed, but the serpent's dooming howl was all she could hear. She wrenched away.
Long-nailed claws thrust out and snagged her, yanking her up against the vile creature's body.
She slammed her fists into its iron-plated scales. She kicked at it. But the harder she struggled, the louder it yowled with maniacal pleasure.
Suddenly, all noise ceased. A deadly silence filled the void.
The thing, its eyes mirroring the inferno smoldering in its mouth, moved to her ear. "Rachel," it mocked in an erupting whisper. "Rachel."
Oh, God, It knows my name.

((chapter 4))

"RACHEL."

She bolted upright. Hair tumbled across her face. Flinging it aside, she found her new husband hovering a mere breath away. The lamp he held aloft created eerie shadows, and its golden light outlined him, making him appear equally as large as the Norse pirate. Worse, his expression was cloaked in hellish blackness. She couldn't read his intent. But whatever was there, *he'd come*.

She hoped he couldn't detect her panic. "Yes?"

"It's morning. Time to fix breakfast. I've already started a fire in the stove."

It was morning? Time to get up? "Thank you," she said, indescribable relief flooding her every sense. Her Viking had come to *wake* her, *not* to ravage or kill.

"Homer's right. You sure do have a mess of hair." Jake turned and walked out of the cabin before Rachel could ascertain if his last remark was meant as a compliment.

Probably not. After all, he'd just spent their wedding night in the barn. She knew she should be grateful, especially after her nightmare, but she had this hollow sinking feeling that she'd been found wanting.

Well, she decided, tossing off the covers, she'd just have to change his mind, show him that she was a truly capable person. And desirable. Before, back in Peoria, she'd always been considered quite worthy. After all, she'd had, not one, but two marriage proposals, hadn't she?

She jumped out of bed. "I'll get breakfast on the table

41

and fast. The quickest way to a man's heart is through his stomach.'' He'd certainly shown her that last night.

Smiling, Rachel padded across the cold floor to her clothing trunk in the front room. She withdrew and donned a satin wrapper that complemented the silvery blue of her eyes, then slid her feet into a matching pair of slippers. After finding her brush, she gravitated to the blazing fire in the hearth. She stroked down the length of her hair, enjoying the way the firelight danced through, turning it to spun gold.

Normally, she would've counted every stroke, but today she couldn't spare the time. It was hard to believe that she'd slept at all. But then, to oversleep? And while she had, Mr. Stone had lighted the lamps and built both fires. Hearing a bubbling sound, Rachel spotted the coffeepot on a burner. And on the counterboard lay a slab of bacon. He'd even gone to the smokehouse for her! He really was a very nice person. Maybe he'd slept in the barn only in deference to her exhausted state. The keen sensation of being mothered by the rough-hewn man welled within her. Tears came to her eyes, which she blinked away as the resolve to prove herself solidified. Remembering the vow she'd made to herself upon first sighting this tranquil little valley, she again pledged to be the best homesteading wife any man would be proud to call his own.

Deciding a ribbon in her hair would add a nice touch, she moved back to the trunk and found one the color of her dressing gown. With it, she pulled up the weighty mass and was tying a jaunty bow when she felt a draft.

Her husband filled the doorway of the cabin. He lounged against a stud, his eyes appraising her.

And, as usual, she couldn't quite read his expression. That beard simply had to go. And, besides, for all she knew, a valiantly handsome face might be hiding behind all that hair. With a body like his, could his face be any less?

Suddenly she realized they were staring at each other. Feeling exposed, she scanned the front of her wrapper, but found it securely in place. Then, not wanting to appear flustered, she lifted her chin and matched his gaze again.

"I'm going to start breakfast now. Anything in particular you'd like? I didn't see any chickens. Do we have eggs?"

"Bacon and some of those fluffy biscuits like you made last night would do fine." Jake stared at her another few seconds, then swung around and made a hasty exit.

He certainly is a man of odd habits, Rachel thought, pondering yet another of his abrupt departures.

In a matter of minutes breakfast was ready. As Rachel placed a pan of golden-brown biscuits on the table set with her rose-trimmed china, her crystal, and silverware, Jake came through the door again. His timing was so perfect she wondered if he had been watching through the window. "Please, sit down."

She filled two delicately fluted cups with coffee and started to join him. But when his oversized fingers wouldn't fit through the cup handle, Rachel exchanged it for one of his dented tin mugs—a concession to practicality. She wondered how many more she would be obliged to make in this wilderness so far from Illinois and civilization.

Jake ate in silence, never looking up at her, but, she noticed with satisfaction, he ate with the same zest.

She did her best to keep up. After forcing down two biscuits, some bacon, and a glass of milk, she rose to pour them both another cup of coffee. "I'm feeling very rested today. If you'll tell me where the seed and tools are, I'll do the best I can to plant a garden."

"You needn't bother," he mumbled, not looking at her. "You just rest up. Get your strength back. I'll do it."

"No, really. I'm feeling quite fit. As soon as I clean up the breakfast dishes and dress, I'll get started."

"All right." His gaze lifted to her face. "If you've got yourself set on it, you can help. Soon as I finish my coffee, I'll go out and plow up the field." He scooted back his chair far enough to prop one leg over the other, then, sipping his steaming brew, he leisurely studied her.

Flustered by his inspection, Rachel raised her cup to her lips while smoothing the pink tablecloth.

"That looks real nice," he said. "But when it gets dirty it'll have to be washed."

"Well, of course."

"There's already more work to do around here than a body can keep up with."

"Thank you for your concern, but I'd prefer to keep it on until such time it proves too difficult."

"Suit yourself." Jake downed the last of his coffee, then unfolded himself to his full height. "I'm going to go hitch up Sampson. When you've a mind to, come on out."

Rachel hurried through the dishes, then put on an old gray dress she'd worn as her father's medical assistant, her sturdiest shoes, and a pair of tea-stained afternoon gloves. Then, opening the door she walked out into a rush of chilly air.

A frothy mist played across the meadow, obscuring the lower branches of the surrounding evergreens. Above the trees, the strutting Cascades sparkled in the crystalline light of morning. Simply beautiful! Beside the house, she saw Jake guiding a shovel plow through the sod, ripping a long dark furrow in the dew-laden grass. Wearing no more than a heavy cotton shirt and denim trousers, he seemed oblivious to the cold. Rachel rubbed her arms, assuring herself she would be grateful for the crisp spring weather as soon as she started shoveling and hoeing.

Jake looked up from his plowing and watched the slender young woman come toward him, tiptoeing over the new clods. She appeared hopelessly out of place as she held up the hem of her dress, exposing black silk stockings. The gloves she wore were next to useless, and her head was missing a sunbonnet. "Whoa," he called to Sampson.

Shading serene blue eyes from the morning sun, she looked up at him. "I'm here," she said, stating the obvious. "You certainly are plowing a large plot."

"The garden has to supply enough vegetables for a whole year."

"Of course. I hadn't thought."

Her gaze dropped and a fringe of gold-tipped lashes hid eyes no longer jaundiced—eyes that reminded Jake of a lake he'd once seen from the top of Mount Hood, a deep blue jewel fringed with ice.

She again treated him to the crystal beauty of her eyes. "Where do you want me to start?"

He forgot to answer.

"What do you want me to do?"

She sure had improved after just one night in his bed. Reluctantly, he shifted his gaze to the barn. "You'll need a hoe. There's one inside the barn door." As she turned, he added, "And there's a pair of canvas gloves in the tool box. We're planting a garden, not going to a *sor-ee.*" A smile magically lifted her lusciously full lips, and he knew he'd misspoken the word, *soirée,* which he'd only seen in print.

When Rachel returned, Jake showed her the height and width each row should be, then left her to her task. While tilling the plot, he glanced at her often. She worked with enthusiasm. The girl had spunk, too. No denying it.

When Jake finished plowing, he returned the workhorse, then with shovel in hand, went to join Rachel. As he neared, he noticed her pace had slackened, but she still labored without ceasing.

Jake started to trench at the beginning of a row and soon caught up with the girl, who had visibly flagged. "Here, give me the hoe. I'll do that for a while."

"No, really, I can do it." Her voice was feeble.

"Take my shovel, we'll just trade jobs. All right?"

Jake finished forming the row, then another—all the while sneaking peeks at the girl desperately trying to keep up. Her hands shook from lifting the shovels of dirt, and her skirt had become a hindrance, weighted down with almost as much mud as that which clung to her shoes. She looked pale, like she had the day before, and her lips were turning blue.

"Ma'am? I think you'd better go take a rest."

As she straightened, her face crinkled with a wince. "I'm

fine.'' She drew an uneven breath and jammed the shovel into the ground. "I don't need to rest."

The lady was so determined to show him she was fit, he'd have to carry her back to the house. Jake dropped the hoe and strode down the row toward her. "Those biscuits you make are real tasty."

She eyed him with a dull, unfocused look.

"I've got a bag of dried apricots, and I'd be mighty grateful if you'd bake me a pie even half as good."

"A pie?" Her voice sounded hollow.

"Yeah. If you start now, we could have it for nooning." Jake took the shovel from her hands. "My mouth is already watering just thinking about it."

"A pie . . . Of course." She turned, faltered unsteadily, then lifted her sodden skirt and hobbled away.

Reaching the porch, Rachel dropped down on the edge and removed her shoes with work-numbed fingers. "Thank God," she sighed. Another minute and she would've collapsed.

She looked across the field to the man easily double her size and at least ten times as strong. He shoveled furiously, and he wasn't even breathing hard. He looked up, prompting her to stagger to her feet and up the steps.

Jake didn't come in for the midday meal for several hours, allowing Rachel the extra time to prop up her feet and drink a revitalizing cup of chamomile tea. When he did return, she greeted him with the tempting aroma of sweet apricot pie and a smile. She'd freshly coiffed her hair, and her cheeks were scrubbed to a dewy pink. She saw his eyes widen appreciatively, and she knew she was a success.

As before, Jake ate without conversing. Rachel guessed it was just the way of mountain men. But it was not hers. At home in Peoria, mealtime had always been a time for catching up on the latest news, discussing an interesting medical case, sharing a poem. She missed those moments, which were now her most treasured memories. Stealing a peek at her new husband, she wondered if the two of them would ever find enough in common to create their own memories.

"Mr. Stone—"

"Jake," he corrected.

"Jake. I noticed your books on the mantel. They look well used."

He looked from Rachel to the fireplace. "Yeah. Books are heavy to tote, so those are all I've got."

"Well, no one could fault your choice. Shakespeare and the Bible."

"An old trapper friend passed 'em on to me."

"But you have read them, I presume."

"Sure. Lots of times. Helped stave off cabin fever more often than I can count."

"Cabin fever? What kind of sickness is that?"

"Missy," Jake said with a gravelly chuckle. "Cabin fever is when you're snowed in. Cooped up in some dark little cabin so long you think you'll go crazy."

"Oh, yes." Mindless brick cell walls imprisoned her soul again. She lowered her gaze. "I know what you mean. I was locked away for two months."

Jake's chair groaned as he shifted his weight uneasily. The poor little thing had already been through so much. How would he ever be able to tell her he was sending her back to Homer Dorset? But since his mind was made up, the honorable thing would be to come right out with it. Before he weakened any more over the winsome creature. He'd stalled way too long. Had to tell her . . . and he would, too . . . right after he'd had his pie. No sense spoiling a good pie.

Some big man you are, Jake thought, belittling himself an hour later as he and Rachel toiled once more on the garden plot. All the while he'd been putting away half that tangy pie, he hadn't worked up the nerve to tell her. But it was partly her fault. Her luminous eyes had looked so compellingly anxious as he took his first bite, how could he spoil her pleasure by saying he was taking her back?

Between bites he'd again noted all her other endeavors to

make the cabin more homey. A clever little figurine of a child feeding a duck even stood on the mantel.

And now, once again, here she was striving to keep up, laboring in a field whose harvest she would have no share in. *He had to tell her.*

Jake stopped and turned to face the young woman lagging far behind. When she saw him she flashed a plucky smile and increased her pace. How could he tell her? She was trying so hard. What the hell, he just wouldn't. He'd just go ahead and keep her. Her spunk and spirit more than made up for her small size. Next time he was in town he'd just have Homer send off for a whole barrel of that quinine stuff.

Jake strolled back to her. With a smile he hoped would show his approval of her efforts, he reached for the shovel in her hand. "Let's trade jobs for a spell."

"I'm sorry—I'll try—harder," she sputtered through heaving breaths.

"Don't fret yourself. You're doing just fine." He handed her the hoe and stepped out of the way. As she walked past him, he scanned her graceful form, taking a second look. Though just a slip of a girl, she was pleasingly proportioned—maybe a bit leggy, but he liked that in a woman. Yes, and this morning when her hair was swirled across the pillow, it was all he could do to keep his hands off of it. And later, when she was brushing it, and the firelight set it aflame, it was so glorious, a rainbow would look common beside it. Yes, keeping her was definitely the right thing to do.

Filled with renewed energy, Jake doubled his pace. He wanted to catch up fast, to get a closer look. As he closed the gap, a line from one of Old Will's verses came to mind. *When that mine eye is famish'd for a look, Or heart in love with sighs himself doth smother.* He paused a few feet behind her to feast his own famished eyes.

She straightened, and a shapely breast thrust against her bodice as she raised a hand to her brow.

He envisioned the delicate turn of her body lying upon his bed amid the furs. He could feel the sleek smoothness of her creamy skin. Her silken hair laced through his fingers. Her full, soft lips . . . hot . . . moist . . .

Rachel swayed. Then, like a shot dear, she crumpled.

Round and round she whirled, deeper and deeper into the inky sea. So relaxed, so carefree. A delicious dizziness caused a tickle in her belly, and she had an almost irresistible urge to laugh. She inhaled deeply.

Then it struck her. She could breath! She'd been so afraid to jump, but instead of being swallowed in an icy shroud, she'd entered a warm, wonderful silkiness.

Strange, she didn't remember leaping. But she must have. Looking up through the whirling funnel, she saw a dot of light far above. It grew wider, brighter. The ship must still be aflame, but she didn't care. Let it and every evil thing on it burn.

But what about the Viking? Did she really want him to die? Of course she did. No! Maybe. She didn't know.

She needed to take another look. To see his eyes.

She swam, no, soared toward the surface with the grace and speed of a ship's prow-maiden slicing through the waves. A sheer white gown clung to her, caressing every curve.

A hand suddenly appeared. *It captured her around the waist, lifted her up, ripping her from the water, crushing her against iron-hard flesh—against the burnished magnificence of the Viking's bared chest.*

Every nerve, every sense sparked to life. Her breath quickened. She knew she should try to fight him off, but instead she looked up into radiance. The fearsome blazing beard had diffused into a soft aura, framing the verdant passion of messianic eyes.

Effortlessly her mystic pagan whisked her up and away, above the fluffiest clouds. Then tenderly, he lowered her into enveloping billows as she beheld his adoring splendor.

Why, then, did he fade from her with the same sureness that the night claims a winter sun?

In a panic, her gaze darted after him. She didn't want him

*to leave. She wanted him to stay. Whisper his hands over
her like a cool, curious breeze. No, not cool, a hot, seeking
tempest. If only she could open her mouth to call him back.
Her arms wouldn't rise up to him, either. How would he
know she wanted him?*

*Out of the blackness he suddenly reappeared, a gentle
smile gracing his princely features. Somehow he'd understood her silent but passionate plea. Now there was nothing
but him, his godlike body lowering over her own yearning
flesh. He smelled intoxicatingly of cedar and the incense of
his virility. His hands went to her throat and slid over her
robe with agonizing slowness.*

*Wave after fiery wave shot through her, as the tips of his
fingers flared into bolts of lightning, turning her into a
living flame. A goddess. For Odin. She spun into a dervish
of tormented ecstasy. She desperately needed to quench
herself with him. But her clothes defied him. She would help
him if only she could get her hands to move. She needed to
be as bare as he. To drape the sleekness of this golden god
over her torrid body.*

*Finally she felt the confining garments being slipped from
her. At last she was free to receive her lover.*

But where was he?

Again he was gone. He'd left her. How could he? *Barren
wind washed its cold desolation over her.*

Suddenly, savagely, she was being yanked by the foot.

My God. The serpent. It had her. It was dragging her
away. Laughing fiendishly. Where was Odin? Why didn't
he save her?

*Then she remembered. Her Viking was the dragon. He'd
tricked her again.*

*Her screams had no sound, her kicks no power. Or did
they?*

The snorting serpent released her.

She dove for the water again.

Once more, steely claws snagged her.

No! She shrieked. *This time she heard her scream. She
kicked the viperous creature in the gut.*

* * *

The way Rachel came awake screaming and kicking, a body'd think someone was trying to rape her. Not that the thought hadn't crossed his mind. "Take it easy, I'm just taking your boot off."

Those thickly ruffled lashes flipped up and her terrified gaze darted around, searching, until she found him sitting near the foot of the bed.

He smiled uneasily and shrugged. "Sorry if I scared you. You fainted, and I was just trying to help you rest easier."

The frightened storm in her eyes calmed and those pristine lakes returned. "I fainted?" she said in a husky murmur. "I don't faint." Then her gaze drifted down to her sleeveless underthing, that flimsy piece of nothing that dipped real low and had the good sense to reach only to her knees. Her eyes widened. "What happened to my dress?" She grabbed the fur quilt and flapped it over her.

Jake ran his hand across his mouth to wipe away a grin before he answered. "Over there in the corner. It's got mud all over it."

"It does?"

By her tone it was obvious she didn't understand about her clothes or about how unfit she was. *Or* how hard it was going to be to keep his hands off her now that he'd seen the swell of her flirty breasts. Seen, hell. He'd made damn sure his hands meandered to each crest as he took a long sweet time undoing her dress. His gaze drifted down to where the fur quilt now rose and fell with her breathing and wished she hadn't been so quick to hide that bewitching body. A sigh slid past the disappointment clogging his throat, disappointment that he knew was going to cost him a lot of sleep. "Look, you just get some rest. I shouldn't have let you work out there in the first place."

Her eyes darkened to troubled pools. "But—I—"

Every fiber in his body ached for the want of her. He knew he had to get out fast before he lost all control. "I'll be out working on the garden if you need anything."

Nodding, she closed her eyes. She looked pitifully defeated as she rolled onto her side, facing the wall.

The sight tore at him. He'd waited so long to see a woman in his bed, and the very look of her, the curve of her hip beneath the quilt . . . Forget it, Jake. He inhaled a lungful and turned to leave. And, damn it, she could never stand up to farm life. Damn it to hell, anyway.

Rachel lay watching the rain sheet down the windowpane. She should get up, but how could she face this man, her husband? She heard him rummaging about. Logs banged one on top of the other as he built the morning fire.

Last evening when he had awakened her for supper, she'd remembered, to her utmost embarrassment, that she'd fainted. *Swooned.* How miserably she'd failed.

During the meal he'd prepared for them, she'd thought of no excuse that would've made her look better in his eyes. And he'd been his usual silent self, except for one noticeable difference—he totally avoided looking at her. When she'd risen to clear the table, he spoke to some vague spot above her head when he ordered her back to bed.

He'd thought she was unfit for farm life, and she'd more than proved him right. But still, she *was* his wife. That was an irrefutable fact. Somehow, they would have to come to some kind of an understanding. Maybe if she told him about her father's money waiting in the bank in Santa Fe, he would feel less cheated. Using only a small portion, he could hire someone to do her heavier chores until she regained her strength. But a transfer of funds would probably take months—much too long to help her now.

But of course, she thought with a swell of hope, any banker would surely advance her a portion for a fee.

But could she trust Jake? If he knew about the money, he could take it and do with it as he wished. As her husband, he had the right. Which was he, valiant Viking or the devil's own dragon? She pulled the plush fur quilt up to her chin. Maybe she'd better wait a while before deciding.

Rachel eased out of bed and onto her feet, feeling for the

first time in her life every unforgiving muscle stretched across every bone. But then she'd never shoveled a mountain of dirt before, either.

After inching into her dressing gown and looping the tie with achy fingers, she walked into the main room as gracefully as her woodlike legs would allow.

"Good morning," she said, attempting cheeriness.

Jake turned from the wood stove with a steaming cup in his hand. "How do you feel?" He eyed her jerky advance.

"Oh, fine, really. Just a little stiff."

"You look stove up worse'n an eighty-year-old man."

And a good morning to you, too, she thought, her irritation pricked with each agonizing step. "I'll start breakfast now. Would you like fried potatoes today?"

"Yeah!" His enthusiasm over food never seemed to diminish. Placing his cup on the table, he retrieved the coarse-haired buffalo coat and put it on. In it, his very presence filled the room. No Viking chieftain could have ever looked more invincible. "I'll be out in the barn if you need me." His relaxed tone, the gentle timbre, disavowed his awesome size as he strode out into the rain.

The entire time Rachel prepared breakfast, she vacillated over the matter of her inheritance. Jake would certainly look upon her in a more favorable light if he knew. But what if she needed it to escape? Oh, Papa, she pleaded, hoping for a piece of wisdom. But all she heard was the same old platitude. *Do what is honorable.*

Maybe Papa's right, she thought. Jake had been a perfect gentleman, very undemanding—considering the fact that he'd been denied his husbandly rights two nights in a row.

But, then, that niggling thought resurfaced. Maybe he wasn't so wonderful after all. Maybe he simply found her too unattractive to bother with. The idea slapped her in the face.

Instant anger flared as, once again, Jake strolled in the door and sat down just as Rachel transferred the food from the stove to the table. Another coincidence? Not blamed likely! He was nothing but an old peeping tom. Vengefully she filled his cup to the brim. He'd either have to bend over the table to slurp some out before he picked it up, or he'd have a devil of a time getting the boiling hot coffee to his lips without slopping some on his hand. Rachel hoped he would opt for the latter.

After giving her a disconcerted look, Jake chose to slurp.

Again, with great gusto, he ate enough to feed a whole family. When he finally finished, he laid down his fork and spoke for the first time since he'd walked in the door. "Could I have some more coffee?"

Rachel filled his cup more carefully this time, since he glared at her all the while she poured. She also refilled hers, then sat down to return his stare with one of her own.

"Missy," he said, then paused to take a deep breath. "There's something I've been putting off telling you."

His use of the term *missy* aggravated her. "Yes?"

She watched his gaze waver then drop to his weather-toughened hands. "I'm afraid you're just not working out. I'm going to have to take you back."

"Back?" Rachel lurched forward. *"Where?"*

"Back to Dorset. He'll have to find you another husband, one that doesn't need a sturdy woman. I think maybe it's best I catch a lumber schooner headed for San Francisco. There's a chance I can find a willing female down there, one who's down on her luck and would be glad for a roof over her head."

Rachel wrenched to her feet, ignoring her protesting muscles. "You can't trade me off like some old mule. I'm your wife. Your *legal* wife."

Jake looked up at her with a weak smile. "I think we can get around that. As long as we catch Homer before he sends the certificate off to Oregon City."

"What you're saying is preposterous."

"No, I'm sure Dorset'll go along. Don't you worry about a thing. There is one thing, though." Jake looked down at his hands again. "I will need to keep you here till the land recorder comes through. No more'n a few weeks. Or I won't be able to get title to the rest of my homestead."

"The gall. The unmitigated gall—"

A loud banging on the door interrupted Rachel.

Looking as if he were escaping a loaded gun, Jake rushed to it and opened it to a gangling young man drenched by the rain.

"Your new woman's gotta come," he said, water dripping off his hat and down his rain slicker. "Right now!"

"Hold on there. Is that you, Harland?"

"Yeah, it's me," he said, doffing his drooping hat. "But I ain't got time to jaw with you. Pa said if I didn't have her back in two hours he'd have my hide."

Rachel joined them. "What's the problem?"

"Donald pushed Gus outa the hayloft, and he fell on his leg real bad. The bone was stickin' out the skin somethin' awful. Pa and Orletta tried to fix it, but now it's all swoll up, and Gus is burnin' with the fever."

Jake moved between her and the young man. "What's that—"

"Please don't interrupt," Rachel said. She stepped past Jake. "How long since the injury occurred?"

"Yesterd'y mornin'."

"I see. And Orletta lives with you?"

"Yeah, she's married to my pa."

Rachel swung to Jake. "Go hitch up the wagon while I get dressed." She hurried to her clothing trunk.

Dumbfounded, Jake stared after her.

"Whatcha waitin' on?" The lanky boy pulled at Jake's arm. "We gotta hurry."

chapter 5

"LAND sakes, girl. Just look at you." Orletta, the very worldly woman who'd taken a special liking to Rachel during the long voyage, left the protection of the porch and ran through the downpour to the wagon rolling to a stop. "You're soaked plumb to the bone. Let me help you down and into the house before you catch your death."

"No, Miss Letty," young Harland said. "You get on in outa the rain. I'll get Miss Stone down. No sense in havin' two wet females on my hands."

"You're right, *boy*." Orletta gave Rachel a conspiratorial wink and swooped up her burgundy wool skirt to race back up the porch steps. "You ain't man enough to handle one, let alone two."

"Orletta!" barked a middle-aged man. He and another young man strode toward them from the direction of the barn. "That's the kind of talk what's got August laid up." Reaching the buckboard, he tipped his felt hat at Rachel. Water in the brim spilled onto his boots. "Name's Amos Colfax, ma'am. A friend of Jake's. Let me help you down."

"Thank you, Mr. Colfax. Mr. Stone bade me send you his regards." Clutching her medical bag with one hand, she offered the other to the man whose sturdy but rounded features instilled her with immediate trust. An accompanying smile spread jauntily across his sun-browned face added a sparkle to his umber eyes. Even his balding head, round as a baby's bottom, looked kissable.

"No. Let me, Pa," said the young man standing next to Mr. Colfax. He reached for Rachel.

"No." Harland, having jumped down from the buck-board, pushed between the others. "I brung her, I get her down."

"That ain't fair," said the other brother as he shoved back at Harland. "You been with her all mornin'."

Rachel pulled in her hand to avoid being the subject of a tug-of-war.

"That's right. I saw her first," Harland said as he banged a bony hip into his brother.

"And she's goin' to be the last thing you see," the other said, flinging a fist.

"Boys!" Amos deftly blocked the blow. "That'll be enough. You'll be havin' Mrs. Stone thinkin' we're nothin' but backwoods ruffians. Now, get back. The both of you."

With crestfallen expressions on raw-boned, freckled faces that bore no resemblance to their father's, they both took backward steps to avoid their father's jabbing elbows.

"You'll have to excuse the boys. They don't get to see a pretty new face very often. Donald, tend the horses." Without further ado, Mr. Colfax reached up and swung her down, then ushered her into the house so fast her feet barely tapped the soggy ground.

"Rachel, honey, come on over by the fire and dry out before you go in to see Gussy. Would you like some coffee to warm you up?" Orletta asked with that overly familiar voice she used even when she was busy mothering some-one.

"Yes, that would be nice." Rachel dropped the hood of her forest-green cloak and tidied the coils of her hairdo before untying and removing the wet garment. "What do you want me to do with this, Orletta? It's dripping."

"Harland, take Rachel's cloak and drape it over the chair by the fire."

"Yes, ma'am." Oblivious of his own soaked clothing, he smiled as he carefully spread out her mantle.

"I can't tell you how much we appreciate you comin' out in weather like this," Mr. Colfax said, handing Rachel a flannel towel to dry herself. "But Orletta says you're real learned when it comes to doctorin'. And that your pa left you all his medicines and purges and such.''

"Yes, it's been most fortuitous since several of us caught malaria. We almost depleted my supply of quinine.'' Finished with the towel, Rachel handed it back to her host.

"Orletta says you helped your pa out some.'' Mr. Colfax continued to smile, but his eyes betrayed his concern.

"Almost every day since I was fourteen. So you see, I have garnered a goodly sum of medical knowledge.''

"You don't look much older than that now,'' Harland observed with a hopeful raise of his brows.

"That's a sweet thing to say, but I'm twenty-three.''

"See, Amos, I told you,'' Orletta said. After handing Rachel temptingly hot coffee in a thick earthenware cup, she entwined her arms through one of her husband's. "Well, now, what do you think of my man? Ain't he a looker?''

"Ah, go on, Letty.'' His grin deepened as he ducked his head and shrugged.

Rachel couldn't help but smile. He really was cute in a cuddly sort of way. He and Orletta were a perfect match. Like his, her big frame was softened by generous padding. She wasn't plump, just wonderfully rounded in all the right places. Even with her thick black hair pulled back into a severe knot her bold features exuded a sensuous welcome.

Rachel felt so lacking around this woman, and knew that when Jake saw her, he would be even more disappointed that he hadn't been in Independence on the day the women arrived.

A feeling of worthlessness shriveled her insides as she sipped the steaming brew. "Harland said his oldest brother has broken a leg?''

"Yeah.'' Amos gave Orletta a knowing scowl. "The boys was squabbling up in the hayloft and Gus fell out.''

"It weren't my fault,'' Harland countered.

"Nobody's blaming you.'' Amos turned his attention to Rachel again. "I just want my son's leg fixed up. In forty-seven we come clear across this country without gettin' so much as a hangnail. Then, just when things was startin' to get easy, my Celia up and passed away on me. And now this. My firstborn could end up a cripple—if he don't die first.''

"Now, Amos.'' Orletta gave his arm a comforting squeeze. "Stop your frettin'. We got Rachel here. She'll fix him right up. Won't you?''

"I'm warmed up sufficiently,'' she said, handing her emptied cup to Orletta. "If you would be so kind as to take me to August.''

The room they entered was warmed by a fireplace, and at the far end lay Gus in a four-poster cherrywood bed. A matching chiffonier, polished to a high shine, stood against the rough-barked side wall. The expertly crafted pieces, the only ones of their kind she had seen in the cabin, reminded Rachel of her own parent's bedroom furniture.

"How ya doin', Gussy?'' Orletta said.

"I told you not to call me Gussy—'specially in front of company.'' He looked at Rachel with eyes of that same expressive brown as his father's.

"Sounds to me like you're feelin' mighty spry for someone in need of a doctor,'' Orletta countered. "I think I'll just send this purty little lady on home.''

"How do you do, August?'' Rachel placed her hand to his brow. It radiated heat. "My name is Miss Chambers—I mean, Mrs. Stone. I'd like to help, if I can.'' She unwrapped the leg, and it was as festered as she knew it would be. Placing her black bag on the bedstand, she searched through it until she located a jar filled with a powdery substance labeled Dragon's Claw. "Gus has a bit of a fever. Orletta, would you please add a teaspoon of this to a cup of hot water? And—here it is—twelve drops of laudanum. A little something for the pain.''

"Sure thing. Be back in a shake.''

Gus looked up at Rachel with a hopeful smile. "I heared laudanum makes you feel real good.''

"It should ease the pain somewhat.''

"It really don't hurt much. Just feels kinda tingly. How does it look?'' he asked with only a hint of a quaver.

"It's abscessed, but I don't see any sign of mortification. I think we've caught it in time."

"Thank you, Jesus! You don't know how good that makes me feel. I was sure you'd say my leg had to come off. I been pretendin' I wasn't, but I was real scared."

"I won't lie to you. It's serious. First, I need to get the swelling down. I'm going to have to lance and drain it before I can check on how your bones are set."

"You really know what you're doin'?"

"Yes, I do."

"Then do your worst. I can take it."

Rachel's gaze moved from the badly festered leg to the young man's face, set in an expression of bravado, and smiled. "Instead, how about if I try to do my best?"

The wistful cry of a night owl invaded the silence of the third watch. The rain had stopped around midnight, and now the only other sound was an occasional moan from Rachel's patient. Only slightly over-warm, he lay in a drugged sleep. Taking Gus's wrist, she checked his pulse. The rate of his heartbeat now, too, was normal.

Rachel stood and stretched her stiff back and legs. It had been a long day and night. After the abscess had been drained, she had straightened the bones of his lower leg with the help of Amos and Orletta. But, because of the infection, she had not been able to splint and bind it completely. Instead, she'd strapped his leg on a board and rigged it to the bedposts and a hook in the ceiling.

Rachel tested the poultice pressed across the wound. It was cold. Picking up the lantern, she went to the kitchen to make another.

Orletta, sheathed in a ruby-red wrapper, came into the room as Rachel dipped a fresh cloth strip into a strong tea of indigo weed simmering on the stove.

"Thought I heard you up stirrin'. How's Gussy?"

"The swelling is almost gone and the red streaks up his leg have all but disappeared. It's lucky you sent for me when you did." Rachel wagged her head. "One more day—"

"Have a cup o' coffee. I'll fix that poultice."

With a weary smile, Rachel dropped into a chair.

"I've been wantin' to get you alone. And that ain't easy to do around here." A generous grin plumped Orletta's cheeks. "Amos says that man of yours is as big as a bear, but you don't look no worse for the wear. Is he treatin' you all right?"

"Mr. Stone didn't come for me until the day before yesterday. And, well, things haven't been going too well."

Tossing the steaming wad of cloth back and forth between her hands, Orletta said, "Let me put this on the boy's leg, and I'll be right back. We need to talk." When she returned, she poured herself a cup and joined Rachel at the table.

Hovering over tightly clenched hands, Rachel watched her knuckles whiten. She didn't want to tell her degrading story, but she desperately needed to vent her confusion and agony. A lone tear trickled down.

Orletta lifted her friend's chin and wiped it away.

"Forgive me," Rachel said, straightening. "I guess I'm more tired than I thought."

"I was really hopin' things would work out for you. After what you been through."

"It's been hard for you, too."

"Yeah, but I had it comin'." Orletta covered Rachel's hands with her own. "So, tell me, what's the trouble?"

"Oh, Letty. I was still yellow from the fever, and I've lost so much weight I look just awful."

"But, honey, you're still purty as a newborn calf. You told him you'd been sick, didn't you?"

"He knew. And he *knows* malaria can reoccur. He doesn't think I'm fit for farm life."

"So the son of a bitch don't think he got his money's worth. I'd like to know what any of 'em thought they was buyin' for that piddly sum."

Rachel's eyes widened at Orletta's words. "I'm sorry. I

should've asked how you're doing with your new husband.''

"Oh, you needn't worry about me. Amos is a real honeybun. But some o' them others sure didn't look like much. Guess I'm just mad cuz Amos said Jake was a fair man. If the man thought you wasn't fit, he shouldn't have married you. There's no end to bachelors out here who would jump at the chance. But I guess the bastard was more interested in his honeymoon than anything else.''

"No, he's not that bad. He hasn't . . . you know.'' Rachel's gaze slid away a second as she shrugged. "But the storekeeper misled him.'' As she told Orletta all that had happened since she met Jake, the worldly woman's expressive dark eyes took on a hard glitter.

When Rachel finished, Orletta arched a brow. "So this is Amos's best friend? I'd sure hate to meet one of his enemies. The man weds you—and believe me, I know men—he'll bed you 'fore he sends you packin'. Which, by the by, robs you of your most valuable asset. But first, he has to get you to file for *your* land, before he throws you off it. Now that's what I call a gentleman of the first water.''

"What do you mean, *my* land?''

"Sugar, you're not goin' to believe this.'' Orletta moved closer, her voice a conspiring whisper. "Amos let it slip out the other day. It seems there's this land act, and it gives a man three hundred and twenty free acres. If he's married, his wife can file, too, for just as much. Not him—her. Imagine, this poor ignorant trollop is gonna be a woman of means, a property owner.''

Giddy from lack of sleep the women became tickled by the irony and began to titter. They tried to smother the sound with their hands. But soon the ridiculousness of the situation proved too much, and they rocked with laughter.

Finally, wiping away tears, Rachel took a deep breath. She looked at Orletta's own wet cheeks and collapsed into giggles again.

Her friend joined her for another round before shuddering to a stop. "So, he says he's sending you back. Well, a body don't always get just exactly what he 'spects, does he? Your Jake thinks he's holdin' the winnin' hand, right now. But if you play your cards right—who knows?''

"I don't want to beat him out of anything. I just want my due. We did stand up before a justice of the peace, and those words must have some meaning. Even in Oregon.''

"Mornin'," Amos called as Rachel came into the common room. He sat with his family at the table.

She'd dozed off sometime before dawn and hadn't heard them rise for the day. "Good morning," she returned as the aromas of frying bacon and fresh brew enhanced her welcome.

"Mornin'," Donald and Harland chorused in return.

"I checked on you a few minutes ago," Orletta said, sopping a biscuit in the last of her egg, "but you and Gussy looked so peaceful, I didn't have the heart to wake you. How about a couple o' eggs?" She headed for the stove.

"Yes, please," Rachel said as she plucked a cup from a shelf, poured some coffee, and sat down.

"You know," Amos said, "that bed in there is the one Gus and the other boys was born in. Letty says he's doin' better. That so? Be a shame to have him die in it.''

"Yes, Mr. Colfax. I'm very pleased with his progress.''

"Call me Amos. Most ever'body does.''

"Thank you, I'd like that. Your son's fever is gone, and the wound is no longer discolored. As long as August's leg is kept immobile till the wound heals, he should be fit as a fiddle in seven or eight weeks.''

"Fiddle." Amos's eyes widened with twinkles of merriment. "You said the magic word." He sprang to his feet. "Come on, boys, we got some celebratin' to do.''

At the stove, Orletta looked over her shoulder and chuckled as Harland beat the others to a wooden chest against the wall. He grabbed up a harmonica and rose it to his lips. Out came the little ditty "Jimmy Cracked Corn.''

A toothy grin split Donald's face as he retrieved a dulcimer, then came back and shoved the breakfast dishes aside to make room for the instrument. It barely hit the table before his fingers began to pluck, and his foot started tapping to the beat of the lively tune.

Amos withdrew a violin and bow. Catching the melody, he jigged toward his sons.

"Here's your breakfast," Orletta yelled above the music as she brought a plate of bacon, eggs, and biscuits.

Donald began to sing the words in a surprisingly clear baritone, and Orletta's husky alto joined in.

It was hard to listen, eat, and laugh at the same time, but putting aside her table manners, Rachel managed. On the fourth time through, Harland led the little band into the bedroom where Gus lay. Abandoning the dulcimer, Donald grabbed a guitar out of the chest and followed.

Orletta sat down across from Rachel. "Ain't they a sight?" Leaning closer, she lowered her tone. "You know, I never intended to stay out here in these backwoods with that old man and a bunch of wild boys, but he makes life so much fun, I think I'm fallin' in love with the old coot."

Rachel looked from Orletta to the open doorway. She could see Amos bobbing up and down to the music. He blocked her view of the others, but she imagined the smile on Gus's face as she heard his tenor voice harmonize with Donald's more mellow tone.

"Yes, Orletta. God is certainly smiling on you."

"He sure is. And I don't know why." The happy look faded from her face. "I know I don't deserve it."

Rachel reached across and squeezed her hand. "You're a better person than you know. I'll always be grateful to you for the way you kept the sailors away from me. Be happy Orletta. It's in Amos's eyes. He loves you, too." She got up and walked to where the dulcimer rested. "Do you think Donald would mind if I tinker with it?"

"No. Do you play?"

"Not really. My music teacher thought only three instruments were suited to *refined* young ladies—the harpsichord, pianoforte, and the harp. But one of my classmates had a dulcimer in her home." Rachel smiled, remembering.

"Whenever we felt really wicked, we would sneak it out behind the woodshed and play it. Now you know my darkest secret."

"Well, it's sure not worth much, not a usable one."

"Usable?"

"You know—to tease with . . . to dangle."

"Sorry. I'll try to come up with a better one." If she told Orletta about the unseemly dreams she'd been having lately, she was sure her friend would find them a much more *useful* secret. Rachel felt uncommonly carnal as she placed her hands on the once forbidden dulcimer.

Amos, ahead of the two boys, capered back into the room and shouted to Rachel over the music. "Do you play?"

"I only know a few basic chords."

"Think you could follow along?"

"Not to anything as fast as 'Jimmy Cracked Corn'."

"How about, 'My Darlin''? Could you follow that?"

Rachel smiled into his exuberant face. "Yes. I've played it many times on the piano. I'm sure I can." Turning back to the dulcimer, her eyes met Orletta's. She winked as if they truly did have a wicked secret.

Always before, the gentle, lilting tune had warmed Rachel, but as they played and sang the sentimental words, memories of her mother and father intruded. She saw them, and other friends, all gathered around the piano, singing as she accompanied. So many pleasant evenings spent with dear hearts—and Gordon, ever-persistent Gordon.

Amos stopped playing. "Are you lost, Rachel? Donald, show her the chord."

"I'm sorry, I lost track."

Donald circled her with his arms and, taking her fingers in his hands, plucked the strings, his body rubbing hers.

Rachel stiffened. "It really isn't necessary."

"*Donald,*" Amos warned.

The young man stepped back and spread his arms in a gesture of innocence.

As they resumed playing, Donald again reached around

her and plucked out the melody while she chorded. Gradually, he leaned close again.

She shrank from him, but he deftly filled the void.

Not to be outdone, Harland crowded in on the other side until he was only inches from Rachel's ear. He played solely for her while the others sang the romantic verse:

> I see my darlin', in each ray of summer sunlight—
> I see my darlin' in the leaves of fall—
> I see her walkin' in the rainy April sadness—
> And hear her name in every bluebird call.

Rachel felt like a trapped rabbit. Had Orletta told them about her problem with Jake and given them the idea that she was available for courting? She looked to her friend and Amos for help, but found that they were sharing a private moment. The sight sent a pang of loneliness to her heart. Why couldn't Jake have been nice like Amos?

She didn't want to cause a scene, but—She threw her hands out and shoved both ways.

The two jumped back.

"Boys! What're you doin' to Miss Rachel?" Amos roared.

She broke out of their hovering circle. "Really, it wasn't anyone's fault. I'm just tired."

"'Course you are." Orletta got up from the table and came toward her. "You've been up all night."

"You're welcome to use my bed," offered Donald, with a slack-jawed grin. "It's the one next to the window."

"Mine's a lot softer," Harland urged. "You'll sleep much better in mine."

"She can choose whatever bed she wants," Amos said, silencing them. "Harland, you go muck out the stalls, and Donald, finish those rabbit hutches."

"Now?" they wailed in perfect harmony.

"Yes, now!" He pointed at the door until they trudged out. "You'll have to forgive the boys, missy. They're feelin' their oats. But you can hardly blame 'em. You sing just like an angel.''

"Thank you, Amos. That's very flattering."

"Just speakin' the truth."

"Come along, angel," Orletta said. "Let's get you to bed before that halo of yours gets to saggin' any more."

Riding up to the Colfax homestead on his prized stallion, Jake saw no sign of life except for a few chickens scratching in the grass. But before he could dismount, an exceptionally handsome woman came out the door. The tightly cinched red checked apron made a striking contrast to the somber gray of her dress, and her black hair, braided into a crown, shone like spit-polished boots.

"Howdy. The name's Jake Stone."

"Thought as much." Her smile was generous but did not reach eyes he knew were taking his measure. "The name's Orletta. Amos's new wife."

"Pleased to meet you." Jake tipped his hat.

"Amos is out in the barn." Her rock-hard gaze shifted in that direction, then softened. "Here he comes now."

Jake turned and saw Amos hurrying out the door to meet him and Harland running to catch up.

"Howdy," Amos said as he neared. "Reckon you're wonderin' what come o' your wife."

For some reason Jake couldn't look Amos in the eye. He settled his gaze on a speckled hen instead. "Thought I'd better come see if she ran off like Hank Reins's bride did."

"Oh, really? Which one of the girls married him?" Lifting her skirts, Orletta stepped off the porch.

"Smitty said she was a redhead. Don't remember the name."

"Belle," Orletta spat, nodding her head in a knowing manner. "She planned to jump ship in San Francisco, but the weather was too bad to make port. She was fit to be tied."

"Let me give Prince a drink," Harland offered as he reached up and rubbed the animal's velvety muzzle.

"Sure, go ahead."

"Pa says Kyle McLean's bought a racehorse. Supposed to be the fastest thing this side of St. Louis."

"Oh? What's its name?"

"Pega . . . Pega something."

"Pegasus," Amos finished for the boy.

"Pa, didn't McLean say he's bringin' him here to race Prince?"

"That's what I heard."

"If he does," Harland said, raising his cheek from the animal's neck, "can I be the one to ride Prince?"

"Ain't polite to ask," his pa chided.

"I don't mind, Amos." Looking into the eager eyes of the skinny, freckle-faced kid, Jake smiled. "Sure you can. But try not to take on any more weight between now and then. You're starting to sprout up faster'n a weed."

"Here we stand jawin'," Amos said. "Come on in and set a spell. Orletta, ain't it 'bout time for noonin'?"

"Almost. Come inside. I'll heat you up some coffee before I finish up."

Seated at the table with Amos, Jake followed every move the voluptuous woman made.

She reached high for cups and a full breast followed provocatively, then she smiled lazily at them while pouring the brew. Her hips gyrating, the checks on her apron danced crazily as she came toward them.

Suddenly aware he was gawking, he darted a glance at Amos to see if the older man had noticed his lusting eyes. But to his relief, Amos was also enjoying the view.

Jake cleared his throat and mumbled "Thank you" as Orletta set down two cups of thick leftover coffee.

Amos smiled up at her and patted her behind when she turned back to the stove. "Ain't she somethin'?"

"Yeah, seems like you got a real winner there."

"Yup. 'Cept she's got the boys so fired up, I may have to run 'em off to get any peace around here."

A chuckle rumbled up from Jake's chest as he shot a glance at the generously rounded cause of the trouble.

"If it hadn't been for your little Rachel, all their squabblin' would've cost Gus his leg."

"Where is Rachel?" Jake half expected Amos to say he'd repaid her by taking her back to Independence.

"She's asleep in the boys' room. She spent the night with my boy."

"What?" Jake roared. He might not intend to keep her, but he sure wasn't handing her over to some randy young buck free of charge.

"No, no," Amos said, waving his hands to erase Jake's assumption. "Rachel spent the night puttin' poultices on August's leg. We owe her a lot."

"Oh." Noticing he'd risen half out of the chair, Jake sat down again. "Well, I'm glad she could help out."

"Help?" Orletta interjected, turning from a stir-pot. "She didn't *help*. *She* brought his fever down. *She* cleaned out the infection, straightened his bones. We mostly just stood around wringin' our hands."

"Really?"

"Yes, really." Orletta stalked toward him, hands on her hips.

Jake knew she was ready to do battle, but he couldn't fathom what he'd said to set her off.

"Rachel says you plan to turn her out."

"Orletta," Amos scolded. "Jake's our guest."

"You're right." Her hands dropped from her waist. "I apologize. Dinner's ready. I'll go round up the boys."

Amos watched Orletta until the door closed behind her. "You'll have to excuse her. She's like a mother hen when it comes to your purty little wife."

"Well, I'm sorry, but I do plan to take Rachel back to Dorset, let him find her someone else willing to pay her passage. You said yourself—she's little, too frail for farm life." The matter settled, Jake sipped his coffee.

"As big as you are, you ought to be able to make up the difference," Amos argued. "And her knowin' all there is about doctorin' more'n makes up for any shortcomin's."

Jake leaned forward. "Yesterday, after she left with your

boy, I looked in the trunk she pulled her medical bag from. It's full of doctor books and bottles, steel knives and tweezers and such.''

"Don't you know anything about her? Where she comes from? Who her people are?''

"No." Jake settled back in his chair. "But you gotta understand, I thought she was a whore. Homer said all the women Griffin brought back were bought out of prison.''

"Yeah, that's right. But with her, it was a mistake.''

"I know *now*. But Homer tricked me into marrying her by telling me what a great bedwarmer she'd make.''

"Well, it looks like you got the last laugh 'cause she's the only doctor this side of Salem.''

"Then she *is* a doctor?''

"'Course not. They don't make doctors outa women. But she's helped out her pa ever'day since she was just a kid, and that makes her more doctor, in my book, then some young upstart fresh out of a fancy eastern school.''

"Well, then, it sounds to me like I'd be doing her a favor if I sent her back so she can marry a town man.''

"Jake. *You're* married to her. You can't just send her packin'. And 'sides, she's such a sweet little thing, why in tarnation would you want to?''

"Sure, you can say that. You already got three sons to carry on after you. And Orletta—that's one fine, healthy-looking woman.''

Amos's mouth twisted down. His eyes narrowed. "Don't you know nothin' about women at all? Sure, Griffin didn't bring back women like we asked for. But since I *do* already have my sons, I was willin' to take her. She's good company, and I'm growin' right fond of her. But if she comes up pregnant, I'll never be all the way sure the baby's mine." Amos pointed a finger at Jake's face. "Is that the kind of wife you want?''

"No, 'course not," he mumbled.

"I'm countin' on you to do right by that sweet li'l gal in there. And from what Orletta says, you got some apologizin' to do.''

"I haven't done anything. I haven't even touched her." He briefly envisioned Rachel's bared neck and shoulders, of his hands running over skin smoother than river rock. He'd never been so tempted in his life.

"And you better not, either," Amos commanded. "Till you say you're sorry and start treatin' her right."

Propping one leg over the other, Jake studied Amos's stubborn look of anger, a marked contrast to his normally beaming expression. Amos's protectiveness suddenly struck him as very funny, and he grinned. "If I didn't know better, I'd think you were her pa."

"Well," he sputtered, "someone has to—" His words were cut short by the thundering sound of stomping boots as Harland and Donald burst through the door.

After the noon meal Jake accompanied Amos and Orletta as they took Gus his dinner. Eyeing the ropes suspending the professionally bound leg to the ceiling, Jake was impressed. "Did Rachel do all this?"

"We helped," Amos said, smiling down at his oldest son. He placed a wooden bowl of stew on Gus's lap as Orletta plumped the pillows propping up the young man.

"Where's my angel of mercy?" The young man's strong voice confirmed his rapidly returning health.

"You plumb wore her out," Amos said. "She's asleep."

"Looks like you're all tied up, here." Chuckling, Jake tested the tautness of the ropes. "Don't reckon you'll be free to go hunting tonight."

"*Funny.*" Gus tried to look irritated, but his round face broke into a wide grin.

"Well, I do expect you to be in your finest form for the foot race on the Fourth of July. Last year you cost me a ten-dollar gold piece when you let Ben Stockton beat you."

"Pa says he got one of them women off the boat, so I 'spect he'll be too wore out to make much of a showin'. Ain't that right, Letty?" Gus said with a snicker.

"Ben's pa, Ellis, was so scared someone would file on the land next to his," Amos added, "he put up the money to send for one of the brides. You can bet old Mabel has raised more'n a few bumps on his head for lettin' Ben bring that sort of female into her house.''

Orletta's face clouded over. Noticing her expression, Gus said, ''I wouldn't mind takin' a few bumps if Ben's wife is half as nice as you.'' He turned back to Jake. ''And don't you worry. I'll be good as new 'fore summer.''

''Thanks to Rachel,'' Orletta added pointedly.

''Yeah, but for a minute yesterday, I thought it was all over, Jake. The way your wife attacked me with them sharp scissors of hers.''

''Those were really fine scissors, weren't they?'' Orletta buried her hands in the medical bag sitting on the stand and drew out a gleaming instrument. She pointed it at Jake. ''Time I repaid Rachel. Come along, Mr. Stone.''

''Why?'' Jake stared at the sharp-tipped instrument.

''Never you mind.'' Motioning with her hands, Orletta shooed Amos and Jake out of the room ahead of her, then grabbed a chair from the dining table and pulled it to the center of the floor. ''Have a seat, Jake.''

''Why?'' The woman was acting mighty peculiar.

''It's time you had a shearing. Sit.''

''You want to give me a haircut?''

''First, I'm getting rid of that awful beard. Sit.''

''But I've had it for years.''

''Then it's high time you got rid of it.''

''But it keeps me warm in the winter.''

''It's spring. Sit.''

''You might as well give in,'' Amos said. ''She won't shut up till you do.''

''You look like a bear with all that hair. And it'll be in your favor when you talk to Rachel about stayin'.''

''But I never said I was going to ask her to stay.''

''Amos.'' Orletta turned to her husband. ''Set him straight. I'm goin' out for some water.'' Grabbing the bucket handle, she walked out the door.

''What's she talking about?''

Amos pulled another chair from the table. Placing it before Jake's, he straddled it. ''Sit.''

"All right. Long as your woman's out of range."

"Jake, there's a slight hitch in the land act. I don't know what fool made such a mistake, but the extra acres you get if you're married ain't yours. It's your wife what puts her name on the paper. She's the legal owner."

Jake leaned closer. "You sure? Never heard of such a thing."

"It's a pure fact. Ask any woman in the territory. They're all gettin' right uppity. Think they're rich now. Anyway, if you want that woods north of your valley, you'd best get on the good side of your wife."

"That reminds me. Did you know Charley Bone and Leland Cooter filed on the acreage between me and McLean's forest land? And they got brides off the boat."

"Yeah, I heard. Paid for by McLean. And I just found out that Roy and Hannah Thornton don't own the hotel in town. They're just runnin' it for the *big man*."

"Really? You know, last winter, we were sitting there in Roy's saloon—make that McLean's. Anyway, Peterson started talking about pulling up stakes for California. And Roy plunked down two shiny gold eagles and started dickering. When I saw Peterson was really selling out, I stepped in and bought his milk cow, or Roy would've bought her."

"And Peterson's place is just west of yours."

"Yeah, I know."

Orletta came in the door, her bucket heavy with water.

Amos jumped up. "Here, let me take that for you. You want me to pour you some in the kettle?"

She flattered him with a smile. "Thank you, sweetie. But it depends." She turned her rich brown eyes on Jake. "Is our guest ready?"

Jake looked from her to Amos, who now stood with the bucket poised over a cast-iron kettle.

Amos raised his eyebrows and his bright eyes seemed to be laughing.

Jake looked back at Orletta, who waited, arms folded hard across her chest. "All right, all right. Get at it."

Brightening, she snatched the scissors from the table with one hand and grabbed Jake's beard with the other.

After a few cuts, Amos left, saying he was going to go check on Donald. But Jake knew he really walked out so he wouldn't have to witness Jake's humiliation.

Orletta kept pace with the quick clip of the scissors, offering Jake a steady stream of advice: be gentle, flatter her, treat her with respect, take lots of baths, be helpful, truthful. . . .

Jake clenched his teeth together and let her preach on. After all, she did have one hand locked onto his hair while the other wielded a lethal weapon.

⟪ chapter 6 ⟫

A HAND slid up Rachel's back. Would those boys give her no peace?

She flung her arm out and threw it off. "Get away."

It returned to her hip.

Lurching up, she swung around. A stranger sat on the bed, staring at her. "My God! Who are you?"

"It's me, Jake."

The voice sounded familiar, but it couldn't be him. A very attractive, smooth-faced man had spoken. From the capable squared chin, to his intelligent eyes, his face displayed a pleasing balance. Wide, clearly defined cheekbones were softened by lips that glided into an easy, flawless grin. *Jake's grin.*

"It is you."

"Yeah."

He was so close that for the first time she noticed that his eyes were every bit as green as her Viking's.

"You came up fighting. Have Amos's boys been giving you trouble?" A frown formed lines above his straight nose.

"Not really. Amos and Orletta keep them in line." She noticed how nicely his freshly cut hair feathered his brow.

"Well, if they do, you let me know. I'll knock their heads together."

"I had no idea you were such a handsome man." The brazen words leapt out before she could retrieve them.

A blush crept up Jake's face. His gaze faltered. "Orletta thought I'd look more civilized this way."

"Oh, I see. You did it for Orletta."

"*No*. I did it for you."

"I find that hard to believe." She hardened her gaze. "Since you plan to discard me like an ill-fitting shoe."

"Oh, yeah. That." Jake's own gaze wavered. "Well, I've been thinking it over. I think I overreacted when you swooned. It was my fault for letting you work so soon after being sick with malaria."

"Yes, but one has to wonder how you'll act if the fever actually returns." Her words cut with razor sharpness. "And most likely, it will. You promised to take me in sickness and in health. Do you plan to honor that vow? If not, speak now. I never want the subject brought up again."

Jake was obviously shocked by her outburst; his eyes widened, then narrowed. "You've got a lot more spunk than I first gave you credit for. That's good. But if we're setting things straight, there's one thing you better know right off. I'm the man here. Not you. Now, get up. I want to get home before dark. And your hair," he added more softly, "it's lopsided." He stood and sauntered out the door.

Openmouthed, Rachel reached up to her hair and found he was right. After rearranging it, she rose and ran her hands down the skirt of her brown woolsey dress.

Time to go home. She stopped short. Was that remote farm really going to be home? And was this outlandish mountain man really going to be her husband? Till death do them part? Her mind skipped to Jake's newly unveiled features, and her heart fluttered. Maybe he truly was trying to make up for his boorish behavior.

Yes, she thought, I suppose it's his way of saying he's sorry. And aren't we supposed to forgive those who trespass against us? But haven't I already had more than my share to forgive these past few months?

Once outside, anxiety added to Rachel's turmoil as she and Jake said their good-byes to the rambunctious family. She was leaving Orletta's protective nest to once again ride into the unfamiliar territory of her wifely duty. Jake was more subtle than Amos's boys, but, nonetheless, his newly groomed face did little to hide what was on his mind. Her.

And the discovery of her every intimate detail. As soon as possible.

Shading her eyes from the afternoon sun, Orletta looked up at Rachel seated on the buckboard wagon. "Don't worry about a thing. I'll take good care of Gus, just like Jake's gonna take good care of you. Ain't that right, Jake?" Orletta's eyes glinted as she looked in his direction.

"Sure thing, Letty." Jake took the liberty of covering Rachel's tightly knit hands with one of his and squeezed. "I'm going to take real good care of our little gal. And thanks again, Amos, for the laying hens. Fresh eggs in the morning are going to taste mighty good."

"It's the least I could offer after what Rachel did for Gus. And that's a real feisty rooster. Watch your rear."

Jake eyed the five squawking chickens trapped in rabbit hutches in the back of the wagon. "He'd better not get too feisty or he'll end up on the table for Sunday dinner."

"Just remember," Amos said, "if you want to keep those hens layin', you gotta keep the cocky little bastard around." Remembering a lady was present, Amos tipped his hat. "Pardon my language, ma'am."

Rachel managed a wan smile. Yes, she thought, I'm very good at forgiving. Too good. If I'd refused to forgive Jake, I could be riding back to Independence instead, back to safety.

"Harland," Jake said, looking at the skinny kid. "I'm leaving Prince here for a few days, so you can start working with him. But be careful, I don't want him coming up lame."

"Don't worry. I'll ride him like he had glass legs."

"See you do," Amos charged. "It's time we turned the tide on McLean. He's gotten way too big for his britches."

"Prince can take him! Prince can take any horse alive. Can't he, Jake?" Harland's eyes sparked with excitement, unlike Donald's, whose mournful gaze never left Rachel.

"Sure, kid," Jake said. "Guess we'd better get going." He slapped the reins and the team started to walk.

"Come back soon," Amos called.

"We will," Jake returned. "And don't make strangers of yourselves, either."

On this trip, unlike their first, Jake eased the tension by asking questions. He asked her where she came from and about her parents. She offered a brief recitation. The tragic details were still too recent to discuss with a near stranger. She also didn't mention the money in Santa Fe. Maybe later.

"You said you were a trapper. Where have you been?" she asked, shifting the conversation from herself.

"I've seen pretty much all of it. Yellowstone country and the Rockies, and on over into Blackfoot and Crow country. Pa taught me how to track and trap when I was just a sprout up on the Wind River. We did all right. We got by." His last words had a wistful ring to them.

"You miss it, don't you?"

He smiled slightly, and his eyes took on a faraway look. "I wish you could've seen a rendezvous back then. Indians coming from everywhere. Even as far west as The Dalles. All dressed up in their feathers and beads, strutting around, showing off. And the likes of Jedadiah Smith, and crazy old Mike Fink, and Frenchies like Lebec. All of us coming together, trading with each other, selling to the fur companies. No one lording it over anyone else. It was something to see." Jake's last words trailed off, and Rachel could sense the depth of his loss.

Taking a deep breath, he looked at her and grinned wide before continuing in a rush. "No sense in chewing over what can't be. Mountains are all trapped out. Those days are gone forever."

Rachel dared to feel encouraged by this new insight into her husband's values. For him to desire a life free of bigotry was a lofty ideal, indeed. This was no rapist, no pillager, this was a man to be trusted . . . maybe.

They arrived home much too quickly to suit Rachel.

Jack lowered her from the wagon with a renewed look of lust. He didn't remove his hands from her waist, but held her in place while he spoke. "I'm awful hungry. Would you mind fixing supper early?"

She knew what he was hungry for. And it wasn't supper. He just wanted to get it out of the way. Rachel modulated her voice carefully, lest she betray her fear. "What would you like?"

"Doesn't matter. Long as it's quick. You're probably tired, too, huh?"

Isn't he being solicitous? she gibed to herself. "I'll get started, then." She stepped out of his hands.

"Good. I'll go put up the team. Then I'd better get started on a chicken coop. Call me when supper's ready."

Rachel retrieved her medical bag from the rear of the wagon and walked into the cabin. The door to the bedroom stood ajar. She peered at the enormous fur-covered bed. It stared back. Slamming the door, she quickly retreated.

Rachel walked out onto the porch to fetch wood and glanced toward the barn. Jake's Viking-like body stretched as he lifted the collar over Sparky's huge head. Catching herself gawking, she reached down and gathered a few logs. When she straightened up, she heard several bouncy notes from a familiar tune he was whistling. She stole another glance at the man who suddenly seemed less forbidding. In fact, he was wondrously pleasing to look at. Rachel's heart gave a jolt, reminding her to recapture her thoughts. The song, what was that tune? Oh, yes, "Sweet Betsey from Pike."

Jake must have sensed her staring. He turned and smiled. She forgot to look away, and he stepped toward her.

Oh dear, she thought, her apprehension returning. But before she could decide whether to stay or escape inside, the rumble of a galloping horse drew her attention.

A man, slapping reins back and forth across the neck of a stocky workhorse, loped toward them across the meadow. The fine-boned man looked out of place riding bareback on such a heavy-footed beast.

Jake stepped into the open as the man urged the horse up the last knoll. "Jennings, what's the hurry?"

The man jerked hard on the rope halter, and the heaving animal came to a lumbering halt. He vaulted down, his slender face twisted with emotion. "I need the loan of your horse. Got to get to town. Fast."

The man breathed as heavily as the spent animal.

Still carrying the logs, Rachel left the porch and went to the men. No doubt something was terribly wrong.

"What's the matter?" Jake asked.

"I don't have time to talk. I got to get to town for some laudanum. Come on. Help me saddle up Prince."

"I'm sorry, Clayton. Prince isn't here."

"Not here. Oh my God." He searched the area with frantic eyes. "Give me one of your Suffolks, then."

"If all you need is laudanum, we've got some here."

"You have?" Swallowing hard, he brushed a strand of dark hair from his eyes that looked near tears. "Thank God. Get if for me—please."

"What's the problem?" Rachel asked. "Can I help?"

Jake nodded in her direction. "This is my wife, Rachel. She knows doctoring."

The man seemed to notice her for the first time. "Pleased to meet you. Do you know anything about burns?"

She dreaded nothing more. "Yes."

"It's my little girl. My wife was heating water outside to wash clothes. She went inside to tend to the baby, and Becky must've got too close." The man clutched at Jake's arm. "I don't know why. We told her a hundred times. I heard her screamin', but I couldn't get there fast enough." He swallowed hard. "She's real bad. Gotta have somethin' to stop the pain."

"Jake, hitch up the team again," Rachel said as she swung away. "I'll be ready in a minute."

The Jennings homestead was located a mile farther up the road from Independence. Several hundred yards before Clayton Jennings and Rachel reached the cabin, they were met by his young son carrying a toddler.

"What you doin' out here?" his father asked.

"I couldn't stand listenin' to Becky."

"Baby Pris is shiverin'. It's too cold to keep her outside. Hop up on the back of the wagon."

"I can't, Pa," he whined. "You take Prissy with you."

"Wait," Rachel interjected. "Let him stay here with the baby for a couple of minutes." She turned to the boy with her sincerest look. "By the time you walk back to the house, your sister will be sound asleep. I promise."

Rachel rushed into the house and to a side room on the heels of Mr. Jennings. The child, whose cries had diminished to a pitiful mewling, lay on a bed with a sheet draped lightly over her. Mrs. Jennings sat beside the child, stroking her forehead and humming a tuneless lullaby.

The woman looked up, her gray eyes wrought with hopelessness. "Why are you back so soon?"

"Jake Stone had laudanum at his place, and his wife's come to help. Emily, this is— Sorry, I forgot your name."

"Please, Mrs. Jennings, move out of the way so I can give your little girl something to make her sleep." Rachel pulled a bottle of ether and a cloth from her bag.

Mrs. Jennings grabbed Rachel's arm, her fingers digging in as she searched Rachel's eyes. "Are you a doctor?"

"My father was, and he taught me." Prying the woman's hand from her arm, she moved past her to the moaning child. "Please, let me by so I can stop the pain."

After administering the ether, Rachel examined the little girl and saw that nothing could be done to save her.

"I'm very sorry." She draped the sheet over the child's body again and looked up into the sunken eyes of the parents. "But I'll see she doesn't suffer. After the ether wears off, I'll give her a very large dose of landanum."

During the long vigil Rachel shared with Emily Jennings, the other woman never spoke. She just sat in a chair Rachel brought into the room and rocked back and forth. Rachel racked her brain to find the right words that would ease the mother's sorrow, but every phrase that came to mind seemed too trite, too useless. Finally she gave up trying and reached into the lady's lap and took her hand. Emily responded by clutching Rachel's with both of hers, and Rachel knew that the simple gesture had met this grieving mother's need in a way no words could have.

Long after the house was still with sleep, Becky faded away. Rachel left Emily to fetch Mr. Jennings, then, giving them privacy, she spent the rest of the night catnapping on the braided rug before the hearth.

The following morning Rachel awakened to the clatter of wood being tossed into the fireplace, then heard the unintelligible chatter of Baby Pris. She rolled over to see Danny holding the tot back with one hand while he struck a match on a stone and held it to a sliver of kindling.

"Here, let me take her." Rachel sat up and reached out for Prissy, whose short black hair curled about her perfectly rounded head. "Come to me."

Just like a little angel, she thought. Like a cherub. Rachel's lips spread into a smile as she remembered how embarrassed Jake had been to admit Cherubim was his middle name before Mr. Dorset would marry them. And so far, she thought wryly, her groom still hadn't received his due. She wondered what he was thinking after a fourth night without his new bride.

The bubbly tot gave her a big hug as the boy eyed her.

"How's my little sister?" he asked in a tight voice. "Is she gonna be all right?"

Rachel's throat knotted. She looked into gray eyes, so like his mother's, and knew she'd have to tell him. "Becky's gone up to heaven to live with Jesus. And he loves little children so much, he'll take very good care of her."

"She died?"

"Yes. And now she doesn't hurt any more because in heaven nobody hurts. She'll have lots of children to play with. She'll be very happy there."

"You mean she won't even miss us?"

"Oh, yes, I'm sure she will. But she knows, someday, she'll see you all again."

"She's comin' back?"

Rachel began to feel inadequate. She reached out and stroked his hair—dark, like his father's, she noticed. "No. But one day when you've lived a full life, and you've turned silver with age, you'll join her."

"That'll be a long, long time. Do you think she'll still remember me?"

"I'm sure she will. You're her one and only brother. That makes you very special to her. Now, how about going out to see if the hens laid any eggs?"

While Rachel prepared breakfast, Prissy insisted on riding her hip. It began to feel really natural. The babe was still clinging to her when she walked into the bedroom to ask the Jenningses if they wanted to eat.

Prissy squealed for her mama and tried to wriggle down. Rachel placed her on the floor, and she ran to her mother's knee and started to clamber up.

Emily shoved her away. "I can't," she croaked. "Take her away. I can't." She pushed at the tot once more and turned her head to the wall.

Clayton scooped up Prissy and ushered Rachel out of the room. "Sorry. Em is takin' this real hard. She won't talk. She won't go to bed. She just sits there. Would you mind stayin' with the kids while I go get Pearly Simpkins? She'll know what to do."

"Of course. I'll stay as long as you need me. But I would appreciate it if you'd go by and tell my husband."

"Sure. I'll take back your wagon and get my horse. Make sure Danny feeds the stock. And I hate to ask this, but would you mind preparin' Becky? I don't think Emily will be up to doin' it."

"How long do you think you'll be?"

"The Simpkinses live just this side of the river, so I'll be gone six or seven hours. Pearly's husband is a preacher of sorts, so maybe he'll come back and—" Clayton took a shuddering breath and his eyes flooded with tears. He looked at the bedroom door, then turned abruptly and strode out of the house.

Since Emily refused to leave the room, Rachel delayed preparing Becky for burial. Instead, after giving her some drug-laced tea, Rachel did the dishes, then restarted the wash that had been abandoned the day before.

Later, while hanging clothes on the lines strung from the

corner of the house to two evergreens, the comical sight of Baby Pris chasing a chicken with a worm in its mouth gave Rachel a much-needed break from the gloom even the bright morning couldn't dispel.

The rumble of a team and wagon coming through the woods enclosing the clearing stole the happy moment. She smoothed her apron over the brown day gown she still wore after two days and nights. At least she'd changed aprons, and it still looked presentable, she thought as she tucked a few stray hairs into the coil at the back of her head.

The beautifully matched pair of chestnut Suffolks, the white blazes on their faces catching the sun, emerged from the trees. Jake! She scooped up Prissy and hurried toward the arriving wagon.

Her gaze met his, and for an instant his princely face jolted her anew. If he'd had the good sense to shave before now, she thought as he closed the distance between them, he wouldn't have had to buy a bride. Every unattached female from Missouri to Oregon would've set her cap for him.

"Howdy," he said as he reined the team to a stop. "I hear things haven't gone too well."

Bouncing up and down in Rachel's arms, Prissy chattered excitedly.

"Have you met Baby Pris?" she asked while watching her husband jump down with the grace of a man half his size.

"Yeah, I was by here just the other day when I came to pick up my stock." He wiped his hands on his trousers, then swung the tot into his arms. "How's my little girl been?"

She answered by grabbing his nose. Pulling her moist little hand away, he put it to his mouth. She squealed with delight when he nuzzled it.

Glimpsing this gentle, playful side of Jake, Rachel was amazed by yet another facet of the man.

"Is Emily in the house?" he asked, looking at her over the springy disarray of Prissy's curls.

"Yes. She's still in the room with the little girl. She

wouldn't leave. But I slipped some laudanum in her drink, so she's finally getting some sleep.''

"That's good. Where's the boy?"

"Danny said he wanted to go fishing. I said he could. I hope his parents won't mind.''

"No. Sounds like the best place for him right now. Folks'll be coming this afternoon. I told Clayton to go by the Colfaxes' for Prince. And I'm sure Amos sent one of his boys to tell folks 'tween here and town about little Becky.''

"Mr. Jennings asked me to get her ready for burial, but I'd like to finish the wash and get some food cooked ahead.''

"Folks won't be coming for another three or four hours. You've got plenty of time. Here, take the squirt. I need to find some clean lumber to build a coffin.'' Jake handed Prissy back to her. Then, as if it were the most natural thing in the world, he brushed Rachel's cheek with the back of his hand. And his eyes softened to that same deep glow she'd seen before . . . in her dreams.

((chapter 7))

JAKE stopped digging and looked out of the grave hole. "Here comes a wagon. Looks like your pa and Sublette. And who's that up there with 'em?"

Danny ran from beneath the shade of the pines and partway down the knoll. "It's Mr. Grills. And there's a passel o' folks ridin' in the back, too."

Jake tossed the shovel onto a dirt pile, then hoisted himself out of the pit and joined the boy. Raising a hand, he shaded his eyes from the mid-afternoon sun. "Looks like Tom Baker. And they brought their wives, too. That's good. They'll be a comfort to your ma. Let's go on down."

Jake, with Danny tagging along, reached the cabin in time to help the women down from the wagon bed. "Afternoon, Mattie. Let me give you a hand," he said, swinging the fleshy one with frizzy yellow hair to the ground.

Her enormous blue eyes bugged. "That you, Jake? Land o' Goshen, ain't you a handsome devil without that beard."

Jake's face burned. He wasn't used to having women fawn over his looks.

Suddenly, her expression hardened. "But you went and married one of them *women* Griffin brought back, didn't you?"

Jake chose to ignore her baiting question. He turned and reached for Edna, Carson Grills's wee bit of a wife, crisply starched as always. "Glad you ladies could come."

"Of course we'd come." Edna lifted her chin high in the air. "The Jenningses emigrated on the same wagon train with us last year. Emily's one of us."

"And how are you today, Mrs. Simpkins?" Jake hoped when he eased the bosomy older woman down that at least she would favor him with one of her toothy grins.

He was disappointed.

"Thank you," she responded with as chilly a tone as the other two.

Clayton Jennings jumped down and walked to the rear of the wagon. "Where's Emily?"

"I've been up digging the grave. But last I knew, she was still asleep in there with your little girl."

"Clayton, why don't you let us women go into her first," said Mrs. Simpkins with the smile she'd denied Jake.

Jake detected relief in Jennings's voice when he spoke. "If you think that's best." He then turned to Jake. "Where's the grave?"

"Up there." Jake pointed to the tree-shaded hill behind the cabin. "And her coffin's beside the barn."

As one, the men all gravitated to the barn, away from the sorrow awaiting in the house. Sublette Simpkins, the slim older man whose face and demeanor bespoke a quiet wisdom, led the way, a Bible in one hand and the other wrapped around Clayton's shoulders.

Jake glanced back to the porch and saw Mattie Baker open the cabin door for the other two. For a second he almost followed them, concerned that they would spurn Rachel, then changed his mind. He wasn't good at smoothing things over with women. He'd probably just make it worse.

Rachel heard voices, then footsteps. She forced open her reluctant eyes. After two days of very little sleep, they felt as if someone had thrown sand in them. Whoever had come, she hoped they wouldn't wake Prissy when they walked through the door. After rocking the tot for over an hour, Rachel had finally settled her down enough to fall asleep in her arms just a few minutes before.

By the time the door closed behind the three women, Rachel had convinced her tired body to stand. Hoping to keep the others quiet while she left the room with Prissy, Rachel smiled in welcome and nodded at the babe. The women did not return her silent greeting, but remained quiet until Rachel returned from putting Prissy in her crib.

"How do you do? I'm Rachel, Mr. Stone's wife."

The women stared at her for a moment before the oldest spoke. "Where's Emily?"

"She's asleep in there." Rachel pointed to the closed door of the bedroom. "If you could get her to come out, I'd appreciate it. I need to prepare Becky."

"That won't be necessary," said the blowzy blonde, emphasizing each word. "We're here now."

Rachel knew she was being rudely dismissed, but at the moment she couldn't muster the energy to care. She turned from them and walked outside, knowing without a doubt her infamy had preceded her.

Spotting the men across the barnyard, she knew she wouldn't feel comfortable in their company, either. Instead, she walked around the house and across the clearing to where a brook meandered through the south end of the meadow. She followed upstream till it entered a sheltering forest.

A felled log lying among some unfurling ferns beckoned. Rachel sank down onto it. Shielded from judging eyes, she breathed deeply of the fresh pine scent and opened herself to the peacefulness of chirping birds and the bubbling brook.

Considerable time slipped by before Rachel decided to take advantage of the stream. She dropped down on the grass at the water's edge and unbuttoned her dress and chemise. Lowering them to her waist, she scooped icy water into her hands and splashed it on her face, letting it run down her neck and over her breasts. She shivered uncontrollably but persevered, until she felt clean and refreshed.

Rachel lifted the edge of her apron and patted herself dry. Running the soft cloth across the chilled thrust of a breast, she had a crazy thought. Would Jake touch her there? And would she feel it to her very core the way she had with her Viking?

Disconcerted by such musings, she quickly slid into her clothing, and with fingers numbed by the frigid water, buttoned both layers.

"Rachel."

At the sound of a male voice, she sprang to her feet and whirled around. A few yards away, Jake stood lounging against the spongy red bark of an old cedar.

"It's time to go up on the hill for the service now."

She desperately wanted to know how long he'd been watching her, but was even more afraid of the answer he might give. She searched his face for some sign, some clue.

"Did you hear me? It's time to go."

He wasn't smiling, and yesterday's lustful glint wasn't in his eyes. Maybe he'd just arrived. But he looked so darned comfortable, a person would think he'd been there a week. "You go ahead. I—uh—need to—fix my hair." Afraid her own expression might betray her, she turned her back to him and began to pull out hairpins.

"Don't be long."

His footsteps were quite audible as he retreated across the twigs and needles covering the ground. As large as he was, how could he have sneaked up on her? He couldn't have. Then why hadn't she heard him approach? Her hands froze in midair. The only time she wouldn't have heard him was when she was splashing water on her . . . !

Rachel spent several minutes regaining her composure sufficiently to meet the ordeal of facing the Jenningses' bitter grief, coupled with the contemptuous rejection of the other mourners. Plus, she must now stand benignly beside the man who had just seen more of her than even her own mother had since childhood.

Coming out of the woods and into the open, Rachel saw a number of people filing up the hill. Two men carried the small coffin, followed by the short older woman and Mr. Jennings, who supported Emily between them. The others trailed after. Jake lagged several yards behind, engrossed in a private conversation with Homer Dorset and Amos Colfax, who must have arrived after she left.

Cutting across the meadow toward them, Rachel noticed that no one held Prissy. She changed direction, veering back to the cabin to retrieve the tot. It wouldn't do to have her awaken to an empty house.

Circling the cabin, Rachel spotted a rider approaching on a stylish horse. The closer the man came, the more impressive he appeared. She hadn't seen anyone so properly attired in gentlemen's riding clothes since she left St. Louis. And this man certainly wore them to their best advantage, from the squared shoulders of the expertly tailored coat to the tight breeches stretched over long muscular legs. Realizing she was staring, Rachel turned to go up the porch steps.

"Madam," the man called, stopping her ascent. "This is the Jennings homestead, isn't it?"

"Yes," she said, looking up into the deepest blue eyes, fringed by noticeably thick black lashes.

"Kyle McLean at your service." Tipping his beaver stovepipe hat, he exposed a pronounced widow's peak that added a debonair flair to his near-perfect features. "I've come to offer my condolences." He dismounted and secured the dapple gray's reins to the split-rail fence.

"That's very kind of you. The mourners are just now walking up the hill for the funeral service."

"It would be my pleasure to accompany you." He crooked a proffered arm and smiled, showing teeth as perfect as Rachel knew they would be. And, of course, he had dimples to add a charming boyish touch.

"That would be very nice, if you wouldn't mind waiting for a moment. I'm going in to get Baby Pris."

"Certainly. Let me assist you."

Followed by Mr. McLean, Rachel went to the children's room. When she entered, Prissy rolled toward the sound, making a happy gurgling noise.

"How's my pretty baby?" Rachel asked, reaching into the crib. "Oh, dear. I think we've had an accident. If Mr. McLean will excuse me, I need to change your nappy."

He made a hasty retreat. "I'll wait in the other room."

Rachel muffled a giggle, then reached for a diaper. "Let

that be a lesson, Priscilla. Men aren't always the stronger sex.''

Mr. McLean stood near the door when Rachel returned with Baby Pris. ''We're ready to go. Aren't we, sweetie?'' She captured and kissed the tot's grasping hand. ''Oh, wait. Would you mind holding Prissy while I get my medical bag?''

The man opened his mouth to refuse, but Rachel thrust the tot into his arms before he could speak. The precocious child wrapped her arms around his neck and prattled some nonsense into his ear. In the few seconds it took Rachel to return from the other bedroom, McLean had relaxed and even seemed to be enjoying the affable tot.

''Let me place my bag in the wagon, then I'll take her.''

''No hurry,'' he said, displaying his engaging smile. ''Prissy and I are getting along just fine.''

Why not? Rachel thought, looking at the two raven-haired spellbinders. They're two peas in a pod. Either one of them could charm the birds out of the trees.

Jake watched them come. McLean, playing every inch the dandy, strolled up the hill with the baby in one arm and Rachel on the other.

Most of the others surrounding the open grave also noticed. Mattie sidled up to Edna and whispered something, her upper lip curling. Edna nodded, one eyebrow spiked.

Sublette Simpkins closed his Bible. ''We'll wait another moment for Mr. McLean to join us.''

Amos stepped close. ''What's he doing with your wife?''

''What he likes doing best. Claim jumping.'' Jake continued to glare at the approaching couple until he captured Rachel's attention. He knew she read his mood when her gaze darted from him to McLean and back again.

''Thank you for your assistance,'' she said, dropping her hand from the interloper's arm. Reaching up, she gathered Prissy to her. ''I'm going to join my husband now.''

As Jake's pretty and noticeably refined lady came to stand where she belonged, he thoroughly enjoyed the shocked look on Kyle McLean's face, especially the way the man's mouth dropped open wide enough to catch a squirrel.

"I'd like to begin," Sublette Simpkins said, opening his Bible, "by reading scripture from First Thessalonians."

Everyone turned toward him except Emily Jennings, who stared at the ground as if in a daze.

"'But I would not have you ignorant, brethren,'" Mr. Simpkins began, "'concerning them which are asleep, that ye sorrow not, even as others which have no hope. . . .'"

Tender words of comfort flowed from his mouth with the empathetic tone of one who truly understood the depth of the bereaved parents' loss. Jake felt tears of compassion fill his own eyes. He heard someone sniffle and knew he wasn't the only one affected.

Suddenly, Emily moaned and flung herself into her husband's arms and pressed her face against his chest. He hugged her to him as she shook with sobs.

Pearly Simpkins patted her back. "That's right, pet; get it out. Get it all out."

Prissy squealed and stretched her arms toward her mother, who stood on the other side of the chasm. To distract her, Rachel stepped behind Jake to block the tot's view and made a game of blowing into each of her ears.

". . . and so we shall always be with the Lord. Therefore comfort one another with these words." Mr. Simpkins closed the book, then raised a hand. "Let us pray." He paused while the group bowed their heads. "Dearest heavenly Father, we come to you today to ask that you take special care of our little Becky. She was such a bright spot in our lives—such a lively, happy child. We will miss her terribly. Please comfort us. Ease our loss. Wrap our dear brother and sister in your love. Take away their pain and leave them with only joyous memories of the precious time that you loaned them this sweet angel. We ask this in the name of our dear Lord and Savior. Amen."

"Amen," the others said in agreement before Tom Baker and Carson Grills stepped forward to lower the pine box into the hole with a set of ropes.

Clayton led his wife to the edge. Kneeling down, he picked up a handful of dirt clods and poured some into her hands. Together, they tossed in the first grains of earth that would blanket the coffin. They stared a long moment, tears running freely down their faces. Then, with arms wrapped around each other, they started down the hill.

Pearly Simpkins took Danny by the hand and led him to the edge. She scooped up some dirt and urged the boy to do the same. With questioning eyes, Danny looked across to Jake.

Jake nodded, and the seven-year-old grabbed a clod and threw it in the direction of the hole, then jerking free of Mrs. Simpkins, he raced down the hill after his parents.

In turn, the rest of those who had come to pay their last respects stepped forward and added to the first layer.

Brushing dirt from his leather gloves, Kyle McLean stepped up to Jake. "I know this isn't the proper time to discuss this, but I've procured what I think is an exceptional racehorse. And I'd—"

"You're right," Jake broke in. "This isn't the time. Step aside. It's time I filled in the grave."

McLean bristled. "Fine. Some other time. I'd better go pay my respects to the Jenningses." Turning to Rachel, he touched the brim of his hat. "Good afternoon, madam."

"Good day," she returned as he made a crisp about-face and strode away. She looked up at Jake. "I'd better go back, too. It's getting too chilly for Baby Pris."

"That won't be necessary," Mattie Baker said as she and Edna Grills came to face Rachel, avoiding even a fleeting glance at Jake. "As we said before, you're no longer needed here."

Edna reached for Prissy. "I'll thank you to give me the baby now."

Jake was surprised by the lack of emotion on Rachel's face as she handed over the tot. She made no reply, just stared after them as they sashayed down the hill.

Amos stepped up to Rachel and took her hand up in both of his. "Now I don't want you to let those two busybodies give you a single minute's unhappiness. They wouldn't know a lady if she come up and bit their nose off.''

Rachel's face softened into a gentle smile. ''That's sweet of you, Mr. Colfax—''

''Amos,'' he corrected, squeezing her hand.

''Amos. But I think you're just a mite prejudiced. And how is August's leg doing?''

''Letty says it's doin' just fine.'' He released her hand, and peered up at Jake. ''Our little angel looks mighty wore out. Take her on home. I'll finish up here.''

''Thanks, old man, I think I'll take you up on that.'' Not to be outdone by Kyle McLean, Jake placed Rachel's hand within the crook of his arm and walked her down the slope. It felt good having her beside him, to feel the warmth of her fingers pressing through his shirtsleeve. A real lady—no snooty airs like those others—a genuine lady. And Amos was right, he was lucky to have her.

When they were within yards of the house, McLean walked out without looking in their direction. Jake watched as he strode to a perfectly proportioned dapple-gray Thoroughbred, obviously the competition. Grudgingly, Jake admired the fluid sequence of motion as the man mounted and kicked the long-legged steed into a canter.

But why had McLean come? Even on an animal as fine as that it would take two hours for McLean to return to town. Four hours was a damned long time to spend on horseback for a two-minute visit, he thought. Jake pursed his lips. The man's got something up his sleeve. ''Yeah, no doubt,'' he said aloud.

''Beg your pardon. What did you say?'' Rachel asked as they stopped beside their wagon.

''Nothing. Just talking to myself. Old habit.''

''Would you mind saying our good-byes to the Jenningses? I would prefer to wait here for you.''

''Sure, but let me help you up on the wagon first.''

Once he had her safely aboard, he turned to leave.

''Wait a minute.'' Rachel reached behind her and hoisted up her medical bag. From it she pulled a vial of laudanum and handed it to Jake. "Tell Mr. Jennings to give his wife two spoonfuls before bedtime for the next few days."

After Jake relayed Rachel's instructions and said good-bye, Clayton insisted on walking outside with him.

He came up to Rachel. "I couldn't let you go without telling you how grateful we are. You just don't know."

"I think I do," she said. "I'm so very sorry we had to meet under such a tragic cloud. Perhaps at a later time . . ."

"Yes. I'm sure Emily would like that." With weary eyes, he followed Jake's climb to the top of the wagon. "Wait a minute. I want to give you something."

He rushed past the side of the cabin and into the smokehouse and returned with a ham tucked under his arm.

"Oh, we couldn't possibly accept that," Rachel said when he held it up to her. "It's too much."

"No, take it. Emily would want you to have it." The man's pleading gaze was as naked as an open wound.

"Take it," Jake ordered. "Thanks, Clayton. We'll surely enjoy it. Sorry, but we gotta get home now to milk the cow." He slapped the reins across the rumps of the horses. "Drop by anytime."

The Jennings homestead left behind, Rachel turned to Jake. "We shouldn't have taken the ham. Their food stores are very low. And except for some salt pork that was the only meat they had."

"The man lost a child today. You wouldn't want him to lose face, too." He saw her mouth open in protest. He cut her off. "If you hadn't taken it, you would've shamed him."

"That's silly. I'd rather he be a little embarrassed than have his children go hungry."

"If a man doesn't feel like a man, he won't be worth anything to himself or his family."

"Just over a ham?"

"Don't worry about it. I'll go out tomorrow and shoot 'em a deer or an elk."

"Would you?" Rachel placed her hand on his forearm. "I feel so sorry for them. They're so poor and so isolated.

And little Becky . . . It was all so . . ." Her voice faded to nothing.

Her agony cut through Jake's own feelings. Shifting the reins to one palm, he drew her to him, bending close until his chin brushed her hair. "I know," he whispered, and felt her melt against him.

"It was so awful," she moaned. "She was so little— so . . ." She swallowed down a sob.

"I know. But she doesn't hurt any more," he said, pressing her closer to him. "I remember reading once about Jesus being in the bosom of his Father, and I try to think of little Becky like that—all snuggled up on Jesus's lap, laughing and chattering. She loved to talk."

Rachel's jerky breathing slowed and steadied. Her next words were barely more than a whisper. "Did she?"

One by one, each bright moment he'd spent playing with the lovable little four-year-old flashed through Jake's mind with vivid clarity. "Yeah. She—she—" No more words of his own would come.

((chapter 8))

RACHEL drifted languidly, blissfully awake. She'd been with her Viking again. But this time had been different. No dragons. Just him and her, Odin and his Valkyrie, wrapped in each other's arms, the wind riffling through their hair as they sailed on a rainbow . . . to Valhalla.

Then she remembered where she was. She turned and looked beside her. In the pale light of a moon sliver, she could see no one else in the bed. To make sure, she ran a cautious hand across the silky fur quilt. Jake wasn't there. He must be sleeping in the barn again. Instantly, she was awash in a sea of loneliness. More than loneliness. She felt utterly rejected. Tears threatened. She sat up and blinked them away with fierce determination. "Don't be such a ninny," she chided. He'd known how tired she was.

Fully awake now, Rachel propped her pillow against the headboard. She leaned into the feathery softness and pulled the enormous fur robe up to her chin to ward off the chill.

Yes, she thought, he couldn't have been nicer about it. Bringing in those extra buckets of water so I could take a bath. And the way he stayed in the barn until I was finished. And I'm sure he did. Not once did I take my eyes off those windows while I was in the tub.

Then he'd helped her prepare supper. And adamantly insisted that she go to bed while he did the dishes. *For the second time in four days.*

He definitely hadn't gotten what he'd bargained for. Amusement trilled within her as Rachel remembered the swath of a smile that had cut across Jake's face that first day when he and Mr. Dorset had walked back into the store after discussing what Jake imagined were her merits.

He certainly isn't the fearsome giant he appeared to be at that meeting, either, thank God. But still, was he really the one she was meant to marry? How could he be? They came from worlds so foreign she was surprised they even spoke the same language. Jacob Obadiah Cherubim Stone— mountain man, trailblazer, homesteader—and Rachel Elizabeth Chambers, the pampered, educated, oh-so-proper lady.

Yes, we're quite a match, she thought. I suppose I'll have to keep a box handy to stand on whenever I want to talk to him. The picture of her dragging a box along by her apron strings seemed so ridiculous, she giggled.

Leaning back, she rested her head on her upraised arms. Yes, I've been whisked out of one life and dropped down into another as surely as I'd been whirled away by some magical dust devil . . . or maybe, she thought, nibbling her lip, whisked here on an ancient Viking ship from over the rainbow.

In her other life she would've ended up marrying Gordon Stillwell or someone very much like him. Polite, sober, with a promising future . . . a dull future. His clothes would be cut to perfection—like the man who'd come to the funeral.

Mr. McLean, the dashing Mr. McLean. In Peoria, a man as obviously successful as he would've been treated with circumspection. But the cut of a man's clothes must not mean much in Oregon. Jake hadn't seemed the least bit concerned when he dismissed the man so rudely. Or maybe Jake was just being reckless because of jealousy. Her lips tipped into an impish grin at the thought. And could a man be jealous over a woman he doesn't truly value or truly want?

Suddenly, Rachel remembered how awkward, how very embarrassed she'd felt when she found Jake watching her at the brook. Her face flushed hot.

Feeling exposed, she buried her arms beneath the fur quilt. One hand brushed the swell of a breast, and again she felt the teasing fingers of icy water stream down her neck, over her shoulders, into the valley of her flesh . . . more sheeting over her breasts, breasts that even now responded by growing taut.

She slid her hands up to the firm mounds and explored the hardened nipples. As her fingers closed over them, a craving ache carved its way to her core. Nothing she'd read in the medical books mentioned that a woman's body reacted so profoundly to the mere thought of a man's touch . . . Jake's touch. If she melted inside at just the thought, what would it be like if he actually did touch all her secret places?

Realizing she was in danger of being engulfed by over-whelming sensations, she contracted the muscles encasing the channel leading to her womb. Instead of ceasing, the quivering need mounted, and for the first time she under-stood the truth in the phrase "but the flesh is weak" . . . which she'd heard preached so often in church.

"Oh, my." Abruptly, she straightened. She had to stop this strange betrayal by her body—had to think about something else. But what . . . ? The women. Yes, those snooty women. Was it always going to be like today? Would she never be free of this slanderous smudge on her reputation? An outcast.

Rachel drew up her legs and hugged them to her. An outcast, she considered, while resting her chin on a knee. But for once being rudely dismissed had been a blessing. She'd been freed of the unpleasant chore of preparing the unfortunate child for burial.

Poor little thing . . . *No you don't.* I must not think of the sadness, only of how little Becky is feeling now, how she's cuddled at Jesus's bosom, feeling safe and warm . . . the way I felt when Jake enfolded me into his.

Her heart fluttered like the wings of a sparrow, and her pulse quickened.

I must cease these unladylike thoughts. Mama would be so shocked. . . . Or would she? Rachel lifted her head from her knees. Maybe not, she thought, seeing her mother for the first time in a new, more adult light. Papa rarely ever passed without touching her . . . a hand on her shoulder, a peck on the cheek. The private looks. And how many times had Rachel caught them embracing?

The picture of her parents wrapped in each other's arms switched to one of her and Jake, pressed body to body, nothing separating them. Skin touching skin. . .

I have to stop this. I'll never go back to sleep. What time is it? She looked out the window to a star-studded night. No hint of dawn. She needed to get some more sleep. Scooting beneath the fur robe, she rolled onto her side and shut her eyes, but within seconds, they popped open again.

This isn't going to work. I'd better go warm some milk. Mother always said there was nothing like warm milk to soothe a body . . . to soothe the *length of my body*. She smiled, enjoying the direction her thoughts took again.

Stop that. Scolding herself, she sat up and swung her feet off the bed.

As Rachel entered the common room, glowing embers from the fireplace attracted her attention. Good, she thought. I'll stoke it up for light. She skirted the silhouette of the rocking chair and made her way to the hearth. After stirring the coals, she tossed on several twigs and a couple of small logs.

With hands before her to absorb the growing warmth, she watched the flames lick their way up through the jumble of wood. She had always taken great pleasure in standing at the fireplace, gazing into the ever-changing blaze. Like a cloud-scattered sunset, no two were exactly the same.

Suddenly, something rustled. Startled, she spun around. Momentarily blinded by the darkness, she stood rigid. As her eyes adjusted to the shadowy light, she saw him. Jake wasn't outside in the barn—he was lying on the floor at her feet, lying on the bearskin rug. The buffalo coat was draped casually over him, exposing his magnificently muscled, gloriously bare chest.

All the sensations she thought she'd left behind in the bedroom assailed her with such intensity, her legs threatened to buckle. Her ripe breasts hardened and peaked, pressing against the constriction of her gown. The sides of her neck pulsed with the throb of her heartbeat. Hot. She was so hot. She reached for the ribbons at her throat and untied them, still unable to take her eyes from the gently breathing mountain of a chest sprinkled with an inviting field of soft golden curls.

The crackling fire flared and his eyes mirrored the leaping flames. *His eyes? He was awake. Watching her.*

A part of her tried to look away, but he beckoned, and she was magnetically drawn to him. She felt giddy, as if she were standing at the edge of a great precipice.

His gaze held her suspended, breathless. Time passed. She didn't know how much. Then, slowly, very slowly he lifted the cover from his body, inviting her to join him. To lie next to him. To touch him. Feel the heady warmth of his bare body pressed against hers. To hold. To enfold.

He rose up on one elbow.

Of their own volition, Rachel's trembling fingers reached for the next set of ribbons that trapped her in the nightgown.

Jake knew he was either dreaming or hallucinating. Outlined by a glowing aura of amber, an alluring vision in the form of his new bride stood before him. Her hair fell in a golden blaze about her, flamed by the elusive firelight.

She wanted him as much as he wanted her; he could see it in her eyes. Wide, staring, smoldering with desire. His pulse thundered and he felt himself harden. He saw a lifetime of need calling him. Daring him to take her as, one by one, she reached for and pulled loose the ties holding the garment.

If he touched her would the spell be broken? The vision vanish? He had to chance it. Slowly, very slowly, he held out his hand to her.

She allowed her gaze to drift to his inviting hand, then slip down his muscled ribs and over the slight rise of a hip that disappeared beneath the buffalo robe. She wanted to slide into the darkness beside his body that exuded more virility than any Viking she could ever conjure. She wanted to touch him, taste skin burnished bronze in the firelight.

Jake watched her fingers move to her shoulders and slip the gown down. Her lips, full and luscious, parted slightly as she let it fall from her gracefully curved body to pool about her feet. His breath caught. Bathed in fireglow, her slender figure seemed to be sheathed in the shimmer of iridescent silk. God, she was beautiful. A golden angel. Her breasts, generous, supple, reached out to him, cocoa-hued nipples, tipped up and waiting. This had to be a dream.

Dream or no, he could wait no longer. Capturing her yielding eyes with his, he reached for her hand. He read only a flicker of hesitation before her fingers tightened around his. He pulled gently, and she followed, dropping to her knees. Her hair billowed, then cascaded down around them like a fiery waterfall as she slid into his arms.

Every place Rachel's skin touched his charged to life. Her legs slipped down his lean length, rubbed past the hot iron-hardness of his manhood, the instrument that she knew could fill her aching need. Her head reeled. Pressing her soft belly against it, she turned to liquid.

Jake reveled in the warmth radiating from her satiny skin as it melded to his. Cradling Rachel on his arm, he folded himself around this delicate beauty. His fingers trailed through the silken strands veiling them. So fine, so fluid. He wanted to dive into it, swim in it. Cool his hot body in its swirl. He buried his face in the tresses floating about her slender neck. Lilacs. Like lilacs in the spring. He breathed deeply of the aphrodisiac before moving toward the full, soft invitation of her lips.

Her body trembled, then stiffened. He hesitated. Careful. If she was the virgin she claimed to be, he'd better move slowly. Gentle her, the way he would a nervous young filly.

"Don't be afraid," he whispered, his lips brushing her ear.

She relaxed, but her body still quivered against his. Her willingness to come to him, to want him, though she was frightened inflamed him with a strange excited tenderness.

Blood rushed to his head in a roar—rushed down, engorging him till he thought he would burst. Never before had he felt such need to take a woman, to pour himself into her.

He felt her tense again and realized he was squeezing too tightly. It took all his resolve to ease the arm pressing the fullness of her bosom to him. His own body quaked from the effort.

Rachel felt him tremble when he loosened his grip and sensed that he was responsive to her, that he cared, would be tender. All her fears fell away, and she floated free.

Jake felt her relax into willing compliance as he ran a hand up her back in soothing circles. Again he buried his hand in her hair, then slowly pressed his lips to her forehead. She was hot, moist, tasted of salt. He could smell her need, that musky perfume of desire, as she pressed her leg between his, pressing against his ravenous manhood.

Rachel tingled as his mouth seared a path across her brow, down her cheek. When his lips reached her jaw, she tipped her head back, freeing the way down her neck. Reaching up, she ran her hands into his ruffled hair and held him close. He smelled of cedar smoke.

Her breath quickened as he sprinkled moist, tantalizing kisses across her shoulders. She waited for his mouth to move lower, willed him to take more of her. When his lips trailed up the other side of her throat, her body cried out from deprivation.

He could feel her hunger, could feel her begging him to take her. Savoring the precious moment, he feathered kisses across her lashes, then found her lips and brushed across their lush softness. He teased with the tip of his tongue until her mouth parted and a moan escaped. At the sound, his heart nearly exploded. He could contain himself no longer. Crushing her to him, he ravaged her lips in a devouring kiss. His tongue entering, probing, searching, retreating, entering.

Rachel never knew a kiss could evoke such stark passion. Recklessly, she drove her tongue past his, into his mouth, joining him in their lover's dance until shuddering waves coursed her body. Groaning with ecstasy, she wrapped her arms around him, pulled him tighter against the need in her breasts and within her intimate sheath damp with desire.

Jake pushed her from him.

Her eyes flew open. Why was he rejecting her? Was she acting so shamelessly that . . . Then she saw his eyes, glazed with desire and roving her body while he removed his arm from beneath her head.

Gently, he eased her down on the thick fur of the bearskin rug, then moved to a yearning breast. At his touch, her eyes widened, then drifted shut. He ran a finger over the tip, watching it peak for him, stretch up for him, only him. No one else had ever touched her softly rounded mounds, claimed them, made them want just him. He was the first. And he would be the last. She was his woman. He lowered his mouth to taste of their wonder.

A piercing sweet pain shot up from her groin. Her hands moved down his powerful frame to his thighs and up again. His body arched against them, and she knew her touch gave him the same pleasure as his did her.

Jake reluctantly left behind the first luscious breast to sample the other before his urgent need would take him elsewhere, that need Rachel's hands fired anew with each trip down his back.

He felt her begin to writhe against him. Her body was asking for him, begging him to come into her. Jake slid his hand down the soft flesh of her abdomen and between her legs.

Even in the midst of her increasing need, she was surprised how easily her legs moved apart to accept him. His finger found her, entered, exploring. Nothing had ever felt like this. She pushed against him, straining for more, much more. No one had ever told her, prepared her. She knew she was panting but couldn't stop. Her hands seared across his body in a seeking frenzy as she exploded, stars flashing behind her eyes.

Then, abruptly, he removed his hand and pulled away.

"No," she moaned. "Not yet." It was too soon.

"I'm still here."

The huskily whispered words compelled her to open her eyes just as he glided himself into her depths.

"Yes . . ." At last, her aching cavern of need was being filled. "Yes . . ."

He began to withdraw. Panicked—she needed him to stay longer—she grabbed his thighs to pull him back. Just as she did, he thrust deeply into her.

A sharp pain ripped through her. Something was terribly wrong. She gasped and shoved at his chest. To her relief, he partially withdrew.

"I'm sorry," he whispered, lowering his body to gently blanket hers. "Just know the pain is over."

Brushing her golden hair aside, he dropped light kisses about her face and neck. A moment later, her inviting lips curled into a smile. The hands grasping his shoulders relaxed and slid around his neck. Thank God, he thought. It would've been hell to pull back now.

He kissed her again, this time full on the mouth. His tongue reached in, filling her, teasing, calling.

She felt herself answering, coming. Her hands cupped his head as she strained to fill him as he filled her.

Then deep inside her he began to move. Slowly, very slowly. Their tongues matched the same taunting rhythm of their bodies, and every fiber of Rachel's being came alive—pulsated. *She wanted more.* She arched upward, meeting him, again and again, taking him deeper, deeper.

He filled her, gorging her till she gasped with each stroke. Her nails dug into his back, but he didn't care. Paradise beckoned.

Rachel crested higher with each frenzied joining. Then suddenly, in a final powerful thrust, Jake reached the other side of her hunger. He erupted, spilling himself, spilling her. Clinging to him, she spiraled into a dizzying shower of stardust as she returned kiss for fevered kiss.

((chapter 9))

AWAKENED by the first rays of dawn slanting through the window, Jake found his bride's head resting on his shoulder, her warm breath whispering across his throat like the wings of a butterfly. She seemed poured into the cocoon his body wove around her as they lay on the bearskin rug.

So warm and smooth, so damned good. God sure knew what He was doing when He made her. Jake swelled with such joy, it was all he could do to keep from crushing her to him. A shudder rocked his constrained body. Certain he'd awakened Rachel, he raised himself up to revel in the glory of her face when she first opened those gorgeous eyes. He wanted to dive into those fathomless high mountain pools. Down, down, and never come up again.

But her eyes did not open. Her long golden lashes remained splayed across delicate cheeks. Her lips, swollen from a night of passion, were parted in a slight pout as her breath came soft and steady. She looked so bewitching, hair swimming about her shoulders in disarray. A few strands clung to the moist cheek that only seconds before had been pressed against his shoulder. Careful not to touch her, Jake brushed aside the strays. She deserved all the rest she could get.

He recalled the stress of her past few days: first, the night spent nursing Gus, saving his leg from putrefaction; then the hopeless vigil at the Jenningses' . . . *then last night. His lips quirked into a grin. Yes, she deserved a lot of rest.*

Gingerly, he unwrapped himself from around her. He'd go out and do the chores, then surprise her with breakfast.

111

Rising to his feet, he watched her face to see if he'd jostled her awake. But not even a flutter. She remained peaceful, eternally angelic. His beautiful jailhouse rose.

Reaching down, he covered her bared shoulder with his heavy buffalo coat, trying not to stare or he'd never leave. A ripple of blue silk caught his eye—the nightgown she'd discarded last night before she'd come to lie with him.

His heart kicked against his ribs. Oh, yes. His angel bride had come to him. Had wanted him—this bear of a mountain man.

The rooster announced the new day, and the cow lowed, reminding Jake of his chores. He snatched his trousers from the elk horns and yanked them on with swift purpose. The sooner he was through, the sooner he could return to her.

Before long, he crept back inside and quietly began fixing breakfast. Flipping the last flapjack, he saw her stretch, then moan in that same electrifying way she had the night before when he'd burst inside her. His heart lurched, and he began to harden as he reached for the skillet. *Hot.* He let out a stupid yelp, and dropped it on the stove. Lord, what a racket.

She bolted up like a scared rabbit, clutching the buffalo coat to her.

"Morning," he mumbled, feeling more like a clumsy oaf all the time.

Her eyes, wide as saucers, relaxed, and she smiled timidly. "Good morning."

Jake made sure he picked up the plate of hotcakes this time, instead of the skillet, and carried it to the table. He set it beside the blackberry jam. "Breakfast is ready."

"Mmm. I can smell it." The music of her words played havoc with his heart as one of her delicate hands slipped from beneath the fur robe and brushed a tangle of hair that had veiled part of her radiance.

He must've gawked too long. Her gaze grew unsteady, then drifted, wandering about until her mouth opened in a gasp. A hand flashed out again, this time to snatch in her nightgown. From the look on her face, a body would've thought she'd just seen a ghost instead of some flimsy piece of silk.

Jake couldn't prevent the grin that swept his face. He tried to squelch it, but it grew broader. He headed for the door. If he laughed now, he might lose everything he'd gained the night before. "I'm going out to get the milk."

He dawdled a bit before coming back inside, as much to regain control of his traitorous funnybone as to give her time to escape into the bedroom and clothe her bewitching body without further embarrassment.

He returned to find her nightgown ribbons neatly tied, and her dressing gown snugly secured around her waist.

She gave him a fleeting glance, the color in her cheeks high. With her free hand clutching the lapels of her wrapper, she poured coffee into his tin mug. Eyes lowered, she moved to her own flowery one and filled it.

Unable to stop watching—her shyness so damned appealing—Jake pulled out his chair and sat down.

After replacing the pot on the stove, she took her own seat and grasped her cup, studying it so intently, one would think she expected it to speak.

Jake helped himself to several slices of bacon and a stack of flapjacks. Then he handed the serving platter to her. "Have some. I fixed 'em special for you."

The look she gave him reminded him of a wary fawn peeking out of a patch of frilly ferns. He detected a slight tremble in her hand when she accepted the plate.

"Thank you," she whispered, taking only one. She then spent a long-spun time buttering it.

Jake searched his brain for something to say that would draw her back to the way things had been the night before. He took several bites, but still couldn't come up with anything. He just didn't have enough experience with women, especially ones with such fine breeding.

Several minutes elapsed, and Rachel still hadn't taken a bite. She just kept spreading jam round and around with one of her fancy knives.

"I guess you don't like flapjacks," he blurted out. "You want me to fix you something else?"

Rachel's stark gaze flashed up to his. "Oh? No. This is fine. Really. Excellent. It was most thoughtful of you. I—" Her eyes lost courage, and she looked down again. She picked up her cup and folded her hands around it. "I—I don't know what to say. I'm so ashamed. I just don't know what came over me last night. I can just imagine what you must think of me."

Jake reached out to her. "There's nothing—"

She held up a hand to ward him off. "Please." Her gaze returned to that blasted cup. "Let me finish." She inhaled deeply. "While I have the courage. I suppose now you must believe what Mr. Dorset said about me. About me being a wanton woman. A soiled dove. I—"

Jake bypassed the trembling wall of her hand and gently lifted her chin.

She still didn't meet his gaze.

"Look at me."

Slowly her lacy lashes rose and she peered up at him from out of tortured eyes.

"What happened last night was a beautiful thing. I know you probably don't think so, me being just a rough-handed mountain man and you being a genteel lady. But I'll never forget it. You coming to me like you did. It meant . . . a lot. More than a lot."

Her questioning eyes drew him until he was sure he glimpsed the enchanting shimmer of her soul, alluring as the lady herself.

"Really." He sounded hoarse even to his own ears as he watched those incredible alpine lakes flood with tears.

Suddenly, he was at her side, reaching for her, and pulling her up into his arms, her lips a soft pillow beneath his mouth. They opened to him. Inviting. She met him with her own tongue, hesitant at first, then boldly. Caressing, teasing.

His hand found the way to her temptingly rounded bottom, pressing her tightly against him, urging her toward his throbbing hunger. Fragrant tresses overflowed his other hand as he captured the back of her head and ground his mouth harder against hers.

Her lips answered his with mounting frenzy. Her arms thrust up around his neck, and she crushed herself against him. The miracle from last night was with him still.

Jake had an unrestrainable urge to laugh. Wrenching his mouth from hers, a chuckle rumbled out as he scooped up his bride and headed for the bedroom.

What a day that had been, Jake thought, sitting on the side of the bed the following morning. He looked out the window at the rapidly growing light as he shoved his second foot into its boot. He'd overslept. Easing off the bed, he glanced over his shoulder at the delectable cause.

Curled up asleep beneath the lush fur, his sweet Rachel looked more dainty, more lovely than anything he'd ever imagined. What had he ever done in this lifetime to be gifted with such a precious creature?

Her wealth of hair hid most of her delicately curved face. Unable to resist, he reached down to brush it aside for one last look before he left.

At his touch, Rachel's lashes rose, and she gazed up at him with loving eyes. "Good morning," she whispered and stretched out an arm to him.

Jake tore his eyes from her to glance out the window. It would be dawn soon. But he couldn't resist going back to her for just one little kiss. "Morning," he said as he dropped down beside her and pulled her into his arms.

"You're already dressed. You should've awakened me."

He brushed her sweet lips with his, relishing their soft welcome—one he'd have to forgo, at least for a little while. Sighing, he moved away. "I'm going hunting for the Jennings family. I should be back in an hour or so."

A frown rippled across her brow.

He smoothed it with his fingers. "Yesterday," he continued, a grin spilling across his face, "I just plumb forgot." Rachel's gaze faltered, and she caught her lower lip between her teeth.

It tickled Jake to watch her cheeks deepen in color. He dared to make them turn even redder. "And yesterday I forgot all about planting. And wood cutting. And fence building. And if the stock hadn't caused such a ruckus, I probably wouldn't have remembered to go out to feed them, either."

Instead of being further embarrassed, Rachel surprised him with an umcommonly lusty lopsided smile. "I wouldn't feel all that guilty if I were you. Considering all that extra time you spent out in the barn when I first arrived."

Jake's mouth dropped open. The minx! She'd come right back at him with a tease of her own. He felt like climbing in with her again to extract his just due for that remark. But the blasted sun was set on rising. He forced his unwilling body from the bed. "Much as I hate it, I gotta go. The deer will only be out in the meadows grazing for a little while longer."

"Deer! How exciting!" She sat up, several tendrils of hair veiling generous breasts. "May I come?"

Tearing his eyes from her endowments, he cleared his throat to speak. Then, like a bolt, it struck him. "You've never been hunting before, have you?"

"No." Clutching the fur quilt to her, she swung her legs off the bed. "But I'll be ever so quiet. You won't even know I'm there. *Please*." She moved toward him, dragging the cover with her. Reaching him, she wrapped one of those lithesome arms around his neck.

How could he refuse? But first he had to ask. "You don't know how to shoot, do you?"

Her smile disappeared. "Are you saying I can't come if I don't know how?"

"That's what I thought." Removing her hand from his neck, he turned for the door. "Get dressed and meet me outside. It's time you had your first lesson."

Apprehension wobbled Rachel's legs as she walked out onto the porch. All she'd wanted to do was watch her mountain man demonstrate his expertise. Have yet another of his virile accomplishments to add to her growing list. But, no. He wanted her to hold one of those frightful things and, worse, fire it. Standing at the top of the steps, she stalled the inevitable by taking her sweet time putting on and tying a bonnet—what did it matter that the sun still had a good half-hour before it topped the Cascades.

Jake had yet to notice her. He stood out in the meadow to the side of the barn, setting bottles on the top rail of the zigzagged pasture fence. After placing the last one, he turned toward the cabin.

Before he could spot her shirking like a useless lump, she started out to meet him at a determined pace . . . that slowed the nearer she came to him and that huge gun he toted.

With an infernally sure stride, Jake met her halfway. Then, without a second's grace, he held out the awful thing.

She told herself not to be a sissy, to take it. But her hands just hung at her sides, growing clammy.

"Take it."

She swallowed. She'd heard of rifles kicking so hard, they left shoulders with bruises the size of platters. "It's so big. Surely you can't expect me to shoot something so powerful."

"Not till you learn to load it. Besides, this Hall carbine doesn't have half the kick of my Hawken."

Where was that smile she'd seen so often the day before? And he stared at her with such deadly earnestness. She sighed and accepted the rifle.

Jake pointed to a lever ahead of the trigger. "Pull on that to breech—break open—the rifle."

The thing looked ominously like another trigger, but without a ring around it. A tremor went through her finger as she eased it back, splitting the rifle almost in two.

As she stared into the opening, Jake dangled a leather pouch before her eyes. "Pour some powder in the hole. Real slow. I'll tell you when to stop."

Taking it, she knew she must control her nervousness, or she'd spill more on the ground than where it belonged.

Steeling herself as she tipped the bag, she pretended that it was nothing more than black sand being dropped down a pipe.

"That's enough." Jake took the pouch from her and handed her a little metal ball. "Shove that down on top of the powder."

"It's not going to cause it to explode, is it?" The whining, cowardly words had tumbled out before she could stop them.

A disgusted silence hung in the air for a few seconds before he repeated, "Shove it down with your thumb."

She rapidly complied, hoping to erase his impatience.

Then he placed a little concaved piece of copper in her palm. "Place the cap over the ball, then bring the barrel back up."

She did exactly as he said this time, without hesitation. But she especially hated the cracking sound as the rifle locked into place again.

"That's all there is to it," he said in a lazy, most irritating rumble.

And the awful moment had arrived. Time to shoot.

But suddenly, Jake took the rifle, swiftly hoisted it to his shoulder, cocked, and fired.

Rachel jumped at the almost deafening explosion and witnessed shards of glass from one of the bottles on the distant fence fly in all directions. A shiver raced up her spine.

Jake shoved the still-smoking rifle back into her hands. Then, from his shirt pocket, he pulled out the gunpowder, and another ball and cap. "Now, load it by yourself."

Rachel looked up into his unwavering eyes, then at the instrument of death in her hands. Fingers stiff with fear, she repeated the steps he'd just taught her. All too soon.

"Now, put the butt tight against your shoulder and aim."

The smooth metal of the barrel felt deceptively cool in her grasp. She looked from it to the bottles. They seemed to have moved farther away. She darted a glance up to Jake.

Standing over her, he waited.

She took a deep, fortifying breath. One, two, three. *Now.* Swiftly, she swung up the rifle while fumbling for the trigger.

"No!" Jake's shout pierced the air.

She nearly leapt out of her skin. She whirled to him.

The man dove away from her, hitting the grass several feet away in a long slide. "Point it the other way!"

She looked down and saw that the carbine was aimed at him. "Oh." She abruptly raised it skyward.

"Don't ever aim at anything you don't plan to shoot."

The impact of the close call turned her insides to jelly. "It was all your fault. You shouldn't have yelled."

Coming to his feet, Jake glared at her. "You were about to shoot and knock your blasted shoulder off. I didn't tell you to fire. I told you to put it *tight* to your shoulder. Which you didn't do."

"I see. Well, I really have no interest in learning how to shoot anyway. And, besides, I'm sure your skill is more than sufficient for our needs."

"Well, you have to. You're not living in some tame eastern city any more. Unless you know how, I can't leave you to go hunting or even ride in for supplies. You have to be able to take care of . . . things while I'm gone."

"Things. Exactly what kind of *things* are you talking about?" Surely there wouldn't be a need to defend herself, Rachel thought.

Jake's eyes seemed to waver—but just for a second. He shrugged nonchalantly. "Like if a fox gets in the chicken coop. Things like that." He stepped to her side. "Position the rifle to your shoulder."

Exhaling heavily, Rachel obeyed and leveled the darned thing toward the bottles again.

Then, from behind, Jake's arms encircled her. His hands engulfed hers as he snugged the rifle butt harder to her. Tucked against his warm chest, protected from the cold wind, she experienced a feeling of absolute safety, and she nearly sagged as she relaxed into him. He would never let any harm come to her. Hadn't he just spent an entire heavenly day showing how much he cared?

Jake felt her melt against him and wondered if he'd be able to keep his mind where it belonged. The crisp breeze feathered her lilac scent across his face, and her bare neck looked particularly tender beneath that silly bonnet. He ordered his attention to return to her hands . . . so tiny and white. Again, he had to jerk himself up by his bootstraps before he could concentrate on the rifle. He adjusted the position of her hands for better balance. "Look down the barrel and target one of the bottles."

Her teasing body pressed closer. "I think I'm going to really like learning to shoot."

His mouth leaned for her neck and almost reached it. He halted with a groan. "You've got to stop smelling so good, or we'll never get anything done around here."

"Is that a promise?" A naughty hip moved against him.

He jerked in a breath. "Cut that out. This is serious business. Now, cock and fire."

She straightened—thank God. "Oh, all right. I'm looking at the bottle. Now what?"

"Hold your breath and very gently squeeze the trigger."

All of a sudden it was just her and the rifle again. She willed her finger to pull, but it wouldn't obey, any more than her legs would have if she'd told them to leap off a cliff. After what seemed like an hour of trying, she expelled her breath. "I can't. It's too loud."

"I'm here," he brushed across her ear. "Trust me." His finger moved over hers and he slowly squeezed.

The rifle exploded with no more than a small buck.

Profound relief bubbled out of her on a light laugh. But the bottle remained standing.

"That wasn't so bad, now was it?" Jake gave her a quick hug.

"No," she said, swinging to face him. "In fact, it was quite thrilling. Give me the fixings for another load."

With a snort he grinned before complying.

While she reloaded, a sense of confidence and power

grew within. She could do this—and anything else this land, this man, this life tossed her way. Lifting the gun to fire, she felt his eyes on her. And she knew that when next she looked at them, they'd spark with love and approval. Holding her breath, she aimed at the center of the fattest bottle and gently, steadily pulled the trigger.

And it blasted into a million glorious pieces!

Throwing her arms wide, Rachel jumped up and down, squealing in a most unladylike manner, but she couldn't have cared less. She swung around to share her thrilling victory with that devastatingly handsome husband of hers. ''What fool ever said farm life was dull? Pass me another load!''

((chapter 10))

ACROSS the brilliant azure sky, a succession of great white puffs floated toward the distant Cascades. A truly gorgeous sight, Rachel thought. Occasionally one blocked the sun, but she felt her laundry would have ample time to dry before darker, more ominous clouds appeared on the western horizon. In the six weeks since she'd arrived in Oregon, she'd come to realize that it rained more often than not. And rain played havoc with her schedule.

Monday was wash day, and here it was almost noon on Wednesday and she'd just hung out the sheets. They almost sparkled as they flared in the light breeze.

Too bad there was no nearby neighbor to see how clean and white they were. Out here, away from town, it would be much more difficult for her to erase decent folk's misconceptions of her. Unconsciously, Rachel reached up to check the tidiness of her neatly coiled bun.

Yes, she wished someone would come to see all she and Jake had accomplished in the past month, despite the persistent drizzles. The times she and Jake had gone to check on Gus, Amos and Orletta had promised to visit as soon as they weren't too busy, but they had yet to come. Rachel understood, this was spring planting time.

She took a moment from her chore to survey the acreage outstretched below the knoll the house and barn stood on. The sprouting vegetable garden covered most of the clearing to the east. She remembered how long she'd argued that she'd regained her health before Jake would even allow her

to weed it. He never forgot that she'd fainted that first day.
Even now she cringed at the thought.

She'd always prided herself on her fitness. After living so
many years with her mother's infirmity and after attending
so many ill patients, she could never consider weakness
attractive. She'd never been one of those girls who cinched
themselves so tightly into a corset that they swooned at the
least provocation. And besides, Father had allowed her to
wear one only to social functions, except when she'd
attended Mrs. White's Academy for Young Ladies.

The brick-red rooster crowed, then strutted along the
paddock railing between the barn and the storage shed.
Rachel's gaze wandered to the new chicken coop attached
to the shed in lean-to fashion. It was elevated several feet
above the ground. Jake had built it rain-tight, and when the
door was barred, the chickens were quite safe from night-
prowling creatures.

He takes real pride in his work, she thought. He never
does anything halfway. No, he certainly doesn't. A smile
played across her lips at the thought of his passionate lovemaking. By comparison, Gordon Stillwell would've been a
puny second best.

Oh, dear, there I go again, she reproved herself silently.
When am I ever going to get a handle on my wanton
thoughts?

Then, as if the reprimand had never entered her brain, she
turned around and searched across the multiplying rows of
newly planted fruit saplings until her eyes found the one
who always stole her breath. Jake. She shivered deep within
as she watched muscles ripple across his back when he
leaned into the shovel.

What an incredible month this had been, building something solid and worthwhile by day—that was what was
really important, she kept telling herself—and then the
nights filled with joys so indescribable she couldn't believe
no one had ever prepared her.

All the poets she'd ever read, and all the silly giggles that
she'd ever heard pass between newlyweds only hinted at the

all-consuming lust she felt for her man. And his desire for her was every bit as strong, she was sure.

But, no matter how she rationalized, there was still that niggling doubt. Did he love her, too? That night when she had been forced to refuse him because of her monthly flow, he had looked almost angry, as if he blamed her for not conceiving. Then after asking how many days he'd have to wait, he'd said, "Well, guess I'd better get some sleep. If I can." He'd dropped a quick peck on her cheek and rolled over, turning his back to her. And for the first time since they'd first made love, Rachel hadn't spent the night nestled against his shoulder, hadn't felt the comfort of his protective warmth . . . hadn't felt wanted.

He'd been as polite and helpful as always during the day, but that spark, that extra something, was missing. But as soon as her time had passed, Jake was again as amorous as ever, even more so, if that were possible. And again, he sang those little wagon-train ditties while he worked. He'd just had a hard time with the privation. That's all it was. He loved her even if he'd never said the words. Of course he did. She was so certain, that when he came in at noon she would tell him about the money in Santa Fe.

"Stop lollygagging," she scolded herself aloud. "Can't start dinner till you get this wash hung out." She filled herself with one last look at Jake, then reached down. From the laundry basket, Rachel picked up a tightly wrung wad—her pink tablecloth. She shook it out then pinned it to the line. "It's been a month, Jake Stone," she said, feeling triumphant, "and I'm still covering the table with linens."

She knew he appreciated the nicety, though he never said anything about it. She'd seen him run his hand across the tightly woven fabric more than once. And before he knows it, she thought, I'll have him wearing fine linen shirts and a tailor-made suit. And when we walk into Sunday Meeting, everyone will turn their heads, and say, "Here comes that handsome couple, Mr. and Mrs. Stone."

Rachel retrieved one of Jake's shirts, the one he'd worn when he insisted on taking her out for her first shooting lesson. The whole idea had frightened her. But, before long, she'd loved the feeling of power it gave her.

Later, when Jake had taken her hunting, he spotted a deer, and with his hand steadying the barrel, she got her first kill. Then he showed her how to dress out the poor creature. That chore she didn't think she'd ever grow to like. However, in this primitive country one had to make adjustments.

Yes, she thought with a chuckle, I take him one step toward gentility and he takes me two steps back. But I love it. Love him.

After hanging the general washing, Rachel came to her undergarments. She had saved space to hide them on the second line behind the sheets. Jake had seen every inch of her body, but somehow it still seemed indelicate to let him see her intimate things blowing about willy-nilly.

Up by the house, the billowing sheets caught Jake's attention. He straightened from packing sod atop the roots of a pear sapling, and his gaze fell upon Rachel. Her slender form was clearly outlined as the wind whipped her skirts to the side. Even in the distance, even with her back to him, the sight caused his heart to bang against his ribs. Such a beauty! And such joy she'd brought to his lonely existence.

Funny, he thought. I never knew how empty my life was before her. She fills me, lights all my dark places.

Suddenly uncomfortable with such poetic thoughts—he was beginning to sound like some sissy writer from New York or Boston—he chuckled and returned to work, driving his shovel into the earth. Oh, I don't know, he thought, I'll bet she'd really like to hear pretty words like that. Maybe some night, when we're all wrapped around each other . . .

"Naw." He felt the heat rise to his face. "Maybe I'll just write her a nice little poem instead."

Yes, that's what he'd do. Sometime . . . when he could find a piece of quality paper, a good quill. . . Yeah, one of these days.

He looked up again, but could see only the top of her head as she moved within the rows of laundry. A knowing grin spread across his face. Here we are, in the middle of the deepest woods and she's still hiding her underdrawers. The birds didn't care, and by now she couldn't possibly still be shy with him. Or could she? Females were sure hard to figure sometimes. Especially the genteel ones.

The stallion whinnied, dragging Jake back to the present. Up on the knoll, the spirited animal trotted in a high-tailed prance from one end of his paddock to the other. Jake surveyed the clearing but saw nothing to warrant the horse's excitement.

Returning to his chore, Jake dropped the root ball of a sapling into the hole and tamped dirt around it.

Prince's piercing whinny split the air again.

Jake's head jerked upward to the knoll. He saw Rachel move toward the edge, her hand raised to shade her eyes. Then, scooping up her gray skirt, she raced to the house. He swung around to see the cause of her hasty retreat.

Although they were too distant to identify, a wagonload of people were coming.

Glancing back toward the cabin, Jake caught but a flash of Rachel as she dashed inside. "Just like a woman. Always worried about her appearance." Amused, he shook his head and tossed the shovel aside, then strode toward the house, stepping past several rows of trees no thicker than his finger before climbing the rise. At the well, he pulled off his work gloves and drew a bucket of water to wash off the dirt. He then ran hands through his shock of blond hair in a hurried attempt to tame it, just as the team and wagon started up the hill.

Jake could easily see the people now. John Riggins, the owner of the dock, warehouse, and ferry in Independence, drove the freight wagon. Homer Dorset rode beside him. On crates in the back sat Coke Lyons, the sawmill owner, and Sam Dooley, along with a brassy-haired floozy, an oversized plume flowing from her peacock-blue bonnet. Jake vaguely recognized her, but from where, he couldn't remember.

"Howdy," Jake called, waving a hand in greeting.

"Howdy," they returned as they rolled to a stop.

"Looks like the city fathers have come calling. Is there trouble stirring?"

"No, no," Homer said, a smile lighting his pudgy face. "Actually, we've dropped by with a proposition that we think will benefit us all."

"Yeah," agreed Coke Lyons, twirling an end of his red moustache. "And we think you're really gonna like it."

"Well," said Jake, "you've sure whetted my curiosity. Hop down and come on in so we can talk."

"Where's the little lady?" Homer asked.

"Inside. Most likely putting on a pot of coffee."

"Good. I think maybe we'd better discuss our business before we go in to her. Don't you agree, boys?"

The others nodded and mumbled their agreement.

Jake rested an arm on a wagon wheel. "Well, get on with it before she starts wondering what we're up to."

"It's like this," Dorset began, then hesitated. "No, Sam, you tell him."

The ruddy-faced blacksmith wagged his burly head. "No. It's your idea. You tell him."

"Oh, hell, I'll tell him," Coke said, a half-grin tilting his stiff moustache. "It's like this, Jake. A few weeks back, one of the Colfax boys came into town. He said you weren't real taken with your new bride."

Jake opened his mouth to protest.

Not noticing, the rawboned man continued. "The boy also told us about your bride's skill at doctorin'. And with all the accidents that plague me durin' loggin' season, it'd be mighty comfortin' to have someone like that close at hand. Even if she is just a woman. So, since you was of a mind to put her aside anyway, we brought you what we think is a most surpassing replacement."

All eyes turned on the peroxided blonde, and she smiled back with a slash of bright red.

"Jake, I'd like you to meet Goldy. McLean sent her to us from his Loggers' Heavenly Haven in Astoria."

"Ain't we met before?" The woman's words flowed

sensuously slow. "But you had a beard then. Remember? Last year while you was workin' the loggin' schooners."

"How've you been, Goldy?" Jake hoped his voice sounded nonchalant.

"Not too good. Business has dropped off next to nothin'. Everyone's runnin' off to California."

"Well," Homer said. "Looks like you two's already friends. So, what do you say?"

"You boys seem to have put a lot of effort into this." Hiding his mounting anger, Jake forced a smile. "And Kyle McLean? You say he's willing to give up one of his best girls for my Rachel?"

"Yeah," John Riggins said, joining in. "McLean said it'd be real good for business. Settlers all up and down the Willamette would have to come in to *our* town to see *our* doctor. And when they do, you know they're going to take care of their other needs as well." Beneath bushy brows, Riggins's deep-set blue eyes fairly sparkled with the expectation of prosperity.

"I hate to disappoint you," Jake drawled, while wishing the bastard McLean'd had the guts to show his cowardly face. "But you're about a month too late. Rachel is my *legal* wife." He aimed his last words at the pig-faced justice of the peace.

"That can be fixed," Homer said with a reassuring nod. "When we hit on this plan, I held off sending your marriage license down to Oregon City. And Sam, here, says he's willing to forget he was the witness."

"That right, Sam?" Jake shifted his attention to the blacksmith.

"None of this sits too well with me," he said, not meeting Jake's eyes, "but I've agreed to go along, if it's what *you* want."

"Sam's havin' a hard time gettin' into the spirit of things," Coke said. "Once we get the little lady to town, he'll see it was the smart thing to do."

"Speaking of town, where would she be staying?"

"McLean said she'd be welcome to stay in one of the rooms above his restaurant. Free of charge."

"I'll bet." Jake snorted, pushing off the wagon wheel.

"She's welcome to stay in the room behind my store again," Homer said, in an assuaging tone. "And of course, as soon as possible, we'll build a house for her. Isn't that right, boys?"

The others first looked confused, but quickly rallied. "Sure," they said, their mumbles tumbling over each other.

"Yeah," Homer continued, "we'll build it on that lot between me and the hotel. We'll be able to keep a close eye on her, see no harm comes to her."

"She's worth that much to you? That you'd even build her a house?" Jake's anger turned to ice. He'd string 'em along. See if there was any more to McLean's scheme. "Well, let's get a better look at what you plan to trade for this prize." He turned to the woman dressed in a low-cut velvet suit the same bright blue as her bonnet. "Stand up, Goldy."

"Sure thing, honey." She streamed up to her feet and rested a hand on a jutting hip. Then, eyes half-closed, lips parted, she treated Jake to a come-hither look.

"Yeah. She looks healthy on the surface, but will she stand up to field work? Do you have all your teeth, Goldy?"

The woman abruptly dropped her seductive pose. "*What? Kyle didn't say nothin' 'bout workin' in the fields.*"

"He's just joshin' you," Homer said, then turned to Jake. "You can't fool an ol' horse trader like me. You think you've got the upper hand, and you want to sweeten the pot. All right, what's it gonna take?"

Rachel's whole body rocked with rage. *How dare they? Who do they think they are?*

She strode away from the open window above the kitchen counter and headed for the rifle racked above the door. "How dare they!" She could find no other words strong enough to express her revulsion. She lifted it down and checked the load. Then flinging the door wide, she stalked outside. "Get out of here!" she railed, pointing the weapon at the despicable louts. "Turn that wagon around and get out."

"Now, Rachel. No sense in getting all worked up." Jake spread his hands in a disarming gesture.

"You! Shut up!" She nailed him with a glare, then aimed the gun at the driver and moved to the edge of the porch. "I said, get that thing off my land."

Jake took a step toward her.

She swerved the barrel toward his chest.

He stopped. "Now, honey, this is no way to treat our guests."

"Don't you honey me, you—you— Get your damned horse and get out with the rest of 'em."

"You can't talk to me like that."

"Shut up or I'll shoot you where you stand."

"Sounds like the little woman's got you henpecked, Jake. If I was you I'd—"

Rachel cocked the rifle and aimed it at the man with the silly-looking orange moustache.

His mouth clamped shut.

Finally taking her seriously, the driver slapped the traces across the horses' backs. "Giddyup."

The people riding in the back grabbed at a side rail as the team jolted the wagon to a start. On a fast roll down the hill, they picked up more speed and were a number of yards away when Rachel heard the woman begin to laugh.

The sound pierced her like a knife, incensing her further. She turned to find Jake hadn't moved. He stood rigidly in place, and his face seemed carved in oak. But she didn't care. Nothing could surpass her own rage.

"Why are you still here? Get your horse and get out."

"Wait a minute. You've got it all wrong."

"No. You're what's wrong. You and that heathen bunch of lowlifes you run with."

"I've had about enough of you shaming me in front of my friends." He started for her.

"One more step and you're dead."

She feared he would keep coming, but with hands balled into tight fists, he stopped. "Fine!" he snapped between clenched teeth. "Don't know whatever made me want to work myself to death on some worthless piece of land anyway. It's all yours, woman."

Rachel remained on the porch, rifle resting in the crook of her arm, while Jake stalked into the barn and whistled.

Prince trotted inside from his paddock.

Moments later, Jake came out leading his now saddled black stallion and headed toward her.

"Stay back."

"If you don't mind," he spat, "I'll be getting *my* coat and some of *my* food."

She couldn't deny him that, she supposed. "All right. But be quick about it." She stepped aside to let him pass.

In a flash, he shoved the gun barrel to the side. It went off, slamming the bullet into the barn door.

"Just so you know, I'm leaving because I want to. No woman runs me off my own place unless I want to go." Then, thrusting the spent weapon to her, he said, "Keep it. You're going to need it."

⟪ chapter 11 ⟫

IN *the black stillness of a moonless night, she turned the ship's wheel slowly, edging close to the slumbering dragon ship. Closer, till it slid within a hair's breadth.*

Just who did he think he was? He was no more immortal than she? Raper! Pillager! Liar, cheat. She'd show him!

Again she scanned the silent deck of her enemy. No movement, no sound came from the shadows, no light peeked from the smallest cranny. She bared her teeth in an avenging smile. The Viking was hers.

She swooped up her skirt and tucked its length within the wide leather belt at her waist, then checked the cutlass sheathed at her side. Tonight the Viking would die.

She leapt onto the railing, grabbed a nearby rope, and swung in an exhilarating glide across the onyx water to the devil's ship. On cat's feet she landed, her tawny hair aswirl. She drew the wide, wickedly curved sword from its scabbard and turned in a ready crouch, peering into the darkness to find where the despoiler hid.

Then she saw them—stairs leading to a door below. Her body pulsed with new strength as she crept down to it and lowered its cold iron handle.

It lagged open on soundless hinges.

And there, sprawled across stark white sheets, lay the villain, naked as the Judas liar he was, a beguiling sleep stripping him of all power.

Oh, yes, she was going to enjoy this.

She vaulted onto the bed, landing with her feet astride his narrow waist.

He jerked awake, his eyes wide—was that terror? God, she hoped so.

She threw back her head and laughed loud and long. Then leaning so close she could hear his heart thumping, she traced her blade down that arrogant chest, leaving a thin line of blood in its wake. "So. You thought you would have your way with me, then sell me to the highest bidder? Not on your lying black soul," she cried at her haughtiest. "But, since you have such an uncommon interest in examining teeth, I'll show you mine." Sneering, she lowered her head to one of his impudent shoulders and bit into the muscled mass.

He tensed then groaned low.

She frowned. That didn't sound like a moan of pain.

Suddenly, he wrenched her from him by the hair. Then in one fluid movement, she was beneath him. Her power-giving weapon clanged to the floor as his deadly face shadowed hers.

"I think your teeth will do quite nicely." His voice sounded like the roll of thunder.

Fear gripped her with such force she thought she would faint. No! She would never give him that satisfaction again. She clamped her jaws together.

"But first," he said, his eyes penetrating her with evil intent. With one hand still twisted in her hair, he pinned her to the bed, then ripped open her bodice and stripped her to the waist.

She attacked him, scratching and kicking, but her desperate efforts were no more to him than the flailing wings of a moth.

He captured her hands and trapped them above her head. "But first, let me show you mine." With a twisted smile, he dipped to a helpless breast.

Eyes clenched shut, she steeled herself for the pain.

But, instead, she felt the moist tickle of his tongue, circling, teasing, torturing . . . raking across the traitorous tip that eagerly responded by growing taut.

He took it into his mouth, and a tremor shot all the way

to her impatient depths. Of their own volition, her legs parted, inviting in the hardness of his seeking need.

His demanding lips moved up to capture her mouth as he plunged into her.

She felt every hot engorging inch as it traveled the miles it took to reach her sweet torment. She arched against him, legs wrapping around him. She—

A dog barked.

The Viking wrenched from her, leaving her achingly unsated.

Dog?

Her eyes popped open to early morning light, and her gaze darted into every corner. But she found no one lurking. Tossing back the covers, she lunged out of bed and jammed her feet into her slippers, then snatched her blue wrapper from off a hook and tossed it on.

Maybe Jake's back, she thought. No, he doesn't have a dog.

Though she knew full well the bar lay across the door, and the windows were latched, she still grabbed the rifle she now kept leaning on the wall next to her bed. On tiptoe she slipped into the front room, searching every shadow, then sidled up to the window near the hearth and looked out onto the clearing between the house and the barn.

Then she saw it. A shaggy-haired dog, with the markings of a collie but with a stubbier nose, sat on the porch. It was tied to a post. Above, a scrap of paper hung from a nail.

Rachel pushed open the window and searched in every direction. It appeared that whoever had brought the dog was no longer around. Nonetheless, she felt creepy knowing someone had been on her porch while she slept.

The dog barked and swished its tail in a friendly hello.

''Hi ya, fella. How do you do?''

The animal stretched forward as far as the tether would allow, its entire rear end wagging.

''If you're sure there's no one else out there, I'll come and get you.'' Leaning the rifle against the wall, she unbarred the door and opened it. After one more cautious look around, she stepped outside.

The dog danced toward her excitedly.

"You sure are friendly," she said, carefully moving a hand to the dog's head. It responded by wetting her fingers with its pink tongue. "Here, let me get you untied."

Once freed, the dog jumped up on Rachel, expressing its joy. After spending the past two eerie nights alone in the big lonely bed, she felt elated by its friendly enthusiasm.

Reaching deep into its fur, she hugged the dog. After a moment, she eased it away. "Settle down. I need to get that note."

It read, "The dog's name is Duchess." Nothing more. No salutation, no signature—just that. Obviously Jake had left the animal to appease his conscience. No one else would've come skulking around late at night, too ashamed to show his despicable face. A decent person would come calling in the middle of the day, maybe stay for tea.

"Come on, Duchess. Let's go down to the smokehouse and find you something for breakfast." They headed for the windowless log building. There she saw a black-tailed deer hanging nose-down from the branch of a tree.

Looks like Jake's feeling too guilty to leave me without plenty of meat, either, she thought, striding toward the carcass. "Thinks I can't make it on my own. Well, he's got another think coming. *I can.* And *I will.* I'm through being some pitiful, weak, obedient little girl. From now on I'm in charge of me. No one's ever going to throw me in jail again like I have no say. No one's going to treat me like some old cow to be bought and sold, to be married off to anyone with gold jingling in their pockets."

Rachel swung around, her gaze targeting the road where it disappeared into the forest. "Do you hear that, Jake?" she railed to the distant stand of trees. "I'm going to do just fine without you. Better!"

A chilly wind whipped at her legs. Looking up, she noticed the dreary gray sky. She pulled her dressing gown more tightly around her and hurried into the smokehouse.

* * *

During the next three days, Duchess proved to be a gentle and loving companion. Not only had she filled part of the huge void Jake left in his wake, Rachel mused while gathering eggs, but her sensitive ears made it possible for Rachel to sleep in peace at night—except, of course, when she was plagued by dreams that turned her body into a hungering, quivering shell. Her delicate task forgotten, Rachel crushed an egg in her suddenly tense hand.

As she wiped the goo onto her apron, the dog began a high-pitched barking that shattered the mid-morning calm.

Rachel ran out and saw a rider approaching across the open field. As he neared, she noticed he was a youth, no more than sixteen or seventeen.

Reaching the yard, the boy reined the horse to a halt. "Hey, Duchess. Ain't that you? Stop your barkin'. It's me, Robby." Pointing to himself, the sandy-haired boy grinned.

Rachel moved forward, finding the boy nonthreatening. "How do you do. My name is Mrs. Stone."

"Figured as much. What you doin' with Bennet's bitch?"

"My husband brought her here for me. Won't you step down and come in for some refreshment?"

"Can't. Don't have time. Where's Jake?"

"He's not here right now. Maybe I can help you."

"Mr. Dorset sent me to tell all the men with the new brides that Mr. Best, the land recorder, is here."

"Oh, dear. I don't know when my husband will be back. How long will Mr. Best be in town?"

"No more'n a couple of days. Look, you'd best come in without him. You don't need him, anyway, to sign for land."

"But I can't. I don't know how to drive a team of horses, even if I knew how to hitch them."

"Oh, well, look. I'm headin' on up to Cooter and Bone's place. I'll have 'em pick you up on their way into town. I'm sure they wouldn't mind."

"Thank you. I'd appreciate that."

As Robby wheeled his horse around and started down the hill at a fast trot, his words, ''you don't need him anyway,'' echoed in Rachel's head. That's right, she thought, I don't need Jake. She'd proved that during the past week, hadn't she? She'd milked the cow, fed the stock, dug those darned holes for the trees. She hadn't quite gotten the hang of splitting logs, but before she ran out of firewood, she'd have that mastered, too. She didn't need Jake. And once she learned how to drive a wagon team, anything she couldn't do for herself, she'd hire done from town.

Money. That's one thing she would need. Jake had placed only two ten-dollar gold pieces on the table before he left. While in town, she would see about getting her own funds sent from the bank in Santa Fe. Her own money for her own life. Without Jake and his contemptuous betrayal, his lying kisses . . . Without the comfort of his arms about her, his warm body next to hers at night. Never to see that dear face again.

A renegade tear slid down her cheek.

''Stop that,'' she whispered, roughly rubbing it away. ''He's gone. Get used to it.''

Near noon, while waiting on the porch in one of the rockers for her ride to arrive, Rachel heard a shrill cackle only Rose, one of the coarser women she'd met on her journey, could make.

Duchess, lying at Rachel's feet, tilted her head, obviously puzzled by the strange noise.

Rachel stood, followed by the dog, and walked to the step and looked down the hill. She spotted the wagon the same instant Duchess leapt down and raced to the edge of the knoll, barking as she ran.

Shading her eyes with a white-gloved hand, Rachel identified Rose sitting in the back, her light brown hair kinky as ever and her sensitive skin splotchy from the sun. Worse, she wore a red dress that accentuated the less than attractive complexion. Rose had her arms wrapped around some man whose back was turned.

Rachel then peered at the other woman sitting up on the

seat. A flamboyant pink bonnet hid her. As the wagon rolled
nearer, Rachel saw that it was Esther—tiny, wiry, with her
large flirty mahogany eyes.

Those two had certainly not been the prettiest of the
women Rachel had traveled with to Oregon. But by the time
they reached port, at least half the crew were vying for their
favors, with which they'd been more than generous.

Considering them crude in word and manner, Rachel had
carefully avoided their company during the trip. Now, she
realized with dismay, she would be forced to endure their
uncouth behavior for the three-hour ride to Independence.

She smoothed the skirt of the intricately tucked and
pleated blue gabardine dress and wondered what good her
Sunday best would do if she arrived in town with those
loudmouthed strumpets. She'd even worn her corset—for
nothing.

As the wagon came up the hill, Rachel got her first look
at the men, neither of whom appeared overly intelligent.
The one up front beside Esther had a square head covered
by stringy black hair. His small eyes were set too close
together and he needed a shave—altogether a slovenly
person. The other appeared neater, but his forehead was far
too high, his chin too weak, and his teeth protruded over his
bottom lip.

Unaware that she watched, they all jabbered at once.
Rachel caught the sun's reflection off a bottle as the driver
lifted it to his mouth, then passed it to Esther.

Oh, my God! They're drinking liquor. Never again, she
vowed, with a lift of her chin. Before I leave town today, I'll
hire someone to teach me to drive a wagon.

"It's Rachel," yelled Rose over the yapping dog.

"Damn if it ain't." Flashing a mouthful of teeth, Esther
waved. "Hey, Rachel!"

She forced a smile and raised a hand in return as they
crested the hill, then she whistled for the yapping dog.
Duchess appeared reluctant to give up, but after one last
bark, she turned and trotted back to her mistress.

Rachel checked the clasp at her waist from which her

chatelaine bag hung by a small chain, then stepped off the porch. "It was so good of you to come by for me. You don't know how much I appreciate it."

"Hear your man's gone. I think it's time me and Esther taught you how to keep one at home." Rose's laughter pierced the air, accompanied by guffawing from the men.

"Rose is just foolin' with you," Esther said in a patronizing whine.

"Where's Jake off to?" the unshaven driver asked.

"He's tending some business about a horse race."

"Oh, yeah? I heard about that. There'll be a passel o' money changin' hands when that race takes place."

The man accepted her lie without question. Good, she thought. She'd use it on everyone else, too.

Esther flung her arm over the man's shoulder. "This is my dashin' new husband, Charley Bone."

"And this is mine," Rose caterwauled, hugging the other man's long bony head to her stingy breasts. "Leland . . . Leland Cooter. Ain't that the funniest name?"

Leland giggled and nibbled at one of the sparse mounds with his rabbitlike teeth.

"How do you do," Rachel said, her disgust with the motley foursome mounting.

"We're doin' just fine," Leland said with a suggestive twang. He and Rose seemed a fitting match.

Against her better judgment, Rachel stepped forward. "I'm ready to go if one of you gentlemen will help me up."

"Ain't you takin' anything with you?" Esther asked. "We'll be spendin' the night in town."

"Oh, dear. What'll I do about Ginger?"

"Who's Ginger?" asked Charley, gazing about him.

"My cow. She's supposed to be milked twice a day."

"Forget the cow," Leland said, raising his head from Rose's chest. "I ain't missin' a night in town for no cow."

"He's right," Charley concurred. "It ain't gonna kill her to miss a milkin'."

Sitting with Rose and Leland on a blanket cushioned by straw, the ride to town was as distasteful as Rachel had imagined. The crude language, the vulgar fondling of one another, and the embarrassing questions they directed at her were almost more than she could bear without protest.

When they reached the river, the young ferry operator, who'd stared at her so rudely when she crossed the first time, recognized her. "You're the one Jake bought, ain't you." He said the words without a hint of inflection or any expression on his skinny face. What kind of place was this Oregon? Words like those should stir some kind of emotion.

"I'm Mrs. Stone, if that's what you mean," she answered crisply. "And with whom am I speaking?"

She'd impressed him enough to cause his dark brows to raise. "Buddy Riggins, ma'am. My pa owns the ferry, and we own the dock and the warehouse over there." He pointed across the swift-running river to the west bank.

Following where he directed, Rachel took her first perceiving look at Independence. The buildings of the tree-shaded hamlet lined a packed-dirt road running inland from the Willamette River. On the north side of the road stood the long building Buddy Riggins referred to, then the smithy and livery stables, then the hotel and Dorset's dry-goods store. On the other side of the road, the sawmill blocked the view of any other buildings that might be beyond. She thought she saw the tip of a church steeple among the firs, but couldn't be sure.

"Well, let's get this wagon on the raft," the young man said as he grabbed the halter of a scruffy-looking horse.

The drunken revelry of her companions reached the other side of the river ahead of them, and a couple of men walking out of the sawmill office watched the boisterous group draw near. Rachel recognized one of them—the redheaded man with the ridiculous moustache whom she'd threatened to shoot five days earlier. After her straitlaced reaction to his boorishness, she felt exceedingly uncomfortable to be caught in such indecent company. She scooted as far from the others as possible.

As the wagon rolled to a stop before the livery barn, Sam Dooley walked outside wearing his heavy blackened apron.

He pulled a large bandanna from his shirt pocket and wiped his hands, then reached up.

"Afternoon, Mrs. Stone. Help you down?"

She gladly accepted his assistance. He'd been the only one who'd disapproved of the nefarious trade.

"Thank you, Mr. Dooley," she said with what she hoped was a pleasant smile. "By any chance, do you know if the official from the land office is still at the store?"

"Yes, ma'am, I believe he is." From the sincere look accompanying his answer, she sensed his deep regret for having been party to the incident at her home.

Rachel reached up in the wagon for her green cloak and needlepoint valise, then turned to the driver. "Thank you again, Mr. Bone. Do let me know when you plan to leave town tomorrow. I'll be staying at the hotel."

Grateful to turn her back on her unseemly companions, Rachel started up the street in the stately stroll she'd learned to perfection at the young ladies' academy. As if she floated across a calm sea, the hem of her blue gabardine dress skimmed a bare inch above the street.

After gliding past the length of the sawmill bunkhouse, Rachel viewed two homes sitting back from the road. The first appeared barely lived in, but the second had a groomed lawn bordered by a bank of flowers in a radiant celebration of spring. A tidy whitewashed picket fence surrounded the yard. The sight reminded her of Peoria, and a wave of loneliness engulfed her. Dragging her eyes away, she looked farther up the street. A small unpainted church stood in quiet beauty among several dogwood trees in full bloom.

There truly was a church in this heathen land. Maybe even an ordained minister. If only she hadn't been too ill to step out of her room on her first stay, most certainly he would've assisted her, seen to it that she was properly wed to a decent Christian man.

But until last week I liked my situation, she thought, the pain of Jake's betrayal stinging her heart anew. Why, Jake? Why did you do this to me? To us?

From behind, Rose's shrieking laughter jerked Rachel's

thoughts back to the problems of the moment. She turned toward the two-storied building with the words Hotel Independence painted across the front, then started toward it. Above its two entrances other signs were printed—one read Saloon, the other, Restaurant. She certainly hoped she could rent a room for the night without stepping into the loathsome imbibing establishment, the memory of her arrest and imprisonment burning afresh.

I'll register later, she decided. Veering away, she headed for the general store. As she walked up the veranda steps, Mr. Dorset came outside.

"Mrs. Stone. Before you go in, I'd like a minute."

"I can't imagine any reason to accommodate you, Mr. Dorset," she said in her most stilted voice.

"Oh, Mrs. Stone. I'm so sorry." He nervously twisted a ring around one of his sausagelike fingers. "We just didn't realize . . . you know."

"No, Mr. Dorset, I *don't* know." Did he really think a simple apology would be sufficient? she thought, watching him purse his lips and frown.

"By your reaction to our proposal the other day, me and the others realized things wasn't like the Colfax boy said. We dropped by there on the way back and learned the truth."

"Misled or not, your actions were reprehensible."

"You're absolutely right, Mrs. Stone. I have erred against you, grievously. All I can do is throw myself on the mercy of the fine Christian lady you are."

"Well," she said, weakening. "I'll try. But I don't think I'll ever see you in the same light as before. But perhaps it was all for the best. It afforded me the opportunity to see Jacob Stone's true colors."

"I—uh—where is Jake?"

"He took his leave on the day in question."

Blanching, Mr. Dorset diverted his eyes. "I see. Well, come inside. Mr. Best is waiting. I presume you still want to file on the forest land to the north of you."

"That's why I'm here."

In the center of the store a man sat at a table covered with maps, ledgers, and papers. When Rachel swept in, he stood. He was tall—not nearly as tall as Jake, of course—and slim, his double-breasted coat adding a much-needed fullness to his meager chest. At least, she thought, by the standards I've recently adopted. And his face, though rather aristocratic, seemed a bit too long. His eyes were too close, his lips too thin. His stylish long sideburns only added to the too-refined look.

"How do you do," he said as she stepped up before him. "My name is Harvey Best. May I be of service?"

Two girls dressed in their Sunday best pretended to peruse the bolts of yardage at the rear of the store while stealing peeks at the man's back and giggling. Rachel surmised Mr. Best was the catch of the county.

"Yes, thank you," she said. "My name is Rachel Stone, legal wife of Jacob Stone. I presume that, though he's not present, I may still file on the property adjoining his."

"Yes, that you may," he said with a smile that broadened his narrow looks. "Do sit down, Mrs. Stone. Might I ask the reason your husband is not with you today?"

Rachel eyed the young girls as they obviously waited for her answer. The whole town knows about the scandalous incident . . . about me, she realized. She instinctively straightened. "To be quite frank, Mr. Best, *and young ladies*," she said, including the nosy twosome, "I don't think Mr. Stone will be accompanying me anywhere in the future. May I still file on the land?"

"Of course," the gentleman assured her. "If you can show proof of your marriage."

"I didn't bring the marriage certificate with me, but I'm sure Mr. Dorset can vouch for me. Isn't that right, Mr. Dorset?" She stared pointedly at the round little man.

"Oh, yes. Most certainly."

"That's good enough for me." The official motioned to the chair opposite him. "Now, if you would be so kind as to sit down, we can get started on the paperwork."

By the time Rachel finished filling out the forms, the girls had drifted outside, and Homer Dorset had gone into the storeroom. She leaned forward. "Mr. Best, there's another matter I'd like to speak to you about. I need to transfer some funds from New Mexico. Since I didn't see a bank when I arrived, could you tell me where the nearest one is, and how I would go about contacting it?"

"You've definitely come to the right person. It just so happens that in a very short time, I will be presiding over a banking establishment in this very community. As we speak, a large safe is being shipped here from San Francisco. And in a few days, workers will start construction on a brick building. Across the street," he added with gusto as he pointed out the front window.

"Indeed. Then I am truly fortunate. If I give you the pertinent information, could you take care of it?"

"I'd be honored. To have a lovely lady, such as yourself, as my first customer—what a good omen. Thanks to you, I already feel I will be a great success."

"And I thank you. You've eased my troubled way, as a stranger in a foreign land, and now I, too, see a small measure of success in my future."

Harvey Best's undernourished chest puffed out at the compliment. "You're most welcome. And please know that I will also be at your disposal for any other little problem that might cause you distress." He picked up his quill and dipped it into the inkwell. "Now, what's the name of—"

Rachel raised a gloved hand to silence him as Homer Dorset came into the room dragging a sack of meal. She didn't want to give the busy little man any more reason to interfere in her affairs.

"Perhaps you're staying in town tonight?" Mr. Best asked in a quiet tone.

"Yes. I plan to take a room at the hotel."

"Then why don't we discuss this over supper there?"

"Yes, I would enjoy that," Rachel said, standing. She extended a hand in farewell. "Till this evening."

Following her lead, the land recorder stood and accepted

her proffered hand in both of his. "Would six o'clock be convenient?"

"Yes, that would fine. Good afternoon, Mr. Best. And thank you again for all your gracious help." Without acknowledging Mr. Dorset, Rachel started for the door.

"You're most welcome, Mrs. Stone," Mr. Best called.

For the first time, Rachel noticed how perfectly this kind and helpful gentleman modulated his words. She turned and lifted her hand in a wave before walking outside.

Stepping off the veranda, Rachel looked toward the hotel. On the porch stood Mr. McLean, the gentleman she'd met at the funeral, looking striking in a black suit with a flamboyant red satin waistcoat fitted over a white ruffled shirt. Flashing a clever smile, he tipped his low, wide-brimmed hat as if he'd been waiting for her.

Of course, she thought, Rose and Esther have been bandying my name about in the saloon.

Mr. McLean started toward her. Then his attention was captured by something off to the side, and he stopped.

Out of the corner of her eye, a flash of color also caught Rachel's attention. From the lovely yard across the street two women, one in a pink floral cotton and the other in daffodil yellow, rushed through the gate of the picket fence. On closer examination, Rachel saw they were two of the women who had snubbed her at the Jenningses' funeral— the generously padded blonde and the petite auburn-haired one who had taken Baby Pris from her.

"Yoo-hoo," the large one called, waving her hand. Her big eyes seemed to be looking directly at Rachel.

"Are you addressing me?"

"Yes, we are," the smaller, older one said as they approached. "We've come to offer our most sincere apologies for our unneighborly behavior last month at the burying."

"Yes," the other concurred. "We're so very sorry. But you must understand, we were led to believe that Jake had married one of those . . . those soiled doves that awful Mr. Griffin brought here from St. Louis."

"I suppose it was an honest mistake." Rachel looked into their faces. They both seemed sincere. If she had been misinformed as they were, would she have acted any differently? She hoped so, but, thinking back, if prostitutes had been brought into Peoria to marry the local citizenry, she doubted she would have reacted any better.

"Please, let us introduce ourselves," the small one said in a crisp but pleasant tone. "My name is Mrs. Grills. My husband is the foreman of the sawmill."

"Yes, and I'm Mattie Baker. We homestead just the other side of the river. Please, do join us for tea. We'd be grateful for another chance to get acquainted."

"Yes, come along. It's time you had a proper welcome to Independence." Mrs. Grills threaded an arm through Rachel's. "And from what we've just heard, I think you could use a bit of female companionship about now."

Hesitating, Rachel looked once more toward Mr. McLean, who seemed to be watching with intent interest. He certainly was the most prosperous-looking man she'd seen since she'd arrived in Oregon, and, she had to admit, the handsomest man she'd ever seen anywhere, anytime. Perhaps too handsome. And, come to think of it, *wasn't he the one who'd supplied that Goldy person for the trade*?

Rachel turned back to the women. "Yes, ladies, I'd very much enjoy a cup of tea about now."

"I'm sure," offered Mrs. Baker with a sad-eyed smile, "after your trials of late, a sympathetic ear is just what you need."

The other agreed with a brisk nod. "And if you're staying in town tonight, you'll be staying with me. That hotel is no place for a lady."

((chapter 12))

PROMPTLY at five minutes before six, according to the Grills's mantel clock, Rachel stepped out the door. As she reached the gate, she touched one of the curls brushing her cheek and smiled. How nice of Edna Grills to loan her a curling iron. Such a kind lady. Looking toward the hotel, she spotted Mr. Best coming her way.

Dressed in his somber charcoal coat and matching trousers, he tipped his stovepipe hat. "There you are," he said, his long legs swiftly closing the gap. "When I heard you hadn't taken a room, I was afraid you'd left town."

"Why, Mr. Best, I'd never be so rude to such a kind gentleman." Tilting up her head, she favored him with a practiced smile before placing her gloved hand in the crook of his arm. "It's just that Mrs. Grills graciously offered me the hospitality of her home."

"Good for her," he said as they strolled toward the restaurant. "The rooms at the hotel really aren't suitable for a refined young lady."

"Mrs. Grills thinks my farm is unsuitable, too. She wants me to move in with her family until a house is built. But, of course, I couldn't."

"Personally, I think it's a most sensible idea."

"But I'd hate giving up land so newly acquired." And everything else that goes with it, her unruly emotions wailed.

Upon reaching the restaurant, Mr. Best opened the door, then lavishly flourishing his top hat, invited her to precede him.

A bit overdone, Rachel thought of his exaggerated courtesy. "Thank you," she said, walking inside.

Starched white cloths covered a scattered group of tables in the otherwise unadorned room. Near the entrance sat two men in dirty work clothes. Skirting them widely, Mr. Best escorted Rachel to a table at the other end.

"I'm afraid," he said, seating her in a chair facing away from the men, "the restaurant receives most of its revenue from the meals it serves to the unmarried sawmill workers. I hope that will someday change."

"I don't mind. Of late, I've become quite accustomed to a simpler life."

Taking the seat opposite her, Mr. Best stood his hat on the empty chair beside him, then carefully straightened the bow of his black silk cravat. In the flow of the lamp on their table, his eyes mirrored the charcoal of his suit. Rachel realized they must be gray, gray to match his gray coat and trousers, his gray plaid waistcoat. How boring!

Shocked by her lack of charity, she lowered her lashes and proceeded to remove her gloves, resolving all the while to be especially kind to this poor man. She looked up as Mr. Best cleared his throat.

"Please don't think me forward," he began, "but in your own best interest, I feel I should mention that there's been talk about town of your misfortune. I bring this up only to make it possible for you and I to speak freely about your predicament." He laid a thin hand on hers.

"Yes, I suppose there'll be gossip for some time." Rachel deftly slid her hand from beneath his. "But I'm sure my life will eventually return to normal."

"Of course. And I'm here to help in any way I can."

"Thank you. I appreciate it. Now, about your help." Loosening the drawstring of her small chatelaine purse, she withdrew and unfolded a piece of paper. "The bank's name is the Mercantile Bank of Santa Fe. The account is in my father's name, Walter B. Chambers. But I have both his and my mother's death certificates. And as their only child, I foresee no trouble claiming the funds. Am I not correct?"

"I see no insurmountable problems."

"Good." She passed the statement to Mr. Best. "The account number and the amount are both clearly printed."

Looking at it, his mouth gaped. "Is this correct?"

"Yes."

He drew a pair of wire-rimmed spectacles from his breast pocket, put them on, and took a closer look. "I—uh, never expected this much."

"With the sale of our house in Illinois, and my father's savings, it did mount up a bit."

"Madam, I'd hardly call twenty-seven thousand six hundred and eighty-six dollars a bit."

"I trust you *will* keep this transaction confidential."

"Of course." He folded the paper and stuffed it, along with his reading glasses, into his breast pocket. "But it may take several months. In the meantime, if you need money to tide you over, don't hesitate to come to me."

"Thank you. For now, I'd appreciate it if you would cover my purchases at the store."

"I'll speak to Homer first thing in the morning. Oh, here comes Mrs. Thornton to take our order. Since I know what's best, I'll order for both of us."

After the stocky middle-aged woman left, Mr. Best placed his bony fingers over hers once more. "I'm sure you'll find her cooking quite adequate."

Deliberately, Rachel removed her compromised hand from the table. "Sir, I don't mean to be rude, but I *am* a married woman."

"If you'll entrust your future to me, when I return to Oregon City I'll speak to an attorney about having that remedied." He glanced in the direction of the sawmill workers, then resumed in a quieter but more intense tone. "If you will but agree, I'll see you're freed from your backwoods husband *and* from those false charges that were levied against you in St. Louis. If necessary, I'll plead your case all the way to the governor. And I am not without influence. I've personally made his honor's acquaintance."

"It's kind of you to offer, Mr. Best. I suppose I should seek legal advice."

"Rest assured, your good name being restored is my most earnest desire, and I'll not rest until it's accomplished."

"My goodness, Mr. Best. One would think you were my own personal knight in shining armor."

A smile burst across his elongated features. "That I am, Mrs. Stone. But I would ask one small favor in return."

"What is that, Mr. Best?" she asked, surprised that he expected some special remuneration.

"I would appreciate it if you would call me by my given name—Harvey. If I'm not being too forward."

Relieved that his request was so simple to grant, she smiled. "Yes, Harvey. I think I could do that quite easily. And you may call me Rachel."

During supper, she was gratified that Harvey, looking almost pompous in his stiffly starched standup collar, monopolized the conversation. Her privacy had been invaded enough for one day. Much too often she'd been reminded of how completely Jake had shattered her most precious dreams.

"I am gratified to say the future that lies before me is bright, indeed. Because of my diligence and foresight, vistas of opportunity are spreading before me. . . ." Harvey droned on about his accomplishments since he'd arrived in Oregon two years ago: about how fortunate he'd been to be appointed to the post of land recorder, how it had placed him in the enviable position of meeting the territory's most influential people, how his ability had been noticed by important people who were now entrusting him with the responsibility of a bank—the presidency, no less.

Mr. Best was obviously interested in her, or he wouldn't be trying so hard to impress her. And he would be a secure future, a second chance. So, why didn't she want it?

". . . perhaps I'll run for Congress when Oregon is made a state. Or even governor. Of course, I'd need the right wife beside me. I hope one as refined and beautiful as, say, yourself."

Rachel flawlessly picked up her cue. "Why, Mr. Best, how you do flatter. I'm sure there are any number of young ladies eminently more suitable. Less encumbered—if you know what I mean?"

"You underestimate yourself." Harvey leaned forward. "I travel extensively, and I've found no one who suits me—save the one with whom I'm enjoying this delightful evening."

Rachel leveled her gaze on him. "Mr. Best, I do believe the conversation is becoming too precipitous for a first meeting. Don't you agree?"

Harvey settled back in his seat again and sighed. "Yes, I suppose I've overstepped myself. But in this primitive land . . . Say you'll forgive my brashness."

She allowed her expression to gentle. "Certainly."

His face brightened immeasurably. "Then, dare I hope that you'll see me again?"

"Good evening, Mrs. Stone, Harvey. Enjoying your meal?"

So involved with Harvey, Rachel hadn't noticed Mr. McLean's approach. "Yes, thank you." She peered up into his heavily lashed eyes, which were midnight-blue in the soft light. "It was quite adequate."

"Harvey," McLean said, placing a familiar hand on the other man's shoulder though his eyes remained fixed on Rachel. "If I'd known you were bringing this fair lady for supper, I would've had the cook prepare something special."

"Mrs. Thornton has served us in a pleasurable manner," Rachel said, feeling the weight of his stare.

"I hate to intrude on your evening, Mrs. Stone. But I must steal away your supper companion. And I'm afraid Harvey will be occupied for the remainder of the evening."

Harvey's face hardened. "Are you sure it can't wait?"

"'Fraid not." For the first time, Mr. McLean looked in the other man's direction. "A business associate is waiting for you in my office. But don't worry, I'll see the lady safely to her lodgings."

"I'm so sorry to desert you." Disappointment rang in Harvey's words. He stood slowly, then lifted her hand to his lips in a farewell gesture. "Till we meet again." On the way toward the kitchen door, he hesitated a moment and glanced back with a baleful look.

Rachel favored him with a sympathetic smile.

Mere seconds after Harvey Best's unhappy departure, Mrs. Thornton bustled into the dining room. She carried a wine bottle, two goblets, and a fancy little round box.

"Perfect timing, Hannah," Mr. McLean said as he took the seat beside Rachel. He relieved the waitress of the crystal stemware and placed one goblet before Rachel and the other before himself. "I understand congratulations are in order. I thought we might celebrate with a toast."

"Congratulations?" she said, watching the stout woman hand him the tapered bottle. Rachel read the label in astonished silence. *Champagne. From France.*

"Didn't you acquire three hundred twenty acres of virgin forest land today?" he said, accepting from Mrs. Thornton the box covered with pink ribbons and ecru lace. "That will be all, Hannah."

"Yes, sir," the older woman said with a swift glance at Rachel, one that caused a slight uneasiness.

A lazy grin dimpled McLean's cheeks as he turned his attention to Rachel. "That calls for a toast. And I can think of nothing more appropriate for the occasion."

"That's very kind of you, sir, but I don't drink alcoholic beverages."

"No lady I've ever met could say no to champagne," he said.

"You don't understand. It's against my religion."

"If Christ offered it to you, would you refuse?"

"Well, no, of course not."

He pushed vigorously on the cork with his thumbs. It popped out with a loud bang, and the bubbly liquid spewed out of control. The startled pair laughed as too late they raised hands to ward off the sudden spray.

Quickly tipping the bottle, McLean filled her glass, then

his. "Jesus not only offered it, his first miracle was to turn water into wine. Surely you remember that."

"Yes, of course. But—" Her lips parted at his casual disregard of her beliefs. But then, what he said was true, she rationalized. And it did show that he'd read the Bible.

"I see my logic has left you speechless."

By the pleased look on his debonair face, Rachel knew he thoroughly enjoyed his little victory.

Without taking his eyes from her, he removed the lid from the box and lifted it toward her. "I find that nothing complements champagne better than bonbons. Have one."

A childlike grin spread across her face, but with a concerted effort she softened it into a more demure smile. "My, what a wonderful surprise," she said, reaching for a creamy chocolate. "Thank you. I do believe I will."

She crunched through the hard chocolate shell to the smooth center that tasted of orange and exotic spices. She savored the experience, but too soon the bonbon vanished.

"Try the champagne. I'm sure you'll like that equally well." As Harvey had done earlier in the evening, McLean seemed determined to entertain her.

Rachel lifted the goblet to her lips, half expecting a bolt of lightning to strike her dead. She took her first sip. The effervescence tickled her as if it were alive. In joyous surprise, she almost opened her mouth. Instead, she swallowed, and the lively fluid warmed her within quite pleasurably. She felt deliciously wicked.

Mr. McLean looked exceptionally smug as he relaxed in his chair. "I see you approve my choice of vintage."

"Vintage? Oh. Yes, the champagne is quite nice."

"Then it's time I propose a toast." He sat erect and raised his glass. "To the most elegant lady ever to grace the shores of the Willamette, and to her good fortune." He lifted his glass to his lips and downed the contents.

Rachel took another sip. "Thank you for that flattering toast. I—"

"In this frontier," he said, overriding her words, "to see

one with your quality, your loveliness, it's truly rare. But, surely you know what an exceptional woman you are."

Heat rose to her cheeks and she felt giddy, light-headed. "Mr. McLean, you're making me blush."

"But you know it's true. I haven't been able to get you out of my mind since I first saw you at the Jenningses'."

His statement triggered a flurry of memories and emotions spanning the past month. But they stopped abruptly at the recollection of the floozy the men had brought to her home. *Goldy. One of McLean's girls.*

Rachel met his gaze squarely. "Mr. McLean," she began pointedly while placing her drink on the table. "No doubt you are a charming, clever man. But I now recall your part in the unsavory attempt to have me dispossessed by one of your—your *women*."

Rachel attempted to rise, but McLean stayed her. She glared at the offending hand on her arm.

After a moment he removed it. "I know what you must think. But I was totally misinformed. I was led to believe that you *wanted* to be freed from Stone. It was obvious when I saw you with him that you were far too genteel for him. Far too cultured. So, when they came to me and asked if I'd find a substitute, I was more than glad to help you out."

"You didn't find their request immoral?"

"I thought it more immoral for you to be tied to that oaf of a mountain man for the rest of your life."

Oaf? Rachel bristled at the affront to Jake. She knew the tenderness of his caress, how gentle his lips could be, moving on hers. "From what I gathered, *that person* works for you in a house of ill repute. Do you also find that not immoral?"

McLean arched a raven's wing of a brow. "I'm afraid you're treading in an area you know very little about."

"I may know more than you think. You forget the cloud under which I arrived."

"Then, if you're so knowledgeable, you're aware that men have certain needs. Needs that sometimes must be fulfilled in a less than ideal manner. As you know, there's a dire shortage of women in the west. And in my small way, I have done what I could. But if you find this particular enterprise so distasteful, I'll gladly disengage myself. I'll tell Harvey to sell the offending establishment.''

What kind of fool did he take her for? "I think Mr. McLean, it's time we talked about something else.''

"I see you don't believe what I say.''

Returning his challenge, Rachel lifted her chin. "Mr. McLean, I find it ludicrous that you would conduct your business according to my whim.''

"But, Mrs. Stone, I don't consider your desires mere whims. And *my* most earnest wish is to be worthy of your trust and respect.''

"Why? We're scarcely more than passing acquaintances.''

He took her hand in his and gave her his most serious look thus far. "You, my dear lady, are the first woman I've seen since I came to Oregon whom I would be proud to have on my arm, anywhere. The governor's mansion, the White House.''

"My goodness. You do have ambitious dreams.'' She removed her hand from his and picked up her gloves. "But I think it's time I returned to Mrs. Grills's home. I'll have enough explaining to do as it is. A married lady, going to supper with one gentleman and returning with another.''

"Oh—of course.'' His engaging grin returned as he rose to help her from her seat. "For some things it's too late, for others too soon. But I'm a patient man.'' He took her arm and wrapped it within the crook of his. Then placing a proprietorial hand over it, he led her toward the exit.

Rachel was surprised to see that the restaurant had emptied of the other diners without her noticing. But what could she expect? She'd just been the recipient of some of the most aggressive courting she'd experienced in her twenty-three years. And not from just one man, but two. And she wasn't even free to accept either of them.

"Be sure to thank Mr. Best for me. It was a lovely

supper," she said, belatedly remembering the man who, in comparison to the worldly Kyle McLean, was a bit of a fop.

He opened the door and ushered her outside. "Of course, if it'll make you happy."

As they started down the porch steps, the saloon doors swung open, and a man staggered out, accompanied by the sounds of drunken laughter. Rose's voice pierced above the rest. Just the thought of returning home with her and the other three debauchers caused Rachel to shudder.

As if he could read her mind, Mr. McLean said, "It would be my pleasure to take you home tomorrow."

She turned and looked at him. At the moment any offer seemed preferable to what awaited her. But, of course, it was out of the question. She could not ride into the wilderness with a stranger, especially one who owned a whorehouse—even if he was prosperous.

"I see by your expression you find my offer less than proper. I understand. I'll arrange for more acceptable transportation for you." Steering her past the inebriated man, he led her up the street toward the Grillses' house.

"Thank you, but I planned to ask the Stockton boy to return with me. There are a few things I need help with."

"Fine. But I don't think the boy has his own wagon. Tell him he can use the one behind the hotel."

Overcome by his generosity, she looked up into his face and softened. "I can't believe how kind all you people have been. Mrs. Grills inviting a stranger to stay in her home. Mr. Best arranging for my funds to be transferred and helping me to sort out the rest of my affairs, and now you. You're willing to trust a team and wagon to me. I've never known such hospitality."

"But, don't you know, Mrs. Stone, word of your good deeds precedes you. Everyone has heard of your compassion and diligence in helping those in need. You should allow us to reciprocate. Provide that house for you here in town, so we can show you what really good neighbors we can be."

"Neighbors. It's been . . . so long." Her throat closed with emotion.

"Come along, little lady," he said, wrapping an arm around her shoulders. "I think it's time we got you in out of the cold."

Pressed against his solid warmth, she became aware of the night chill for the first time. "You really are a very nice man, aren't you?"

"You mean you're just now noticing?" A chuckle rumbled forth. Reaching the garden gate, he opened it and escorted her to the front door before he released her. "I'm leaving for Oregon City first thing in the morning, but if you need anything at all, ask the Thorntons at the hotel. I'll leave instructions with them."

"I don't think that will be necessary. But thank you for the kind thought." She extended her hand. "Good night, Mr. McLean. It's been a pleasure."

He raised it to his lips. "The pleasure's been all mine. Till the next time." Then, slowly, he turned and strode away.

Reaching for the door handle, Rachel took a deep breath before facing Edna Grills. The motherly woman would certainly have something to say about her returning with a second escort. *And slightly tipsy at that.* A giggle burst forth . . . then dried up as she came face to face with the good woman, who'd obviously waited up for her.

"You've certainly enjoyed yourself," Edna said, closing the door behind Rachel. "Two gentlemen in one evening. My word."

Hoping the red rushing to her cheeks didn't show in the dim light, Rachel returned Edna's stare. "Mr. McLean sent Mr. Best on some business matter. Then Mr. McLean offered to accompany me to my lodgings in his stead. All perfectly innocent, I assure you."

"I wonder. Mr. McLean has his fingers in too many pies to suit me. And now he's ordering Mr. Best around? Humph," she snorted while pulling her robe sash tighter. "Mr. Best is supposed to be in the employ of the territory,

not some lackey of Mr. McLean's. That McLean simply
doesn't look trustworthy. And that red vest he wore today.
No upstanding citizen would be caught out on the street in
one, especially not in broad daylight. The other women and
I have told our daughters to keep their distance.''

Uncomfortable, Rachel edged toward the stairs.

In a sudden change of demeanor, Edna's disapproving
stare changed to one of glowing warmth. ''But Mr. Best is
another story. There hasn't been one whisper of gossip
about him. His dress and decorum are always impeccable.''

''I'll keep that in mind.'' Then, hoping to put an end to
the subject, she asked, ''What time are church services
held? I plan to learn how to drive a team between now and
then, and I'd like to attend.''

''Wonderful!'' Edna's small dark eyes brightened. ''Come
Saturday. Spend the night. I'll introduce you around. The
ladies will be dying to meet you. And bring that doctor's
bag with you. A few of the women have complaints.''

((chapter 13))

BENEATH an overcast sky, the Redman homestead lay hidden in the darkness, save for the squares of light coming from the cabin's windows. Normally Jake would have sought shelter before nightfall, but he felt an unaccountable need to see his old friends. Besides, he knew they'd always welcome him with open arms no matter how untimely his visit.

A hound yipped incessantly as Jake rode into the yard.

"Who's out there?"

Jake recognized Wayne's voice, but was surprised by the hostility in it. "It's me, Jake. Jake Stone."

"Well, I'll be. Come on in."

As Jake rode closer, he saw his friend from the wagon-train days standing in the deep shadows of the log house. A rifle rested in the crook of the lanky man's arm.

"You're sure acting jumpy tonight."

"Tell you later. Climb on down. Let's get a look at you." Redman flung open the cabin door and leaned in. "Mary, Davy. Come see who's here."

Before Jake's feet hit the ground, Mary and their oldest son rushed out to greet him. All three wrapped him in hugs, and Mary planted a noisy kiss on his cheek.

"Come on in. I want to get a better look at you." She pulled him inside. "My, my." The slender, fair-haired woman stretched up on her toes, drawing nearer his face. "Ain't you the handsomest one. See, Davy, he's shaved off his beard."

Frowning, the towheaded boy reached up. "It's gone!"

161

Jake grabbed his hand. "Come on, folks. Can't a man get rid of some whiskers without everyone taking on?"

"It's just that we didn't know you was hidin' such a fine face under all that hair." Mary turned to her husband. "Wayne, ain't he good-lookin'?"

The creases in her husband's craggy face deepened as he burst into laughter and slapped Jake on the back. "Yeah, he's purty as a picture."

"All right, that's enough." Jake shrugged off Wayne's hand. "I come calling, and this is the way I get treated?"

"Sit down, sit down," Wayne invited in a lazy drawl. "It's been a coon's age."

"You're always hungry," Mary laughed. "How about some coffee and a big slice of apple pie?"

His favorite. "My mouth's watering already."

"Davy," Wayne said, "run out and put up Jake's horse."

Jake sat down at the table across from his friend while Mary poured cups of steaming brew. He watched her, reacquainting himself with the graceful way she moved, her daintiness. She had always seemed miscast as a farmer's wife. Jake had wondered more than once why Wayne had chosen her—the weathered man's angular build and height so overshadowed her.

"Well, now," Wayne said. "What brings you up this way? Thought you'd be real busy about now. What with spring plantin'—and ain't your bride comin' some time soon?"

"Wayne. Don't you know anything?" his wife said as she set down the cups. "Jake's already got his wife. Ain't that right?"

"Yeah. But how'd you know?" He hadn't planned to discuss Rachel with them . . . or had he? Had he really thought they wouldn't ask about the bride he sent away for?

"I figure it'd take somethin' mighty important to get you to shave off that beard." Faint lines feathered from her gray eyes as she smiled smugly.

Jake rubbed his jaw. "Well, I'm kinda getting used to it now."

"How old is she? What's she look like?" Wayne asked with a teasing grin.

"Don't pay him no mind," Mary said as she placed a huge wedge of pie in front of him. "Where's she from?"

"Thanks." Jake picked up his fork and cut off a piece of the flaky crust. "Some town in Illinois. She's a city girl. Her father was a doctor."

"Really? Why would a girl like that sign up to be a mail-order bride?"

"That's easy," Wayne said with a chuckle. "She's either old or ugly."

"No, it's nothing like that. She's really very pretty. A lot like you, Mary, tiny. Looks like she'd break real easy. But she's real plucky. She tries real hard."

A serious expression replaced Wayne's amused one. "Then you're pleased with her. That's good, 'cause I thought sendin' off for a wife was a dumb way to pick someone you planned to spend the rest of your life with." He captured Mary's waist and drew her to him. "It's hard work livin' with a woman—even one you're madly in love with. Ain't that right, sweetums?" he said, hugging her close.

"No harder than livin' with some bull-headed man." Mary pulled out of her husband's grasp and took the seat at the end of the table.

"Well, we aren't exactly living together," Jake blurted out. He had to tell someone—get it off his chest. After almost a week of keeping to himself, spending his nights alone in the woods, talking to friends might help him work through all the troubling thoughts that kept him awake most of the night . . . all the lonely feelings. Absently, he held his fork aloft. "She got real mad about something, and, well, she insulted me and my friends. And a man can't have a wife shaming him in front of his friends, can he?"

"No," Wayne agreed. "A wife needs to respect her man."

"Yeah, that's the way I felt." Jake nodded firmly.

"Sounds to me like there's a story here that needs

tellin'," Mary said, crinkling her brow. "What happened?"

"Well . . . Ah, hell, you don't want to hear about my troubles. How're things going around here? Did you ever get that dock built?"

"*Jake.*" Mary's voice was brittle. "What did you men do to make her so mad?"

Jake had a hard time meeting her eyes. "Well, you see, some of the boys came out from town, and they wanted to well . . . It sounds kinda bad unless you know why."

"Why don't you just start from the beginning. And don't leave out anything." Mary settled back and took a sip of coffee.

"The beginning? Yeah, I guess that's probably best. Well, you see, I was over on the coast, loading logs on schooners. I was hoping to make a little extra before the brides arrived. Anyway, a chain broke, and a big cedar log rolled flat over me. Must've cracked a couple of ribs. I couldn't sit a horse for three or four weeks."

Mary grimaced. "What's that got to do with a wife that hasn't even arrived yet? Get on with it."

"All right," Jake said, knowing already whose side she'd take. "The brides arrived two weeks before I got back. And there was just the one left waiting. She'd had malaria and . . ."

Jake gave them all the facts. He told them about all the misunderstandings and frustrations of the first days, then the way they had settled into an easy, really friendly relationship. He even told them he'd come to think very highly of her. He did, however, leave out a number of details. He didn't speak about how much he'd grown to count on seeing her first thing in the morning, or how his heart leapfrogged every time he caught sight of her walking out of the house, and how her hair caught the fire of the setting sun. Nor did he tell them that her lilting voice was more pleasing than the cleverest lark, or how soft she felt when he hugged her to him. That he missed the very smell of her.

Finally, he finished giving them the misbegotten details of that last day. ". . . and there was no reasoning with her.

I tried, but she was just too pig-headed to listen. And besides, I wasn't about to grovel like a dog. And how am I ever going to face the men in town after the way she ran 'em off?''

"Now, let's see if I've got it," Mary said, the gray of her eyes turning to steel. "Your new bride buried both her parents on the way to New Mexico, was mistaken for a prostitute while she was mercifully caring for a trollop. Then she's falsely imprisoned until Mr. Griffin buys her out. She catches malaria on the way, then is given no choice in who she's gonna marry. Am I right so far?"

"Yeah, sounds like it," Jake said, pricked with uneasiness.

Mary leaned forward, holding him with her stare. "She marries you anyway, 'cause she ain't got no other choice. She has to put up with you and everyone else thinking she's a harlot. And just when things is startin' to look better, she hears you and them other heathens talkin' about tradin' her off for some tart?" Without softening her penetrating gaze, Mary leaned back in her chair. "You're lucky she didn't shoot the whole devil-taking bunch of you."

"Now, Mary." Wayne placed a cajoling hand on her arm. "Jake said he was just leadin' those men on. He didn't have no intention of goin' along with 'em. Did you?"

"No. But like I said, she puffed up and there was no reasoning with her. She should've had the decency to at least listen to me."

"Decency? For heaven's sake, Jake. No woman with any self-respect would've acted any different. Now, you've got to go back there. And face her. *And apologize.* And hope to God she'll take you back. From what you've said about her, she sounds like a charitable person, the way she's always helpin' others out."

"You expect me to go crawling back, asking for her charity?"

"I thought you wanted a wife and children."

"I do—I mean, I did. I don't know."

Leaning forward, Mary slid a small hand atop Jake's arm

and squeezed. "You've spent two years provin' up your land so's it'd be fit for a wife. And now, at long last, you got one. And from what it sounds like, you're real partial to her. Ain't you?"

Jake's gaze dropped to her hand on his forearm. "Yeah, I suppose so. She's . . ." His voice faded away.

Mary gave him a last pat and straightened with a determined look. "Then you got no choice. You gotta go back and make it right with her. Tell him, Wayne."

Redman took a breath before he spoke. "She's right. You got too much at stake here. We're talkin' about the rest of your life. If you love her at all, you gotta."

"There's more to it than that. . . ." Jake inhaled slowly before continuing. "She's a real lady. Been to school. You ought to see all the books she brought with her. If she'd had any kind of choice at all, she wouldn't have picked an ignorant mountain man like me."

"That's not necessarily so," Mary said. "Ever since I knowed you, you always seemed real educated. Remember how, out on the trail, you used to read Shakespeare to us."

"And," added Wayne, "I never once heard you say *ain't*."

"That's only because a mountain man by the name of Cecil Parrish took a liking to me when I was just a kid. He was the black sheep of some uppity Boston family, and he'd knock me upside the head if I didn't use proper English. But it's not like I had real schooling."

Redman raised a finger. "Yeah, but you know all you need to about homesteadin' and huntin'. You've led whole wagon trains across half a continent. Hell, man, I've even heard you talkin' that Indian gibberish. How many tongues *do* you know?"

"Oh, I can get by in five or six."

"Now that takes a heap of learnin'. So, I want you to stop sellin' yourself short. You can hold your head high in anybody's company."

Jake opened his mouth to protest, but was interrupted by

Mary, rising from the table. "Better go fetch you some bedding," she said, turning away.

"Well, how're things going around here?" Jake asked as Mary left the room.

"Not so good."

"From what I could see when I rode in, everything looks shipshape. What's the problem?"

"You might call it a plague."

"A plague?" Jake leaned forward, cradling his cup in both hands.

"Yeah. A plague of accidents. 'Specially if you live along the river or a good-sized fork. Mysterious fires breakin' out in the middle of the night. Work animals disappearin', never to be found again. Sanford, upstream? His fence was *accidentally* busted down and his neighbor's herd of cows just happened to wander into Sanford's newly planted orchard. The hay burners ate his saplin's down to the ground before he knew they was there."

"Who do you reckon is behind it?"

"No one I could swear to. But it don't take much smarts to figure out why. The price of timber has shot up since they struck gold in California. San Francisco's beggin' for lumber and payin' hard cash."

"Yeah, I know. I took one of the logging schooners down there last summer."

"Well, far as the big lumbermen is concerned, us homesteaders is just in the way. They figure to force us out like we was nothin' but piss ants."

"They can't all be in on it. I've met most of 'em, and they wouldn't go along with that kind of a deal."

"Kyle McLean would. He's opened two new sawmills along the Columbia in the past year."

"Queer you should mention him. He opened a hotel in Independence last fall. He didn't let on that he owned it, though. I just found out a few weeks ago. And I wouldn't be surprised if he has a share in the sawmill there, too."

"You mean he's movin' up the Willamette, too? I thought he was just operatin' up and down the Columbia."

"Hell, he's got the timber rights to a huge tract of land just to the north of me, and he's lusting after more. Folks down my way are starting to get real edgy."

"Have you had any mysterious accidents?"

"No. Not yet."

"Well, you better keep a close eye out. 'Cause, sure as I'm sittin' here, they'll be startin'."

Sweet memories, painful memories assaulted Jake as he lay on the downy pallet before the hearth. Whether his eyes were closed or open he could see Rachel, her streaming locks shimmering in the firelight. Her face dusky with desire. Wanting him. Coming to him.

Jake jerked up on an elbow, turned, and slammed his fist into the pillow before settling down again. He would not let thoughts of her rob him of one more night's sleep. After all, if he swallowed his pride, just this once, he'd see her soon enough. He'd head for home tomorrow. Besides, by now, she'd probably be all simmered down.

Yeah, he thought, gaining confidence in his decision. By now she's found out how hard it is to run the place by herself. Hell, she'll be so glad to have me back, I probably won't even have to apologize. The idea of admitting he'd done something wrong didn't sit well.

Propping his head on his arms, he wondered if Rachel was as haunted by thoughts of him as he was of her. Did she think of him when she rolled over in their big bed? He remembered that last morning when he'd awakened to find her curled against him, her head resting peacefully on his arm, baring her delicately curved neck. So creamy white. Waiting to be kissed.

Only one amber strand lay in the way. Lifting it aside, he'd leaned down and trailed the length of her neck with his lips. Stopping at the nape, he had run the tip of his tongue in a small circle, tasting her.

She'd turned to meet him, with adoring eyes.

God, how he loved her.

She'd reached into his hair, and the taut bud of a supple breast had trailed up his chest.

An exploding spark raced down Jake's spine.

"Stop it!" he growled. He had to think of something else, or he'd never get any sleep.

McLean. Think about McLean.

Maybe before Jake left tomorrow he'd have Wayne take him around to some of the homesteads that'd had "accidents." Maybe go into Oregon City, check the records, talk to the law. Yeah, he thought, the man needs looking into.

Remembering the last time he'd seen McLean, Jake's jaw muscles tightened. The bastard had strutted up the hill with Rachel on his arm like he owned her. McLean sure looked shocked when she left him and came to stand by me— nothing but a crude dirt farmer, he thought. But she did care for this ol' clodbuster. It was in her eyes when she looked at me. In the urgency of her touch when she'd pull me to her.

His skin burned at the thought of her hot, frenzied hands running up and down his back as he thrust into her.

Rachel woke with a start, feeling hollow, empty . . . desperately missing the wholeness that only Jake could give. She crossed her legs and squeezed in an attempt to stop the throbbing ache. Grabbing her quilt, she crushed it to her until the overwhelming desire began to ebb.

"I hate you, Jacob Stone," she groaned. "You did this to me."

She heard a rustling sound and searched for its origin. The muted shapes in the darkened room were strange, scary. Then she remembered where she was—at the Grillses' in town, in their daughter, Dinah's room. In the faint light, she looked to the bed on the opposite wall. To her relief, the girl's chest rose and fell in the even cadence of slumber.

Rachel rolled over, still hugging the quilt to her. How many more times would she awaken in a rush of heat? How much longer would it be before her body let her get a full night's sleep? Feeling utterly forsaken, tears welled.

How many more times would she cry?

I will forget you, she stormed in silence. *I will.*

A balmy breeze stole gently across the crystalline tropical bay, frothing her tresses, ruffling the flounces of her skirts. She toyed with the sleek satin, the gorgeously extravagant, sensually daring creation ashimmer with that tender pink found only within the recesses of a seashell. She mused over which was more beautiful, the gown or the horizon as the dipping sun splayed a riot of color across sky and sea . . . or him.

The very sight of him held her in a hush of sublime serenity.

In the magical twilight, his godlike physique gleamed gold, and stardust feathered his hair. His eyes, more alluring than a gemlike lagoon, wooed her, dared her to come, to explore their secret depths.

Her senses a swirling passion-filled waltz, she moved closer.

His dazzling white blouse lay open almost to the waist, catching the air, enticing her with its bewitching imitation of the breeze-filled sails of his trim sloop.

She couldn't resist the temptation to reach past the silk to the smooth, hard haven of his chest. She stretched forth a hand.

He filled it, instead, with a jewel-encrusted goblet. The lace dripping from his sleeve washed across her wrist, sending a tingly wave all the way to her expectant heart.

"Champagne for my lady." Her Viking breathed the words softly in a husky whisper, a faint smile curling the corners of his beckoning lips.

Champagne for my lady, he said. But his eyes . . . they whispered much, much more. They said, I do love you. I'm yours, forever, and ever . . . and ever. . . .

⟨⟨ chapter 14 ⟩⟩

AFTER two days of trying to get past the governor's bespectacled snob of a clerk, Jake lost all patience. He stalked out past the great white columns and down the steps of the courthouse.

Oregon City's getting as bad as some damnable eastern town, he thought as he walked toward the livery barn. Snooty little dandies with their spiteful little rules.

He'd ride out to Captain Ainsworth's big house. Jake didn't like the idea of asking anyone for a special favor, but Ainsworth owed him a few. So, maybe just this once— because he needed to get home to Rachel. How he could've walked out on her like that, he just didn't know. Her so spindly, so frail. Alone. No one to chop firewood for her, to tote the feed bags. No one to protect her from wolves and bears.

That's not exactly true, he rationalized as he walked into the stable. I left a dog to keep the wild animals away.

Riding down Leland Road toward Ainsworth's mansion, Jake's thoughts drifted back to where they always did now—to Rachel. Rachel, swishing around in the kitchen, a spot of flour on her cute little nose. . . . Rachel in the barn. The scent of lilac water filling his nostrils when he knelt around her, hands over hers, teaching her how to milk the cow. Hearing her high-pitched laughter when the first squirt *ping'd* into the pail. . . The morning he'd gone hunting and had come home to find her drying her honey-gold hair by the fire, dressed only in a skimpy chemise. As she ran nimble fingers through her hair, the dampened filmy material clung temptingly to her ripe breasts.

Jake's heart jumped in his chest when he remembered the invitation in eyes turned dusky, the sensuous grace as she moved toward him.

"I didn't think you'd be back so soon." Her words had flowed, low, sultry.

"I got lucky," he said, feeling luckier all the time. He drew her to him, and buried his hands in her cool silken hair that spoke of woodsmoke and roses. Her breasts overflowed the low-cut shift as they pressed against his chest. She moaned and circled his neck with her bare arms, and he slowly moved to her soft, moist lips and tasted their sweetness.

Suddenly, she pulled back. "It's broad daylight, Jake. What will people say?"

Every time he remembered that day, and Rachel's wide-eyed horror at the thought of being caught making love in the middle of the day, he chuckled. He repeated her words with those same panicked inflections. "What will people say?"

Prince perked his ears and swung his head around.

"Settle down, boy." Jake leaned forward and patted his sleek jet neck. Then, as he gazed unseeingly down the road, his mouth dropped into a slack grin. "Yeah, that sure turned into one lucky day."

The gleaming white Ainsworth mansion, its impressive Grecian columns supporting a wide veranda, came into view. It was a fitting home for the owner of the most successful steamboat line on the rivers. It bespoke prosperity—prosperity of the industrious, the ambitious, the clever.

But not too clever, McLean, thought Jake as he reined his horse into the wide lane that led to the manor house.

A manservant opened the door in answer to his knock. Upon viewing the coarsely dressed woodsman, he stretched to his full, if meager, height and sniffed as if searching for an offending odor. "If it's work you want, you're to go round to the back door."

"I'm not looking for work," Jake said, barely restraining himself from grabbing the snooty runt by his stiffly starched collar. "I'm here to see the captain."

"Do you have an appointment?"

"No, but I'm sure he'll see me."

"Captain Ainsworth is occupied with important business at the moment. He couldn't possibly be bothered with the likes of you."

Jake leaned down till his face was within lethal inches of the servant's. "I just spent two days at the mercy of another rude little bastard. I'm through wasting my time."

The butler's eyes widened with fear.

"Now, you high-step on in there and tell your boss Jake Stone is here to see him."

Jake had to smile as he watched the slight man almost run to do his bidding.

Within seconds Captain Ainsworth came out of the drawing room and across the marble tile of the entry. He extended both hands in a hearty handshake. "Stone, is that really you? I hardly recognize you without the beard. How've you been?"

"Fine, Captain. And you?"

"Couldn't be better," said the robust middle-aged man. "Come on in. The governor's here. Have you met him?"

"*The governor's here?* No, but I'd sure like to."

"Yes, John's a fine man, fine man." Ainsworth turned to the butler standing submissively to the side. "Get a whiskey for my friend here. We'll be in the drawing room."

The servant's mouth dropped open, then clamped shut as he hurried off.

"Governor Gaines," Ainsworth said when they entered the stylishly appointed room, "I'd like you to meet Jake Stone, a man to whom I owe a great deal of my success."

The governor, though in his fifties, looked surprisingly trim and fit. Jake enjoyed the thought that it was probably due to his recent marriage to a pretty young schoolteacher.

Governor Gaines extended a hand. "How do you do, Mr.

Stone. The captain has mentioned your talent for diplomacy more than once.''

''I think you must have me mixed up with someone else. I'm not a politician.''

''You may not see yourself as one,'' the governor said with a slight smile, ''but nonetheless, your powers of persuasion among the natives of this land have not gone unnoticed. You have aided immeasurably in our efforts to trade along the waterways. To bring civilization and prosperity to this wondrous new land.''

It was obvious to Jake why John Gaines had been appointed governor of the territory. Everything that came out of the man's mouth sounded like a Fourth of July speech.

''I don't think I can take all the credit, Your Honor. You see, trading comes as natural to a Chinook as eating.''

''Nonetheless, my good man, we owe you a great debt. If ever we can do anything in return, don't hesitate to ask.''

''Glad to hear you say that, sir.'' A smile brightened Jake's face as the one on the governor's dimmed slightly. ''You see, I've been trying to get an appointment to see you for two days, now.''

Captain Ainsworth broke in. ''Gentlemen, why don't we all take a seat?'' He motioned to velvet upholstered chairs.

As they did, the butler returned with a small glass of whiskey and, with sidecast eyes, handed it to Jake.

''Thanks.'' He nodded and downed the fiery liquid.

''That will be all, Thomas,'' the captain said as Jake handed the empty glass back to the butler.

After the servant left the room, Ainsworth said, ''What seems to be the problem, Stone? Anything I can do to help?''

''How much do either of you know about Kyle McLean?''

The captain shrugged. ''Oh, he showed up here three or four summers ago with what seemed like limitless funds. He acquired a number of enterprises, mostly the kind that meet man's more carnal needs. Last year he built a couple of those newfangled steam-powered sawmills, and he's fast becoming my best customer. We ship thousands of board feet for him every month.''

"Do you know how he came by his fortune?" Jake asked.

"No. He keeps his personal affairs private." The captain turned to the governor. "Do you know more?"

"Not enough. And I'm beginning to have my doubts about the man. Judge Skinner says he came to Oregon with generous assets. Struck it rich in California, or so they say."

"Well, Your Honor," Jake said. "There are some very odd happenings I think you should know about. Wayne Redman, a friend of mine, showed me a burned-out homestead the other day. . . ." He spent the next few minutes relaying his suspicions as both listened intently. ". . . and what I'd like to do," he finished, "is look at the homestead records."

"Let me take care of that, Mr. Stone," Governor Gaines said. "I think you would be of more service if you would keep an eye out for me up the Willamette. Maybe we can get enough evidence to put a stop to him before there are any more mysterious 'accidents.'"

"Of course, I'd be glad to, Your Honor. Fact is, McLean's shipped in some fancy eastern horse and wants to pit him against my Thoroughbred. I was planning to set up a race for Independence Day. It'll look real natural for me to ride the valley, letting folks know. I could leave a note for him at the Oregon House before I leave town today."

"Wonderful idea. I love a good race. We'll be sure to have it whether Mr. McLean is still among the free or not." Gaines stood and the other two did likewise. "Thank you, Mr. Stone," he said, shaking Jake's hand. "I know I can count on you. When you've gathered sufficient evidence, please report to the captain here, and he'll summon me. I can't stress enough the importance of secrecy until we're ready to make our move. Mr. McLean has acquired a number of important friends, especially among the Democrats."

Always the politician, Jake thought with a smirk.

"Jake," Ainsworth said. "Let me show you out."

They walked out of the room and to the front door.

Stepping outside, Jake turned back on impulse. "Captain?"

"Yes?"

"Can I trust the governor?"

"Yes, Jake, we both can. He's a man of good character. A man of high principles."

"I'll be counting on that."

Rachel sighed with relief as she closed the lid of the last trunk. She shoved the fully packed chest toward the center of the wagon bed with all her strength until it thudded against the other chests. Edna had convinced her of the dangers of living so isolated. She had decided to move into town, and was even leaving a day early, refusing to spend one more forsaken night on the farm, especially now that the dog was gone. The day before when she'd taken Ginger and the chickens to the Jenningses' for safekeeping, she'd also taken Duchess because she couldn't imagine Edna Grills allowing the long-haired animal in her tidy yard. But she would fetch her loyal pet as soon as her new house was built.

Rachel eyed a heavy mass of clouds that had been gathering for the past couple of hours. "Better get moving," she murmured as she walked to the front of the wagon and gripped the bridle at the side of Sparky's head. Making a clicking sound, she led the team and wagon away from the house. She was especially pleased at how efficiently she'd hitched the horses and backed the rig up to the porch. Robby Stockton would have been proud of her.

The lack of movement in the yard drew her attention. She looked across to the barn and the now vacant paddocks. Her gaze then wandered to the eerily silent chicken coop. The farm had already begun to look abandoned, dead, the way she often felt. And she'd come to this place with such hopes.

She stepped past the horses to take a last look at the

sprouting garden—proof that there was still life. The first promise of a bountiful harvest.

But not her harvest.

She swallowed at a catch in her throat and turned away, only to notice the fledgling orchards of apples and pears below. She would not be here to taste their sweet fruit, either. Tears threatened. She blinked them away as she diverted her gaze to Mt. Hood to the north, so tall snow still capped it in pristine white. It filled her, as always, with the majesty of God's creation. All around her, in the meadow and the forest, His hand was at work. "But what about me?"

No! Rachel shut her eyes, squeezing out the last hint of moisture. God had not tried to trade me for a strumpet. *Jake had.*

She swept her attention to the forest land north of the clearing. Her land—signed and recorded. And if Jacob Stone wanted it as much as he'd professed, she'd get her freedom without a fight. And she'd better not hear him complain about what it cost to bring her here, either. It had been nothing compared to what his despicable duplicity had cost her. The lying Judas!

Her rage spiked for a few seconds before she regained her composure. Lying? Had he lied to her? Not once had he told her he loved her. She'd just been an out-and-out fool.

One of the horses snorted, and the team took several steps forward, pulling the rattling wagon along.

"Whoa!" Rachel rushed to them and placed a staying hand on Sampson's neck. "Getting antsy, are you? Well, let me change clothes first." She scanned the sky. "Those clouds are rolling in really fast."

She dashed into the house, ripped off her soiled clothes, washed, and dressed. Once freshly attired, she ran her fawn-gloved hand over the rich brown of her serge dress so close in color to the pair of Suffolks. Then suddenly feeling quite foolish, she rolled her eyes. "To match my costume to a work team, that's the height of vanity."

After collecting her dirty clothes from the floor, Rachel

smoothed the wrinkles from the fur quilt. She allowed her hand to glide over its silkiness for a moment before turning to leave. At the doorway, she took one last look at the cedar-lined room and the big sturdy bed where she'd spent the most unforgettable nights of her life.

Nothing would ever be the same again. Now that she'd experienced Jake's touch—found the fullness of her own true passion with him—could she ever hope to find another who would even begin to replace him? Or, after this disaster, could she ever again give herself so freely? She'd been so sure of Jake's love. And she'd been so very, very wrong. The aching hollow would be with her forever.

"No!" Whirling around, she walked out of the bedroom. "It's not going to be like that. Tomorrow when I wake up at the Grillses', I won't even remember Jake. No old yearnings, just a lifetime of new beginnings."

Jake had been watching the sky for the past hour, wondering if he would reach home before the ominously dark clouds dumped a flood of rain on him. One large drop hit the brim of his brown felt hat just as he reached the rise overlooking his homestead.

Prince broke into a canter, and Jake allowed the horse to stretch out into a gallop as they crossed the clearing. Eager as the stallion was, the animal couldn't want to get home half as much as he did.

Passing by the rows of fruit trees, Jake noticed that Rachel had continued planting. A good sign, further evidence that she was as interested in the farm as he. And now that she'd had a chance to cool down, she'd be easier to talk to. He knew she cared about the life they were making together, and she must have missed having him around the place as much as he missed being there. She'd want to make up. He was almost sure.

Nearing the knoll, Jake noticed Sampson and Sparky hitched to the wagon. Puzzled, he reined Prince to a walk. "Wonder where she's been? Probably off tending someone."

Just as Jake crested the rise, Rachel came out onto the porch amid the swirling skirts of a chestnut-colored dress. Though she had yet to remove the tan bonnet covering her luscious amber hair, the sight of her still caused Jake's heart to lurch. She turned in his direction, and with an irrepressible grin, he raised a hand in greeting.

Jake. Rachel's heart leapt with joy, and her hand flew to her breast. *My husband.*

Quickly, reason returned and she stiffened with resolve. She looked at him with new eyes, eyes not fooled by his handsome face and masterful body or by that devastating boyish grin. And just look at him, she thought. Waving at me like some long-lost lover just returning home. *How dare he?*

She walked to the edge of the porch. Did he really think she was so simpleminded that she would forget what he'd done in less than two weeks? Hardly. And after all her sleepless nights? And now that she'd finally made up her mind to leave him and the farm behind, he'd decided to come home? How dare he! Never mind the fact that she'd nearly broken her back loading those blamed trunks!

The joyous expression on Jake's face turned icy-cold.

The instant change startled Rachel, frightened her. What if she were wrong? Maybe he doesn't want her to stay, after all. Maybe the only reason he smiled was because he saw all her things packed and ready to go. Nonplussed, Rachel reached for the ribbons of her bonnet and nervously tightened the bow before descending the steps.

Jake's breath locked deep in his chest. Every one of her damned trunks was crammed onto the wagon bed. And where were the chickens? And Ginger? And why in hell wasn't Duchess barking?

Even before Prince stopped, Jake vaulted to the ground and strode to the starched-up hussy. Her brows crimped, and she clutched onto a wheel hub, soiling one of her prissy gloves. She looked scared. She should be, damn her. And damn those haunting blue eyes.

He felt his hands ball up as he trapped her with a narrow

glare. He spoke each word with precise clarity. "Where do you think you're going?"

Flinching, she cowered against the spokes. But just for an instant. Then she thrust herself from the wagon and stretched to her fullest height, eyes flashing, pert chin jutting upward. "And what business is it of yours, Mr. Stone?"

Her fierce challenge threw him for a moment. It looked as if she intended to continue just where they'd left off, even after he'd been gone all this time. Well, one ruffled-up banty hen wasn't about to run him off his place again. "I asked you a question. I expect a civilized answer."

"You have the nerve to talk about being civilized?"

He stepped within inches of her and enjoyed watching her gaze veer away, even if it was for just a second. "That's right. I'm not civilized. So I suggest you answer me while you still can."

The black clouds above rumbled forebodingly.

Even while she backed up a step, she gave a defiant little sniff. "Very well, if you feel you must know, I'm moving into town. I'll be staying with the Grillses until a house is built for me."

"Grillses?" Jake blurted out. Was this some kind of joke? "Are we talking about the same snooty Edna Grills who snubbed you at the funeral?"

Her breath caught, and one of her brows shot up. "That's all behind me now. Just like you." She moved away, stepping to the side. "Now if you'll—"

Without warning, the rain came down as if someone had suddenly overturned a thousand water-filled barrels on them.

Rachel gasped as her bonnet bill drooped over her eyes. "Good heavens!" Picking up her skirts, she dashed for the house, leaving the horses, the wagon, and all her belongings in the drenching downpour.

Jake stared after her until she'd slammed through the door, then slowly shook his head and grabbed Sparky's collar. "Just like a woman. Guess it's up to me to get you boys and all this truck into the barn.'' He whistled for Prince, and the stallion followed along behind.

After unhitching the animals and feeding them, he grabbed a bottle of whiskey he kept in a box with his horse liniment. To ward off the cold, he told himself as he sloshed through the fierce storm from the barn to the house.

Rachel had brushed most of the moisture from her clothing, had a lively blaze going, and was at the hearth blotting her bonnet when she heard the pound of Jake's boots on the steps. Her panicked pulse boomed in her ears, crowding out the sound. Placing a shaky hand to her breast, she inhaled deeply to steel herself for the next battle.

But he took plenty of time stomping off the rain before walking in the door, his shoulders barely missing the sides.

She'd forgotten how incredibly he filled the room.

He hung his wilted hat on an elk horn, then wheeled about and headed for the stove.

Then she saw it.

A bottle of whiskey dangled from his hand.

Victory was hers. Truth, honor, everything was on her side, and he knew it.

Jake grabbed a tin cup from the now almost bare shelf above the range. Then, without looking at her, he took it to the table, scraped back a chair, and sat down. She watched him uncork the bottle and poor the cup at least half-full. Yes, she would be the conqueror, the vanquisher.

Crossing the bearskin rug, she moved toward him as he downed a sizable amount. With just the table between them, she stopped. ''As I was saying, I will be settling in town. I've left the animals with the Jenningses.''

He looked at her, his face an unreadable mask as he took another gulp.

Almost undaunted, she continued. ''And since I've already filed on the forest land you wanted so much that you even agreed to marry me, you'll let me go, freely, without protest, or I'll never sign it over to you. In exchange for my signature, I will expect yours on some annulment papers.''

She waited for an answer, some kind of acknowledgment,

but all he did was pour himself another drink. The damp hair at his temples was starting to curl in the most endearing way. A tremor tickled from her bosom down to the center of her need. Her whole being tensed with anticipation. No! she railed inwardly, scolding her insubordinate body. Don't you dare betray me now.

In a flash she remembered how the champagne she'd had with Mr. McLean had numbed her, and she realized why Jake was drinking. Well, she could stop her baser feelings just as easily as he could. Easier. She turned on her heel and went for one of her goblets, then realized they were all packed and on the wagon. Instead she whisked a second dented metal cup from the high shelf. Returning, she plopped down across from him and reached for the bottle.

As her hand touched the cool glass container, Jake's closed over it. "What do you think you're doing?"

She tilted her head to the side and challenged him with her eyes. "I daresay, are you stingy as well?"

He let go, and downed his drink while she poured herself a full portion. The way he was putting it away, she'd better get her share while she had the chance. As soon as she put the bottle down, he grabbed it and refilled his own cup, also to the rim.

Jake kept his head lowered, letting a fringe of hair shield his eyes as he watched Rachel raise the whiskey to her lips. Her nostrils flared, and she jerked back slightly.

Just as he thought, she'd never even had a whiff of it before. He was going to enjoy this.

It smelled horrible, and Rachel thought it probably tasted worse, but she couldn't back down now. She'd simply swallow it fast. She held her breath and tossed back a mouthful.

Her eyes popped and her mouth opened in a mute protest as her hands flew to her throat.

Jake couldn't help grinning. "What's the matter?" he drawled. "You look like you saw a—"

Her eyes began to glaze over like a dead rabbit's, one

hand snatched at the air, trying to reach him as she worked her mouth. But still no sound or breath broke forth.

She was choking to death! Jake lurched to his feet and charged around the table. He snatched her out of the chair and slapped her back until she began to cough. Thank God.

Jake eased himself into her chair, pulling her onto his lap. He massaged her back until the spasms had almost subsided. "That's my girl," he crooned, brushing a tear from her cheek. "Always jumping in without looking. Remind me never to take you swimming."

The humiliation of making a helpless fool of herself instantly transformed into rage. She sprang off his lap and whirled around to face the arrogant beast! "To begin with—" The words croaked out in a gravelly whisper. She cleared her throat. Then, jamming her hands onto her hips, she started again. "To begin with, I *am not* your girl. And, believe me, it makes my going a whole lot easier, knowing you think I'm nothing but a—a—precipitous fool. I can't wait till this interminable storm stops." She flung him her haughtiest look and stalked around to the other side of the table and took the seat he'd vacated.

He stared at her with stony eyes for what seemed forever, but she did not give him the satisfaction of wavering. He dropped his gaze first. Another victory.

Suddenly he reached across the table and grabbed his half-empty cup of whiskey. "With so much else wrong with me, I sure don't want to be thought of as wasteful, too." He downed half the liquid as if it were water, then smiled at her as he wiped a hand across his smug mouth.

"You're right." Rachel scooped up her own cup. Keeping her gaze riveted to his own cocksure one, she took a sip, this time more carefully, letting the fiery liquid trickle slowly past her throat. She prepared for another explosion, but, to her surprise, all she felt was a rather pleasant warmth trailing down. She smiled with all the audacity she could deliver and dabbed at her lips with the back of her hand, then took another most relaxing, most enjoyable dram.

Sitting across from each other, they drank in silence, the

only noise coming from the rain and wind lashing at the windows and from the fireplace as the flames slowly died amid the crackle of burning spruce.

Seeing that prim stiffness disappear from Rachel's back as she propped herself up by her elbows, and watching her mischievous neck, as often as not, forget to hold up her head was more entertaining than that vaudeville act Jake had seen last year in San Francisco. The defiance had disappeared from her face, too, and a wicked little smile flickered now and again as she traced a finger along the rim of her cup. It looked like the war was about over.

Eyes agleam, a titter erupted from Rachel. She slapped a hand over her mouth. Partially unpropped, she almost fell over. Righting herself, she giggled again.

Jake chuckled and poured her a bit more whiskey.

With only the slightest wobble, she picked up her drink with a merry flourish. "Di' I ever tell you," she said, her words tumbling haphazardly over each other, "how funny y'all looked tha' day when I came marching ou' wi' the rifle? Never saw a more scared bunch o' men. And you, my dashing pirate," she said with a wildly pointing finger, "your eyes almos' jumped righ' outa your head."

Yes, sir, things were sure going his way. Jake caught her hand in his. Leaning forward, he brushed his lips across her tender palm.

She giggled again and retrieved her hand. "Now, now, we'll 'ave none o'that." She made a pitiful attempt at a glower.

But no matter how she screwed up her face, she was the most beautiful creature he'd every seen. Or wanted. And he was getting closer all the time. "You want to talk about someone looking scared? That first time you ever saw me. Remember? At Dorset's store. You looked like you were going to faint dead away."

"Did not." Pulling herself up straight, she grabbed onto the table to steady herself.

"Sure you did. You turned whiter than a snow rabbit." *Whiter than your skin would look right now on that bear fur.*

"Well, 'f I did," she slurred and attempted a stern stare until her eyes almost crossed—but then his own weren't seeing all that clear, either. "'F I looked scared, it certainly wasn' o' you. I jus' woke up from a . . . wicked . . . dream. The malaria, you know."

Jake's mouth slid into an easy grin. At the moment, he'd agree with anything she said.

Rachel felt light and heavy, incredibly sure of herself yet dizzy. She broke into another bout of laughter.

Looking much too sure of himself, Jake reached across and again enfolded her hand in his, drawing it toward him, drawing her.

Think you're catching me off guard, do you? she thought smugly as she started to move out of reach.

His grip tightened. "You're scared of me, all right." His words were an out-and-out challenge. "If you weren't, you wouldn't pull away."

She relaxed the hand he held and, with her free one, swiped at a bothersome tendril of hair blocking a most pleasing view of her husband—her Viking. "Do you see me pulling away?"

Without taking his eyes from her, Jake again pressed his lips to her palm, his tongue tracing a scintillating circle that telegraphed his desire to every tip, every crevice of her body. A soft moan slipped from her lips as she slowly closed her eyes.

The next thing she knew, Jake was standing beside her, lifting her out of the chair. "Getting scared now?" His teasing whisper tickled her ear.

The room began to sway worse than the deck of a ship. She leaned into him for support, melted against him as his arms slid around her, crushing her to him. Mercy me, but he felt good . . . but she couldn't let that keep her from winning. "I wasn't the one who tucked his tail and ran."

"Well, I'm back now."

She felt the constrained power of his desire press against her soft, yielding belly and a delicious curl tickled downward to her innermost depths. She felt herself go moist, and all other thoughts vanished, leaving nothing but him . . . the smell, the feel, the very male essence of him. *He certainly was back.* She circled his neck with her arms and tipped her head away until his devastatingly handsome face came almost into focus. Smiling her most suggestive smile, she heard his breath catch as she moved in an ever-so-deft tease against him. "Yes, you cer'ainly are." She wished her tongue would work better.

A lopsided grin appeared on his face—a maddeningly smug one.

So, he thinks he has me now, does he? We'll just see who has who—whom. Rachel twirled out of his grasp and waltzed away, reveling in the collapse of his overly confident expression. She fanned herself with her skirts, making sure she displayed a generous amount of leg. "Myyy, i's warm in here."

Jake stepped toward her, but his hands caught only air as she danced farther away. Then, with her own cocked smile dimpling one cheek, she traipsed back toward him, watching his eyes spark to life again. Just outside his reach, she flung herself around again while tossing a smile in his direction. "This dress's chafing me drea'fully. Woul' you min' helping me wi' the buttons?"

When his overeager fingers began fumbling with the tiny circles of bone, she barely contained her mirth. Hearing him grumble something under his breath as he tugged at the stubborn fasteners, she exploded into laughter.

"Hold still, dammit—I mean, angel face."

When he'd reached the ones at her waist, she spoke in mocking tones. "Would it bother you'f I took down my hair? Those mean ol' pins are stabbing me."

"Yeah, do it," he said in a rush, his breath a warm breeze on her exposed neck. His fingers became more frantic as they wrestled with the last buttons.

Pulling the pins out, she let them fall where they might in careless abandon. She could always find them later. After the last one hit the floor, she shook out her hair, letting it spill down her bare back.

"Done," he breathed. Sweeping the mass to the side, his hands meandered up her spine, then began to peel the dress from her shoulders.

Not so fast, my gallant pirate. Rachel whirled away again, her tresses and skirts becoming the wings of her flight. Halfway to the fireplace, she stopped abruptly, turned, and challenged him with a commanding stare as she shrugged out of the spilling dress. She kicked it across the room. "Yes, tha's much better." She then untied the strings at her waist and stepped out of her petticoats. These she sent soaring toward the nearest rocking chair. Her aim was true, and she looked back to Jake with triumph. The stunned look on his face infused her with even more daring. Toying with the ribbons lacing her skimpy camisole, she hiked a brow. "Frightfully hot, don't you think?"

"Uh—yes—hot." He ripped at the buttons of his tan shirt. One popped and shot across the room, ricocheting off the enamel coffeepot. He shrugged, a chortle rumbling from his throat. Then, getting into the spirit of the moment, he tore off his shirt and slung it across the other rocker.

The bawdy chuckle that rolled out of him infected Rachel. She joined in with her own reckless mirth at their new game.

Within seconds both had shed and sailed the remainder of their apparel about the room, shoes and all. Rachel was particularly proud that not one, but both her black silk stockings now dangled from the spikes of the elk rack. Still tittering, she looked at Jake.

Then, suddenly, as he sauntered toward her, he seemed astoundingly naked, almost as shockingly nude as she.

Hiding her shyness in a flash of genius, Rachel raced to the hearth and grabbed up the bearskin rug lying before it. She dropped the ferocious-looking head over hers and swathed herself in its dark fur, clasping onto the huge clawed paws as if they were her own hands. *"Grrr."* Taking wide swipes at Jake, she lumbered toward him. She growled again and thumped her chest with a once-savage paw. "I Bear Woman. Come from Grea' Spirit. Take you to cedar heaven. You be my slave till Sun God no longer rises in the east.''

With a gleaming grin, Jake spread his magnificent arms. ''Who am I to argue with Bear Woman? I'm all yours.'' Then, in a dizzying blur, he swooped her up, bearskin and all, kicked open the bedroom door, and tossed her on the bed.

She fell in a tangle of fur almost as fuzzy and confusing as her arms and legs and her impishly ponderous head.

Jake's great shadow spread over her.

She couldn't let *him* take *her* and be the *winner*. She rolled to the side just as he dropped down. Snatching up a bear claw, she dragged her protector with her as she vaulted up and straddled Jake. She would be the commander, the captain, the master. ''I am . . .'' The room began to spin. ''Bear Woman . . .'' It spiraled like a merry-go-round, teetering through an empty black sky. ''I—''

''Rachel?'' Jake's hands gripped her shoulders.

She grasped helplessly at his chest, trying desperately to hold on. But, try as she might, she still floated into the darkness, soaring down on a long, delicious, hazy giggle.

From somewhere in the bottomless void, she heard a distant, plaintive cry. *''Rachel, no.''*

chapter 15

A PAINFUL yank on Rachel's hair jolted her awake. Her eyes sprang open, and cruel shards of light stabbed into them. She reached to free the hair from between her husband's arm and his slowly heaving chest.

Husband? What was that rat doing in her bed? She flung off the covers and leapt to her feet . . . and staggered into the wall. Her skull threatened to explode, and her legs started to buckle. She grabbed onto the bedstead with one hand and her temple with the other. Closing her eyes, she attempted to unscramble her thoughts. The first image to emerge out of the muddle was one of herself, *buck-naked,* fanning her cotton underdrawers about as if they were some elegant plume. She gasped in anguished embarrassment, then darted a peek at her sleeping husband, but found him undisturbed by her strangled cry.

Peering down at her nudity, then at his bare shoulders exposed above the fur quilt, flashes from the night before again assaulted her . . . outrageous, disgraceful pictures . . . her flaunting her hips before him as if they were a scrap of cheap red silk—and Jake acting like a thick-horned bull. She'd thrown herself at him worse than any whore—at least worse than any of the stories she'd heard the women tell aboard ship—and most shameful of all, without so much as a shred of an apology from the rogue.

Besieged with guilt, she glanced around. The very walls mocked her. How would she ever be able to face him again? She had to get out of here, *now.*

Still hanging on to her hammering head, she tiptoed around the bed and out of the room, carefully taking the time to silently shut the door behind her.

A telltale array of clothing strewn about the common room greeted her. A moan escaped as yet more memories taunted her. How on earth would she ever be able to look anyone in the eye again? Ignoring the scattering of hairpins pricking her feet, she yanked on each piece of clothing as she retrieved it, starting with her lace-trimmed underdrawers draped so indelicately over Jake's denim trousers. *She simply had to get out of this place.*

Without taking the time to button her dress or shoes, she raced out to the barn to hitch the team, to escape.

The sun rode high in the sky when Jake wandered outside looking for Rachel. Shading his squinting eyes with a trembly hand, he scoured the grounds. Hellfire and damnation, he'd sure drunk more'n his share last night.

Then a slow grin swept his face. But it had been worth it. Rachel had been magnificent. And, more important, he'd ended up back in their bed. Too bad she had to pass out like that. The smile slackened, then he shrugged. "Next time . . . Where in tarnation is she?" Careful not to jar his throbbing head, Jake edged toward the barn. "Milking the cow, maybe?" Swinging a door wide, he remembered that Ginger was gone. *"And so's the wagon and team."*

Jake frowned and rubbed a hand across his burning eyes as he tried to make sense of things. He could've sworn they'd made up. They'd drunk together, laughed together, things couldn't have been better. *But she was gone.* His legs didn't want to hold his weight. He leaned heavily against the barn door as his brain cleared. She'd obviously awakened this morning with a hangover . . . *and blaming him.*

He snorted. "You can just bet she's convinced herself that I forced that 'devil's brew' down her, that I led her down some sinful path. Lord knows, once she's all nested in at that snooty Edna Grills's, she'll probably pretend that nothing even happened last night. Shoot,'' he muttered, ''she'll probably even deny Bear Woman ever existed.''

His ire rising, he stalked toward the house. But his stride began to slow as if someone had poured lead into his legs. He felt curiously hollow, strangely empty. He stepped inside and grabbed the bottle of whiskey from the table. ''A little hair of the dog might help.''

Collapsing onto the nearest chair, Jake took a swig, finishing off the bottle. He eyed the two dented tin cups cozied up to each other on the table. ''Yeah, well that was last night. Her leaving like she did proves she's back to being nothing but a snooty prig.'' And if she thought he was going to go crawling to her, beg her to forgive him for . . . *for what*? He didn't force her to drink. ''Force her, hell—I couldn't stop her.''

The team had moved toward town at a sluggish rate due to mud caused by the prior evening's downpour. But, except for a nagging dread that Jake would catch up to her, sneer at her with those knowing eyes, Rachel appreciated the slower pace. It gave her time—time to properly arrange her clothing, twist her hair into some semblance of a knot, time to breathe in vast amounts of the crisp, blustery air, to clear her head, compose herself, think. And after much thought, she knew the only way to get past this episode was to erase it *and* Jake from her life. The move to the Grillses' was a necessity now—she could never go back.

She welcomed the feathery drizzle that began to moisten her face as she neared the ferryboat dock. In the minutes it took for the Riggins boy to pulley her across the dark swollen river, the rain had turned into a steady sprinkle. Fetching a crocheted shawl, she covered her head before driving off the planked wharf and into the puddled ruts of the main street.

As the wagon wheels churned through the muck, Rachel envisioned bogging down before the pointing fingers of the entire town.

But the powerful horses leaned into their collars and

continued without slowing the pace one iota. Maybe it would be all right. Maybe this truly would be a fresh start.

Noticing that she was slumping, Rachel sat taller on the wooden bench as she passed the men filing out of the sawmill at the end of their shorter workday, this being Saturday. She spotted Edna's husband, Carson, and their near-grown son, Peter. She reined in. "On your way home?"

Mr. Grills, a big man whose muscular body was showing signs of middle-age padding, turned in her direction and shielded his eyes from the rain with a beefy hand. "How do, Miss Rachel. See you made it into town all by yourself."

Rachel ignored the hint of surprise in his voice. "Hop on, and I'll give you and Peter a ride home."

"Thanks," they chimed as they ran to climb up on the wagon seat.

"Sure glad you made it before it was too late," Mr. Grills said, as he settled down.

"Too late for what?" Rachel knew she hadn't set a definite hour of arrival.

"Supper. Edna's cooked up a little supper party."

Rachel felt the weight of weariness bearing down, but knew she'd have to endure it in secret. She gave the two men the brightest smile she could conjure. "Why, that was very nice of her."

"See the framework going up next to the store?" Mr. Grills pointed at the empty lot between Mr. Dorset's Merchantile and the hotel. "That's where I've got the mill workers building your house."

"Already? You folks really are serious about me moving to town, aren't you?" Rachel veered the horses to the side of the Grillses' home and pulled back on the reins. "Whoa." She reached back for her carpetbag.

"Don't worry about anything," Mr. Grills said. "Me'n Peter'll get your trunks in."

"Thank you, but I'll only need the two in the back. The others can just be stored out of the way someplace."

Peter had jumped down and was now standing at her side,

his chest thrusting out and a solemn expression on his smooth face. "Here, let me hand you down 'fore the rain soaks you through. Let us men worry about the rest."

Rachel almost laughed, the strapping lad's attempt at manhood was so endearingly funny. She managed to turn her mirth into a gracious smile. As much as she hated to admit it on this sorry day, at times the opposite sex could be very sweet and quite handy to have around.

Once inside the sunny yellow kitchen, warmth radiated from the cook stove, and Rachel realized how chilled she was. She moved to where lids jangled atop steaming pots and held up her hands.

"Rachel!" Edna swept into the room. Petite yet elegant, she wore a teal satin gown with a high lace collar and looked every inch the matron of the manor. "You're here. Good. We've invited a few guests for supper. They'll be here in a couple of hours." After a candid perusal of the bedraggled younger woman, she grasped the satchel and took Rachel by the hand. "Come along. You need to freshen up."

Sometime later, the sharp patter of high-heeled shoes reached the top of the stairs, waking Rachel from a stolen nap. Edna's voice called through the door. "Rachel, dear, our guests will be arriving soon."

"I'll be down in a moment," Rachel returned. She rose feeling somewhat refreshed and lit the lamp in the darkening room before slipping into her dusty blue alpaca dress with its dramatic vee-cut lace-filled bodice. Then, after checking the upsweep of her hairdo, she screwed on her most treasured possessions, a pair of sapphire ear bobs. She swung her head back and forth before the mirror, watching the dangling gems catch the light. When her father had presented the pair to her on her sixteenth birthday, he'd said he selected them because they matched so perfectly the shade of her eyes. And hadn't Jake once said her eyes were like pure mountain lakes edged with the frost of morning?

Tears welled, turning them as crystalline as the precious stones she wore. Forget Jake! Tonight's for new beginnings, new friends. Just the idea that he might show up and make a scene in front of her new neighbors made her want to hide under the bed. But she wouldn't. Somehow she would face *with dignity* whatever the evening wrought. With a forced lift of the chin, she whirled away from the mirror and walked out the door.

Edna's voice floated up the stairwell. "Carson, Mr. Best is coming through the gate. I'll be busy in the kitchen, so be a dear and entertain him."

"Harvey Best?" Rachel heard him croak. "Is that dandy coming for dinner?"

"I invited him as a supper partner for Rachel. And, dear, you shouldn't make fun of a man just because he takes pride in his appearance."

"I know what you're up to, Edy. So, before you get too carried away, remember Rachel's married to Jake Stone. And I don't see him taking your matchmaking too friendly-like."

"Mr. Stone callously abandoned that poor little thing upstairs. And I don't intend for her to waste away—" Interrupted by a knock at the door, she lowered her voice. "Now, you be cordial to him. He's a guest in our home."

So, Rachel thought, moving in means Edna plans to take charge of this "poor little thing." We'll just see about that. She placed the squared toe of her kid slipper on the first step, then hesitated just long enough to regain her ladylike deportment before descending the steps in a stately fashion. Oh, well, she thought with resigned charity as she reached the bottom, Edna means well. She sighed, then sailed into the tastefully selected blues and pinks of the lamp-lit parlor. "Good evening, gentlemen."

Despite the many possibilities for calamity, supper turned out to be a pleasant affair. Although Harvey sent her a few meaning-filled looks, he maintained himself in a congenial and proper manner. Edna, sitting opposite her husband, kept him in check with an occasional stern nod. Another couple, the Rigginses, had joined them and proved to be a pure delight despite the fact that Mr. Riggins had been among the wagonload of businessmen on that fateful day. Maureen chattered and tittered like a happy sparrow about everything and nothing while her quiet husband gazed at her with adoring eyes. And thank the moon, the stars, the planets, and every raindrop that ever kissed the Willamette Valley, Jake Stone did not appear.

Rachel fairly floated with relief as Dinah, Edna's pretty fourteen-year-old, who was acting as serving girl, cleared away the dessert dishes.

"John." Carson turned to Mr. Riggins while taking a pouch of tobacco from his breast pocket. "From what I hear, there's going to be big doings here soon. Kyle McLean's bringing his new Thoroughbred to race Jake Stone's Prince."

"_Ladies,_" Edna said, staring pointedly at her husband as she came to her feet. "Would you care to join me in the parlor while the men have their smoke?"

The men stood politely as Rachel gratefully rose.

But before she could escape, Harvey spoke. "Rachel, I must be going in a few minutes. If you wouldn't mind, I'd like to speak to you about a business matter now, if it would be convenient."

"Of course. On the front porch?"

"Yes, that would be fine."

"I'll run upstairs for my wrap and join you outside."

When Rachel went out the door to meet him, he was standing near the front gate, peering up at a cluster of stars that peeked through the receding clouds.

Upon seeing her, he rushed back to assist her off the porch step. "Have I told you how beautiful you are tonight?" he said, taking one of her hands into both of his.

"Yes, I believe you did." He really was a dear man, she decided. A real gentleman. And so attentive he seemed almost anxious.

"You're even more beautiful in the moonlight. I've been longing to get you alone all evening. And finally my patience has been gloriously rewarded."

His ardor was a bit too cloying for her taste. She tilted her head and lifted a brow. "Really?"

He took her other hand. "Madam, I assure you, my intentions are most honorable. I merely wanted time alone with you to tell you my good news."

He bent closer, and Rachel had to admit that he really was attractive, in a refined sort of way. But if he only had flaxen hair, or if he was just a little bigger, a little stronger, a little . . . something.

"Without mentioning you by name, I spoke to Belton Cruthers, a lawyer friend of mine in Salem, about your unique circumstances. He says he can arrange for you to present your case before the governor. Cruthers sees absolutely no reason why Governor Gaines would not grant you an annulment. Personally, I think that's best. It would wipe any taint from your name forever. And that, of course, is of utmost importance to both of us."

"Both of us? I see." On the pretext of adjusting her shawl, Rachel withdrew her hands from his long, slender fingers—fingers that now seemed like claws. "Making sure my name is pristine is very important to you, isn't it?"

"Of course. Isn't it to you?"

"It's just that after all that's happened, I don't—"

"I know you've been through a lot. But trust me, one day you'll be glad I was concerned. You agree, don't you?"

She gazed down the street at the church, silhouetted in the moonlight. Could the word *annulment* truly make her pure again? After last night?

"I see I'm going to have to take charge." Harvey took her hands more firmly this time, recapturing her attention. "I'll make all the arrangements and personally escort you to Oregon City. You needn't bother your pretty little head."

He seemed so certain he wanted her. If he only knew.

"Rachel?" he asked, squeezing her fingers.

"Uh—yes, yes. That'll be fine. And I thank you for your generous efforts."

He released a hand and tilted her chin up to him.

For a frigid second Rachel thought he intended to kiss her. She froze.

His gaze wavered. ''Soon, Rachel. This will all be behind us, and then the future will be ours for the taking.'' He raised the hand he still held and brushed it with his lips. ''I must be going now, but I'll keep in touch.''

Rachel watched as he turned and strode down the walk and out the gate. When he disappeared into the darkness, she felt like a bird being released from its cage. She knew she should appreciate his attentions, even desire them. He was assuredly every mother's dream for her daughter. But she could already hear him ordering her about. And worse, after being with Jake, how could she ever let him touch her with those namby-pamby hands? How could she lie beneath his bony body?

She shuddered and searched the night again. *Where is Jake? Why hasn't the rat come for me?*

((chapter))
16

JAKE kept his leggy horse at a slow, easy gait as he rode toward town. He cursed the unceasing ache just behind his eyes, and knew he'd never again laugh at any man who said his wife drove him to drink. Nearing the Colfax cutoff, he stretched his stiff back. "Well, one thing's for damn sure. I won't end up like this again over her."

At the broken silence, Prince whinnied low. Jake patted the animal's sleek neck. "Yeah, that's right. We're going into town and settle this once and for all." He looked down what seemed an endless road of torture and uncertainty. After an indecisive moment, he reined the horse onto Amos's wagon trail. "She can just wait till I damn well feel like showing up. I have real business, important business that needs tending first."

Jake found Amos and Orletta sitting on the front porch taking advantage of the "day of rest." Upon seeing Jake, Amos grinned, displaying his typical good-natured congeniality. But Orletta's surprised smile vanished as suddenly as it had appeared, and Jake knew he would've been better off just going on into town.

"Howdy," he said, swinging down from Prince.

"Jake." Amos came to his feet. "Been a spell."

Orletta also rose, her dark eyes flashing. "'Bout time you got back."

Amos's smile drooped and he turned to his wife. "Letty, why don't you go in and warm up the coffee?"

Her reluctance apparent, she stared at him for several seconds before turning. "Whatever you say, *dear*."

After she'd gone, Amos motioned for Jake to take the chair Orletta had just vacated, then took his own.

"Where're the boys?" Jake asked, easing himself down.

"Fishin'."

"Good day for it."

The older man eyed the sunny sky. "Looks like it."

Amos was obviously not his usual talkative self, so Jake decided to get straight to business. "Just got back from Oregon City yesterday. Been to see the governor."

"Really?" Amos sounded honestly interested.

"That's right. We had a little talk about McLean and his rampant prosperity, and the way he's been acquiring land earmarked for homesteads. Governor Gaines is going to take a real close look at some of McLean's deeds."

Amos snorted and chuckled. "I can already see good ol' land recorder Best squirmin' like a worm on a hook."

Jake nodded, grinning. "The governor has asked me to keep an eye on McLean's doings down this way. I need you to keep this under your hat—don't tell anyone, not even your wife. But you get around a lot, so if you come up with anything interesting, be sure and let me know."

"Well, for starters," Amos said, leaning closer, "McLean's buildin' a bank in town. And, wonder of wonders, he's hired Best to run it for him."

Puzzled, Jake frowned. "Independence isn't large enough for a bank."

"You noticed," Amos said with a smug twist of the mouth. "Methinks McLean has plans for our little burg."

"You know that horse race McLean's been wanting? I left a note at the hotel where McLean lives in Oregon City, setting it up for the Fourth of July. We can make a big do of it. That way it'll look natural for me to be nosing around, since I'll be inviting folks in for it."

"Yeah!" Amos slapped his knee. "We could make a real ripsnortin' day of it." Then his rounded features creased into a frown. "If you haven't actually talked to him, are you sure he'll show?"

Jake settled back with a grin. "He'll be there. He's too

proud a man not to . . . 'specially since I mentioned that, if he wasn't up to taking a licking, he could just leave word at Dorset's store.''

"Oh, yeah,'' the other said, his eyes sparking with prankish humor. "He'll show, all right.''

Both broke into laughter as the door opened. Coming out with her hip-swaying walk, Orletta looked sexy even in the conservatively cut blue striped dress, but her expression hadn't sweetened one bit. She handed each of the men a tin mug. "Coffee was still hot from noonin'.'' As they mumbled their thanks, she leaned against a porch post and looked from Jake to Amos. "I see you haven't told him?''

"Not yet,'' Amos said, irritation marking his words.

"Told me what?'' Jake asked, but from the scowl on Amos's face he wasn't sure he really wanted to know.

Amos looked at Orletta a moment, then turned to Jake. "I was in town yesterday afternoon, and Homer told me somethin' that's gonna get you all head-up.'' His eyes narrowed. "Leastways, if you got any sense, it will.''

Jake returned Amos's intense stare. "Spit it out.''

"They're building a house next to the store, 'tween it and the hotel. Homer says it's for Rachel. She moved into town yesterday and is stayin' at the Grillses' till it's finished.''

Jake made certain his face showed no expression. "I think I heard something about it.''

Amos's mouth went slack, then clamped shut. Taking a long breath, he leaned back in his chair. "Well, so's you won't think I'm holdin' anything back, the lot the house is bein' built on, it belongs to McLean.''

Jake shot to his feet. His forgotten mug clanged to the floor, splattering coffee all over the porch.

Undaunted, Orletta grabbed his lapels. "It's about time you got mad. Now, you get yourself on into town and apologize to that sweet little girl. And you get her to home where she belongs.''

"*I'll get her, all right,*'' Jake rasped. He wrenched Orletta's hand away and started down the steps.

Amos jumped up. "Hold on there, boy. No sense goin'

off half-cocked. McLean may be tryin' to cut in, but right now this's still just between you an' her. Now, I know you never woulda traded Rachel off for some whore—'' Halting in mid-sentence, his eyes darted guiltily to Orletta before returning to Jake. ''But that's what Rachel thinks you's about to do. So you go on in there, real easy-like, an' make it right with her. You know, give her a hangdog look. Women just can't resist a man that looks all whopped.''

Orletta's hands went to her hips. ''Is that so?''

Amos grabbed her around the waist and hugged her to him. Shrugging, he gave her his most rascally grin, then turned back to Jake. ''Now, get goin', give it your best.''

Jake shook his head slowly and chuckled. ''I never knew keeping a female happy was going to be so much work.''

Amos's eyes twinkled as he squeezed Orletta's waist. ''Son,'' he spouted, bursting into laughter, ''you don't know the half of it.''

Orletta's mouth gaped, then her sensuously full lips spread into a grin. ''You're going to pay for that, *Mr. Soon-to-be-sleepin'-in-the-barn*.'' She stepped off the porch as Jake swung up into the saddle. ''Wait a minute. I been hoardin' a bottle of real French perfume. I want you to give it to Rachel. Women always like presents.''

As they floated across the river, the scrawny Riggins boy acted polite enough, but more than once Jake caught the kid giving him scampish looks. Jake clenched his fists and stared at Buddy with wolf-mean eyes. When the boy ducked his head in a cower, he didn't care. Hell, if it was going to be like this everywhere he went, someone was bound to end up eating splinters before the day was out.

At the dock, Jake unloaded and led the horse up the road past the warehouses. His pace steadily slowed as he tried to remember the speech he'd been memorizing all the way into town. But it was useless. All those fine words had vanished like a wisp of smoke. As he passed the saw works, his gaze wandered to the Grillses' well-kept home with its tidy white picket fence bordered by a neat row of town flowers.

Everything in perfect order, just like Edna Grills. . . . And Rachel?

As if struck with a sudden case of the clumsies, Jake's hands and feet seemed to turn into blocks of wood, all fumbles and stumbles. He slid his brown felt hat from his head and ran sweaty fingers through his hair, trying to smooth down the unruly thatch that never would stay in place. He was only yards away. What was he going to say? He felt for the perfume in his shirt pocket, making sure it was still there.

Then he saw it—the framework of the house that the town was building for Rachel—the house sitting on *McLean's* property. Rage exploded within, igniting him with renewed power. The throbbing at his temples magnified, blinding him. He stopped till his vision cleared.

A door banged open, catching Jake's attention. He turned to see a mill worker come wheeling out of the hotel saloon. Then he noticed that sorry sore-infested team and wagon of Charley Bone's standing between the unfinished house and the hotel. McLean's man was inside. Jake veered toward the two-story building. He really did need to talk to Bone, especially if the polecat was drunk. Maybe the man would let something slip about his dealings with McLean.

Besides, Jake thought as he looped Prince's reins around the hitching rail, a stiff shot of whiskey might take away this damnable headache. Climbing the steps up to the porch, he stomped the mud from his boots, then took one last look over his shoulder at the Grillses' trim home across from Dorset's store. "Yeah, and maybe a shot'll help me remember that blamed speech, too."

Walking into the dim, stale-smelling room, Jake couldn't make out the man who called, "Well, if it ain't the wanderin' husband."

A caterwaul of laughter erupted as Jake's vision adjusted enough to see Bone and his rabbit-toothed cohort sprawled at a table near the door with two scrawny floozies in flashy satin gowns. He clenched his teeth together to keep from demanding that Bone stand up and face him like a man.

Instead, he sauntered over. "Howdy." Forcing his lips to curve upward, he added, "Heard you two got married and took up homesteading north of me. Are these your new brides?"

The slatternly foursome burst into laughter again, as the frizzy-haired woman squeezing Cooter's undernourished leg howled at a head-splitting pitch.

When the noise died down, Charley Bone straightened from a slouch and spread his arm to encompass the women. "Tha's right," he slurred and pointed at the cow-eyed one. "This here's my sweet wife, Esther. And that's Rose."

Jake nodded at each of them, determined not to show his disgust as he wondered how his fair Rachel could ever have been in jail with the likes of them. "Pleased to make your acquaintance." He compelled his gaze to linger a second before turning back to Bone. "You and Leland home-steading—That mean you aren't working for Kyle McLean any more?"

Bone shot Cooter a menacing look. "We don't work for Mr. McLean," he rasped in a rush of words. "Never did. Who told you that?"

Jake shrugged nonchalantly. "Don't remember. But what difference does it make? The way you're taking on, you'd think he was a criminal or something." At the pop-eyed looks on their faces, Jake turned toward the bar to keep them from seeing his grin. He knew he shouldn't have said that. It'd probably draw their suspicion, but it felt too good not to.

His smile collapsed as quickly as it had appeared. Behind the vacant bar lounged the brassy-haired whore from Astoria. She studied him with half-closed eyes and a come-hither smile.

"Well, if it ain't Jake Stone." The words meandered luringly past Goldy's bright red lips. "What's your plea-sure? Stud."

Careful to keep the astonishment from punctuating his voice, he answered, "Whiskey. Two fingers." Propping a booted foot on the rail, he casually leaned an arm on the varnished wooden counter. "Make that three."

She grabbed a glass from a shelf behind her and poured him a drink, inviting him to much more with her smile.

"Surprised to see you still in town," Jake said as she served him. "Thought you'd be back in Astoria by now."

Planting hands on her hips, she quirked a one-sided grin. "I'm still waitin' to see if you're gonna marry me."

"Look, Goldy, I'm sorry you were led to believe that I'd be willing to trade off my wife."

"Yeah. I thought it was a crackpot idea from the start. But Kyle told me to hang in here for a spell longer. Don't know why. Only business I been able to scratch up round this place is a coupla sawmill workers that ain't married. I swear, this is one dead town."

Jake had no doubt as to why McLean was keeping Goldy here—to try to wedge her between him and Rachel. He tossed down the whiskey in a couple of quick gulps and wiped his mouth. "Well, I'm afraid you won't find much action around here. We're mostly just hardworking family men."

Goldy leaned across the bar, allowing the neck of her shiny orange gown to dip so low a man could reach in and grab one of her big tits with no trouble at all. "You know, Jake, I don't think I told you what a eye-filler you turned out to be once you got rid'a all that hair." The slow way the words drawled their way out put Jake in mind of a purring cat, claws hidden, rubbing up against his leg. She reached up to toy with a curl falling over his brow. "Even before, you's my favorite." Her gaze slid to the buttons in his britches. "You bein' so *big* an' all."

Jake backed out of her reach and straightened to his full height. He heard titters from Bone's table, but was pretty sure they were too far away to hear what Goldy had just said. "Guess I'd better be going. Got lots to do."

She smirked knowingly. "On Sunday?"

"Got to get on over to the Grillses'. My wife's waiting for me to pick her up."

"I doubt that, seein' as how I been woke up ever' mornin' this week listenin' to 'em nail together her new house." She leaned across the bar and grabbed his arm, her long nails digging in. "But don't you fret, you big hunk'a handsome. I was brought here jus' special for you. An' I can more'n keep up with anythin' you can whip out."

Jake was beginning to feel like a mouse trapped in her clutches. He took a quick breath, then pulled away and slapped on his hat. "Gotta go." Wheeling around, he almost ran for the exit and from the sound of her throaty laughter.

"Rachel, dear," Edna said as she headed for the front door with scissors and a basket. "Would you like to come outside and help me cut some fresh flowers for the table?"

"Yes, I'd like that." Rachel laid the pillowcase she'd been embroidering on the cherrywood table beside her wing chair and left the parlor to join the older woman. She could use an improvement of mood. Harvey Best had insinuated himself on her that morning, insisting on escorting her to church. And she had no doubt everyone in the congregation had noticed his possessive manner with her. It had been all too embarrassing, all too irritating.

Once outside, Edna led the way to a row of gladiolus, whose various hues rivaled an Oregon rainbow. Spiking upward next to the fence, the elongated clusters of blossoms were almost as tall. "These should look quite impressive in the dining room, don't you think?"

"Yes, very," Rachel said, admiring Edna's taste.

Edna handed her the basket. "Here, hold this while I cut a few." She snipped one and turned to place it across the gently scooped wickerwork, then looked up at Rachel with a questioning frown. "Mr. Best was most disappointed that you didn't stay after church for the potluck. I don't think he believed you had a headache. In fact," she said, reaching for another stalk, "*perturbed* might be more accurate."

"If anyone had a right to be perturbed, 'twas I," Rachel said, brushing a fallen cedar sprig from her pink skirt. "He led everyone to believe that he and I had an understanding. Quite scandalous considering my state.''

"Nonsense!" Edna pointed the scissors dangerously close to Rachel's nose. "All the ladies would be relieved to see you properly settled with someone of Mr. Best's repute."

Reminding herself that the older woman was just trying to be motherly, Rachel sighed and took the flower dangling from Edna's other hand and placed it in the basket. "I don't think Brother Simpkins would agree with you. He gave me a most disapproving look every time he glanced my way."

"Humph." Edna turned back to her task. "Sometimes men are slow as molasses figuring things out. There's times when it takes me weeks to get Carson to see things the way they really are." The tiny woman, an expert at ruling a husband twice her size, snipped another bloom and handed it to Rachel. "Now, getting back to the subject. Next time you see Mr. Best, I want you to apologize to him as sweetly as you can. Flatter his manhood. They all like that."

"But Edna, I don't even know if I—"

"For mercy's sake." The words exploded from Edna as she pointed up the street. "That despicable husband of yours is coming this way."

((chapter 17))

STEPPING off the hotel porch, Jake caught his first enticing glimpse of Rachel, and all thought of Goldy's crude innuendoes flew from his mind. Wearing a breezy pink dress that hugged every curve of her winsome body, Rachel stood in a bower of flowers, with a basketful draped over her arm. There couldn't be a lovelier sight this side of paradise. He pulled his hat from his head and moved toward her. With each step, his heart thudded rhythmically against his ribs, bringing to mind a verse of Ol' Will's:

> For all that beauty that doth cover thee
> Is but the seemly raiment of my heart
> Which in thy breast doth live, as thine in mine

If only he could make those words be true again. He would. He had to. He tried to ignore the mocking presence of that cursed house being built for her, as he swerved across the street toward Rachel . . . *and Edna Grills,* who was wagging a finger at him, her face all scrunched up as if she'd just sniffed scorched eggs.

Upon seeing him, Rachel's eyes widened, and Jake was sure he spotted a flicker of joy. But just as quickly, the color drained from her face.

Her initial reaction pumped confidence into him. She cared.

Then a sickeningly familiar voice called out to him from behind. "Jake. Jake, honey."

He wanted to jump in a ditch, hide behind a tree, anything

to disappear. He sighed and turned. Goldy's peroxide hair and bright orange dress clashed even worse in the full light of afternoon.

"Yoo-hoo, Jake, honey." She walked to the edge of the hotel porch with an exaggerated swing to her hips. "Just wanted to invite you to come by again . . . anytime."

Speechless, he watched her slink her way back into the saloon. His hands itched to wring her pasty neck, but he knew it would only make matters worse. With a powder-dry bitterness in his mouth, he turned and trudged toward the horror-filled eyes of his wife.

"How dare you?" Edna Grills rasped, drawing his attention to her. Her eyes squinted mean-narrow, looking more lethal than usual since her hand had a tight grip on a pair of scissors. "How dare you flaunt that—that *hussy* in front of this poor sweet girl? Haven't you tormented her enough already?"

Jake stopped at the picket fence barricading him from his wife. "Afternoon, Mrs. Grills," he gritted out as his gaze pleaded with Rachel. "I'd like to speak to my wife."

Looking up to his far greater height, tiny Edna stretched on the tips of her toes. "Ab-so-lute-ly not!"

Rachel, who hadn't moved a mouse's whisker since she first saw Jake, laid a hand on the older woman's arm. "Please, Edna," she said in a breathy whisper, "leave us alone for a few minutes. I'll be fine."

Edna's chin jerked in mute disagreement. Finally, she harrumphed. "Very well. Holler if you need me."

Both Jake and Rachel followed her stiff walk with their eyes as she returned to the house. Then Rachel turned back to him, though her gaze didn't quite meet his. "She means well."

"I know."

Silence charged the space between them while Jake waited for her to say something, anything. But she just stared at his chest.

Becoming uncomfortably aware of his navy cotton shirt, he wondered if it was too wrinkled. Did she even care?

Finally, he gave up waiting for her to speak. He filled his lungs with strength-giving air. "I suppose it looked pretty bad, that business a minute ago with Goldy. But I swear, I wasn't in there for more'n five minutes. I didn't even know she was working there."

Rachel's rigid lack of response unnerved him further. "I thought she'd already be back in Astoria by now."

At last, her eyes lifted to his, but her expression remained hard. "I'm sure she's still here waiting to take her turn as the *next* Mrs. Stone."

"Now, Rachel—" Jake started. Then he caught a flash of movement at an open window and saw Edna watching with the fierceness of a mountain cat. He turned back to Rachel, to eyes that had always been an irresistible enticement, but now seemed brittle and colder than a lake in January. "Look, I think maybe this isn't such a good time to talk. I'll come back in a few days when things aren't so—so—" He stopped speaking, not wanting to confirm the tension between them with words. Instead, he reached in his pocket and withdrew a ten-dollar gold piece and handed it across the fence. "In case you need something while you're in town."

Rachel didn't say thanks or anything; she just stared at the money in her hand till a body'd think she didn't know what it was. Jake never felt so unwanted in his life. He turned to go, then remembered the bottle of perfume in his shirt pocket. He pulled it out, then reached across to Rachel's open palm and placed the cut-glass vial on top of the coin. "Hope you like how it smells." Jake pivoted on his heel and strode swiftly to his waiting horse.

In a fierce war of emotions, Rachel watched her husband ride down to the wharf. Jake, Goldy, and Edna all seemed to be battling within her, thrashing her insides, bashing her weary head. Placing a hand to her temple, she felt the sharp angles of the tiny bottle clutched in her fist. *A present from Jake*. She opened her palm and let the prisms catch the light in a shimmer of iridescence. *For me*.

Suddenly, she remembered the overwhelming joy that had leapt within her when she first sighted him. His strong purposeful stride, the way the sun glinted off his flaxen hair, the golden planes of his dear face. Why hadn't she said something, done something to let him know how she felt?

Lifting her gaze from the gift in her palm, she searched down the road for him. But he'd disappeared. An urgency overtook her. She rushed to the gate—but it was too late. He and his horse were being ferried across the river. In agony, she watched as he neared the far shore. A wash of tears prevented her from seeing more.

The next few days passed so slowly Rachel felt sure she'd counted every irritating tick of the noisy mantel clock. With three women working in the small house, the chores were always completed well before noon, leaving the remaining hours to drag by with stitch after tedious stitch of needlework, accompanied by the persistent drone of Edna's advice. At least ten times a day she'd reminded Rachel that Jake's gift only proved that he still thought he could buy her. And, besides, no little dab of perfume could possibly sweeten the stench of his sins.

Oh, maybe Edna's right, she thought, a forgotten embroidery hoop in her hand. Last Monday when Rachel had awakened, she'd felt certain he'd come back, if not for her, surely for the team and wagon. But after jumping at every sound that whole day, she'd finally ventured down to Dooley's Livery Barn, hoping against hope. But Sparky and Sampson were gone—had been since the afternoon before. Jake had returned for them Sunday evening while she was upstairs hiding her tear-swollen face. And now he'd left her sitting here most of the week. Waiting.

"But Harvey . . ." Edna continued as her knitting needles clicked together.

Rachel knew that for the hundredth time this week the woman would be expounding on the virtues of this most eligible territorial official. But, thank heavens, someone knocked.

Edna laid aside the scarf she was knitting and went to answer the door. A moment later, she returned to the parlor with a rather stumpy older woman wearing a drab dress that matched the color and severity of her tightly knotted hair.

"Rachel, dear," Edna said, "I'd like you to meet Mabel Stockton. She and her family have a farm downriver a mile or so." She turned to her guest. "Mabel, this is Rachel Stone, the young lady I told you about."

Rachel stood and extended a hand. "How do you do. I'm so pleased to meet you."

A smile obviously missing, the grim-faced woman hesitated, then curled her lips slightly before taking Rachel's proffered hand. "Oh, yes, I've heard about you and your misfortune. You're the one my Robby taught to drive a wagon—not like that tart I got at my house."

"Now, Mabel, dear," Edna interjected, guiding the other woman to the navy velvet settee. "I'm sure everything's going to work out just fine. I've seen your new daughter-in-law, and she seems to be a perfectly mannered girl."

"Oh, yes," Mrs. Stockton sneered, her thin lips bowing downward. "She's a smart one all right. Has my husband and the boys eatin' right outa her hand. And lazy? That girl ain't seen the mornin' side'a noon yet. And she's always askin' sly questions about what we got and such. But she's bound to show her true colors soon. And when she does, I'll be there to catch her."

Edna urged her to sit, then she and Rachel took their own chairs. "Rachel, dear, I suppose you've guessed by now that Mabel's son, Ben, married one of those less desirable women from St. Louis. And, of course, the deed was done before this poor woman knew the truth. And now she's forced to share her roof with a . . . you know."

"Not for long," Mrs. Stockton spat. "In fact, that's why I dropped by. To invite y'all to a barn raisin' Saturday week. Ben's new house is near finished, and once his barn is up, he can move that lazy chit outa my house. 'Course, I don't know who's gonna cook him his meals."

Rachel knew who Mrs. Stockton was talking about—

Sarah Beth—angelically blond, with the most innocent blue eyes, the sweetest voice. And the most cleverly treacherous mind of anyone Rachel had ever met. Of course, Sarah Beth had snagged herself a young husband lacking in worldly wisdom. But she was sure the schemer hadn't counted on such a formidable mother-in-law. Her respect for Mrs. Stockton mounted with the woman's every venomous word. She would truly enjoy watching Sarah Beth meet her match for a change. "Thank you for the invitation. I'd truly enjoy coming to your barn raising. I haven't been to one in ages."

"Yes," Edna concurred, "tell your husband we'll all be there. There hasn't been a real get-together since last fall. We'll make it a real hoedown. Have you asked Amos Colfax and his boys to come play for the dance afterward?"

"Robby's ridin' out their way tomorrow when he makes deliveries for Mr. Dorset." Mrs. Stockton turned her small faded eyes from Edna to Rachel. "That reminds me. Mr. Dorset said he had a letter for you at his store." A thin white brow spiked. "From Mr. Best."

"Oh, really?" Rachel said, standing. "It must concern a business matter he's tending for me." She felt suddenly anxious to leave now that the flint-eyed woman's attention had shifted to her. "If you don't mind, I'll go over and pick it up. And maybe I'll look for some material to make a dress for the barn dance."

Walking across the deserted street, Rachel surveyed the partially roofed dwelling that would be hers. Since no workmen were about, she assumed they'd gone home for the noon meal. She entered Dorset's Merchantile and found the front room vacant. Then, shuffling and banging noises drew her to the inner door that stood ajar.

With the help of Robby Stockton, Mr. Dorset hauled in a crate from a wagon out back. His pudgy face streamed with sweat. "Howdy, Miss Rachel. Be right with you."

"Thank you, but there's no rush. Whenever you have a free moment." She turned and walked over to the bolts of fabric stacked on the table along the back wall.

Puffing from the exercise, Mr. Dorset came in and began

to sort through a stack of mail on the counter. "I suppose Mrs. Stockton told you about the letter from Harvey Best." After a few seconds, he pulled out a white envelope. "Here it is. Anything else before I get back to work?"

Rachel took the letter and perused the envelope as she answered. "I'm looking for some material. It'll take a while to decide. I'll let you know when I'm ready."

Mr. Dorset pulled a red bandanna from his back pocket and wiped his face. "Fine."

Noticing nothing on the envelope but her name and the town's, Rachel experienced a burst of righteous anger. Had that old snoop opened her mail? "Mr. Dorset? How is it you knew this letter was from Mr. Best?"

Stuffing the kerchief in his breeches, he grinned smugly. "Why, the handwriting, of course. Nobody makes capital letters half as fancy as Harvey. Now, if you'll excuse me, I need to get back. No tellin' where that boy'll put things."

Whether the gossipy little man had opened her letter or not, he'd made certain that shrew Mrs. Stockton knew about it and Lord only knows who else.

Rachel closed her eyes to calm herself while he left the room, then looked down at the elegantly swirled, oversized letters. She shook her head. Harvey Best. He certainly did work at impressing folks with his education. Just as Rachel tore open the envelope, a splintery shattering sound, immediately followed by loud swearing from Mr. Dorset, disturbed her. She decided to step out onto the porch. After shutting the door behind her, she withdrew the missive and found a newspaper clipping also enclosed, but decided to read Harvey's elaborately scrolled words first:

My Dearest Rachel,

I trust you are well. I had urgent business up the Columbia or I would have delivered this message in person. It seems the Whigs and Democrats are vying over the location of the capital. The government offices are at this moment being moved to Salem, therefore I

cannot arrange an appointment with Governor Gaines
as quickly as I had hoped. But I assure you, I will
expedite the matter within the fortnight.

In the meantime, I found an interesting essay published in last week's *Oregonian*. After recalling your
rather abrupt and independent leavetaking from church,
I thought this paragraph might prove enlightening and
beneficial to a more pleasurable and fulfilling future
for both of us.

> Your most ardent servant,
> H.B.

So, Rachel thought, aggravated but curious, you think I
need some enlightening. She placed the small neatly cut
square of printed paper in front of the letter and read:

> A man—poet, prophet, or whatever he may be—readily
> persuades himself of his right to all the worship that is
> voluntarily tendered. Despise woman? No! She is the most
> admirable handiwork of God, in her true place and character.
> Her place is at man's side. Her office, that of sympathizer:
> the unreserved, unquestioning believer, the recognition
> given, in pity, through woman's heart, lest man should
> utterly lose faith in himself; the echo of God's own voice,
> pronouncing, "It is well done!" All the separate action of
> woman is, and even has been, and always shall be, false,
> foolish, vain, destructive of her own best and holiest
> qualities, void of every good effect and productive of
> intolerable mischiefs.

As the full, outlandishly arrogant meaning of the words
penetrated, outrage stopped her breathing for a few blood-
racing seconds. Then Rachel exploded. "You pompous
ass," she railed and viciously crumpled the papers in her
hand. "You puffed-up scarecrow." She opened her mouth
to spew more rage but was stopped by the sight of two men
rumbling her way atop a freight wagon loaded with red
bricks. Just before reaching her, they turned onto a cleared
lot across the street, the one between the mill bunkhouse

and Coke Lyons's home—the site of the new bank. *Harvey's bank.*

With her heart rapidly thrusting fury to every taut muscle in her body, she swung her gaze about. This would be her new life? Her anger burst again into words. "So, I'm to move into a house between the gossipy little pig and the brazen-haired tart? While Harvey dictates my every breath from over at the bank?" Her foot tapped angrily of its own volition. "And let's not forget Edna and her harpy friends, right across the street, watching my every move."

"What's that?" hollered one of the teamsters unloading the bricks.

She waved them off. "No. Nothing." She spun around and went back into the store. Seeing a trash barrel in the corner, she tossed the hateful letter into it.

She stalked to the fabric table and started sorting through the array. But her fury wouldn't quell. Suddenly, a blue plaid similar to one of Jake's shirts assaulted her eye. "Oooh," she almost growled, shoving the odious bolt aside. "Everything I said about the rest of them goes double for you, Jake Stone. If you think you can turn me into a simpering, lovesick mouse for one stinking bottle of perfume . . . If you think . . . I'll have you know . . . And that goes for the rest of 'em, too! I'll get the annulment, then *I'll decide where I'm going to live and with whom, if anyone.*"

Yes, she thought with vehemence as her temper began to dissipate. A new confidence grew within her, a peace. "Yes," she sighed aloud this time and began to look in earnest for something pretty for a dress—one to celebrate her freedom. She would be a new, independent Rachel in a beautiful new creation, when she danced in the new barn.

Just as she spotted some polished cotton dyed a creamy beige and joyously splayed with sprigs of peach blossoms, Mr. Dorset emerged from the storeroom.

"Have you found what you want yet?"

Rachel looked up at his overheated face; her emotions

had tempered to a level that she could now almost tolerate him again. "Why, yes, Mr. Dorset." Gathering up the bolt, she carried it to the counter. "Seven yards will do nicely."

He smiled at her and nodded, the wispy curl at the top of his near-bald pate bobbing. "You couldn't have picked anything that's gonna go with your colorin' better. You'll sure have the heads turnin'."

Rachel raised a mischievous brow. "I do hope so."

"I've got some satin ribbon the same pink as the darkest flowers," he said as he flipped the bolt over and over, unwinding the fabric. "It would go real good."

"Well then, give me three yards of that, too."

While measuring the material from the tip of his nose to the end of his extended hand, Mr. Dorset began to speak in rushed, gossipy tones. "Clayton Jennings was just in a few minutes ago. Come to get a sack of lye. Most his stock up and dropped dead."

"*What?* Did he say anything about my cow? I left Ginger with him."

"Nope. He just said when him and his family got home from town yesterday all his animals was dead. Even the chickens."

"Good heavens! Did he say what killed them?"

"He's not sure. That's why he wants to bury 'em soon's possible and cover 'em in lye—in case it's somethin' catchin'."

Rachel's throat tightened in a knot of empathy. "This is dreadful. That family has so little as it is."

"I know. They don't give me hardly no business a'tall."

"And you say Mr. Jennings doesn't know what caused it?"

"Mighty queer. He says they looked fine when he and the missus left home. That's another queer thing. Harvey Best sent word to have 'em meet him here yesterday. But he's not even due back till next week sometime."

"That *is* odd." Rachel glanced out the window at the Grillses' house. "I have a veterinary book of my father's—"

"A what?" he said, interrupting.

"A book for doctoring animals. I think I'll rent a rig and ride out there. Maybe I can discover the reason they died." Rachel chewed on her lip. "It shouldn't have happened so suddenly. Oh, and would you please wrap up twenty pounds of beans and ten of flour to take with me? I'll be back for it after I see about a horse and buggy."

Rachel started toward the livery barn, grateful that she wore nothing better than a brown work dress. Examining dead animals would not be a pretty business.

"This is my lucky day," a rich, deep voice called from the hotel, startling Rachel to a halt.

Mr. McLean looked as dashingly handsome as ever. "Good afternoon." He leaned against a porch post, his black suit coat nonchalantly flaring to display a lace-fronted shirt and a midnight satin brocade waistcoat. He wore no cravat and the neck of his shirt was casually unbuttoned. His smile, however, appeared genuinely pleased. "Where might the pretty lady be off to in such a hurry?" He sauntered down the steps toward her. "I'd count it a supreme pleasure to accompany you."

"How nice to see you. But I don't think you'd enjoy going where I'm off to."

"Don't be too sure. You'd be surprised how varied my interests can be." His deep blue eyes held hers intently.

Goldy came quickly to mind. She looked past him to the saloon. "Yes, I can imagine. Good day to you, Mr. McLean." She turned and began to walk away.

Matching her stride, he caught her arm and presumptuously folded it within his. "At least let me walk you to your destination."

"I'm afraid it'll be a short walk." She looked up at him and pointed to the livery barn only a score of yards past the hotel. "I'm going in to rent a rig to drive out to the Jenningses'. They've had some trouble. Their stock have all died. I hope I'll be able to discover the cause."

"That's terrible." Shock rang in his voice as he steered

her toward the gaping doors. ''If you don't mind the company, I think I'll go along. Maybe there's something I can do for that luckless family. Besides,'' he said with a teasing slowness, ''someone as delicious as you shouldn't go riding alone out in the forest. Who knows what hungry wild creatures might be lurking about out there?''

((chapter 18))

RACHEL looked up from the veterinary book and stole a glance at Kyle McLean as he guided the bony rent-horse up the road. His wide-brimmed hat was set at a jaunty angle, and a smug smile dimpled his cheek. He'd insisted on driving her, and, certain that nothing short of an ugly scene would have deterred him, Rachel had relented.

When Mr. McLean had first seen the shabby, rickety buggy, he'd given it a look of disdain. But the expensively clothed man's distaste for it had not daunted him—nor had Edna's stony expression when they had gone to tell her where they were going.

And here I am, Rachel chided inwardly, once more allowing someone else to take charge of me. She eyed the picnic basket at her feet and wondered again at how quickly Mr. McLean could entice others to do his bidding. He'd managed to get Mrs. Thornton at the hotel to fill the cloth-covered wicker with foodstuffs in the few minutes it took Mr. Dooley to hitch the rangy horse. "We'll be hungry long before we ever get back," he'd said matter-of-factly.

Well, he might have his way about everything else, but Rachel had made certain he didn't have the pleasure of conversing with her on their way to the Jenningses'. She'd told him that she needed to study her father's textbook and had done exactly that ever since.

Rachel knew the importance of arriving at the Jenningses' before Clayton covered the stock with lime. But as they passed the cutoff to the Colfaxes's, she looked down it with longing, wishing she had the time to drop by. She'd like to sit down and have a long talk with Orletta. Her friend had a way of seeing things through wise, uncluttered eyes. Rachel could also tell her about the barn raising. Anxious about the ''good'' ladies' reception of her, Orletta hadn't stepped foot in Independence since she'd married Amos. But with Rachel and all the Colfax men there to ease the way, it would be the perfect time for her to get acquainted.

Maybe I'll ask Mr. McLean to stop by on the way home, Rachel thought as she dragged her gaze back to the book. On second thought, she decided to wait till another time. Who knows what that bunch might say to Mr. McLean, since they were such good friends of Jake's?

Later, passing the wagon ruts to her place, Rachel held her breath and made a concerted effort not to look down them, for fear—or was it hope?—that she'd catch sight of her husband. After the extended moment elapsed without hearing anything but the chirping of a few sparrows and the persistent clatter of the horse and rig rolling over packed earth, she exhaled and relaxed. And, for the first time since she'd buried herself in the book on her lap, she allowed herself to admit that she'd kept her eyes occupied to avoid watching for Jake at every curve and hill.

She purposefully closed the book and looked up. ''We're making much better time than I do in the wagon.''

''Scrawny-looking as the nag is,'' Mr. McLean said, nodding at the rawboned horse, ''he moves along at a good clip on those long, knobby legs.'' Shifting the reins to one hand, he pulled a filigreed gold watch from his pocket and flipped up the cover. ''It's only two-fifteen, and we didn't leave until after noon. If your examination doesn't take too long, we'll have time to enjoy a leisurely picnic supper and still get back to town before dark.''

''I've never actually examined an animal before, but it couldn't be that much different from a person.''

He turned to her with an unaccountable smile. ''Really?'' Then his expression changed as quickly as a thespian switches masks. ''Did I mention that back home in Maryland I'd seen an epidemic of lung carbuncle?''

"No, you didn't."

"Yes. Bad business. It's not only deadly to animals, but to people, too. We had to destroy every animal for miles around."

"Well, let's hope it's not that. Fortunately, the book is very precise, and it would be simple to diagnose."

"I suppose it would. But, you can never be too careful." His gaze returned to the road ahead.

"That's true, but it's best not to jump to conclusions before we get there." She placed a hand on his arm. "I was thinking, you mentioned you wanted to help the Jenningses. I'm sure others will, too. Particularly since it's been such a short time since they buried their little girl. The Stocktons are having a barn raising Saturday after next. Brother Simpkins could ask for animal donations. I'm sure with all the spring birthings, folks wouldn't mind giving some piglets or maybe even a calf."

"Probably. But I doubt Jennings would accept 'em. He's never struck me as the type to take charity."

Rachel was stunned into silence. His words were almost identical to those Jake had used the time she'd tried to refuse Mr. Jennings's ham. Her shock soon turned to irritation as, once again, she hadn't been able to keep thoughts of Jake from crashing through her defenses.

She retorted with a most logical answer. "When Mr. Jennings arrived in Oregon, I'm sure they held a barn raising for him, didn't they?"

"Sure. I suppose so." His tone was unconvincing.

"He took charity then without his manhood being damaged. I'm sure if it were put to him just right," she said, giving Mr. McLean her most winning smile, "he'd be willing to be the recipient of an 'animal raising.' "

Hesitation flickered in his eyes. "Look, don't you say anything to him. While we're there, I'll take him aside and see what I can do."

"Then there's nothing to worry about." She arched a confident brow. "You have such a talent for persuasion."

A short time later, they broke out of the forest and onto

the Jenningses' cleared land. Rachel's gaze climbed the distant knoll and found the lone wooden cross.

"Jennings must be digging over yonder. See that big pile of dirt?" Mr. McLean pointed past the barn to the north pasture and reined the horse toward it.

As they stopped beside the hill of rich brown clods, Rachel's gaze fastened onto the carcass of her spotted cow. Poor, sweet Ginger lying stiff-legged in death. She then noticed a scattering of dead hogs, a number of baby pigs, and a bull calf beyond the large hole. Several feet below the surface worked two men, Mr. Jennings, a weariness ravaging his fine-boned features, and . . . *Jake,* who glared back at her with a malice surpassing even her lethal Viking.

Clutching the side of the buggy, her fingers tore through the rotten leather. She wrenched her gaze from Jake and veered it to Mr. Jennings. "Good day," she croaked. "I don't mean to intrude, but Mr. Dorset told me about the sudden deaths of your animals. He said you didn't know the cause."

"Yeah," Jake said, drawing her back. But his volcanic attention followed Mr. McLean's rather jerky descent to the ground. "Mighty strange."

Jake's glaring stare followed Mr. McLean, who circled the buggy to Rachel and helped her down with a noticeably tight-lipped smile.

Both Jake and Mr. Jennings climbed out of the hole and began slapping mud from their britches.

Rachel looked skyward, begging for divine assistance, then with practiced grace, she stepped toward the two men with Mr. McLean following close behind. "Mr. Jennings?" He and Jake stopped dusting themselves and looked up. "If you would like," she continued, "I'll examine your animals. It's quite possible that I can determine the cause of their deaths."

Mr. Jennings looked toward the carnage then back to her. "I'd 'preciate that," he said, swiping a strand of dark hair from his worried eyes.

She walked past the hole, knowing without a doubt that everyone watched. She envisioned herself jumping in and pulling the dirt over her. But reason told her that would only draw more attention. Attempting to ignore the men's scrutiny and the churning of her stomach, she knelt beside the dead cow. After shooing away the flies, she pried open its stiff mouth. The smell of death gagged her, but she persisted. Anything was better than rejoining the men.

"I've been told," she heard Mr. McLean say in a casual tone, "that there's some sort of animal sickness going around. I've heard of several cases up north."

Wondering why he hadn't mentioned it to her on the trip there, Rachel looked in his direction. But her husband, now facing the other two, blocked her view. By the bunching of Jake's shoulder muscles, she sensed he was close to violence. She tensed, awaiting his retort.

Instead, Mr. Jennings spoke. "You don't say. Where would that be?"

"Outside of Portland."

"Up near that sawmill you're putting in?" The contrast between Jake's low, smooth words and his battle-ready stance jangled Rachel's nerves further.

Mr. McLean answered with equal calmness. "Why, yes, I heard about it from my workers."

The muscles rippled down Jake's arms. He looked as if he would explode into action any second.

"Mr. Jennings," Rachel called, hoping to expel the tension. "Would you come here a moment?"

"Did you find something?" He and the other two skirted the hole, coming to stand above where she knelt, their legs fencing her.

"Nothing thus far. Did the animals have a good appetite the last time you fed them?"

"Yeah. That's what so queer. They weren't at all off their feed."

Running a hand along the cow's underside, Rachel felt for lumps or lesions, but could find none. She edged to the rear of the cow and again found nothing out of the ordinary.

As she began to rise, both Jake and Mr. McLean grabbed an arm and swiftly lifted her up. Her heart tripped over itself and skipped a beat. "Thank you," she whispered, feeling like a meaty bone caught between two dogs. She stepped out of their grasps, and wiped at her hands.

Jake whipped out his handkerchief and placed it in her palms before she knew it.

"Thank you," she whispered, afraid to look up at him, fearing what she might see—or not see—in his expression.

"Well, what do you think?" Mr. Jennings asked.

"I think they either ate or drank something poisonous." Keeping her eyes decidedly on the homesteader, she shoved the kerchief in Jake's direction.

She felt the solid warmth of his hand as he took it. She hoped he didn't feel her tremble. "Could I see their feed?" she quickly asked.

"Sure. But it's good dry grain, not even startin' to sour," Mr. Jennings said and led the way toward the barn.

"So, you think it looks more like poison than some mysterious sickness?" Jake's tone was strangely light as he moved to her side, and Rachel swore he was about to smile.

"I'm no expert, but that's what it looks like to me."

"But, as the lady says," Mr. McLean said with a curt tightness to his voice, "all she really knows is what she read in her father's animal book on the way out here."

"Knowing *my wife* as well as I do," Jake returned with equal intensity, "she doesn't make mistakes."

Rachel increased the pace.

When they reached the barn, she and Jake sifted through the feed bin, perilously close, but could find nothing amiss.

"Maybe something's wrong with their water," Rachel said, turning to Mr. Jennings.

"I already checked the creek. It looks clear to me."

"Possibly something fouled it upstream." Rachel started out the barn door.

"Anything's possible," Jake said, following behind. "Right, McLean?"

As he reached her side, Mr. McLean's jaw muscles clenched then abruptly relaxed, and he turned, smirking. "I know one thing that's not possible—and that's the chance that your black stallion could ever beat my gray."

"I take it you got my message in Oregon City."

"Yes, and I'll be sure to have my Thoroughbred, Pegasus, here well before Independence Day, so the sporting men can get a look at him. I would've brought him with me this time, but I was late. I barely caught a sternwheeler this morning, just as it pulled away from the Salem dock."

"So, you just got here this morning." Jake sounded almost friendly as he looked down at Mr. McLean, but he walked entirely too close.

"Yes." The other leaned away just the slightest bit. "I needed to check on a business matter."

"As busy as you are, I'm surprised you could take the time to bring my wife all the way out here."

"I'm never too busy to assist a lady in need," Mr. McLean said, taking a step closer to Rachel.

Knowing instinctively that he'd crossed some invisible line of challenge, Rachel quickly swung around, placing herself between him and Jake. "Speaking of need, Mr. McLean, weren't you going to talk to Mr. Jennings?"

It obviously took a second for him to grasp her meaning. "Yes, that's right." Another second elapsed before his eyes, glinting like shards of blue glass, softened and lowered from her husband to her.

No doubt Mr. Jennings also noticed the hostility between the two men. He'd stopped and turned, eyeing one then the other. "Then why don't me an' Mr. McLean walk on up to the house. I'll have my wife put on a pot of coffee."

Her escort's gaze left her and returned to her husband. "I'll only be a few moments."

"Take your time," Jake drawled. "*My wife and I* will be down at the creek looking for anything suspicious."

Rachel's gratitude knew no bounds when the other two walked away, putting distance between Jake and Mr. McLean. It was one thing to daydream about a couple of handsome swains battling for her favor, but the calamitous reality held absolutely no romance. Competent as Mr. McLean looked, he seemed a poor match for Jake's awesome strength.

"You ready?" A smile flickered, but his eyes . . . Did they betray a sadness? A regret?

Rachel swallowed and stepped ahead of him, starting toward the tree-crowded creek that slashed a dark swath across the meadow.

They followed a worn, narrow path down to the wide stream but found nothing save a few trout swimming in the clear water of a quiet eddy.

"Maybe there's something upstream." Without waiting for an answer, Rachel gathered her skirts and stepped across some gnarled tree roots that stretched to the edge.

"Yeah." Jake picked up a smooth stone and sent it skittering across the water. "Maybe."

Walking proved difficult for Rachel in her slick-bottomed leather shoes. Boulders obstructed the way, and roots, deceptively covered with sand, waited to trip her, while branches snagged her hair and clothing.

Following closer behind than she realized, Jake caught her by the shoulder just as she stumbled over a jutting stone. She fell back against his chest with a thud. His other hand crossed over her, steadying her against him. "Better watch your step," he whispered into her hair.

She found herself swaddled in his comforting strength, breathing in the very smell of him. A wave of yearning washed through her, building, until it crested beneath his touch. And the way his arm lay across her breast, she had no doubt he could count the thumping of her ever-increasing pulse. Worse, she realized as she came to her senses, if it weren't for the gurgling stream, he'd probably be able to hear her betraying heart. She moved out of his hands.

He hesitated a second before releasing her. She heard him exhale heavily and knew that he, too, had been holding his breath. Without daring to glance at him, Rachel ducked under a low tree branch and continued along the bank.

In a silence as strained as an overtuned violin, they followed the brook out of the meadow and into a forest of tall evergreens. Continuing on, they worked their way through a tangle of ferns, searching both sides of the creek. Other than a sprinkling of animal imprints, the only thing she found was the tracks of a couple of horses crossing at one point. Unable to stand the tension any longer, Rachel finally thought of something to say that she hoped wouldn't sound like meaningless prattle. She turned toward Jake and made her eyes meet his. "I suppose you heard about the barn raising Saturday after next."

He stopped walking. "No."

Her gaze escaped to the red trunk of a giant cedar. But she determinedly forced it back to him. "The Stockton family is having one for their son." By his expectant expression, she realized that she had misled him into thinking she was asking him to escort her. She quickly added, "With all the neighbors gathering, it would be a good time to ask them to donate some animals to the Jenningses. Have an animal raising, so to speak."

Jake's face smoothed into unreadable planes, and Rachel's heart lurched at the pain she sensed he hid. She swung around and started up the creek again.

After a moment, she heard a twig break directly behind her. Jake had again closed the distance between them.

"Yeah," he said in a casual tone, "if it was put to Clayton like that, like something as natural as a barn raising, I think he'd accept it."

She looked back at him, and though she felt like crying from the sheer want of him, she managed a smile. "I'm so glad you think so. Mr. McLean is talking to Mr. Jennings about it right now."

Instantly, Rachel realized her mistake as a look of malice raked down Jake's face. "Yeah? Well, I'm sure he'll make short work of that."

At the scoffing remark, Rachel started to defend Kyle McLean, but knowing it would only stoke Jake's anger, she looked ahead again and increased her pace.

Jake watched the sway of brown skirt as she moved onward in that graceful way of hers. He followed after, though he knew there was no sense in going any farther. He'd already found what he was looking for back a piece—the two sets of horse tracks he'd known would be there. They'd crossed the creek just about where he suspected they would. As lazy as Bone and Cooter were, he knew they would've taken the most direct route from their place to Clayton's.

Rachel walked into a shaft of sunlight that streaked through a stand of fir. The hair piled atop her head shimmered, reminding him, as it always did when it turned to golden fire, of the first night she'd come to him. He began to ache down low. He would give anything to take her in his arms and cover her face with kisses, tell her how much he wanted her, loved her.

From the hurt that reshaped her eyes every time she looked at him, he was almost sure she felt the same way. But what if he was wrong? What if her pain was caused not by the love of him, but just the opposite? And as much as it stuck in his craw, he could almost understand how any unwitting lady could be charmed by McLean. The bastard reeked of money and highfalutin manners.

He'd give a winter's worth of furs to tell her what that silver-tongued snake was really like. But, as naïve as she was, Jake couldn't trust her to keep the investigation a secret. If nothing else, McLean would know something was wrong just by looking into those gorgeous eyes of hers.

And besides, if she chose Jake, it had to be because she wanted to, not because she was running from McLean.

Suddenly, the trees and ferns lining the stream gave way to a tiny glade blanketed with tender grass and dappled with light. A log lay at an angle near the brook, and a footpath led away through the woods toward the Jenningses' homestead. *This is the exact spot where he had first glimpsed the enchantress that was Rachel*—the day of the funeral when he'd found her splashing water on her face, watched it slide down to her throat, down the slender column of her neck.

Watched the trickles play across her full upturned breasts. He'd seen the tips tighten into pouty little buds as she shivered from the chill. He'd been awed by everything about her, the gentle slope of her shoulders, the delicacy of her arms, silken skin sheathing a porcelainlike back that gradually narrowed to her tiny waist.

He would never forget how incredibly lucky he'd felt. How undeserving.

"Jake?" Rachel's voice sounded high, thin. She stood a mere arm's length away, her eyes holding that same look a doe gets in mating season—frightened and nervous, yet seeking, eager.

He had no doubt she, too, remembered. He stepped into the space separating them.

Breath catching, she moved back slightly. "The water looks clear here, too."

It took real effort to turn his gaze from her, but he did long enough to scan the stream. Returning to her, he noticed a pulsing at a tender place just below her jaw. When her fluttery hand rose to hide the spot, he dragged his gaze up to eyes much darker than usual. "Yeah, clear."

Hand still at her throat, she backed up another step and peered off to the side. "I don't understand. Nowhere in the book is there such a lack of symptoms for any deadly disease. Even colic in horses shows a tremendous amount of stress preceding death. As far as I can see, only a very lethal poison could cause death so suddenly." Her words came fast and breathy. "Is there any reason someone could want to poison Mr. Jennings's stock? Someone who hates him?"

Jake didn't want to talk about this. He wanted to gather her up and crush her to him. To lay her down on the cool grass, to . . . "No. Clayton's highly thought of."

He watched the thick fringe of golden lashes rise as she slid her gaze slowly to his chest then up to his face. "You're probably right. I'm presuming far too much."

It took all his willpower not to grab her. Instead, he stepped near and raised an unhurried hand to her cheek. "You tried, and that's what counts."

She didn't pull away. And though the pressure was almost imperceptible, he felt her lean into his palm.

A shiver ran up his spine as he reached for her.

"Rachel!"

Feeling as if he'd been punched in the jaw, Jake jerked his head in the direction of the sound.

The distant call was unmistakably McLean's. "Rachel!"

Jake swung his gaze to her. She had backed away and now stared up the path cutting through the trees. You'd think her husband was about to catch her with her lover instead of the other way around.

Jake's wrath returned with blood-roiling force, then turned glacial. Just what kind of a claim did the bastard have on her anyway? He grabbed Rachel by the arm and yanked her to him. "Why the hell'd you come out here with McLean?"

She flinched at the words pelting her. Then her eyes widened, and she opened her mouth as if to speak.

"Rachel!" McLean called again.

Jake sliced a glance toward the nearing voice, then turned to his wife again. To his surprise, her guilty expression had changed to one of cat-eyed anger.

"Let go. You're hurting me."

He looked down at his hand clamped onto her, knuckles turning white. Feeling wretched for holding her so tightly, he abruptly released her fragile arms. "But I still want an answer. What are you doing with that bastard?"

"For your information, Mr. McLean has always been a perfect gentleman." She wrenched her skirts to the side and stalked away up the path to the Jenningses'. Then, suddenly, she stopped and whirled around, her eyes flashing with fury. "Can Goldy say the same about you?"

But before he could think of a good answer, she had melted into the trees.

((chapter))
19

HE'D done it again. And after getting so close. "That damned close," Jake moaned bitterly, holding up a barely separated thumb and forefinger. He looked down the narrow curving path that swallowed Rachel as she ran to meet McLean and cursed himself again. *"You damned stupid fool."*

Jake had held his temper all the time the son of a bitch had stood there looking so smug. How he'd wanted to smear that cocksure grin off the bastard's face. "Hell, smear his whole damned face off." But he hadn't. He'd held himself in check. So, why in tarnation couldn't he have managed just a little longer? She'd been so close to surrendering to him. So damned close.

Jake jammed his hands into his pockets and started up the trail. Seeing a fallen pine cone, he gave it a savage kick and watched with grim satisfaction as it splattered against a tree trunk.

Breaking out of the woods, he strode across the Jenningses' wheat field. Halfway to the cabin, he spotted the rear of the livery buggy leaving the farmyard in the opposite direction. His anger fought a losing battle with the despair gnawing at his insides. He slowed to a heavy-footed trudge as his gaze followed the rig until it disappeared into the forest.

His attention swung to Clayton, who had already returned to the burial pit. Jake watched his neighbor toss another shovelful of the rich dirt onto the growing pile, and his step faltered. He really didn't want to face Clayton. The whole business with Rachel and McLean had been a mess. He'd much rather just ride out. But he knew he couldn't.

Reaching the hole, Jake grabbed a pick then jumped in beside the other man, but didn't say a word. And, thankfully, neither did his neighbor, not until they were both huffing from the strenuous labor.

"I think it's big enough," Clayton said and tossed his shovel onto the dirt pile.

"Yeah, looks like it."

They hoisted themselves out and walked to the nearest carcass.

"You know," Clayton said, grabbing the hind legs of a piglet and pitching it into the hole. "It's mighty queer."

"What?" Waiting for the question he was sure would be about him and Rachel, Jake also flung in a dead animal.

Clayton picked up another baby pig. "Mr. McLean's only been out here twice. Both times right after somethin' bad's happened. And both times he offered me a job in Portland loading ships. He even threw in a house this time."

"That's what McLean wanted to talk to you about?" Surprised yet not, Jake stopped working and turned toward the other man.

"Yeah. An' this time I think I'm gonna take him up on it. I spent all I had on that bull calf over there," he said, pointing to a carcass half the size of what had been Ginger. "Don't have the money to replace my hogs. And I don't know what to say about your cow."

"There's nothing to say. She was a sweet-natured critter, and I'll miss her. But I'm sure her milk is more of a loss to your family than me."

"Well, it's lucky you took your dog home, or she might be layin' here, too. My Em, she's comin' real undone. She ain't near got over Becky. And now this. Like I said, we best just move on. We sure ain't had no luck here."

Jake was sorely tempted to tell Clayton that he was sure McLean had ordered the poisoning of the animals. But the man would be so head-up he'd try to kill McLean for sure and most likely end up dead or in jail. No, it would have to wait until he had enough evidence to put McLean behind bars—let that bastard rot away in some damp, rat-infested cell instead of Clayton.

But Jake couldn't just stand by and let his neighbor give up, either. He placed a hand on the smaller man's arm. "These animals were deliberately poisoned by someone."

Creases lined Clayton's refined features. "I know. But who? Why?"

"I'm a good tracker. Give me two weeks to turn up the culprits before you give up. Just two weeks."

"Even if you do find 'em, it won't bring back my stock. I still won't be able to feed my family."

"Don't worry. If the mangy curs don't have any money, we'll skin 'em and sell their hides."

Clayton nodded slowly, determinedly. "Yeah. You hold 'em. I'll do the skinnin'."

Rachel was hardly in the mood for a picnic, but there she sat on a red-checked tablecloth next to Mr. McLean, trying to choke down Mrs. Thornton's fried chicken and potato salad. The idea of begging off and giving further credence to his suspicions was unthinkable. By the overconfident look decorating his face when she'd rushed out of the forest—practically colliding with him—he'd obviously assumed she'd had another row with her husband.

However, gentleman that he was, he had yet to mention it. Instead, for the past half-hour he'd been talking about the elegant furnishings and cultural entertainment he planned to import once his lumber business really started to boom. He also spoke of a trip to the Far East to purchase some rare teaks and mahoganies, even intimated that the two of them might enjoy taking the journey together, to lands with exotic names like Sumatra and Malaya and Siam.

"Speaking of culture," he continued, "Captain Ainsworth—he's the biggest steamship-line owner on the Columbia—is giving a ball for the governor and his young schoolmarm of a bride next month. It'll be the closest thing to a social gathering this primitive territory can produce.

Anyone who's anyone at all will be invited. It would be an excellent opportunity to introduce you and give these bumpkins a chance to see what a real lady looks like.''

Rachel had been only half listening, but from his expectant stare she knew he awaited a response. She ran his last words through her mind and realized he'd asked her to a governor's ball. ''Mr. McLean, I—''

''Don't you think it's time we dispensed with these cumbersome formalities? Call me Kyle, for God's sake.''

Uncomfortable under the intensity of his stare, Rachel avoided looking at him. She peered slightly to his left. ''It's very kind of you, *Kyle,* to invite me to this ball. Where did you say it would be held?''

''At Ainsworth's mansion outside of Oregon City.''

''Oregon City? Dear heavens! I couldn't possibly travel that far with you. It would be most unseemly in any case, but even more so since I'm married to another.''

Kyle wiped chicken grease from his fingers and picked up her hand. ''Believe me, none of this need worry you. I have the ear of the governor's secretary. I'll have him speak to Governor Gaines about you. And I'm positive he'll convince the governor to give you an annulment. You have my word, when you arrive for the ball, *accompanied by a proper escort,* the papers will be ready for you to sign.''

Rachel knew she should be grateful that this obviously successful, powerfully connected gentleman was courting her. She had little hope that things could ever work out between her and Jake. They simply weren't compatible . . . well, for the most part, she thought, experiencing an all too familiar craving. She shifted slightly, attempting to squelch a flutter of desire. Looking squarely at Kyle, she wondered if one day she would have the same reaction when she thought of him. He was incredibly attractive, but something was missing, especially in his eyes. ''I thank you. A quick annulment would certainly simplify my life.''

Kyle placed his other hand over hers and drew it closer. ''You'd be surprised by all that I have to offer.''

Yes, I bet I would, she thought as she watched the pupils

of his eyes enlarge, the pace of his breathing increase. At
least he would be a less repugnant bed partner than Harvey.
Harvey! *Kyle's paid man.* And now he'd just told her about
another government employee who also did his bidding.
Bordellos? Bribed officials? She pulled away. "This secretary follows your wishes the same as Mr. Best?"

Kyle's eyes flicked wide, then settled into unreadable
politeness, but his lips had tightened slightly. "Yes, both
men are sometimes in my employ. But then, so will you be
the first time you tend an injury at the sawmill."

"I don't understand."

"I'm Coke Lyons's silent partner. Since I own the hotel
and have a bank under construction, I thought folks around
town might get nervous if they knew I owned the saw works
as well. Plus an extensive tract of land to the east."

His smug, lopsided smile didn't amuse Rachel in the
least. She climbed to her feet before Kyle could rise and
assist her. "Yes. I could see how they might begin to feel a
bit surrounded."

Kyle stepped close, a pained expression in his deep blue
eyes as he lifted her chin. "Please don't misunderstand me.
I want very much for you to hold me in the highest regard.
If the fact that I've not disclosed my partnership bothers
you, I'll make it public. It's of little consequence."

Of course. Anything to appease the lady, to gain the
proper adornment for his aspiring arm. "How you handle
your business is really your own affair," she said as further
seeds of mistrust sprouted. "And, speaking of business,
don't you think it's a bit odd about Harvey?"

His hand dropped from her chin. "What about Harvey?"

Rachel enjoyed the idea that she now controlled the
moment. "Didn't you know? It was Harvey who asked the
Jennings to come to town in the first place, the day their
stock was poisoned. Something about their homestead
papers."

"Just a coincidence, I'm sure."

"But the odd part is, he wasn't there to meet them. Point
of fact, he's not even due for another week or so."

"You don't say? That is strange. But I'm sure someone just made a mistake about the date."

He was right, of course. She was becoming entirely too suspicious. Another thing she could thank Jake for. "Yes, most likely. I seem to question everything of late."

"That's understandable, considering your past unjust treatment."

She attempted a smile.

"We'd better be getting back," he said, looking at the sun. "I need to catch the *Oregon Belle* when it returns this evening." He reached down and picked up the corners of the tablecloth—food, plates, bowls, and all. Rachel was sure dishes broke as they crashed together. Then, taking her by the arm, he hastily steered her toward the buggy.

"I thought you had business in Independence."

"I took care of that," he said. Then his voice slowed to an enticingly low murmur, "before you came sashaying by."

She stopped and jerked loose. *"I was not sashaying."*

Kyle burst out laughing, causing her to feel foolish.

She smiled and repeated far more calmly, "I was not sashaying."

"You're absolutely right," he said, helping her into the buggy. His amused expression relaxed into a lopsided grin. "And I'm *not* Simon Legree."

Rachel chuckled at the audacity of her previous distrusting thoughts while Kyle hopped aboard. Of course he wasn't some greedy, corrupt ogre. He'd always been more than kind and generous with her. And hadn't he offered to help the Jennings family? "By the way, how'd your talk with Mr. Jennings go?"

"Fine, but don't change the subject. Do you know that's the first time you've let me hear your delightful laugh today?" He picked up the traces and flicked them across the gelding's spiny back. "And I'll be looking forward to hearing much more of that musical laughter at the barn dance Saturday week. It's sure to put those amateur hoe-down players to shame."

* * *

Following the horse tracks he'd discovered, Jake came into a small clearing in the woods shortly before sundown. A board-and-batten shack and a three-sided shelter with an attached corral filled the deeply shadowed area.

Jake pulled his rifle from its scabbard. After checking the load, he dismounted and tied Prince behind a thick clump of brush. He scanned the clearing from some movement, listened for voices. The only sign of life he saw was a couple of silhouetted horses standing in the shelter. He crouched low in the fading light and moved closer, though he was almost sure no one was home. By now the lamps should have been lit inside the house.

Coming up behind the shack, he peeked in a small window but could see next to nothing in the darkness. He straightened and walked around to the front.

Both horses whinnied and trotted to the fence.

Jake backed against the cabin wall, a finger pressed against the trigger of his rifle.

From the woods, Prince echoed the other animals with a rumbly nicker.

Jake flinched and glanced intently about, then he noticed that Bone's shambly wagon and team were missing. The place most likely stood empty. Relaxing, he opened the door. The rancid odor of spoiled meat greeted him, and his stomach recoiled. He reached into his pocket, pulled out a sulfur match and struck it on the seam of his pants. In the dim flare, he found a lantern among the dirty clutter on the table. He lit the wick, illuminating the room.

A reeking mess surrounded him, and his first instinct was to escape. Tin plates and pots with dried-on food covered the tables and stove, heaps of dirty clothes filled the corners, and at one end of the room lay two mattresses strewn with rumpled blankets. Jake's skin itched. "The whole place has gotta be crawling with lice."

As he picked up the lantern and started for the door, he noticed a dead rat across the room next to a saddle. "My God, they're even too lazy to build a place to keep their

tack. And if that's so . . .'' He turned back and held the
lantern high. Casting light into all the nooks in the room, he
slowly walked around.

Within seconds he found the proof he was looking for.
Against the wall next to the stove slumped a half-empty
burlap bag with an unmistakable skull-and-crossbones in-
signia printed on it. Jake reached inside and scooped up a
handful of oats that were undoubtedly laced with strych-
nine. Releasing the grain, he dusted off his hands and
straightened the bag to find the distributor's name. It
wouldn't be too difficult to find the merchant who stocked
that particular brand of rat poison. And as unforgettable as
those two slop buckets were, it wouldn't take much for the
storekeeper to recall when he sold it to them.

Jake replaced the lantern on the table and started for the
door and some fresh air. He now had all the evidence
needed to have Bone and Cooter arrested. Those two
sniveling cowards would talk. He'd see to that. They'd be
begging to incriminate McLean and Best, and whoever else
the son of a bitch had on his payroll.

Outside, he breathed deeply of the crisp evening breezes.
He felt victorious, as if he'd just brought down a killer
grizzly. ''Yes!'' he shouted and raced to his horse.

Come first light, he'd head for Oregon City. In no time,
that scheming Romeo and his bunch would be locked
behind bars. And Jake could get back in time to sweet-talk
Rachel into going to the barn raising with him.

*Ensconced on the walls, an array of flaming candles
enlivened the mahogany paneling to the richest shades of
port and claret. She felt so nestled within the warm
welcome, so coddled by the gentle rise and fall of the ship's
cabin, that a symphony swelled within her. Its melody gave
flight to her bare feet. She pirouetted across the lush
Persian carpet until, reaching the bed, she slowed to a stop
and peered once again at the evening gown lying upon it. A
gift from him . . . a gift to wear on their trip to Valhalla.*

Her eyes misted with quicksilver emotion. Then in joyous

wonder, she swooped up the gossamer of midnight black. Hugging it to her bare form, she spun away again in a dizzying waltz that turned a hundred flickering lights into a whir of liquid gold. The breezy creation flowed around her, clinging in a silky caress. Deliciously, she and the gown melted into one.

Gradually, the sliding chiffon became his hands, his sumptuous touch, and a shower of anticipation cascaded over her, through her, sparking her every craving inch.

A sudden impatience erupted. She stepped into the pooling Grecian confection, slipped its rapturous coolness up the length of her warm, lithe body, and clasped a shimmering diamond brooch in the silk draping one of her nude shoulders.

Then raising her head, she caught her reflection in the gilt-framed looking glass, and her heart began an untamed drumbeat. She moved toward the mirror, watching the sheer fabric ripple across her every curve, whispering promises— promises she knew her Viking would answer.

Her tresses, swept up by an ebony velvet rope, tumbled in streaming ringlets of molten gold, tracing her brow, her petal-pink cheeks, the tender nape of her neck.

But it was her eyes that verily intrigued her. They mocked as they drew her into their knowing amusement, beckoning her to come explore dark, sultry labyrinths of veiled secrets.

Was this really her? A mysteriously ethereal yet pagan enchantress? Goddess yet temptress?

Yes!

She ran out into the starlit night. On deck, she looked for him, but all was masked in shadows except for a linen-covered table, its settings of crystal and china gleaming in the circle of light cast by a silver candelabra.

She moved toward it, reveling in the smooth hardness of the deck beneath her feet, the kiss of the salty sea mist on her unclothed arms, the intoxication of her spiraling expectations.

As she neared the table, a hand, flashing a red-gemmed ring, moved into the light, then came a frilly lace cuff, *spilling from a silhouetted sleeve. Her breath caught. She hesitated, then lifted her eyes to the ruffled white shirt ashine in the dazzle of candlelight.*

He stepped into full view. His black attire molded alluringly to his magnificent physique.

She peered up into his face.

He smiled, a generous . . . vain smile?

She squeezed her eyes shut and looked again. It wasn't her Viking. It was Kyle! She was here with Kyle. Alone on a ship in the middle of the ocean. And the gown—this sheer bit of nothing—was from him.

"Diana." His voice rushed over her. "You've become my Diana. My wild goddess of the forest. My tigress for the hunt. With you I'll rule the heavens and the earth."

Caught in a vortex of shame and bewilderment, she stepped back, out of the revealing illumination. With hesitation, she returned the rapier stare of the raven-haired stalker. "Where are you taking me?"

Eyes bluer than the deepest sea narrowed slightly. "What a strange question. To the governor's annulment barn dance, of course."

"Oh. Yes. I recall." How could she have forgotten? Feeling foolish, she lowered her gaze, then noticed the gown again. "I couldn't possibly wear this to the dance."

He strode around the table with his usual lordly grace, looking supremely handsome. And considering her own exceptionally exotic appearance tonight, they really should be a perfect match. He took her hands in his, while his gaze lapped downward. "The gown was meant to enchant me alone." Releasing her, his fingers grazed up her arms.

She tried to conjure a future with him, but icy slivers of panic raced ahead of his gliding touch. Then remembering his promise, she stiffened. "Where's the chaperone?"

"Chaperone? Darling girl, there's no need. We're alone on our own sailing Eden. Adam and Eve." His teeth sparkled in the fickle light as his lips spread in a slow grin. "And I have some very special fruit I'd like to share with

you. But first—'' Turning to the table, he picked up a tall, tapered bottle. ''Refreshment for my lady.''

A drink? *Absolutely not! Not after the last time. She moved away, toward the railing. ''Thank you. But I couldn't possibly. I don't drink.'' Any more.*

The cork popped out of the bottle.

At the sound, she turned and watched the bubbles fizz forth as Kyle poured champagne into the stemware.

Glasses filled, he looked up at her with half-closed eyes, his head tilted, his mouth curved into a one-sided grin. ''From what I hear, you can be most enchanting after a few drinks.''

Merciful heavens! He knows! The blood drained from her face. She reached for the railing to steady herself and looked out across the moon-dusted sea. The desire to jump overboard and put an end to this unbearable humiliation overwhelmed her.

''My dear,'' Kyle said.

She heard him step up behind her.

''You shouldn't be upset that I know. It only makes me want you more.'' His breath washed over her neck.

The spot turned to ice. The frost spread to her arms, down her back, all the way to her feet. She froze solid, unable to move, unable to resist.

A hand moved over her shoulder and slid beneath the flimsy fabric and cupped a breast.

Heart thundering, she tried to open her mouth to scream, but no sound emerged.

He pulled her to him and slipped the strap from her shoulder.

Desperately she tried to lift her arms to save the gown, but it slid down her body as if she were marble. Only her panting told her she was alive.

''You're so beautiful,'' he whispered. His tongue traced her ear while both hands roamed at will. ''You're so—'' Suddenly, he pushed her to the side. ''What the hell is that?'' *He peered into the inky night.*

She darted a look across the water. And there, sails filled

*with a great wind spawned from the bellows of hell, came
the roaring, fire-spewing dragon ship. Haloed in its red
glow, it came straight toward them.*

Then she saw him.

*Leaning forward in a fierce stance, her Viking stood on
the prow-neck of the beast. Firelight reflected off every
tensed muscle of his brawny body; he held a thick-bladed
lance in one hand.*

Her heart leapt out to him, and her arms followed.

*His eyes found hers. But, to her horror, they were filled
with malice.*

*Then she realized. She was standing beside his sworn
enemy. Naked. She reached down to swoop up the gown, but
a wind caught it, and it skittered along the deck. Heaven
help her. She snatched at it, but it soared over the rail and
up into the sky like a black-winged flag, signaling her
degradation.*

*The Viking, riding his fire-mouthed dragon, sliced through
the water toward them at unbelievable speed. She had to
think fast. How could she explain her presence on Kyle's
ship? She didn't know herself how she'd gotten there. How
could she hope to convince him of her loyalty?*

At her side, Kyle chuckled.

*Her gaze swung to his face, which was illumined by the
nearing vessel. His eyes shone with pleasure and . . .
sublime confidence?*

*His gaze drifted languidly to her. "Forgive the interrup-
tion, pet. I'll be but a moment. This fool barbarian thinks
he's a match for me." He walked to the table and plucked
a candle from the stand.*

*She watched in numb fascination as he strode toward the
stern . . . and lit the wick of a port-side cannon.*

*"No!" She bolted forward, trying to reach the big gun
before it fired.*

*Too late. A deafening explosion stopped her. Chest
heaving, she watched the dragon ship's main mast topple in
a swirl of smoke and flame into the sea.*

She swung her attention back to Kyle to find him setting another fuse ablaze, then another.

A second cannon ball splintered the hull near the bow.

Her gaze swung to her Viking. Still balanced on the monster, he looked down at the water rushing into the gaping hole.

The last thunderous combustion followed within seconds, sending its missile of destruction into the dragon's mouth. A tremendous explosion shot starbursts into the night sky, sending a rain of fire down to devour the sinking remains.

The air, the ship, the sea—all seemed consumed in flames.

Her Viking. Where was her lover? She raced along the length of the rail, looking, searching the watery grave. Eyes straining, she still saw nothing. She must have missed him. She rushed back . . . and slammed into Kyle.

He wrapped his arms around her, trapping her nakedness against him. "It's all right, my sweet beauty. I've saved you from the savage."

She pounded her fists against his chest. "You've killed him!" Her wail echoed over and over, bouncing across the waves as she shoved at him and fought to free herself.

He threw back his head and laughed at her impotent struggling. She was his toy, his helpless plaything.

She'd rather die. He'd murdered her lover.

Without warning, he thrust her from him. She staggered but regained her balance as he drew a small silver pistol from his coat.

In a panic, she jumped back and threw up her hands to block the bullet. After a silent moment, she peered around and found that the weapon was not aimed at her, but at the water. She ran to the side.

Just below her, the Viking surfaced in a powerful thrust. Meeting her vast relief with a menacing challenge, he grappled a rope ladder and began to climb.

Blood spurted from his forehead even before she heard the shot. She saw the stunned look on his face.

His hands reached for her, but clutched only air.

She stretched forward, trying to catch him, to save him.
Their fingers touched but for one electric second before
he sank away, slowly, agonizingly. The water swallowed
him. Took him down, deep, into a bottomless, pitiless hell.
She slashed at the cruel silence in anguish. "Jake."

Rachel bolted up in bed. Her gaze darted wildly about.
Seeing the shadowed figure of Dinah asleep in the bed next
to her, she leaned back against the headboard and exhaled
hard against the racing beats of her heart. It had only been
a dream. A horrible, horrible nightmare. One that could
never really happen. Or could it?

❲ chapter 20 ❳

GOVERNOR Gaines had not been pleased to see Jake in person, and Jake left his office feeling strangled by the reprimands of a reasoning man. But with Captain Ainsworth out of town, Jake'd had no choice. Then the governor refused to make a move until solid evidence pointed directly to McLean himself. Everything proper and legal.

"Bad business, being too precipitous," Gaines had said. "When one is after the head, cutting off a couple of fingers would not suffice, it would only warn off the leaders."

Yes, but Gaines would be surprised how the twisting of a couple of those fingers could point them right to the head.

But, no. "Keep your eyes and ears open," the governor had ordered. "Watch every move the culprits make. In the meantime, Mr. Best's records are quietly being examined."

Walking down the steps of the capitol building, Jake caught Best watching him before the man abruptly walked inside. Odd coincidence. Shaking it off, Jake walked down toward the wharf. As he passed Pillow and Drew's jewelry shop, a display of ladies' rings caught his attention. He stopped and looked in the window. Gems of every color stared back at him. One gleamed with a translucent blue almost the color of Rachel's eyes. Another, a square-cut stone, captured the same brilliance as her molten hair in the firelight. And the pearls, smooth and creamy, reminded him of her skin. Maybe if he bought her a ring, she'd see how much he cared. Wanted her. Just her.

He reached in his pocket and pulled out forty-three dollars in coins and twenty in bank notes. If he spent it, he'd have to do some lumberjacking for a while. But if it made Rachel forget about Goldy, it'd be worth it.

"Well, I be adrift in a fog. That you, Jake?" The jaunty but thin voice had a Cajun cadence.

Swinging around, he recognized the good-natured Pacquing kid. She looked very much the boy, as usual, with her hair tucked up in her hat, and her sloppy shirt and dungarees hiding any hint of a female curve on the leggy girl. "Georgie. It's been a while. See you haven't drowned yet. Still shooting the rapids up at The Dalles?"

Those spicy Cajun eyes sparkled with her laughter. "Yeah. And it doesn't look like a log's rolled over you, either. Except, maybe, your beard. Hardly recognized you. You turned into one fine looker. Think I marry you myself."

"Sorry. I'm already taken."

"For sure? When?"

"In April."

"So that's why you be looking at ladies' rings."

"Yeah. Thought I'd surprise her. And, you know, if you'd start dressing like a girl, there'd be a peck of fellas lined up at your door with a ring or two."

"Eh? They have to catch my boat first. Besides," she said as she swiped a coppery wisp from her smoothly tanned forehead, "how do you know what I look like in a dress?"

"You forget. I saw you and your pa last year at Trader Clerou's burying."

"And, saints preserve us, the trouble that's caused me ever since. That Mrs. Kleinsasser saw me. And now every time we dock in Portland she and her gossipy friends start pestering Papa about turning me into some sissified girl." She pulled her floppy, misshapen hat farther down, almost concealing the dramatic flare of her brows. "They almost drive him to drink again."

"How is ol' Louie doing?"

"Fine, the best." She grinned wide with that bold, expressive Paquing mouth. "In fact, even Cadie begins to believe Papa's finally able to stand on his own again. My other brother, Jocko, has a pilot's job waiting for Cadie back on the Mississippi, and he plans to leave soon as we get back to the *Dream Ellen*."

"Where are you and Louie going?"

"Up your way. You seen the new *Willamette* that's just been launched on your river? Papa and me, we go to pilot it for the next month or so for one of his friends."

"That's a pretty fancy boat. It's even got a salon."

"*Oui.* I know. Let's just hope word doesn't get out."

That was an odd thing for the girl to say. Jake peered down into large lustrous eyes only slightly darker than her copper hair.

She must have noticed his puzzlement. The serious expression on her face transformed into a churlish smile. "Riverboat gamblers. Always looking for some new sheep to shear. And Papa . . ." She shook her head. "You know what he's like after a few drinks."

"Well, you don't have anything to worry about. Nothing but homesteaders and lumberjacks up our way. Unless a few show up for the Fourth of July. I'm racing my black Thoroughbred against one Kyle McLean imported. We plan to make a real hoopla out of it. Be sure and lay over then."

"You promise Prince wins, I'll be there with bells on."

"And in a dress?" Joshing, Jake grabbed the droopy brim of her hat as if to jerk it off.

She ducked out of reach. "Hey, if it takes that to see McLean get his comeuppance—at least once—I'll dress up fit for a cotillion. He ruins the river with his damn steam saws."

Jake's teasing grin faded. "What do you mean?"

"The noise," she said with an exasperated roll of her wide eyes. "You can hear that high whine for miles. Enough to drive a saint to sin. I think it's the reason people are pulling out below the gorge."

"Is that what they said?"

"No. They say they leave 'cause of bad luck with their animals and fire and such. But everyone has bad luck now and again. I say it's the noise." Grabbing his arm, she skipped up on her toes. "Hey. Let's quit this talk and go in and find your bride something real pretty."

Jake chuckled as he allowed her to drag him into the shop filled with glass cases. "You know about jewelry?"

"Sure. Before my mama died, she packed me off to a fancy finishing school for a couple of terms. I can set a table and curtsy with the best of 'em."

The array of rings astounded Jake. He didn't know how he would choose, even with Georgie's help. But when he told Mr. Drew, a white-haired man with a perpetually sad smile, how much he had to spend, the selection shrank to a few.

Georgie modeled them on tanned but still gracefully tapered fingers. The rings were all pretty, but none had the spirit and sparkle of his Rachel.

"All I can say, Jake," Georgie said, after he'd asked her to try on the blue sapphire for the third time, "is I want to meet this wife of yours. She must be some lady to make you go on like this. But for pity's sake, pick one of the blamed things."

"Oh, I guess the one you have on. It's as close to the color of her eyes as I'm going to get."

"Good. Done." She yanked it off and slapped it into Mr. Drew's hand. "Wrap it, please. Before he changes his mind again."

"It's just"—Jake hesitated, savoring the picture of Rachel—"her eyes are deep blue near the center, then toward the edge they feather to icy silver."

Georgie shoved her hands in her pockets. "You sound like some old lovesick moose." She twisted around, looking as if she'd just sucked on a lemon.

Jake smashed in her rumpled hat even further. "You'll grow up someday and fall in love. Then you'll understand."

She squirreled out from under him. "Whatdaya mean, grow up? I'll be eighteen in four months." Her gaze drifted out the window. "Well, like I said, I can't wait to meet her. And from the way Mr. Best is gawking in at you, I'd say you had an admirer of your own."

Jake swung around and, for the second time today, caught the man staring at him from across the street, A body would've thought Jake had his Hawken pointed at Best, the way the land recorder spun away, then veered toward the Oregon House . . . McLean's headquarters when he was in town.

Rachel grew to hate the slow, incessant ticking of the mantel clock, but even more its night chimings. She often heard the unerring bongs at eleven or twelve, and worse, on occasion, she'd still be awake after it struck one or even two. Fortunately, Dinah slept heavily, or the turnings of Rachel's restless, yearning body would've disturbed her. One hope—or was it a desire for retribution?—was that Jake suffered at least a fraction of what she did. But logic told her he didn't, couldn't, or he would've come for her.

The terrible dream she'd endured the night after the fiasco at the Jenningses' had been relegated to another of her foolish imaginings, until the afternoon when she'd been called to doctor a mill worker. The man had been stabbed by a splintered log. All the while she'd stitched and dressed his wound, she'd felt the strangle of one of Kyle McLean's far-reaching tentacles.

Later, as she watched the slow track of the moon crossing another midnight sky, she struggled with hard questions. Was Kyle the ambitious yet generous gentleman he seemed to be when with her, or the devious villain Jake saw?

Each dawn was a blessed relief. She could fill her daylight hours with housekeeping chores and the making of her new dress. Especially the dress. Although she tried to discipline her thoughts, to keep them free of Jake, every fitting was taken, every stitch was sewn, with his pleasure in mind. And no matter what she'd told Edna *and herself* about making a good impression on the community, she could not deny the truth. She'd frivolously used some of her best lace to trim the rather daringly cut bodice of the cotton frock just on the chance of seeing that certain light come into his eyes.

That niggling hope that Jake would come, boots all

polished, a bouquet of flowers in hand, to ask her to the barn raising, would not be doused even by the fact that Kyle McLean had made known his intention to escort her . . . that is, until Mrs. Simpkins's arrival with an infected toe.

The chipmunk-cheeked woman couldn't wait to tell Rachel that she and her husband had called on the Jennings family, to discover that Jake had left his animals with them and gone away. The news squelched all her foolish school-girl hopes. And worse, Rachel just knew the stupid swollen toe was merely the busybody's excuse to keep the gossip pot stirring.

To add insult to injury, that same afternoon while she and Edna stood peeling potatoes at the bright yellow kitchen table, Dinah dropped off a note from Harvey stating he'd heard about the barn raising and would make it a point to be back in time to escort her . . . and with a delightful surprise.

Edna, vastly more thrilled than she, forgot her manners, ripped the missive from Rachel, and read it. After a quick scan, her face grew red, and she sheepishly handed it back. But a motherly smile persisted. "Forgive me, but I just had to be sure. Thank goodness, he's forgiven your rude behavior that day after church." She flung her arms around Rachel and gave her a big hug.

Rachel stiffened and stepped out of the embrace. "Harvey may have forgiven me, but I haven't done likewise."

Edna's dark eyes sharpened. "Whatever could you have to forgive?"

Rachel moved back to the work table and began hacking at another potato. "This isn't the first word I've had from him since he left town."

Edna idly picked up her own paring knife. "You never mentioned another letter."

"I was so blasted furious at the time, if I'd said anything, there's no telling what blasphemy would've come out of my mouth. That man," she said as she viciously gouged out a rotten spot, "had the audacity to send me an essay on the correct and acceptable place of a woman."

Laughter burst forth as Edna nodded knowingly. "Was it the one printed in the *Oregonian* last month?"

"I don't know. I suppose."

"Mattie Baker showed it to me. We got the biggest laugh out of it."

Rachel shot a disbelieving glance her way. "You thought it humorous to say a woman's place is to worship her man? Why, it's almost sacrilegious. And then to read that anything a woman does on her own is foolish, vain, and destructive? If Harvey had been within reach, I would've gladly wrung his scrawny neck like a Sunday chicken."

Edna placed a quieting hand over hers. "Or slice him up like what used to be Wednesday's potatoes?"

Rachel looked down and saw the mangled remains of her work. "Oh, dear, I really butchered them, didn't I?"

"Sit down." Still grinning, Edna pushed Rachel into a chair and took her own. "Mattie and I were laughing at what a fine job the author's wife had done convincing him that he was the holy prince of his realm. That woman must have him so hornswoggled she does exactly what she wants *and* . . ." Edna raised a perky brow. "Sees that he does, too."

"That's all well and good. But to have someone I barely know send it to me in the mail—"

Edna patted Rachel's hand as if the younger woman were a hopelessly ignorant child. "My dear, it only proves what I've said all along. Mr. Best is very interested in you. And when he comes, I want you to be on your best behavior." She shrugged happily. "I wonder what the surprise is."

Rachel couldn't hide the agitation in her tone. "Annulment papers for me to sign, no doubt."

"Wake up! Wake up!"

Rachel's eyes opened with a start. She glanced about until she found Dinah standing at their bedroom window in the rosy glow cast by the pink ruffled curtains.

"Come quick, before it's gone! A rainbow!" In her

lavender nightgown, with her russet hair catching the early light, young Dinah was a match for any mere rainbow.

Still sleepy, Rachel groaned her objection before throwing off the colorful quilt. Joining the exuberant girl, she looked out and witnessed one of God's most thrilling creations—a shimmering arc that just kissed the tips of the distant trees. Even the firs seemed to strut as they sparkled from a recent rain. A truly magical sight.

"See!" Dinah's shrill pitch stabbed into Rachel's ears. "Isn't it just the prettiest one you ever saw?" She clutched Rachel's waist and hugged her tight. "It's a sign. I'm going to meet the handsomest boy in the whole world today. And we're going to dance and dance. . . ."

Catching the joy of Dinah's enthusiasm, Rachel smiled and returned the girl's embrace. "You're right. It's a perfect day for a barn raising. Nothing would dare go awry on such a gorgeous day!" After all, she told herself for the hundredth time since she'd received Harvey's note, what could be so terrible about *both* Kyle and Harvey coming to escort her? They were gentlemen. She could handle it.

Nothing could go wrong? Fudge and fiddlesticks. Ticks and toads. Rachel paced the blue and gray length of the hooked parlor rug. Three hours earlier, the Grills family had left for the festivities. And here she waited in yards and yards of peach blossoms floating on creamy beige and scads of expensive ruffles framing the swell of her bosom. And for what? Neither of her "gentlemen" had shown up. She'd even spent an hour arranging her curls and the coral bows.

She placed cooling hands to her cheeks and walked to the kitchen to put on the kettle. She needed a soothing cup of tea. While stoking up the fire in the cook stove, she heard a loud knocking. Joy and anger rallied for supremacy as she leaned the poker against the wall. Wondering which one had *finally* arrived, she walked to the front of the house and opened the door . . . to an out-of-breath Harvey with his hat in fidgety fingers.

"Thank providence, you're still here," he gushed. "I'm

dreadfully sorry to be late. I had every intention of arriving early. The *Willamette* was supposed to depart from Salem by eight this morning, and it's only about fifteen miles. But they couldn't find the captain. That pretty-faced boy of his looked all over town for him. Then, when Captain Pacquing finally did show up, *an hour and a half late* and looking like he'd been on a drunken spree, something was wrong with the damned engine.'' Harvey's eyes widened, and he gasped. "Oh, forgive my language. It's just that it's been such a bad start to what I hoped would be a most marvelous day. Please forgive me."

How could she stay angry at someone so desperate to please her . . . even if he did send that despicable article? "Of course, Harvey. I understand. But I'm surprised I didn't hear the whistle when the ship arrived."

"It never did! I finally took it upon myself to drive here as fast as I could." He turned and pointed to a stylish but sweat-dampened bay mare. Hitched behind the animal stood a surprisingly splendid two-passenger buggy with bright red spokes and a lustrous black leather bonnet virtually dripping with fringe. "See?"

She stepped out the door. "My, you certainly look the part of the prosperous banker in that fancy rig. And isn't that horse a hackney? Docked tail and all?"

"So, you approve of the buggy," he said with a rather conceited smile. "It's yours."

"Don't be silly."

"I'm serious. It's merely my pleasure to deliver it."

She looked at the rig, then back at him. "You're being ridiculous."

He spread his arm wide. "No, really. In foul weather or fair, you can now come and go as you please."

"But where did it come from? And what's the price?"

"You needn't worry your pretty little head about that."

How she hated that tiresome phrase. She gave him her weariest frown.

"Really," he insisted, taking her hand.

She pulled free. "Surely you don't expect me to accept such an expensive gift from you."

"Well, uh, it's not from me, exactly."

Was it Jake? her mind flashed. Of course not, you foolish ninny. "Then who?"

"The townfolk plan to pitch in and reimburse Mr. McLean when they sell their cash crops in the fall."

"McLean?" her voice grated in her outrage. "This is too much. Won't you people ever stop meddling in my life?"

Harvey snapped soldier erect, and his voice rang with a stern reprimand. "Where *is* that lovely young lady I'd come to admire so?"

Mollified, Rachel sighed, then managed a smile. "Forgive my lack of manners. But concerning the gift, I need time to think about it. For now, let me get my things, and we'll be on our way."

When she returned, Harvey drove them past the church to the first crossroad and turned south.

"How far is it?" she asked, making polite conversation.

"Only a mile or so." He turned and grinned. "Not nearly far enough since I haven't seen you in two weeks."

And I feel the distance stretching, Rachel thought as she arranged her skirts. "I do hope Orletta Colfax will be there," she said in a deliberate change of subject. "I sent her a note, urging her to come. And Edna has agreed to befriend her and introduce her to some of the other ladies."

Harvey's smile became brittle. "You really shouldn't bother with her and the rest of that Colfax bunch. They're so . . . uncultured."

"But she's my friend."

"My dear, if we're going to have any hope of clearing the taint from your reputation, you must dispense with these unsuitable associations."

"I'm sorry you feel that way. But I couldn't possibly. Orletta was an unwavering friend to me when I desperately needed one. I won't turn my back on her when she needs me."

"You're entirely too altruistic for your own good. But I

love you for it anyway.'' Shifting the reins to one hand, he took hers and squeezed it as his eyes flitted between her face and décolletage. ''And have I told you how breathtakingly beautiful you look in that dress?''

''Thank you,'' she murmured as she slipped her hand from his. She suddenly felt far too underclothed. But, then, the low-cut bodice hadn't been designed for his eyes.

As if reading her thoughts, Harvey moved his gaze from her to the road ahead and asked in a constrained voice, ''By chance, I saw Jacob Stone in Oregon City last week. Have you heard anything of him since that time?''

The thought of discussing Jake with Harvey caused her chest to tighten. Why did he have to bring up the subject today of all days? ''No,'' she said with as little emotion as possible, hoping her casual response would satisfy him.

It must have. He remained oddly silent thereafter.

The staccato of tapping hammers reached Rachel's ears a half-mile before she and Harvey rolled into the clearing. It was near noon, and Ben Stockton's barn raising was well under way. Men crawled along the upper beams of the giant framework, much like ants on a skeleton. They worked together with great speed, nailing boards to cover its nakedness before nightfall.

The pungent smell of fresh-cut wood floated on the air, mingling with the aroma of the many casseroles lining two makeshift tables. The women were busy removing lids and adding serving spoons, filling glasses and cups, and slicing meat and bread in preparation for the noon meal.

Rachel felt a squiggle of uneasiness, arriving at a second gathering escorted by Harvey. But of course, he didn't mind a bit. While he walked—no—strutted around to help her down, Rachel's eyes searched among the women until she found Orletta. Her friend seemed quite at home, pouring coffee into tin cups. Then Rachel noticed tiny Edna on the other side of the table filling glasses from a pitcher of lemonade.

Edna saw Rachel and waved, then said something to Orletta, who looked up with a quirky grin.

Rachel returned their greetings, warmed more by the knowledge that Edna had honored her word to set her prejudices aside, than by the friendly welcome.

Rachel's arrival with Harvey also caused a stir among the other women. The abundantly endowed Mattie Baker wagged a wooden spoon.

"Rachel, give me your hand."

She'd momentarily forgotten about Harvey. With outstretched arms, he waited to help her from the small carriage. Unlike the other men, who were dressed in work clothes, he wore his usual gray business suit.

"Thank you, Harvey," she said with a perfunctory smile.

After assisting her down, he wrapped her arm within his and led her toward rows of dining tables and benches made of boards laid across barrels and kegs.

Edna intercepted them. "You finally got here. I was just about to send Peter home for you. We're just about to call the men in for dinner."

Mattie, along with a couple of the women Rachel had met at church, came forward. "Rachel, dear, I'm so glad you made it in time for noonin'. You, too, Mr. Best." A full smile caused the corners of her big blue eyes to crinkle. Then they widened as she peered past Harvey. "That sure is a fine-looking horse and buggy, Mr. Best."

"I—uh. Actually, it's Rachel's."

"Rachel's?" Mattie raised her brows and turned to Edna, who returned her questioning stare.

"Mattie, you haven't introduced us," said a tired-looking dishwater blonde standing beside her.

"Oh, yeah. Mrs. Stone—Mrs. Loomis. Geneva, here, is the mother of Dinah's friends, Chloe and Mardell."

"And three others," she said with a dubious chuckle.

"How nice to meet you." Rachel extended her hand.

"Mr. Best," Mattie said, "would you mind goin' over and hollerin' up the men? It's time to eat."

"Of course, Mrs. Baker." He removed Rachel's trapped hand from his arm and turned to her. "I'll be back in just a minute. Save a place at the table for me."

After he'd gone, Mattie spoke again, this time in an intense whisper. "Now, Rachel, tell us about that horse and buggy." She and the others crowded closer.

"I don't know what to say. You probably know more about it than I do."

Nothing but puzzled expressions answered her.

Edna's gaze suddenly veered past Rachel. "Come on, girls. The men are coming. We'd better get back to work."

Rachel had hoped to eat with the Colfaxes or the Grills family, but Harvey had steered her to a table where Kyle's flame-haired sawmill partner sat with Hannah Thornton and a droopy-jowled man with a potbelly.

Coke Lyons stood and tipped his hat. "It'd be a pleasure to share our table with such a fine lady."

"Howdy," drawled the other man, bumping his protruding stomach against an unnailed table plank as he rose. Liquid slopped from the glasses before Hannah could resettle the board. "The name's Roy Thornton. I run the hotel. Believe you already met my wife." He turned slightly and extended a hand toward the work-worn woman.

With a nod, Mrs. Thornton returned Rachel's smile.

Along with the others, Rachel filled her plate from the bounty on the table, and had raised her fork to her mouth with a first bite of pork roast when Mrs. Simpkins, three tables down, clanged the inside of a triangle with a rod.

"Sublette will be sayin' grace now," she said, and the clatter of forks dropping on plates resounded down the line.

Her husband stood, and everyone bowed their heads. "Almighty God, we've gathered here today in Christian love and charity to build a barn for young Ben and his new wife. We ask that you bless our undertaking. We also ask that you remember the Jennings family in their time of need. Thank you for the gracious generosity of folks sharing out of their abundance with this poor blighted family. They have been restored far more than they ever dreamed. Bless this food that it might give us the strength to complete this work today. In the name of Jesus Christ. Amen."

Before Brother Simpkins dropped to his seat, the sounds

of congenial chatter and the clinking of utensils again filled the air.

Grateful tears rimmed Rachel's eyes as she pictured folks riding out to the Jenningses' with their gifts before they'd even been asked. She looked through a blur at the dear people who had not only saved that family but were providing her with a house and a horse and buggy. Brushing the wetness from her eyes, she noticed the handlebars of Mr. Lyons's flamboyant mustache seesaw as he chewed.

He caught her staring and grinned unabashedly. "You know," he said, putting his fork down. "That day we rode out to your place, we thought we was going out there on a mission of mercy. A lady of your fine breeding and all. We thought you'd jump at the chance to get back to civilization."

"I see." Rachel trapped his deep-set blue eyes within her steady gaze. "You think a lady of breeding is exempt from her marriage vows if her surroundings seem unsuitable?"

The others at the table turned to him.

Lyons's face flushed, rivaling the color of his hair. "Guess we jumped the gun a might. It's just, we didn't want someone with your doctorin' skills goin' to waste out in the wilderness. We just didn't think."

Rachel arched a brow. "No, you certainly did not. But I've chosen to put that unpleasantness behind me. Shall we make a pact to never speak of it again?" For the first time, she favored him with a slight smile.

Under the table, Harvey reached over and patted Rachel's hand. She wasn't sure if the gesture was one of congratulation or reprimand. After all, Mr. Lyons would be important to Harvey's success as a banker.

"Mr. McLean said he was having some shipping problems on the Columbia," Harvey said, changing the subject.

With the conversation redirected to business, Rachel finished her dinner in peace. While enjoying the feast, she looked down the tables and saw the Colfax boys scattered here and there. Harland sat next to Dinah Grills, who looked like a young bud ready to be plucked in pink and lavender.

Rachel then spotted Amos absorbed in a heated conversation with Carson Grills and another man. Her gaze roved the other tables until she found Sarah Beth, looking totally angelic in baby blue gauze. Her flaxen hair, falling in ringlets on either side of her delicately rounded cheeks, added to her look of sublime innocence.

On one side of Sarah Beth sat a man whose square face and solid build reminded Rachel of an older Robby Stockton. That must be Ben, she thought. He seemed enthralled by her every coquettish gesture. But Mabel Stockton, to the right, glowered so, her look alone would sour milk.

Rachel turned and peered at the nearby completed wood-framed house located on a small rise to the west, upwind of the barnyard smells. She had no doubt Sarah Beth could hardly wait to get into her own home and out from under her mother-in-law's nose.

After lunch the men and half-grown boys jumped up and went back to work. Harvey removed his coat and cravat, rolled up his sleeves, and joined them. With a doubtful scowl, Ben Stockton gave him a hammer and a sack of nails and assigned him the task of nailing siding to the bottom level. Rachel couldn't help smiling as Harvey ineptly began to pound, missing the nail head more often than not. She doubted if he'd ever held a hammer in his hand before. But even after banging his thumb, he never lost his good humor, and the other men began to treat him like one of them. Even Carson Grills joked with him.

After cleaning up the dinner mess, the women set up a quilting frame to stitch a quilt with the Double Wedding Ring pattern they had finished piecing together that morning. It would symbolize the beginning of Ben and Sarah Beth's life together in their new home. As they worked, the women chatted easily, including Rachel and Orletta. She would've felt more comfortable, though, had the absence of Jake's and Harvey's names not been so evident.

Half an hour before the sun slipped behind the forested coast hills, the last nail was driven into the last board. Looming like a great winged bird, the completed barn cast a giant shadow across the meadow. The men weary, their skin itching from sweat and sawdust, trudged down to the stream to wash up and put on clean shirts while the women hurried to set the tables with food and dishes.

The men returned from the creek with a spring in their steps, revived by the frigid water and the knowledge that after supper they would initiate the barn with a boot-tapping, skirt-swirling, frolicsome dance. Heading for the tables, they laughed and joshed and jostled one another.

Harvey, his hair parted and slicked back and his cravat neatly retied, made a beeline for Rachel. A wide grin reached up to his eager eyes. "Have you got my supper ready, woman? I'm so hungry, I could eat a horse."

His earthy choice of phrase amused Rachel, and she laughed. "Come this way, kind sir. I have your place set." Then the insinuation that she was his woman hit, rankling her. She opened her mouth to retort, but Amos stepped up, looking almost silly in a bowler hat.

"Well, missy," he said, one arm outstretched while the other swayed as if he were playing a violin. "You set to do-si-do around the room with all the young bucks?"

"I sure am," she said, her own enthusiasm mounting as the time drew nearer.

"You will favor us with a song or two, won't you?"

"What? Oh, no. I couldn't."

"Sure you can," he said with a straight face. Then before she could repeat her refusal, he asked, "Have you heard from Jake? He was supposed to be back days ago."

"No, I haven't." A sudden uneasiness reminded her of her most recent nightmare.

"Queer." He tipped his hat, then after a quick glance at Harvey, he whirled and jigged away toward his wife.

Harvey literally blanched as his eyes followed Amos's jaunty retreat. After a number of seconds, he turned back to Rachel. "Surely you're not getting up on the stage with those coarse fellows."

"No, Harvey," she said, noting the return of his snootiness. "That is not my intention."

Something caught his attention. His gaze cut away and riveted to a spot behind her.

She swung around to see Kyle McLean ride in on his magnificent gray stallion.

"Come along," Harvey said. "We'd better go sit down."

From her seat at the table, Rachel had a clear view of Mr. McLean as he dismounted and strode to where the Stockton family sat. As always, she was impressed by the stylish cut of his suit, and more, its perfect fit.

"Rachel, pass me the bread," Harvey said, with a rough edge to his voice.

She lowered her gaze to Harvey seated across from her, his back to Kyle. He'd lost all track of his former good humor. And not even a "please," she thought as she picked up the basket and handed it to him. His impeccable manners were decidedly beginning to slip.

Then he took it from her without a "thank you" as he turned and glanced at Mr. McLean.

Methinks, Rachel mused, my friend is jealous. A far more dashing, far more successful gentleman has arrived.

But where's Jake?

((chapter 21))

BEN Stockton's father clanged on the iron triangle for silence. When all the diners turned to listen, he stepped next to Kyle McLean, who stood beside Ben and Sarah Beth.

"I thought you folks'd like to know," the older man said. "Mr. McLean, here, just gave my boy and his new wife *one hundred dollars*. A stake to help 'em get started in their new place. Now, that deserves a big applause."

Already in a merry mood, everyone clapped with enthusiasm—except Harvey, Rachel noticed, and Amos, who sat with his family at the next table. She knew why Harvey wasn't thrilled, but the scowl on Amos's face puzzled her. She could not conceive that a man with Colfax's fun-loving temperament held petty grudges. But then, she hadn't thought Jake would, either.

As the applause subsided, Ben hugged Sarah Beth to him. "I want to thank Mr. McLean, too. It's goin' to come in right handy for me and the little missus, here."

Sarah Beth's face was radiant as she smiled up at their benefactor. "Oh, yes, Mr. McLean. And I want you to come back out here again, just as soon as we're settled. I want to personally show my appreciation." Her last words came out distinctly. She paused before adding more quickly, "By fixing you a real home-cooked meal."

The smile on Kyle's face went slack, then his dimples emerged again as he studied her. "I'll be sure to take you up on that." He stared another second, then swung his attention to Ben. "I'm real partial to home-cooked food."

Kyle's gaze then found Rachel. He nodded a greeting.

She returned it, then quickly averted her eyes, embarrassed at being caught staring.

She swiveled back around to find Harvey glaring at her.

Rachel refused to be intimidated. "I see I'm not the only one receiving the reward of Mr. McLean's generosity," she quipped. "It would appear that he's a very public-spirited man. Don't you agree, Harvey?"

He looked from her to Kyle and back again. His attempt at a smile looked more like a grimace. "So it would seem."

Leaving the Stocktons behind, Kyle started straight for Rachel, eyeing her with those dark blue eyes framed by that thicket of black lashes.

Harvey pretended not to notice him until Rachel said, "Good evening, Mr. McLean."

Unsmiling, Harvey leaned around. "Kyle. Glad you could make it."

"Yes, me too." Kyle's gaze still remained on Rachel. "Good evening, my lady. I was detained by urgent matters." He turned toward Harvey, his eyes following after a moment. "I'd like to speak to you in the morning about that business we discussed last week in Oregon City. My office at nine."

The color again drained from Harvey's face. Just the thought of meeting with Kyle seemed to distress him. "Fine. I'll see you then." Harvey picked up his fork, and his hand trembled noticeably.

In contrast, McLean looked relaxed as he continued to stand behind the unnerved man. "Good evening, Hannah," he said, two manicured fingers touching his black felt hat in an abbreviated gesture. "Roy, Coke."

"Have a seat," Mr. Lyons said, motioning to an empty spot across the table. "Plenty of room next to Mrs. Stone."

"Why, thanks. I could use a bit of refreshment." He walked around to the other side as Rachel scooted closer to Hannah to make more space. He stepped over the bench and eased himself down, while removing and placing his hat beside him. Running fingers through the abundance of his jet-black hair, he combed back any mussed strands.

Hannah rose. "I'll go get you a plate, Mr. McLean. Do you want lemonade or coffee?"

"I'd love a glass of lemonade."

The charm of his sparkling grin was wasted on the older woman. Without returning his smile, she walked away.

"It's fortunate that you sat here," Rachel began, turning in Kyle's direction.

"I couldn't agree more. I'm seated next to the loveliest lady in the territory."

Out of the corner of her eye, Rachel saw a vein bulge at Harvey's temple. "What a charming thing to say. But I was speaking of a need to discuss the matter of the buggy."

Lines creased Kyle's brow. "Why? Is there something wrong with it?"

"No, absolutely not. It's really quite perfect. And the mare is elegant. And I thank you for all your trouble, but I can't possibly accept such an extravagant gift."

Kyle looked at Harvey, then back to her. "Didn't Best explain? It was purchased so you would be able to traverse the roads, even in bad weather."

"I explained that," Harvey said, his indignation evident.

"That's not the point," Rachel said. "Surely you know how improper it would be for me to accept it. Especially since—"

"Do you think anyone's going to care how you came by it when they're in need? They'll just want you to come. Fast."

"He's right, ma'am," Mr. Thornton said. "You need it."

"I'm not denying that," she said.

Before she could continue, Pearly Simpkins stood and announced it was time to say grace.

It was probably for the best, Rachel decided. She'd find a moment alone with him. It would be much easier to come to an agreement when he was by himself. One that would let her keep both the buggy *and* her good name.

By the time dinner was over, Rachel was sure Kyle had been to Ireland and kissed the Blarney Stone. He'd spent the entire time expounding on the glorious future of Oregon and how it paled in the glory of her presence. She couldn't help but enjoy the flattery. Mr. Thornton and Mr. Lyons also appeared amused, but not Hannah. Her face was almost as sullen as Harvey's, her expression causing Rachel to recall the one that had clouded Amos's face earlier.

"You must join me on a trip up the mighty Columbia—"

Interrupting Kyle's invitation, Pearly Simpkins stood. "Women, it's time to clear the tables. And you men start totin' them benches into the barn."

No one waited to be told twice. They all scrambled up and started to work in an excited rush.

"Rachel," Orletta called from several yards away. She looked almost matronly in blue and gray striped gingham. Almost. "Could you come help me a minute?"

"Of course." Rachel threaded her way through the other women, who bustled back and forth between the tables and their wagons carrying leftover food and dirty dishes.

"This big ol' pot is just too heavy for poor little ol' me to carry all by myself," Orletta said with a coy pout.

Joining the game, Rachel stared at the near-empty iron kettle with wide-eyed amazement. "Oh, my, yes, I can see that. Let me give you a hand."

Sweeping their skirts up to avoid the sides of the sooty kettle, the women shared the handle as they carried it to the Colfax wagon and hoisted it up on the bed.

Rachel turned to start back, but Orletta stayed her with a hand. "Not yet. I been wantin' to get you alone. What you doin' messin' around with them two yahoos? Amos says ain't neither of 'em fit to wipe your shoes."

"I saw the way Amos glared at Kyle McLean when he rode in. Why doesn't he like him?"

"He didn't say. But from what I seen of McLean, he looks to be slipperier'n a greased pig."

"Well, so far, he's always been a perfect gentleman around me. And generous. He loaned me his wagon one day so I wouldn't have to ride home with Esther and Rose and their husbands. Have you seen them since they got married?"

"No. But I saw who they got hitched to. That was enough for me."

"Anyway, Kyle loaned me the wagon, and now he's brought a buggy for me to use on my medical calls. I plan to —"

"*Kyle,* is it? Now, you listen here, sweetie. A man like McLean don't do nothin' for nothin'. They always want somethin' in return. And I think it's you."

"Yes, I know. He's made that quite clear. So has Mr. Best. And they're both determined to get my marriage to Jake annulled."

"Speakin' of Jake, Clayton Jennings said he only went to Oregon City for two or three days. If you said somethin' to keep him away, that'd be a real shame. He loves you somethin' fierce. And he's a sight better than either of them two phony—"

"Come on, Orletta." Rachel took her well-meaning friend by the hand. "Everyone's already gone inside."

"Everybody but that mealymouth, Harvey Best. Now, if that ain't a fine figure of a man if I ever saw one," she said with a sarcastic snort as she pointed toward the barn door. "He's waitin' there to walk you in—makin' sure everybody knows you're with him. 'Specially your most *generous* friend, Kyle McLean. Of course, if Sarah Beth has her way, he'll be spreadin' some of it her way. She's been droolin' after him like he was the fatted lamb."

"Listen, Orletta. Harvey said everyone in the community is going to pitch in and help pay for the horse and buggy after harvest."

"Really? I heard folks admirin' that rig all day, but I ain't heard no one say they was gonna pay for it."

"Are you sure?"

"Talk to Amos. Ask him. And while you're at it, ask him about McLean. And that stuffed shirt over there, too." Orletta tossed her head in Harvey's direction. "And Rachel," she said, her voice losing its harshness, "talk to Amos about Jake. And really listen to what he has to say."

"Lovely evening for a dance," Harvey said, as the two

women walked up to him. By the lightness in his tone, he'd obviously regained control of his good humor, sorely lacking since Kyle had arrived on the scene.

Relieved that he wouldn't put a damper on the merry time Rachel hoped to have, she said, "You promised the first dance to me, so we'd better run. Sounds like they're starting to play 'Golden Slippers.'"

Harvey's face lit up like the rows of lanterns suspended from the rafters as they rushed, hand in hand, through the open door. Couples were standing in squares, filling the vast floor of the high-ceilinged barn. At the far end, standing on a platform made from the table planks, Amos, his three boys, and another fiddler played the lively tune. A skinny man Rachel had seen with Geneva Loomis stood in front, tapping his boot to the beat.

"Over here." The summons came from the right side, near the front door. Robby Stockton beckoned with both hands. "We need a fourth couple." Mardell Loomis stood next to him, and the Simpkinses and the Bennetts formed the other two sides.

"Come on," Rachel said and pulled Harvey into the square just as the lanky man on the stage, his angular features almost skeletal, began the first call of the night.

> First old buck and the pretty little girl,
> Down the center with the butterfly whirl,

Rachel and the others clapped while Robby and Mardell stepped to the middle, twirled, and moved back into place.

> Lady go right and gent go left,
> And right around the outside now,

Turning away from Harvey, Rachel threaded hand over hand while looking around the room. She spotted Dinah Grills, Chloe Loomis, and twin girls parading with young men Rachel had yet to meet. Wondering what Harland thought of Dinah on another young man's arm, she glanced up to the stage. The boy's mouth flew back and forth across his harmonica, not missing a note, but his eyes followed Dinah's banana curls as they bounced down her back.

> Promenade your lady. Promenade your lady.
> Promenade your lady. All the way around.

Then across the heads of the other dancers, Rachel caught sight of Kyle McLean. Taller than most, his raven hair flaring from his widow's peak was easy to spot. A smirk dimpled one cheek. He held the older Mrs. Stockton's hands as he gamboled around he square, but he watched Sarah Beth. She skipped impishly along, promenading just ahead of him with her husband, Ben. Now I see why Harvey's temperament improved so dramatically, Rachel thought.

She looked back at the childishly happy Harvey and could easily see why Edna championed him. Caught up in the machinations of the dance, he high-stepped with enthusiasm to the rapid music. She had to admit, he'd been behaving quite admirably all afternoon, slipping into snobbery only a time or two. A good catch. Solid. Trustworthy.

"Second old buck and the pretty little girl," the caller continued with a lilting cadence, "down the center with the butterfly whirl. . . ."

Harvey swung Rachel into the center of the square and twirled her around. The fact that he was soon to be bank president must have slipped his mind. He laughed far more loudly than was considered tasteful as they stepped back to their place.

At the end of "Golden Slippers," the musicians whipped into the "Arkansas Traveler" without missing a beat, then on to the lively "Turkey in the Straw."

Flushed and breathless from the exhilarating tempo, Rachel felt her heaving bosom strain against the bodice of her dress. When the music stopped, she demurely placed a hand over her heart before smiling up into Harvey's eager eyes. "My, I am thirsty."

"Me, too." He pulled out a kerchief and wiped the moisture from his forehead. "I'll get us some punch and be right back."

I know you will, Rachel thought indulgently as she watched him join others converging on the serving table.

Edna, looking pert as ever in green and blue plaid, stepped up to Rachel. A confident smile decorated her petite features. "There's no doubt." She shielded her mouth with a hand as her gaze slid in Harvey's direction. "No doubt at all. Mr. Best is purely smitten with you."

A loud clanging sound errupted from the stage where the elder Stockton rang for silence. Kyle McLean stood beside him as Ellis Stockton raised his hand. "Folks. Ladies and gentlemen. Mr. McLean, here, has an announcement to make."

Kyle took a step forward. "I assume by now," he said in a voice loud enough to carry to the far end of the barn, "you've all had an eyeful of my recent acquisition—my Thoroughbred racehorse, Pegasus."

He pulled a folded piece of paper from his breast pocket and waved it open with a flourish. "I have here a note from Jake Stone challenging me to a race . . . here in Independence . . . on the Fourth of July!"

Rachel blanched at the mention of Jake's name. But no one seemed to notice.

Instead, enthusiastic cheers, clapping, and boot stomping burst forth.

Rachel forced her hands to slap together several times but could not muster a smile.

". . . add to the occasion," Rachel heard Kyle continue as the thundering applause subsided, "we plan to celebrate the opening of the First Bank of Independence!"

The roar again bounced off the walls.

"We'll be passing the word up and down the river, so ladies, better get to baking. This is going to be a day to be remembered in the history of this fair—dare I say?—*city*.

I've ordered twenty kegs of beer, and they're on their way.''

This time the women did not join the men in their hooting approval.

Kyle raised a hand for quiet. "Yes, I think eighteen fifty-three will be a banner year for Independence. And not the least of the credit, I'm sure, will go to one of our new residents, Miss Rachel.''

Rachel's mouth dropped open. She quickly closed it as all eyes were trained on her.

"Rachel, would you please step up here a moment?''

Her mouth fell open again.

"Go on, Rachel,'' someone said and gave her a shove.

She stumbled forward. Then, seeing no way to gracefully excuse herself, she moved on wooden legs toward the stage. She took Kyle's hand and climbed onto the platform. He continued to hold it as he led her past the grinning faces of the Colfax boys.

Amos stood to the side, an empty punch cup dangling from one finger. His face lacked any expression, a sure sign of his displeasure.

Rachel felt unaccountably guilty.

"I'm sure by now,'' Kyle said, addressing the group once more, "everyone is aware that Independence now has someone with considerable medical skills. And, I'm sure, her presence in Independence will be an incentive to others to settle here rather than at some other landing along the river. Who knows, maybe they'll be wanting to move the capital up here before long.''

"Hear, hear,'' shouted Coke Lyons.

A rumble of chuckling filled the barn.

"Let's show the little lady our appreciation.'' Still holding one of Rachel's hands, McLean spread his other arm expansively. "How about a big round of applause!''

Most of the people responded by clapping heartily, and an embarrassed smile spread broadly across Rachel's face. She glanced nervously about until she noticed Sarah Beth holding a fan just below narrowed eyes. From the jerky way she waved it, Rachel knew she was miffed.

Rachel's gaze moved on until she spotted Harvey, his face all ascrew, his neck craned to see over Homer Dorset's bald head. Rachel knew he worried about more than spilling the two cups of fruit punch he held aloft.

As the applause subsided Rachel nodded several times and said self-consciously, "Thank you . . . thank you."

"You know," Kyle said, turning to Amos, "I don't think I've ever danced with a doctor before. Mr. Colfax, how about playing one of those waltzes?"

"Yeah!" Harland concurred fervently. He thrust his harmonica at the square-dance caller. "Grady, would you play this? I promised Dinah the first waltz." Without waiting for an answer, he leapt off the stage.

"Well?" Kyle said, assisting Rachel off the platform.

She glanced back at Amos. Creases raked Amos's brow as he raised his violin to his chin.

"May I have the honor?" Kyle lifted her hand and held it out, then placed his other at the small of her back.

Still the center of attention, Rachel felt like a bird in a cage. She squared her shoulders. "Thank you, Mr. McLean. I'd be delighted." Raising one side of her skirts as the first smooth strains of the waltz began, she allowed him to glide her across the empty floor.

Her self-consciousness partially dissipated as, one by one, other pairs joined them. She would not be totally comfortable, though, until the music stopped. However, she had to admit that she did love the airy, light-headed feeling of floating and swirling like a feather. Smiling, she looked up at her partner and found him peering intently down at her, a grin playing across his lips.

Her heart lurched. It was the same look she'd seen on Jake's face that first morning after they had been together. That knowing expectation . . . the same look Kyle'd had when he watched Sarah Beth. The man was a bounder. Rachel's own smile faded. "You really are an expert waltzer, Mr. McLean," she said, hoping to distract him.

"Thank you, but I'm sure it's your stylish grace that inspires me." His lustful expression never wavered.

"Oh, I'm sure you'll find other partners equally inspiring." She nodded her head toward Sarah Beth, who waltzed in the arms of her husband, Ben.

Kyle glanced in the silvery blonde's direction, then turned back to Rachel. A low chuckle rumbled out. "Ah, yes, the eager Mrs. Stockton. But you, my dear, are the belle of this ball. Or any other, for that matter."

"You forget, Mr. McLean, that I do not qualify as a belle. I'm a married woman."

"A minor inconvenience. One day soon, you'll forget anyone but me ever existed."

Rachel's brows lifted at his supreme confidence.

"Has anyone ever told you that your eyes sparkle like blue diamonds?" Kyle tossed as he whirled her around.

"You're the first this evening."

"Touché, my beauty."

As they sailed toward the other end of the room, Rachel caught sight of Harvey, and their eyes met. Waiting beside a post, the cups of punch still in his hands, he was a mere turtle compared to the swift Mr. McLean. But in the end, hadn't the turtle won the race? His steadfastness had bested the cocky hare. And like the turtle, Harvey could be counted on. He was, after all, the only one who had actually come for her this morning.

As she looked back at her partner, the music slowed and swelled for the final three notes. Kyle bent into an exaggerated bow, clearing her view of the bandstand, and revealing, in particular, the scowl on Amos's face.

"Play another waltz," Harland called to his pa, one hand still at Dinah's waist.

"Good idea," Kyle said, taking Rachel's hand again just as Harvey Best strode up beside them.

"Your punch is getting warm," Harvey said, offering it to her while staring at Kyle.

"Thank you for holding it," Rachel said, taking it.

"It was my pleasure." His tone lacked warmth.

"Yes, that was very thoughtful of you, Harvey," McLean said, the brittleness in his voice unmistakable. "But would you please hold on to that cup a little longer? Rachel and I are about to start the next waltz."

Harvey stiffened, his face turning red. "Rachel is—"

His words were overridden by Amos's call. "Harland, come on up here. It's Donald's turn to dance. Rachel?"

She didn't look his way. She was afraid to take her eyes off Harvey. Would his jealousy cause him to risk his position at the bank?

"Rachel?" Amos repeated.

Harvey and Kyle turned toward Colfax, freeing Rachel. She took a step forward. "Yes?"

"Come up here and play the dulcimer a while, so's Donald can go dance."

Under normal circumstances Rachel wouldn't have dreamt of exposing her tenuous talent before a roomful of people. But at that moment . . . "You will excuse me." She almost ran to the stage.

"Come on over here, missy." Amos pointed her to where the dulcimer rested on a small table. "We'll do 'My Darlin''. You sing that real purty."

"*Sing?*" Rachel suddenly felt as parched as a powder puff. She swallowed the contents of her cup in three gulps before placing her trembly hands on the instrument.

⦅ chapter 22 ⦆

THE sentimental words of "My Darlin'" wafted on the evening breeze, tugging at Jake's heart, drawing him irresistibly to the barn, to the place where the Riggins boy had said Rachel would be. The doors of the barn stood wide. Light flooded out, creating a welcoming path to guide the weary wayfarer safely home. Home to Rachel.

Jake dismounted and tied Prince to the low branch of a nearby tree, then strode toward the barn. Stepping inside, he scanned the dancing couples, searching for his bride. Then, looking over their heads, he found her on the stage.

The sight of her—the way her hair glowed like a sunlit waterfall—stole his breath. Her wide eyes, dark and luminous, her voice rising in a pure soprano, breasts straining against a lacy bodice. Jake's heart pounded. His blood raced hot and fast, rushing downward, engorging him.

A barnful of people separated Jake from Rachel, but at that moment, he could see no one but her. She stood behind a small table, plucking out the last bars of "My Darlin'" on a dulcimer. The flowered fabric of a long-sleeved dress molded sensuously to her winsome curves. Gathered lace teased the edge of a bodice that dipped invitingly low. And a bounty of skirts swirled about her as she swayed to the final strains of the tune. Utterly feminine.

"Jake."

Someone grabbed his arm. Reluctant to take his eyes from Rachel, he slowly turned to see who kept him from her.

"Jake," Homer Dorset repeated. "It's about time you got back. Where the hell you been?"

Jake returned his gaze to Rachel. "Oregon City. Around," he said absently as the music stopped. He attempted to move on, but Homer gripped his arm even tighter.

"There's something you ought to know before you just walk on in there."

"Later."

"Now."

Perturbed, Jake sighed and turned to Homer. "All right, but make it fast."

"I just thought you oughta know, there's a couple wolves been sniffin' round your claim whilst you been off gallivantin'."

"I haven't been off gallivanting. I've been away on important business. Are you trying to tell me Harvey Best is messing with my homestead papers?"

"No, Rachel. I'm talking about Rachel. Don't you know you can't just walk off and leave a good-lookin' woman out here? Hell, man, this ain't Philadelphia. This is Oregon."

Jake's gaze swung back to his wife. She was being helped off the stage by that bastard Kyle McLean. Fists clenched, Jake jerked his attention back to Dorset. "Get to the point, Homer. What's going on here?"

"Harvey Best's been—"

"One more waltz," came McLean's voice from the other end of the barn as he called up to the musicians.

Further enraged, Jake charged through the crowd, jostling couples as he pushed past. He vaguely heard the murmurs of his neighbors as he neared Rachel.

"Jake." Coming from the bandstand, Amos's voice was loud and demanding.

As he glanced up into the comfortable face of his balding friend, Jake heard Rachel gasp.

"Good to see you," Amos continued. "We was startin' to get worried."

Rachel's mouth hung open. She blinked as if she couldn't

believe her eyes, then abruptly wrenched her hand from
Kyle McLean's.

Jake turned to McLean, who also stared at him with
disbelieving eyes. If possible, he looked even more amazed
than Rachel.

"Evening, Stone," McLean managed in a gravelly croak.

Jake made a concerted effort to keep his own voice
casual. "McLean." After a slight nod of acknowledgment,
he turned to Rachel, who'd regained her composure. "You're
looking mighty pretty tonight. How've you been?"

"Fine, thank you," she said in a rushed whisper.

All the color had fled her face. She looked as pale as she
had that day when he first met her in Dorset's store. So
fragile, so scared. He felt the strongest urge to take her in his
arms, to hold her close until she felt safe again. "Amos," he
said, looking past Rachel to Colfax. "How about that
waltz?"

Amos flipped up his fiddle. "Boys," he said to the others
on stage. "The man's ordered up another waltz."

As Amos slid the horsehair bow across the strings, Jake
took Rachel's tiny hand into his. "Shall we?"

She stumbled slightly as he guided her to the center of the
dance floor. Her skirts fanned the air as she caught them up,
creating a tantalizing breeze.

The haunting scent of French perfume, lilac soap, and
that faint muskiness that spoke of Rachel alone teased his
nostrils. He breathed deeply.

She looked up to him with searching eyes, reaching into
him, penetrating his soul, binding him to her. Then, suddenly, she dropped her gaze and lowered her head.

Jake realized they had been standing poised in the middle
of the floor for several seconds. He knew without looking
that all eyes were on them. After a silent count of one, two,
three, he swept Rachel across the floor.

Jake's feet always doubled in size when he danced.
Tonight was no exception. He felt like a clumsy oaf as
everyone watched. Finally a couple of fellows from the
sawmill moved onto the floor with the Bennett twins, and

Jake breathed easier. He concentrated on the music. Mary Redman had once said that as long as he stayed with the beat and didn't step on his partner's toes, he'd be all right. Nonetheless, he would've been far more sure of his footing if he and Rachel had been walking in the woods.

Jake looked down at her, but, with the way her face still dipped, all he could see was the top of her head. Why won't she look up at me? he wondered. Is she scared of what I might do? No, he didn't think so. Her breathing was steady and the hand he held wasn't clammy. She's probably just embarrassed. His anger from moments before resurfaced. Compared to McLean, he must seem like some backwoods ruffian. Backwoodsman or no, she was his wife, and she owed him an explanation. "Rachel."

He felt her jump. Then she looked up and met his gaze with those transparent blue eyes. "Yes?"

"You know how I feel about McLean. What are you doing dancing with him?"

Her eyes widened, then darkened as they narrowed. "With whom I choose to dance is no longer your concern."

A wave of shock ran up his spine, and he faltered, almost losing the momentum of the waltz. "As long as you're my wife it is," he blustered.

"You gave up that right when you abandoned me, leaving me alone in the wilderness to fend for myself."

"I did no such thing. I left you in a tight house with plenty of food and firewood. I found you a watchdog, and I left you a rifle for protection while I was gone."

"Well! Aren't you the considerate one?"

"I intended to get back in time to take you to the dance, to apologize for yelling at you out at the Jenningses'. But something got in the way." He knew his excuse sounded lame, but he couldn't tell her about the man who'd been stalking him and had run off into the night when Jake went out to challenge him. The same mountain-smart man Jake had been tracking for the better part of the week until he lost his tracks downriver a few miles.

Rachel stopped abruptly, woodenly, and pulled her hand

from his. She held him with a menacing stare. "I understand what a busy man you are. Far too busy to send someone as insignificant as me even the simplest note." Swerving out of the path of another couple, she stalked off the dance floor.

Feeling conspicuously alone, Jake followed. "Rachel," he called above the music.

She whirled to face him. "Mr. Stone." Glaring up, she placed a hand to her temple. "I do believe it's time for me to have a headache. If you'll excuse me, I'm leaving now."

"You can't leave here in the dark by yourself."

"I don't intend to. Mr. Best was kind enough to escort me here, and I'm sure he'll be more than happy to see me safely back to town. I bid you good night."

With her chin hiked up and her back as straight as a broomstick, Rachel whirled around and sped off toward the punch table. After speaking a few words to Mrs. Stockton, she walked to Harvey Best and spoke to him while touching her brow. He smiled and looked in Jake's direction before crooking an arm in a gentlemanly fashion. Placing her hand on his forearm, they walked past the silent onlookers, who stepped back and made a pathway to the entrance.

Jake watched her disappear into the night, puzzled by how quickly she'd slipped out of his hands again. And what the hell was she doing with Harvey Best? Outrage scalded his brain. *Harvey Best?* We'll just see about that.

Stretching into a long stride, Jake reached the door a few seconds later. He started out, but was brought up short by Homer and Sam Dooley, who each grabbed an arm.

"Whoa," Dooley said. "I think you need a little time to simmer down."

"She's getting away." Jake jerked out of Sam's grasp.

"She won't be hard to find. She's stayin' in town at the Grillses'." Homer's whiny pitch grated on Jake's nerves.

"So, I'll talk to her there."

"And just what do you have to say for yourself?" The sharp, harping words came from behind.

Jake swung around and saw Edna Grills, her hands

planted firmly on her hips. "If you don't mind, Edna, this is my business."

"Well, I'm making it mine."

"So am I," Mattie Baker said, looking like some heavy-breasted goose, as she swooped toward him in a white dress piped with yellow.

"You ought to be ashamed of yourself," Edna harangued. "Coming in here, ruining that poor girl's fun, embarrassing her like that."

"I—"

Mattie cut in. "What could a body expect from someone who'd trade a decent, hardworking wife off for a—a you-know-what? He's capable of any manner of despicable behavior."

"Now, Mattie," Homer chided.

"Don't you 'now Mattie' me, Mr. Dorset. From what I hear the whole thing was your idea."

Homer's face scrunched up. "Now that ain't exactly true, Mrs. Baker. And I have apologized to Mrs. Stone. If she forgave me, it seems only fittin' that you should, too."

"Let's get back to the real culprit here," Edna said, glaring up at Jake. "I don't know why God saw fit to hand a fine Christian lady like Rachel over to you—as if she hasn't already suffered enough in her life. Well, she's finished with you. Has been for some time now. What right do you have coming here, acting like you're the injured party? Like she owes you anything?"

Jake jammed his hands into his trouser pockets before one stuffed itself in Edna's big mouth. "If you'll pardon me," he said, sidestepping her.

"No, I won't. Not until you give me your word that you'll leave her alone and let her get an annulment. Give her a chance to make a new life with someone who'll appreciate her, like—"

Carson Grills jerked his wife back from the group surrounding Jake. "That's about enough for one evening." The harshness in his voice matched the stern look on his face. His expression relaxed slightly as he turned to Jake. "I apologize for my wife. I don't know what got into her."

Too angry to accept anyone's apology at the moment, Jake could muster nothing more than a curt nod.

"Get going." Carson pushed Edna toward the other end of the room. "You, too," he added, grabbing Mattie's arm.

During the confrontation, the tune had come to an end. Although Amos put his fiddle into its case, he said, "Square up folks. It's time for the 'Virginia Reel.'"

To Jake's relief, everyone stopped staring at him. Instead, they turned to find their partners, then scurried to the middle of the floor.

Amid the flurry, Amos jumped down from the platform. He skirted the crowd and walked to Jake's end of the room.

As Colfax approached, Homer's pudgy pointing finger punctuated his words. "I tried to warn you, Jake. But, no, you wouldn't listen. You came in like a bull on the prod. You need to go on home and—"

Brushing past Homer, Jake shook Amos's hand. "Glad you're here. I need to see a friendly face about now."

Amos's lips whipped into a grin. "Thought you might." He gave Jake's fingers an extra squeeze.

"I got a jug out in my wagon," Sam offered. "Why don't we go on out and have us a couple o' swigs?"

"Sounds good," Amos said. "How 'bout it, Jake?"

"Sure, why not? Nothing to keep me here." Jake headed outside between Sam and Amos, with Homer taking up the rear.

As they walked to Dooley's buckboard, Jake searched the shadows for Rachel, but she'd already been swallowed into the darkness of the woods.

Sam hefted out an earthenware crock, then jiggled it a few times. "Feels light." He frowned. "Homer, you seen any young bucks hangin' round my wagon?"

"Come to think of it, I did see Robby Stockton sneak out here a while back with one of them Loomis girls."

"Quit your jawing, and pass it over." Jake grabbed it and

pulled out the cork. Tipping it up, he filled his mouth with the fiery liquid.

"Gimme a drink," Amos said, taking it from Jake.

"And what about me?" came a sexy woman's voice.

Jake jumped and turned, expecting to see Goldy.

Instead, Orletta approached.

"Wasn't you goin' to invite me to the party?" she said, with a mock pout.

"Sure." Amos stepped forward and handed her the jug.

After taking a drink, she took a couple of seconds to recover her breath, then handed the jug to Jake. "Well, big fella, you was supposed to make up with Rachel. What happened?"

"What's done is done," Amos said. "But it's high time you got that temper of yours tied down and commenced with some sweet-talkin'."

"Yeah," Sam said, placing a ham-sized hand on Jake's shoulder. "She's a real nice lady. I'm plumb sorry about the part I had in what's come between you two."

"It's more my fault than yours," Jake said. "I should've just come right out and said no to you boys instead of stringing you along like I did. But I just couldn't resist asking to see Goldy's teeth."

Wagging their heads, Sam and Homer chuckled.

"Yeah, that was a good one," Dorset said. "Goldy didn't shut up about it all the way back to town."

"I'm sure ya'll had a good laugh," Orletta said. "But it's time we got back to business. Jake, what are you going to say to her?"

He downed a swig, then wiped his mouth with his shirtsleeve. "Well, I guess I'll just—" He stopped mid-sentence and peered past Sam. "Someone's coming."

The others turned toward the barn, and after a moment Jake recognized the pair coming toward them through the darkness. Robby Stockton and Mardell Loomis.

"Howdy," Sam said.

By the surprised looks on their faces, it was obvious that the young couple had not seen them.

"Howdy," Robby said. "I see we're not the only ones that needed a little fresh air."

Clutching his arm, Mardell giggled and swayed into him.

"You sure that's all you been comin' out here for?" Sam said, pointing to the jug in Jake's hand.

Robby's eyes widened. "I—uh—*Mr. Stone*," he exclaimed as if it were the first time he'd noticed the big man that evening. "Good to see you back. I went out to your place whilst you was gone to help out for a few days. Taught your wife how to hitch up and drive Sampson and Sparky. Small as she is, you oughta see how quick she learned to handle 'em."

"Robby, what about my jug?" Sam said with an edge to his well-deep voice.

The boy ignored him. "But I guess she won't be drivin' the wagon since Mr. McLean gave her that fancy new buggy."

Jake's words split the night like gunshots. *"McLean did what?* He gave my wife a horse and buggy?"

"Yeah," Robby interjected, "And the horse is one of them fancy hackneys with a bobbed tail and all."

McLean, always McLean. Jake eyed the barn and started forward.

"Hold on there, big fella," Orletta said, pressing her palms against Jake's chest. "I talked to Rachel about that rig. She says she thought the townfolks was chippin' in for it so's she'd always be able to get to 'em whenever they was ailin'. I set her straight about that, an' she said she'd be talkin' to the jack-a-dandy."

"What else has he given her?" Jake roared.

Robby took a step back. "Well, uh—he did give her the loan of his spring wagon once."

"Homer moved closer to Jake. "And I hear they was drinkin' some of that French champagne and eatin' little chocolate candies over at the restaurant that first night she come to town. Queer thing about that. She went over there to have supper with Harvey Best . . . but it was McLean who walked her back to the Grilleses' house."

Orletta wheeled to Dorset. "Stop your silly gossip." She turned back to Jake. "I know Rachel better than anyone here, an' I know she'd never do nothin' that weren't right and proper. An' if you got any sense in that thick skull of yours, you'll go to her with your hat in your hand, and ask her to forgive you."

Seeing McLean step out the barn doors, a fiery roar rushed into Jake's head. He shoved past her.

"What's the matter?" she cried.

The slick-talking snake and a blonde in a blue dress ran hand in hand toward the new house. *"McLean,"* Jake roared as he stalked straight for the claim jumper.

The bastard halted, jerking the girl to a stop. She stumbled back against him.

"That's Sarah Beth," Robby said. "What's she doin' out here with him?" He started toward the couple at a run.

The others followed close behind.

"Robby Stockton!" Sarah Beth scolded, placing her hands on her hips as he halted before her. "If you keep sneaking off with Mardell, her mama's going to twist your ears off."

"And what about you?" he blustered.

"Me?" Throwing her hands across her heart, she opened her mouth in a shocked expression as her gaze flitted to the ring of faces surrounding them. "Dear me, what a naughty mind you have. I was merely showing this fine gentleman where I plan to place the furniture his grand gift will allow me to purchase. Isn't that right, Mr. McLean?"

"Why, yes," McLean said, his voice mellow, casual.

Fists knotted, Jake moved within inches and hovered over him. "I understand my wife has also received some of your generosity."

One side of McLean's mouth lifted into a smirk.

"I'll be returning that horse and buggy tomorrow, real personal-like." Jake bent closer. "If you know what I mean." Unable to restrain himself, he grabbed for McLean.

Sam and Amos snared Jake from either side as McLean jumped back, just out of reach.

Leaning nonchalantly against a tree trunk, McLean slipped a hand inside his jacket. "Fine. Bring it back. I'll simply return it when she's free of you. I wouldn't think of allowing such a refined lady to be coarsened by the kind of life you've provided."

McLean's last words cut deep, and no matter how much Jake wanted to believe otherwise, he knew the cur was right. His muscles lost their strength. Rachel was far too fine for him. Nonetheless, he would never let a swindler like McLean know it. "You're right about one thing," he said with force. "*My wife* does need a horse and buggy. I'll buy it from you. How much did you give?"

McLean removed his hand from his coat and let it fall to his side. "A thousand dollars."

Jake wasn't the only one surprised by the steep price; he heard the others gasp. "I don't have that kind of money. I'll find her another buggy. One I can afford."

"I'll tell you what. I heard you were a gambling man. I'll put it up, complete with the registered hackney mare, *plus* a thousand dollars. It's all yours if your horse beats Pegasus on the Fourth of July."

"I already told you I don't have that kind of money to bet," Jake said, wondering what the slickster was up to.

"There's your farm. I'd be willing to take that."

"You can't do that," Homer said, butting in. "Homesteads can't be bought or sold *or* wagered away."

"All I ask," McLean said, "is that you walk away from it. What do you say? Are you man enough to risk it?" His face hardened with the earnestness of his challenge.

Amos squeezed Jake's arm. "Don't do it. All he'll lose is a little jingle in his pockets. You'd lose ever'thing you worked for these past two years."

"Yeah," Orletta added, "and I don't think Rachel would be real partial to settin' up housekeepin' under a tree."

Jake turned to Amos. "Prince can take him. I've never seen a gray yet that could run worth spit."

"Me, neither," Amos said. "But that don't mean it can't never happen."

"How about if I sweeten the pot?" McLean said. "If you win, I'll step aside where Rachel is concerned. And if you lose you do the same."

Ben Stockton's new wife broke in with an angry burst. "I think I've had about all the fresh air I can take for one evening." Tossing her blond head, she sent her ringlets bouncing as she stomped off toward the music-filled barn.

But McLean's eyes never wavered from Jake. "Well, what's your answer?"

Jake was sorely tempted. Ever since he bought Prince off a busted gold miner down in San Francisco, no other horse had come close to besting the spirited stallion. But if Rachel heard she'd become part of a wager, he'd never be able to explain that one away. And all for nothing—McLean would most likely be in jail long before Independence Day.

"Don't do it, Jake," Orletta said before he could speak. "Rachel will never forgive you."

"I'm a gentleman," McLean said. "I'll not bandy it about."

"If you're a gentleman," Orletta scoffed, "I'm the queen of England."

Jake shook his head. "Can't do it."

"I just thought," McLean countered with a smirk, "any man up to buying a wife in the first place, wouldn't be too squeamish about placing her on the block again."

Jake lunged, dragging Amos and Sam with him.

McLean's eyes widened. He leapt back as Jake attempted to wrench free and grab him.

Amos and Sam dug their heels into the earth and managed to stop Jake.

He bellowed, lowered his head, and charged again.

Robby jumped on Jake's back, grabbing him around the head and neck.

Trotting backward out of reach, McLean shoved his hand inside his coat and withdrew something that flashed silver in the moonlight.

"Look out, he's got a gun," Orletta yelled.

Jake didn't care if the son of a bitch had a cannon. He

strained forward while trying to shake off the three men he hauled with him.

Still retreating, McLean raised the short-barreled pistol and aimed. He collided with a tree behind him, and the gun exploded with a sharp crack. It bounced from his hand to the ground.

Mardell Loomis shrieked.

Jake turned to see if the girl had been shot.

McLean took advantage of Jake's inattention and stopped to retrieve the derringer.

Orletta beat him to it. She kicked it out of his reach, then stepped on it, covering it with her skirts.

Robby vaulted off Jake's back and ran to Mardell. He took her by the shoulders. "Are you hurt?"

"Is she shot?" Jake asked as the girl's screams crumbled into sobs.

Tears streaming, she whimpered "No" and ran her hands down her body. "I don't think so."

"What's going on out there?" a man's voice yelled from the entrance of the barn.

"Ever'thing's fine," Homer shouted. Jake noticed that the storekeeper had moved a number of safe yards from the others. "Just a little accident."

Mardell muffled her crying, and the curious man melted back into the large structure.

The wildfire burning within Jake began to subside. His impatient muscles eased, and he unclenched his fists.

Amos and Sam released him, but neither moved more than a foot away.

"Robby," Orletta called from where she stood, the gun still trapped beneath her foot. "Loan your girl a kerchief so's she can clear up her face, then you two get back inside. Now, *scat,*" she said with a wave of her hand before bending to pick up the small double-barreled pistol.

"If you would be so kind." McLean stepped forward and held out his hand. "I'll take my gun now."

"I see it's one of them newfangled derringers," she said, looking at the weapon resting in her palm. She eyed

McLean briefly, then broke it open and plucked out the remaining bullet before handing it back. "Mr. McLean, there ain't gonna be no more business conducted out here, so I suggest you go back inside and find yourself a girl to dance with. An' try an' find an unmarried one this time."

McLean looked at Jake for a long second. "If you all will excuse me—" Turning on his heel, he strode away as stiff as a lieutenant fresh out of West Point.

"I'm not finished with him yet," Jake growled.

"I doubt if he's through with you, either," Amos said. "Better watch your back."

"Don't worry, I intend to. I already scared one sneak thief off the other night. I've spent the last few days trying to catch up to him. He's wearing moccasins, but I don't think he's an Indian. Covers his tracks good as any, though. I lost his trail again this side of Salem."

"So that's what took you so long," Amos said. "Clayton said you was only supposed to be gone a few days."

Homer moved into the circle. "Why would someone be after you?"

Jake exhaled slowly. "No reason." He turned to Amos. "But then, there might be."

Homer sniffed. "What reason?"

Sam's bass voice intervened. "Jake, Roy Thornton was talkin' to me this afternoon. Said a mean-looking cuss come in the saloon this mornin' wearin' moccasins and one of them fringe leather coats. He asked for McLean. When Roy told him McLean wasn't in town, he asked directions to Charley Bone's place. He perked right up when Roy told him it was just past yours. You ever heard of a Crow Dog Catlin?"

"Did you say Crow Dog Catlin?" Orletta's words were ominously hushed.

Amos turned to her. "Do you know him?"

"No," she said, wagging her head slowly. "But I seen his leavin's."

"I've heard of him, too," Jake said, his voice also lowered. "He's a crazy-mean half-breed out of Blackfoot country. Thought he would've gotten himself shot or hung by now.'' Jake looked to where he'd tied his horse. ''Think maybe I'll ride out that way. See what him and those two useless horse thieves are up to.''

Amos placed a hand on Jake's shoulder. ''You don't want to ride out there alone in the middle of the night. Might be a trap. 'Sides, I think we all had enough excitement for one evenin'. Wait till tomorrow, and we'll go with you.''

''Yeah,'' Sam said. ''Why don't you just bed down in Lyons's bunkhouse for tonight? You can put your horse up in my stable free of charge.''

''You're right, I guess. It won't hurt to let Crow Dog wait one more day.'' Jake exhaled heavily. ''I'm more tired than I thought.''

''And first thing in the morning,'' Orletta added, ''before you do anything else, you go on over to the Grillses' and straighten things out with Rachel.''

''I doubt if it would do any good. When it comes to her,'' Jake said as he trudged over to Prince to unloop his reins, ''I never seem to get it right.''

((chapter
23))

ON the short ride back to town, Harvey drove within the glow of overlapping circles from the buggy's two lanterns. Rachel was thankful that he respected her excuse of a headache and remained silent as he maneuvered the hackney carefully past any bad ruts in the road. The darkness beneath the black leather bonnet hid any telltale expression as over and over she relived the moment when Jake first appeared. It was as if her latest nightmare had come true, as if she'd been caught stark naked in the arms of a forbidden lover.

There Jake had stood, so magnificently huge, so powerfully built that every other man seemed puny in his presence. And what was she doing, for heaven's sake, while the whole town watched, waited? Holding on to Kyle McLean. The same man who'd this very day given her a very expensive gift, one she utilized at this very moment. Kyle—the man her husband wholly disliked and distrusted.

But then Jake had taken her hand and folded it within his own strong, but ever-gentle one. That simple act had caused her stomach to drop like a ball and her knees to almost buckle as a bolt of carnal need seized her.

When he walked her to the center of the floor, she looked up and saw that wayward lock of blond hair feathered across his deeply tanned brow . . . so many times she'd brushed that same lock aside. And as often he'd caught her wrist and kissed the heart of her palm when she had.

Then she looked into his rich green eyes and saw the yearning, the need, and, yes, love. For a moment, one suspended moment, she'd felt so enveloped in its wonder nothing else existed. All the hurt and anger, the hollow emptiness she'd suffered these past weeks floated away.

She lingered within a breath of him for how long she couldn't be certain. Then suddenly, she realized they'd never begun to dance. *And neither had anyone else.* Every eye in the room was glued to them. Staring. Seeing the passion in their expressions. The mystical moment vanished. Abashed, Rachel ducked her head and stared at the brown and green plaid of Jake's shirt.

When she met his eyes again, they'd turned as hard and cold as cut emeralds. Then the dreadful accusations began.

Leaning her head against the side of the buggy, Rachel pulled her shawl tight about her and recalled Jake's censures. They chilled her far more than the night breeze.

Turning toward her, Harvey broke the silence. "Are you cold?"

"A bit," she said, sitting upright again.

"It'll be only a couple more minutes. Town's just past the curve ahead."

"I appreciate your willingness to leave the dance without a moment's hesitation."

Harvey guided the mare around the curve, then turned onto the town's main street. As he did, the vaguely outlined buildings came into view. A scattering of lights flickered from a few windows, mostly at the hotel.

"I could never consider any opportunity to spend time alone with you a sacrifice," he said, veering the hackney to the right as they approached the Grillses' home. "Surely, by now, you must know how I covet your company." He reined the animal to a stop. Draping the traces over the front board, he removed his driving gloves and took Rachel's hands.

Even in the darkness she felt the intense heat of Harvey's gaze. Please Lord, she prayed, I don't think I can deal with any more tonight. "I really must be going in now." Rachel attempted to free herself.

Harvey increased the strength of his hold. "Please, I beg of you."

Rachel sensed a marriage proposal looming. "But, I—"

"Please, my dear, do not interrupt. What I have to say will have a bearing on the rest of your life, a positive one, I might humbly add. I would have preferred a more leisurely courtship, long rides in the country, picnics in the shade of an old tree. But, as was evident by this evening's fiasco, circumstances don't permit us the luxury."

"Harvey." Rachel took a deep breath and turned away to avoid his zealous stare. "As I've told you before, I am wed to another. I'm not free to make any promises."

"And I told you I can easily have you released from your marriage contract. Come with me to Salem. Tonight. We could be there in a couple of hours. The governor's there now. You could see him tomorrow." His thumbs dug into her hands. "Then we'd be free to go anywhere we want."

She pulled back. "You're hurting me."

"What?" He glanced down and loosened his grip. "Oh, forgive me. I'm dreadfully sorry."

"Harvey, I'm very grateful for the offer. But I can't simply run away with you in the middle of the night. We'll talk in the morning, when I'm not so exhausted. Now, please," she said, moving out of his grasp, "would you help me down? I'm really very tired."

Harvey caught her shoulders. "I implore you. Leave with me tonight, before it's too late."

Reaching up, she pried off his fingers. "For goodness' sake, Harvey, you're much too overwrought to think clearly. *Please help me down.*"

Alone at last in the darkness of Dinah's bedroom and out of Harvey's clutches, Rachel still felt the confining weight of his entreaties. Trapped, suffocating. Frantically, she stripped away the layers of her clothing and tossed them across a chair, then walked to the window, opened it, and breathed deeply. A soft rush of air ruffled the curtains as it caressed her bare skin, reminding her of a breeze from the

mountains. She looked toward them longingly, but the
sawmill buildings blocked her view.

She hadn't realized until this instant how much she'd
come to treasure the freedom of living on her own hill,
overlooking her own valley, free from prying, demanding
eyes. Even while hiding within the deep shadows of an unlit
room, she felt as if someone watched her from one of the
darkened windows across the street, could see her nakedness.

She now understood the lure that drew so many into the
wilderness, men like her Jake who'd spent most of his life
roaming free. She was sure he knew the wonder of standing
on top of the highest ridge, the sun on is face, and overhead,
a dome of blue sky so vast it touched the very edges of the
world. His choice of a place to spend the rest of his life had
obviously been carefully considered. No one who'd experienced a life as unfettered as his could live in a town or
select one of those homesteads hidden in a forest of tall trees
as the Colfaxes and Jenningses had. Jake needed to see the
mountains, the sky, to see his land spread before him. And
now so did she.

At that moment, someone came out of the barn. As he
walked toward the hotel she recognized that it was Harvey.

He stopped and looked in her direction.

Quickly she ducked behind the curtain.

A number of seconds ticked by before he turned and
walked to the saloon. When he opened the door, light and
sounds of rowdiness flooded out, a woman's raucous laugh
soaring above the rest. Rachel grinned at the thought of
overly proper Harvey being accosted by one as licentious as
Goldy. *Goldy*. Her smile faded. She moved closer to the sill
to listen. But Harvey closed the door behind him, shutting in
the unholy merriment.

Then, the clip-clop of approaching hoofbeats caught her
attention. She looked up the road past the silhouetted church
and watched until a man on horseback became distinguish-
able. Because of his size, she knew immediately that it was

Jake, although his wilted hat brim sagged over his eyes as he slouched in the saddle.

He looked so tired. Sympathy welled within her.

As if he read her thoughts, Jake straightened.

Rachel's gaze measured the width of his Viking-like shoulders and lingered on his muscled-padded chest.

He turned and looked in the direction of the Grillses' home, then veered Prince toward it. Reaching the picket fence, he reined the horse to a stop.

Why hadn't it dawned on her that he might follow her to town? Unconsciously, she placed her hands over her nudity.

Rachel heard the leather creak as Jake dismounted.

My God, he's coming in. Rachel's mind whirled. What should she do? Should she let him in or pretend she wasn't there? No matter what she decided, she'd better get dressed. She ran to retrieve her clothing, but in the dark she misjudged the distance and bumped into the chair.

Its legs scraped loudly.

She rushed back to the window and peeked out to see if Jake had heard.

Still standing at the gate, his hand on the latch, he stared at the front door. But then he turned and walked back to Prince. He unhitched the horse and started walking toward the stable.

He's not coming in, she thought, feeling the cut of disappointment. He's leaving. She swatted aside the curtain blocking her view. If he'd just looked up. Couldn't he tell I was here? Couldn't he feel me?

Rachel hugged herself close as she watched him disappear into the cavelike blackness of the livery barn. Maybe he'll be back. Maybe he just wanted to tend his horse first. Yes, that's it.

Light suddenly shafted through the open doors.

He'll be back, she decided. He has to. She turned to face the dark room. I'd better get something on. Feeling around, she located her trunk and withdrew her silk wrapper, then moved back to the window to watch for Jake.

She stood suspended in place for several minutes. Her

eyes burned with anticipation as she watched the entrance to
the livery. Her temperature rose despite the wash of cool
night air. Reaching up with one hand, she pulled the pins
and ribbons from her hair. As her tresses fell, she slowly
shook them loose, letting them catch the wind.

Clutching the silken garment to her, she continued to
watch. She rubbed its satiny coolness along her hot cheek.
The hem brushed across a breast. It tightened and peaked.

At last the light went out, and Jake emerged.

Her pulse increased. Her breathing quickened. She leaned
forward, willing him to come to her.

He moved out into the street, looked in her direction, then
started toward her.

Her heart nearly burst from her bosom. She jerkily thrust
her arms into her wrapper sleeves and tied the sash.

But wait! Jake turned toward the hotel. Toward the
saloon. Toward Goldy.

How could he? Watching him walk up the hotel steps,
Rachel's nails dug into the window sash.

He stood outside the door.

She held her breath as she waited for him to enter.

Suddenly he turned and strode off the porch. Then in
long, purposeful strides, he came up the street. *Toward her.*

Rachel swung around, her hands flying to her cheeks in
an attempt to crush an irrepressible grin. Bolting, she ran out
the door and down the stairs so fast her feet barely touched
the wood.

A light, she needed a light. She didn't want him to think
she'd been mooning around in the dark.

She started for the parlor. No, a sudden light at the front
of the house would be too obvious. Whirling around, she ran
into the dining room, then on to the kitchen. Brushing her
hand along the shelf above the stove, she found the matches,
then hurriedly lit the lamp on the table.

She listened for his knock, but heard only the squeak of
the gate swinging open. Was there time to start a fire in the
stove for tea water? She jerked open the door and tossed in
all the kindling from the wood box, grabbed the oil can in

the corner, and recklessly sprinkled some over the twigs—
no time to nurse a fire into life. She tossed in a live match.
She managed to slam shut the fire-box door just before she
heard a loud whoosh.

A light tapping sounded at the door.

Rachel's heart flip-flopped. She pulled the tea kettle over
the hot plate, tossed a couple of logs in the stove, grabbed
the lamp, then rushed toward the front of the house.

Another series of knocks sounded just as she reached the
door. She started for the handle, then noticed her excited
breathing. She didn't want him to see her in such a stir.
"Who is it?" she called, stalling to compose herself.

A full five seconds of silence passed.

"It's me, Jake." His voice flowed in a low timbre, close
to a whisper.

Inhaling deeply, she opened the door with shaky hands.

He completely filled the entrance, and in the shaft of
lamplight, his presence seemed awesome, sending her heart
skittering again.

"You came."

"I had to." His words were faint, and after a moment, he
averted his gaze and took a jagged breath.

The haunted look in his eyes tugged at her. "Come in."
He moved past her and she shut the door. "Come to the
kitchen. I have some tea water heating."

She walked ahead of him, excruciatingly aware of every
sway of her hips. Did he notice that she had nothing on
under the wrapper? She knew he wanted her. She'd seen
that same deprived look often enough in her mirror. She
heard his footsteps right behind her. If she but paused, he
would bump into her hungering body. And weren't they
alone with only one small light separating them? How easy
it would be to blow out the lamp's flame and kindle their
own.

But she couldn't. Too much remained unresolved. She
pushed through the door to the kitchen and placed the lamp
on the table. Its glow brought to life the brilliant yellow of

the room, a place too purely bright for lies to hide. Would
they be able to bear it? "Sit down, I'll check the water."

Moving to the stove, she heard a chair scrape back.

"I came to say . . ." His voice trailed away.

Waiting for him to continue, she placed an unsteady hand
above the kettle spout, but felt no steam. His nearness
muddled her thoughts. She couldn't remember what else to
do to prepare for tea. On awkward legs, she turned around
and, after adjusting the skimpy wrapper, slipped into the
chair opposite him. "The water's not ready."

He nodded and looked down at his hands.

Out of nowhere a vision of her commanding Viking took
form. He would never tuck down his head, be afraid to look
at her. He knew what he wanted and took it. Where was he
now when they both needed him? Just the thought of her
Norseman filled her with borrowed strength. It poured into
her soul, bringing an impatience. She straightened and
stared boldly.

His head jerked up, and for a fleeting second she saw the
blaze that was her Viking in his stare. Then his look
wavered. "I—uh—came to apologize. It's just that every
time I see you with . . . I—uh," he stammered again.
Reaching into his shirt pocket, he pulled out the tiniest
package and thrust it to her. "I saw this when I was in
Oregon City. Thought you might like it."

Taking it, Rachel accidentally brushed Jake's hand. She
flinched, and heat rushed to her cheeks. How quickly her
newfound courage collapsed. For fear her eyes would betray
her erratic emotions, she lowered her gaze and concentrated
on opening the string-tied bit of brown paper.

"Have you been making out all right while I was gone?"

Afraid her voice would wobble, she merely nodded as she
peeled back the wrapping.

"You look real good." His words were soft but sure.
"With your hair down like it is now, you're even prettier
than you were in that low-necked dress you had on."

"You liked the dress?" she asked. Glancing up, she
almost lost herself in his yearning expression.

"Yes," he breathed.

Quickly, she diverted her attention to her task as her fumbly fingers unfolded a layer of tissue. In its midst lay a ring. The prisms of its crystal-blue stone danced in the lamplight. "Oh, my." She held it aloft. "Blue sapphire just like my father gave me." Her eyes flooded with tears as she looked past the gift to Jake's dear face. "You bought this for me?"

"Put it on. See if it fits." His words came stronger, more confident.

She slipped the ring on her third finger, the marriage finger. It felt only slightly loose. She swiped the blinding wetness from her eyes and held her hand before the lamp, turning it to catch the light. "It's lovely. So right. Not like the horse and buggy Kyle McLean sent me." Even as the words slipped out, she couldn't believe her incredible blunder. Her glance shot to Jake in time to see the shattering of his joy. How could she have mentioned Kyle in this precious moment?

Jake's hands clamped onto the table edge.

"I'm sorry. I don't know what made me say that."

"But since you have, what did you do to make him think you would accept a fancy rig from him?"

"I didn't—I mean, that's not how it happened. You see, when it arrived, I was told it was a gift from the entire community. For visiting the sick."

"So, you're saying McLean tricked you into taking it?" The arrogance in his tone reminded Rachel of those rude interrogating constables in St. Louis.

"I'm not sure. Harvey Best delivered it. He's the one who told me that story." Even to herself, her defense sounded contrived.

"I see." Jake stood abruptly. "For someone who's been tricked and lied to, you sure were enjoying their company."

Her own anger flaring, she shot to her feet, clutching the lapels of the silk wrapper. Poor excuse or not, she would not allow him to talk to her as if she were a fool. "If by that you mean I was handling the situation in a civilized manner, then—''

''*Civilized?* You thought you should be civilized with a cheating liar like McLean?'' He leaned across the table at eye level with her.

Her instinct told her to back away, but he'd challenged her. She stood her ground. ''He always treats me with respect.''

Jake chuckled but without humor. ''Right. That's what I told him tonight when he wanted me to ante you up as the prize for the horse race. I said, 'McLean, that's real respectful of you.' That was just before he pulled a gun on me.''

''*What?* He wouldn't do such a thing.''

''Believe what you want.'' He shoved his chair up to the table. ''I'm going. I've had about all the civilization I can take for one day.'' He wheeled around.

He was leaving her! Running away again! Not this time. Not till things between them were settled. Rachel sprinted after him, catching him by the arm just before he reached the front door. ''Oh, no you don't. Not like this.'' She turned him around and looked up, but couldn't read his expression in the darkness of the hall. She could only hear his breathing, feel the warmth of his body so near.

''Why not?'' he grated. ''We'll just fight about McLean again.''

She pulled at his arm. ''We don't have to.''

Covering her hand with his, he sighed. ''Maybe not, but someone else is bound to come between us—someone just as citified. When I married you, I took you out of your proper place. I've finally come to understand that I have no right to you. I tried to make you happy. But I . . .''

He was freeing her? Leaving her? ''Please!'' She sprang forward and clutched the front of his shirt. ''Don't! Wait! Not tonight. I need you.''

Jake's breath stopped short. The fear in her voice ripped through his gut as her fingers clawed at him. She was just as scared as he was. He wrapped his arms around her, surrounding her, protecting her.

Rachel moaned a soft mewling sound, and her hands shot up, encircling his neck. "Stay with me."

The words struck Jake's loins with stunning force. He lowered his face into a billow of her hair and breathed deeply. The scent of Rachel stole all reason.

She hugged closer, and he felt the softness of her breasts as they molded to him. He felt her need in the hasty beat of her heart as it thudded against his chest. She wanted him. And God knew he wanted her. Later—he'd think later. Bringing a hand down to cup her rounded bottom, he pressed her against his increasing arousal.

A thrill chased down to Rachel's womb. She laced fingers through his hair and pressed her lips to the top of his bowed head. "You'll stay?" A wispy strand of his blond thatch feathered with her words.

His breath blew hot and moist against the slender column of her neck. "Yeah." He began to move against her tightly pressed body.

"Oh, yes," she crooned and drew his head deeper into the hollow of her shoulder.

"I've missed you." His words drew her gaze, dark and languid, to meet his. Naked desire stampeded through him. He scooped her up. "Which way?"

"Up the stairs. To the left."

The urgency in her voice sent him racing to the top.

A giggle bubbled from Rachel as she nibbled at his ear.

Kicking open the door, he strode to the side of the bed, then lowered her feet to the floor. His hands, his body, reveled in every one of her womanly curves as she slid down.

Going up on her toes, she pulled his face close again. "I missed you, too," she whispered, then traced his lips with her tongue.

Another hot hungry jolt rocked through him.

She felt it. A throaty chuckle poured from her.

He covered her mouth with his in a crushing kiss, and her laughter crumpled into a low moan.

Her lips began to move beneath his with force, challenging his hungry assault with her own demands. Her tongue met his, playing, teasing, then inviting him in.

Her willingness so overwhelmed him, every fiber of his body throbbed. He tightened his grip, and drove deeply into her mouth.

She groaned.

Was he holding her too tight? Hurting her? He forced himself to release her and move back a space.

She frowned and bit her lower lip. Why had he pulled away so abruptly? Did he think her too brazen?

Seeing her hurt expression, Jake brought her hands to his lips. "I didn't mean to be so rough."

"You weren't. But if my noise bothers you—"

"No, don't stop. I love every sound you make." His eyes on her face, he kissed each palm, then made tiny circles with his tongue.

Her lashes drifted shut and a lazy smile played at the corners of her lush lips.

He reached for the tie that held her dressing gown together and pulled it loose. It fell apart, exposing the taut, waiting crests of her full, uptipped breasts.

They beckoned, and her ripe mouth parted enticingly.

The quicksilver touch of Jake's hands slid the silk cloth from Rachel's shoulders, then he took full possession of her breasts. Her breath caught as he rubbed his thumbs across the peaks. She felt them harden beneath his exquisite ministrations. It seemed like centuries since he'd last touched her there. Frantic to join the pleasure, her hands flew to the buttons of Jake's shirt and unfastened them. All the while, his hands telegraphed wave after wave of sweet pain to her core. She jerked the shirttail out of his trousers and shoved past the gaping fabric to explore his every muscle. From the hard ripples at his abdomen, her greedy hands moved up to the swells of his furry chest, then on to his bulging shoulders. Reaching the cords of his neck, she felt the vibration of a soundless groan.

Jake removed is hands from her, leaving behind cold where

he'd been. He lowered her arms to her sides and held her away. He needed another look to be sure it was really her. A shaft of moonlight fell across her loveliness, veiling her perfection in a silver glow. "You're so beautiful," he said, his words husky, thick. When he could bear no more, he released her and took her face into his hands. He gently pressed his mouth to her soft, full lips.

The slowness of Jake's overtures was beginning to drive Rachel crazy. Couldn't he tell she needed him? Now? She reached up and pulled him closer, demanding entrance in his mouth until he opened to her. Testing, teasing, she thrust and parried like a fencer until he again matched her fevered entreaties.

Rachel's flaming insides turned to molten liquid. Her legs trembled. Her head reeled. She swayed against his bared chest, skin touching skin. *She wanted more.* She wrenched her mouth from his and ripped his shirt from his shoulders.

Breathing heavily, his eyes hungry, he stepped back. His hands slipped from her face and down the sides of her warm satiny throat, then meandered downward till they captured her supple breasts again.

Rachel groaned, her breath coming in rapid pants. *"Please."* Her urgency was unmistakable.

After one last second, Jake let go of her and worked his arms out of his sleeves while she grabbed the end of his belt and unhooked it. Unbelieving, he watched her flip her tumbling locks out of the way and begin to claw at the buttons trapping him inside his britches. The intensity of her desire for him sparked a wildfire beyond anything he'd ever known. He grabbed her hands. "Let me. I can do it faster."

Her eyes dark as midnight, she climbed onto the bed. "Hurry."

Hurry? As if he were being timed, he dropped down beside her and jerked off his boots.

He was about to jump up and shuck his trousers when she raised herself up behind him. Throwing her arms around his neck, she rubbed her hardened nipples across his back and, nibbling one shoulder, she ruffled his thick Scandian hair.

Jake took a ragged breath. "If you don't stop that—"

"Stop what?" she whispered, trailing kisses down his arm.

Swinging around, Jake caught her by the shoulders and lowered her to the pillow. "You'd better let me get my britches off, or we're both going to be sorry."

"Is that a promise?"

The naked lust in Rachel's voice brought Jake to the brink. He yanked off his remaining clothes and rolled toward her.

Her heart lurched. She beheld the evidence of his desire, freed, ready to drive past her grinding ache, ready to pierce deep into the throbbing heart of her hunger. Only he had the power to reach to the other side of her need. She opened herself and beckoned with outstretched arms.

Jake spread himself over her, flowing across every inch of skin like a sea of fire, searing, inflaming. Feverishly, she reached for that part of him that had been withheld from her. It pulsated with life as she guided it into her.

Jake buried his hands into her hair and vanquished her in a wrenching kiss. His tongue drove into her mouth. At the same instant, he thrust into her.

Moaning, she arched against him, and raked her fingers across his back.

Jake drew himself out, slowly, feeling her quiver with every inch. Never had she been like this. So bold, so good. He wanted to taste all of her, savor her, but he couldn't slow the raging pitch of his own need. He thrust into her, hard, fast. Again and again. Deeper. He felt her tighten, drawing him, taking him farther . . . until his impatient seed burst forth.

She cried out and wrapped her legs around him, clasping him to her. She held fast, drowning in ecstasy. Then, as if reborn, she soared up into an explosion of stars.

Jake collapsed onto her, then rolled to the side, pulling her close. His desire not fully sated, he molded her to him as he ran his fingers across the hot, moist skin of her back and sprinkled kisses about her damp face.

She returned them, kiss for kiss, as her hand rode down his ribs and over a hip, then back again, reveling in the smooth hardness of his body.

"Rachel," Jake whispered, choked with feelings of love he could not contain. "My sweet, sweet Rachel. I—"

A loud bang shattered the night, followed by excited voices.

Rachel jerked upward. Her heart stopped. "Oh, dear! The Grillses have returned." Pushing Jake aside, she tried to vault off the bed, but he pulled her back.

"Sounds more like they're whooping it up over at the saloon." Jake circled an arm around her.

"No. I don't think so." Rachel scooted out from under him and ran to the window.

Three riders pulled their horses to a wrenching halt in front of the saloon. One of them, Ben Stockton from the barn dance, shot his rifle into the air.

Jake rushed up behind Rachel and held back the curtain as, in a yelling confusion, patrons poured out the door, Harvey included.

"Fire! Fire!" shouted the riders. Pointing toward the river, they galloped off toward the wharf.

Rachel craned her head out the window, with Jake just above doing the same. A bright glow lit the eastern sky.

Jake clutched her shoulders. "My God, it looks like our place!"

((chapter 24))

"I'M going with you," Rachel said as they rushed around in the dark gathering their clothes.

"No. You'd slow me down." Jake searched the floor under the bed. "There it is." He dragged out a boot.

Rachel jerked a gray work dress over her head, then, eyeing him, spoke with emphasis. "I am going. It's as much my home as yours."

The last boot on, Jake headed for the door. "You'd just get in the way, and you might get hurt."

"I will be going—with you or on my own." She jammed her foot into a shoe, not bothering with stockings.

Jake wheeled around. "I'm riding horseback."

She stood to meet his challenge. "So? Saddle me one of Mr. Dooley's."

"I didn't know you could ride."

"There's a lot of things you don't know about me."

"You'll have to keep up. I can't wait for you."

Rachel hadn't exactly lied. She *had* ridden a few times as a girl, but with a sidesaddle and always at a slow gait. The gallop down a dark road in the middle of the night tested every speck of her courage as she clung to the horse.

But, much to Rachel's relief, Jake took pity. He slowed Prince several times and waited for her to catch up. About a mile before the cutoff to their place, Jake reined in until Rachel, riding a short-legged horse, came alongside. "The fire. It's not at our place. It's at the Jenningses'!"

"The Jenningses'?" She looked toward the orange glow. "Not again."

"'Fraid so." He kicked Prince in the flanks. "Come on! We've got farther to ride."

Smoke stung Jake's nostrils as he rode across the clearing to Clayton's place. In the harsh glow of the leaping flames, the cabin alone stood untouched. The barn and outbuildings had already collapsed to burning rubble. As he and Rachel neared, the roar and crackle of the inferno, the snap and crash of crumbling timbers, almost drowned out the excited yells of the men trying to prevent the catastrophe from spreading. Twenty or so formed a bucket brigade from the well to the house. They tossed water on the roof and the sides to douse the embers the hot fire wind whipped toward it.

Jake spotted both McLean and Best in the line, their sleeves rolled up and working with the others. It aggravated his sense of justice. He'd be willing to bet money they'd had something to do with this latest "accident." He pulled his rifle from its scabbard.

McLean spotted him and stared back without expression. But when Best saw Jake, his eyes sprang into a frenzied, almost crazed look in the erratic firelight. Was it because he saw Rachel with Jake? Or because he'd somehow learned of the investigation?

Jake dismounted from his nervously prancing stallion, then helped Rachel down from hers. He handed her both sets of reins. "Please take the horses over by the others and tie 'em good to the fence."

Sighting the Jennings family standing off to the side, Jake strode up to them. "Where do you want me?"

Clayton handed Baby Pris to Emily and moved away from her and his son, drawing Jake with him. "Sure glad you came. Remember what we talked about the last time you was here?" The fitful glow of fire enhanced the grim look on his char-smudged face.

Jake bent nearer. "You mean my suspicions about the poisoning?"

"Yeah. You were right. I didn't want to believe it, but it kept pickin' at my brain."

"You found something else?"

"You might say that." Clayton sounded almost chipper, very odd under the circumstances. "Let me tell you about yesterday first." Clayton edged closer. "I passed Charley Bone on the road. An' he asked if I was goin' to the barn raisin'. When I said yes, he got a queer look in those beady little eyes o' his. That's when I decided to stay home. An', sure enough, t'weren't a half-hour after we turned down the lamps for the night. Three of 'em come ridin' in at a dead run, torches burnin'. Before I could get my rifle, they throwed two fire sticks in on my hay. I did manage to shoot the one headin' for the house. Knocked him right outa the saddle. An' I shot the horse out from under another one. But he got away on Cooter's horse."

"You shot Leland Cooter?"

"You say you shot someone trying to burn you out?" Unnoticed by Jake, McLean had left the bucket brigade and moved close enough to overhear. "Is he dead?"

Jake wheeled around to face his adversary.

"No," Clayton drawled. "I got him tied up in the house. We can deal with him when we get the fire out."

"He's in there alone? With no one watching him?" McLean stepped closer.

"He'll keep," Clayton answered with a shrug.

"I'd better go make sure." McLean bumped past Clayton and raced toward the cabin.

Jake started after him.

Clayton grabbed his arm. "Let him go." A strange smile spread across his face. He looked almost daft.

"But if my suspicions are right, McLean just might shoot the bastard. He's got a gun hidden in his coat."

Clayton shrugged again. "So, let him. It'll just be one more thing we can hang him for. You see, me an' Leland already had a nice little chat. He got real talkative . . . real sudden-like."

Jake's own mouth slid into an easy grin. "You don't say.

By any chance," he asked, looking back at the firefighters,
"did Harvey Best's name happen to come up?"

"Sure did," the other drawled. "Along with a couple
other dandies workin' for the government."

"I like the sound of that. But I still better get in there and
stop McLean. We need Cooter alive."

Best must have sensed they were talking about him. He
turned in their direction.

Clayton waved at him in a disarming manner.

Striding toward the cabin, Jake glanced back at Best and
saw his attention suddenly shift. Jake followed his lead and
saw his wife coming.

"Rachel!" Best stepped out of line and rushed to
intercept her.

A shot rang out above the turbulence.

Forgetting Best, Jake ran for the house, with Clayton at
his heels. Just as they reached the porch, McLean walked
out the door, palming his tiny double-barreled gun.

"I got there just in time," McLean said in a loud,
all-encompassing voice. "I shot the culprit just as he was
sneaking out the back window."

Clayton snorted. "Just makes him one less to hang."

McLean took a backward step. "What do you mean?"

"He means," Jake said, raising the barrel of his rifle till
it aimed at a button on McLean's coat, "Cooter was a real
talker. Already spilled his guts."

Coming from where the horses had been tied upwind,
Rachel had heard a sharp clap only a gun could make and
saw Jake dash toward the sound. Something else had gone
awry. She hurried after him.

Passing Carson Grills cranking a bucket up from the well,
she stopped. "Did you hear the shot?"

"Yeah. It came from the house. Didn't know anyone was
in there, but Mr. McLean just came out." He swung his
gaze in that direction and stopped turning the crank.
"Wonder why Jake's holding a rifle on him."

She picked up her skirt and sprinted to the cabin and up the porch steps. "What's the—"

Kyle's arm ensnared her, slammed her against his chest.

Something cold and hard nudged her temple. *A gun.* She lunged forward.

Kyle's grip held fast. "Your timing couldn't be more perfect, my dear," he said close to her ear. "Now, Stone, if you want to see her take another breath, I'd suggest you hand over that rifle."

Jake seemed frozen except for the muscles in his jaw. He stared from Kyle to Rachel and back again.

Kyle pressed the gun harder to Rachel's head. "Now!"

Jake flinched. Then, slowly, he lowered the barrel.

"What's going on here?" demanded a voice from the men beginning to gather below them.

"Stay back!" Kyle yelled and dragged Rachel backward till he hit the log wall. "Here, Stone! Bring it here!"

Her temple throbbed against the lethal steel. "Kyle, have you gone—"

His arm wrenched against her ribs, stopping her.

Jake's gaze reached out to her. Seeing fear on his face frightened her even more. His eyes never leaving hers, he stepped up and offered the weapon.

"Butt first," Kyle spat as he shifted the pistol to Rachel's chest, freeing his other arm.

A muscle twitched in Jake's jaw again. His eyes hardened to brittle shards as he turned to Kyle. Flipping his Hawken, he slapped the wooden stock into the man's hand.

Kyle's finger moved rapidly to the trigger as he brought the barrel up to her husband's belly. "Back!"

Jake's brows formed a mean shelf over his piercing stare as he gave way by a couple of steps. "Let her go, McLean."

"What is it?" Harvey's voice was pitched high with hysteria as he hesitantly climbed onto the porch. His eyes darted to and fro. *"What's going on?"* He stepped between the two men.

"Get out of the way!" Kyle shouted and jabbed the rifle barrel past him to center on Jake again. Then his voice slid

into strangely relaxed tones. "Seem's as though Mr. Cooter's been telling lies about us, Harvey. Accusing us of some
despicable crimes. So the lady and I are leaving. Taking a
little ride. Isn't that right, Rachel?"

Harvey swallowed, his Adam's apple rubbing against his
stiff collar. His excited expression melted. "What lies?"
His gaze drifted to Rachel. He looked at her with pleading
eyes. Suddenly, they snapped wide, and the veins bulged at
his temple as he lashed back at Kyle. "You're lying! Let her
go! She's mine!" He lunged.

"Get back!" Kyle screamed.

The rifle exploded.

Harvey slammed back into Jake. In shocked silence,
Rachel watched him clutch his chest. Blood spewed past his
spread fingers. He stared at her in wide-eyed disbelief as he
collapsed in Jake's arms. His head slumped forward. His
mouth fell open.

Kyle tossed the spent rifle off the porch.

Dazed, Rachel followed the weapon to the ground. Men
crowded close—Sublette Simpkins, Ben Stockton, and a
blur of others. Their expressions were dark with rage.

Kyle clamped Rachel tighter, then in a halting sideways
walk, hauled her off the porch, making sure he faced Jake
and the others at all times. "Don't follow," he commanded
as he backed toward the horses. "If I so much as hear a twig
snap, she's dead."

Rachel clung to Kyle as the gray stallion sped them down
an unfamiliar wagon trail leading north. Behind them, Kyle
towed Jake's Thoroughbred. He had refused to tell her why
he'd killed Harvey—*murdered* the poor man. Why he'd
taken her hostage. And Jake's face had been twisted,
tortured, his every muscle straining as he'd helplessly
watched Kyle take her. Something had gone terribly,
horribly wrong. But what?

Suddenly, they broke out of the trees and into a small
clearing. Squares of light shone from a small cabin, most
likely Rose's or Esther's. From what Rachel had heard, they

and their husbands were the only people living to the north.

Kyle jerked back on the reins, and the horse came to a skidding halt. In one swift motion, he swung down, pulling Rachel with him. Nearly crushing her rib cage, he toted her along as he secured both horses to a rail.

"Where are we?" she cried, her panic unmistakable.

He ignored her, all pretense of good manners gone.

Just as they reached the door, it swung open.

"What's the hurry?" Bone said, rubbing one hand down his soiled shirt, while holding a rifle in the other. "Heard you comin' half a mile away. Come real close to shootin' you."

"We have to talk." Kyle shoved Rachel inside.

Her stomach bucked from the stench. She'd never seen such filth. Esther sat at a table, her oversized eyes looking uncharacteristically solemn. A man in buckskins stood behind her. His hand rested on the hilt of a hunting knife.

A moan drew Rachel's gaze past him to the far corner. Curled up in a pile of bedding lay Rose. She rose up on an elbow and stretched a grossly bruised arm toward Rachel.

Rachel gasped. Lamplight reflected off the fresh blood splayed across the scrawny woman's face and down the scraps of ripped clothing hanging on her.

"My God!" Rachel started for her.

The stranger snatched her by the shoulder, stopping her. "Don't fret yourself, little mouse," he drawled in a thin voice. "Me an' the whore just been havin' a little fun." A crazy light shone in his sunken eyes as he leered down at her.

She turned icy with fear. The man was surely possessed.

He moved his evil glance to Rose. "Ain't that right?"

She shrank back into the corner, clutching onto a foul blanket. "Sure," she whimpered in a rush. "Sure, Crow Dog." Collapsing, she began to shake with silent sobs.

Crow Dog. The name blasted into Rachel's brain. Her vision dimmed. She felt light-headed. The madman from St. Louis? This had to be a dream—her worst nightmare.

The beast's nails dug into her arm. "What's the matter, little mouse?"

Kyle grabbed her other side. "Sit down, Rachel, and shut up." He pushed her toward the table.

Dropping into a chair, she swept a strand of tumbled hair from her eyes, then met the fear in Esther's, as the skinny woman fidgeted with an empty tin cup.

"You boys been real busy tonight, haven't you?" The anger in Kyle's clipped words was unmistakable. "Me and the whole countryside's been out to the Jenningses' putting out a fire . . . they know you started."

Bone flicked a quick glance from Kyle to the one from hell. "Well, it didn't look like Jennings was gonna move on, the way folks was bringin' him pigs and chickens and such. An' I knew how you was set on gettin' rid o' him. It ain't our fault Jennings was there. He said he was gonna be at the Stocktons'."

Rachel looked at Kyle with belated understanding and felt incredibly stupid. Jake had warned her—over and over.

"I realize you don't have many brains rattling around up there, Bone," Kyle said, sneering, then diverted his gaze to Crow Dog. "But you, Catlin. I thought you'd know better than to leave someone behind who could finger us all."

"Leland talked?" Bone raised his rifle and walked to the window.

"Couldn't be helped," the vile one said, fingering a beaded Indian fetish hanging from his neck. "We was ambushed. They was shootin' at us from ever' which way. Ain't that right, Bone?"

"What?" At the window, Bone cocked his ear their way. "Oh, yeah, sure, that's right."

"Oh, really?" Kyle smiled with sarcasm.

"Yeah," Crow Dog snarled. "Shot my horse out from under me. And now you owe me the price of another outfit."

"Speaking of owing," Kyle ground out. "Jake Stone dropped in this evening to say howdy."

Rachel couldn't believe Kyle's lack of fear as he strode,

stiff as a general, to face the wiry buckskinned hunter. Crow Dog was sure to kill him, then she'd be left to the crazy one. She looked in his eyes.

But, surprisingly, the insane fire had been banked. "I almost had Stone in my sights, but he got wind o' me. Been doggin' my trail for days. Just got shed o' him last night." The wild blue glint crept back into his eyes. His hand edged toward his knife again. "Almost drowned myself in the river doin' it, too."

Had he tried to murder Jake? Rachel stared at the bone-handled knife. Was that the one he'd used to slice off the prostitute's ear in St. Louis? The thought sent shivers to her fingertips.

To Rachel's relief, Kyle had the sense to ease back and spread his arms. Dangerous as he was, the other was a fiend.

"What's done is done," Kyle said. "I suppose you know that twenty men will be riding this way before morning. I've stalled 'em for a little while. Told 'em I'd kill the girl if they followed, but that won't stop 'em too long."

Crow Dog's vile gaze swung to Rachel, and his thin lips stretched into a twisted grin.

"I'm finished here in Oregon." Kyle moved to the table. "You idiots have seen to that."

Esther, who hadn't muttered a word or moved since Rachel entered, dodged as he swept away the dirty clutter.

Kyle drew a scrap of paper and a pencil from an inside coat pocket. "I'm going to have to leave for good. If you'll hold off Stone and the others for a little while, I'll make you rich men. I have more than ten thousand dollars in the safe at my whorehouse in Astoria."

The two looked at each other and wagged their heads.

"I'm not expecting you to put yourselves in danger. I know you have to get out, too—Cooter fingered everyone. All I ask is that you ride a little ways toward Jennings's place. And when you hear them coming, shoot your rifles a few times. Then you can take off into the woods. That's all I ask. What do you say?" He scribbled something on the paper and thrust it at Crow Dog.

A long, bony hand shot out and took it. He stuffed it inside his belt.

"It's a deal, then? Give the note to my man, Bowles. He'll get it for you." Kyle reached across the table and grabbed Rachel's hand. "Come on. Let's go."

Rachel sprang to her feet, more than willing to leave the inhuman beast behind. She glanced back at poor Rose huddled in the corner, but was too afraid to risk asking if the battered woman could also come.

Crow Dog stepped in front of Kyle. "You'll travel faster without the little mouse." He reached for Rachel.

Strangling a scream, she dodged behind Kyle.

Kyle chuckled and pulled her forward. "Fancy her, do you?"

The man burned her with his searing gaze. "Yeah."

"Any other time she'd be yours. But she owes me." Kyle moved past the man, taking her with him. He opened the door and pushed her ahead of him. "And you can bet I'm going to take a sweet long time collecting."

Rachel couldn't shake the horror she'd witnessed at Bone's cabin and before that at the Jenningses'. Her insides continued to quiver for some time as she and Kyle traveled west through the woods in the faint light of the setting moon. This time Rachel rode Prince, but Kyle held her mount's reins as he had before.

When her mind emerged from visions of Harvey and Rose, Rachel knew she should try to escape, but, although Kyle's threat to shoot her wouldn't have stopped her, his "promise" to return her to Crow Dog if she tried had. All strength poured out of her at the mere thought. She'd have to hang on and wait. Jake would come for her. She had no doubt. The others might insist on waiting till morning, but her Jake would come. He'd save her.

A gunshot cracked in the distance behind them and echoed through the still darkness before fading away.

Jake was coming! He'd reached the cabin. Rachel swung in her saddle and listened for further firing. She waited, straining to hear above the pounding in her ears and the crunch of hooves on the twig-strewn ground.

Even Kyle slowed the pace.

Rachel desperately prayed for more shots. She waited for what seemed an eternity. But there was nothing. Nothing but the hollowness of her hopes, her dreams. Her life crumbled about her. Jake was dead. There could be no other explanation for a lone shot.

"Ha! They got that backwoods son of a bitch!" Kyle kicked at his gray stallion until it loped into a canter.

Jake was dead, as dead as if Kyle had pulled the trigger himself. Rachel's soul and body ached to retreat from the torment, to lapse into numbness, but every time she looked at the murderer's insolent back, every time she filled her eyes with him, hatred burst from her with such force, it wouldn't be denied. She clung to the saddle, determined to stay astride as he led her back to the road to Independence.

Once on it, he whipped his horse into a gallop, and the two powerful Thoroughbreds raced toward the river at a pace no other horse in Oregon could've matched—had one been following. But, of course, Jake wasn't. He never would.

Somehow, someway, she'd make Kyle pay. Her fingers tightened around the pummel in a strangling hold. If need be, with her own hands she'd send him to hell.

chapter 25

AS Kyle and Rachel hurtled through the chill night toward Independence, she turned around to see if the horizon held even the faintest promise of morning. But the darkness seemed to go on without end. This night had started so happily with the merriment of the barn dance. Then Jake had returned, and they'd wondrously found each other again.

The deepest ache gnawed at Rachel's heart as she remembered. Tonight he would've said the words, would've told her he loved her. It had been in his touch, his eyes, the passion of his whisper. He would've told her . . . if not for Kyle McLean.

Rachel squeezed her burning eyes shut for a second. She would give anything to be able to collapse into tears. But she couldn't. They would have to wait. Instead, she aimed her gaze at the center of the heinous rogue's back, her cold-stiffened finger jerking the trigger of a nonexistent rifle. McLean. Poisoner, barn burner, leader of scum. Murderer of poor foolish Harvey. . . And with her own ears, she'd heard the shot that ripped away her husband's life. McLean would pay. God help her, she'd find a way.

And the hellish darkness dragged on until, slowing his horse, Kyle gathered in Prince's reins.

As her animal drew abreast, Rachel could barely resist the urge to tear out Kyle's eyes. If she stretched just a little, they would be within reach.

Suddenly, Kyle's hand shot out and grabbed the back of her cascading hair. He yanked her close and leaned within inches of her face, his eyes piercing hers. "We're almost to the dock." His breath pelted her as she clawed at his unyielding fingers. "Make one sound, do anything, and I'll kill the Riggins boy. Then I'll strangle you and throw your body in the river." He jerked harder. "You got that?"

Rachel ignored the pain and returned his look with one of utter contempt, refusing to give in to him in the least.

His jaw snapped shut, and his other hand moved toward her throat.

The same instant, Prince nipped at the other stallion, and both animals squealed and shied.

In a scramble, Kyle thrust her away and grabbed Prince's reins, then nudged his mount forward to gain control.

Rachel's heart still drummed heavily in her chest as they clomped down onto the empty dock. She'd have to be more careful, more subtle. It was vital to stay alive until she reaped her just revenge. She couldn't die until she'd seen him begging for mercy. Oh, God, yes.

"My luck's still holding." Kyle dismounted. "The ferry's on this side. And no one's here." He led the horses onto the raft, then poled them away from the edge.

Rachel searched the opposite shore, hoping to see a light, someone waiting for the return of the firefighters. But all was silent in the predawn darkness.

Then she suddenly realized that the overconfident fool had played into her hands. He had not ordered her to dismount, and he stood directly in front of her, pulling on the tow rope threaded overhead. If she but slammed her heels into Prince's flanks, the horse would bolt, toppling Kyle into the deep, swift water.

Gripping tightly to the saddle horn, she raised her stirruped feet . . . but logic intruded. No doubt she could knock Kyle overboard, but most likely Prince would follow, taking her. And she couldn't swim. But that vile devil probably could. She'd drown, and he'd still get away.

With profound regret, she slowly lowered her legs. Later. She'd find a way later. Maybe someone in town was awake and would be able to help.

After reaching the wharf, Kyle avoided the main street. He skirted north, toward Salem. Then, to Rachel's surprise, once the town lay behind them, he returned to the road going west. Then, in the dim light before dawn, he tied Prince's reins to a saddle ring, and he heeled his stallion into a gallop, racing them toward the coast hills.

Riding into the first hour of morning, they passed no one, and the few sets of wagon tracks veering off provided the only evidence of civilization. Finally, Rachel smelled wood-smoke on the crisp breeze as the lane dwindled to two ruts. She knew that at any moment they would break out of the forest and onto one of the last of the family farms.

She tensed, straining to see around Kyle. She needed to be ready to grab Prince's black mane at the first glimpse of someone, to ram into the other stallion, jump off, scream for help. Folks this deep in the wilderness were always ready for trouble. They'd come running with their rifles.

He slowed the horses to a walk, then, to Rachel's utter dismay, led them off the path and into the brambly under-growth. Looking back at her with a deadly glint in his eyes, he opened his coat and displayed the small gun tucked inside.

Grudgingly, she complied with his unspoken order of silence. She had no intention of causing havoc unless she saw a chance to beat him. She did, however, sweep her gaze from his. Having that Judas goat think she was some dumb obedient lamb galled her.

Within minutes, they began a long rugged climb up the first of the coastal hills. The horses, already winded, weary, and lathered from hours of hard travel, strained with this added effort. Rachel suffered with them. A grinding pain spread from her spine, torturing every joint, and the abrasive action of the saddle rubbed her already tender thighs until they felt like peeled flesh.

Halting abruptly, Kyle dismounted, then turned to Rachel. "The horses need a rest. Get down."

Stiff as old leather, she lowered herself to the ground. Her feet tingled and felt as if they weren't quite touching earth.

Several minutes of walking passed before she sensed them securely beneath her. Bare of stockings, she felt several spots burning, the obvious beginnings of blisters. She gritted her teeth and remained silent as the irritations multiplied.

Sometimes riding, sometimes walking, they climbed one ridge after another. The sun gained strength and beat relentlessly down upon them whenever they broke into a clearing. Kyle stopped once to wipe the sweat streaking his face, and Rachel smiled, reveling in his discomfort. Overheated, he still wouldn't remove his frock coat. She suspected he feared his white shirt might be too easy a target. Even if her Jake were dead, she had no doubt others were tracking them. But she also knew it would've been difficult, if not impossible, for her rescuers to read the trail at night. They couldn't be within twenty miles.

Just as surely as her neighbors followed, so did exhaustion. But Rachel refused to let it overtake her. She pushed herself beyond anything she would have ever dreamt possible. At any moment an opportunity to vanquish Kyle might present itself, and she had to be ready.

Kyle's lack of conversation through the hours added to the tension. Always before he'd been such a talker—always confident, often clever. Was this closed, ruthless man the real Kyle McLean? Or was he merely looking for a place to hide his guilt?

Then Rachel thought of Jake lying dead at the evil Crow Dog's feet. Her heart turned to a leaden lump, pressing heavily on her overworked lungs. Her arms and legs hung heavily from her body. Feeling herself collapsing again, giving up, she jounced herself erect and shook the lamenting weariness from her head. She returned her attention to her enemy, who seemed like a brick wall riding in front of her.

Three hours or so after the sun began its afternoon slide, they crested the last high ridge. A cool, moist breeze touched Rachel's chafed cheeks, bringing a precious moment of relief. She lowered her lids over eyes gravelly with need of sleep and breathed deeply.

"It won't be long now," Kyle said with enthusiasm.

Rachel's lashes sprang open at the first words he'd spoken in hours. *It won't be long now?* She followed the direction of his gaze. Down the tree-covered slope, she saw the vast span of the Pacific Ocean sheeted silver by the sun. My God, why hadn't she realized it? Her throat clogged. The bastard wasn't just running. He must know of a logging schooner along the coast. *Maybe one of his own.*

Now, instead of time dragging, it sped by, hurling her downward to Kyle's victory. Rachel willed his weary dappled gray to stumble as it passed each jagged boulder, prayed it would toss the murdering villain headfirst into one.

But Kyle's animal performed with the same surefootedness as the magnificent midnight stallion beneath her. It seemed no time at all before they had descended the steep timbered inclines to reach the coastal strip.

When they came upon a set of wagon tracks, Rachel could already hear the roar of the surf crashing against the shore and smell the tangy salt air coming through the screen of dark evergreens.

Kyle pulled out his pocket watch and checked the time. Then, without a backward glance, he wheeled his horse, and headed south, nudging the stallion into a faster pace.

South, not north? No doubt remained. He wasn't simply taking a roundabout way to Astoria—he had another destination and even knew what time he needed to be there. *Before high tide.* Frantic new energy poured into her. If someone or something didn't happen along soon, she would have to figure out a way to destroy him by herself.

The dipping sun had lost its power to the first wisps of evening fog just as they reached a cliff overlooking a cove cut into the surrounding forest. Thousands of logs floated in it, creating a cacophony of low thuds as they gently bumped one another. Protecting the still waters from the tides, a peninsula of sand dunes stretched from the southern shoreline, nearly enclosing the inlet. And what Rachel had most

dreaded lay moored alongside a pier near the entrance . . .
a two-masted schooner.

"Bless the Virgin Mary!" Kyle cried. "My ship's still
there." He swung around and smirked.

Rachel flinched before she could stop herself.

"Yes, sir, bless that virgin," he said and presented her
with a grotesque tooth-baring grin. "And any other virgins
that might be handy."

At the thought of his loathsome hands on her, her
stomach roiled with revulsion. She averted her gaze.

He chuckled with confidence.

The sound grated against her already raw nerves.

He led the way to a path that zigzagged downward.
Lower and lower they went, closer and closer to the logging
ship. She felt as if she were being sucked into hell's own pit.
If only the bluff were higher or steeper, she'd willingly
sacrifice her own life to force him off.

Within minutes, they reached a strip of sand edging the
gently lapping water and headed for the dock jutting past
timber on the near side and the devil's ship on the other.

Too soon they reached the planked narrow structure. As
Kyle led them onto it, Rachel's panic mounted to volcanic
proportions. She knew she couldn't allow herself to be taken
aboard. Suddenly she spotted some men—one man cranking a wench, and two others guiding a log out of the water.
Thank God, they would save her. When she and Kyle rode
close, she would scream for help. They could pull him down
before he knew what happened.

But would they act fast enough? She didn't want the
murdering reprobate to kill anyone else for trying to save
her.

They *would* be quick. They had to be. This was her last
chance.

She felt Kyle staring at her. She veered her attention to
his sublimely smug face.

"I wouldn't try anything if I were you. You'd just make
it harder on yourself. You see, I own the ship . . . the

captain . . . *and* the crew.'' Turning forward again, his
shoulders bounced with another chuckle.

His mocking laughter shattered the last of her control.
Fury exploded through her veins, blinded her with its force.
She grabbed her horse's mane and wrenched it in Kyle's
direction. Then, smashing heels into her stallion's sides, she
pierced the air with a shrill war cry.

Prince jumped forward and slammed into the gray's
rump.

The startled animal reared, its hooves thrashing the air. Its
hind legs danced toward the edge of the pier. Ten feet
below, a flotilla of logs waited to crush him under.

Kyle's eyes flared wildly as he clung to the saddle.

A back hoof slipped off. The animal screamed. Its
scrambling front legs returned to the deck just in time to
save itself.

And the devil held fast.

She would have to dislodge him herself. She lashed at her
own frightened mount's flanks again, then yanked her feet
out of the stirrups as Prince slammed alongside Kyle. She
lunged for him.

The last thing Rachel heard as she took Kyle down into
the sea of timber was his shrieking epithet.

''Bitch!''

A fierce throbbing in her head pulled Rachel to con-
sciousness. Her arm and side ached and she lay on something rock-hard . . . but unsteady beneath her. She tried to
open her eyes. They wouldn't obey. One of her hands rested
on the swaying surface. She managed to move her palm
slightly and felt the rough grain of wood. *She was floating?
On a board?* Soft thudding echoed all about.

And cold! She'd never endured such a bone-aching chill.
Starting to shiver, she tugged a musty-smelling blanket
tighter around her.

"The horses took off up the bluff," a man's voice called
in the muted distance. "Want us to chase 'em down?"

"There isn't time. We'll lose the tide. It's imperative I

leave this evening.'' The voice belonged to Kyle McLean.

Kyle? Her eyes wrenched open as the horrors of the past twenty-four hours pierced her like jags of ice. Frustrated rage burst into an already bursting temple as she sat up. She'd killed the monster, and he was still alive.

''Hoist the sails and get this tub moving while I change. Where can I find something dry?'' He sounded closer.

''My cabin,'' called the other. ''In the trunk.''

In the dusky light coming from a small window, Rachel leaned up and quickly surveyed her situation. Sopping wet, she sat in a puddle on the floor of a rude little cabin. The dank cell held only one narrow bunk, a table cluttered with papers and maps, and a couple of trunks chained to the wall. Above, a lantern swayed gently from a ceiling hook, and a rain slicker hung by the door.

Rachel's sensitized ears picked out the sound of footsteps among the other bangs and scrapes of a ship readying for departure. They grew louder. He was coming!

She scrambled halfway to her feet, only to fall again in a heap. One of her legs was numb. Frantically, she reached down to massage it.

The door swung open, and Kyle's silhouetted form filled the undersized portal. ''So, you're going to live after all.'' Ducking, he stepped through and closed the door behind him. ''If it'd been up to me, I would've left you to drown. But my men didn't know you were trying to kill me.''

Brushing aside a string of damp hair, Rachel eyed the drenched polecat, then quickly resumed rubbing the life back into her useless limb.

''You cost me the two horses. I could've gotten two, maybe three thousand for each of 'em in San Francisco.'' Kyle strode toward her.

Blood racing, Rachel thrust her hands out to ward him off.

But he passed her by. He walked to the table against the wall and unscrewed the lid of a small can. Withdrawing a match, he struck it, and lit the lantern above his head.

The mean, cramped room flooded with light.

"I guess I'll have to be extra inventive to make up the difference." He blew out the match. "There is that hefty bank account of yours. Yes, my pet, I know about that. Ran across it in some of Harvey's papers. After I get my hands on it, think I'll offer you to old Chang Sun, a little yellow devil down at the wharf. He'll pay plenty for a pretty little round-eye like you." He stood beneath the light, shadows exaggerating his vile features as he nodded. "Of course, that's after *I've had my fill.*"

His words barely had time to register. The ship lurched beneath her. It was moving! Leaving! She sprang to her feet and lunged for the door.

Before she could wrench it open, Kyle caught her hair and yanked her back against him.

Crying out, she clawed at the punishing fingers.

He tightened his grip, pinning her back against his chest, and reached around with his other hand. Closing it over one of her breasts, he gave a sharp twist.

She bucked against him, tore at his steellike grip.

A low, lusting chuckle taunted her. "This isn't exactly how I thought we'd spend our honeymoon." His crooning words seared her ears like a hot poker. "But a long voyage does sound romantic, doesn't it?"

"Never!" Rachel rammed a heel into his shin.

He yelped and jumped back. An instant later, he spun her around, slammed her up against the door, and ripped open her bodice.

In a wild whir, she battered his face and chest.

He threw himself against her. Straddling her, he caught her wrists and pulled them above her head. He trapped them in one of his, then bent within inches of her straining face and smiled. "Mad as a wet hen, eh? Must be those soaked clothes. Not to worry. I'll have you out of 'em and into a warm bed before you can ruffle another feather."

"Grab that rope!" came a voice from outside the door.

Rachel opened her mouth to scream.

Kyle's lips ground against hers, smothering her cry. The

beast continued his attack on her mouth as he mashed his weight against her.

Heaving against him, she felt his manhood grow hard. The knowledge that her struggling only succeeded in arousing him shocked her into stopping. She froze in place except for her panting gasps.

Kyle released her mouth and smiled. "You're proving to have a lot more spirit than I thought you capable of. We're going to have a lot of fun." He eased away, his leer traveling downward. A hand flashed out and ripped a tear in her flimsy camisole.

She spit in his face and slammed her knee up between his legs.

His eyes flared with stunned pain. He let her go.

Rachel dodged out of the way as the cur stumbled against the door and doubled over, clutching himself, moaning like a wounded bull.

Free! But she had to get past him. Wildly, she looked about for a weapon.

"I'll . . . kill . . . you," he managed between clenched teeth as, hunched over, he staggered toward her.

Rachel could find nothing. Except the lantern. She snatched it and flung it at his face.

But the devil deflected it, batting it against the wall above the cot. It shattered, spilling oil down and all over the bed. Flames chased the splatters with consuming fury.

"You bitch!" Kyle railed. He grabbed the blanket off the floor and stumbled toward the burning bed.

Rachel bolted out the door and ran for the railing, but in the growing darkness, she banged into something. A stack of logs.

"Fire!" yelled someone high up in the forward mast. "Fire in the captain's cabin!"

Two sailors rushed past her, and another came from around the side. They ripped off their jackets and rushed into the blazing room.

Rachel heard them yelling and thrashing at the flames as she reached the end of the log stack. She cut to the rail, prepared to jump across to the dock. But the bow end of the ship had already cleared the pier. She swung around and raced toward the stern.

"Get water!" Kyle yelled from the captain's quarters.

Sneaking past, Rachel looked in the small window at the inferno . . . and tripped over a coil of rope. She sprawled onto the deck.

A circle of light poured over her, and a strong hand gripped her arm and pulled her to her feet. "What's goin' on?" asked a ruddy-faced seaman.

"Fire! They need help! I'll take the lantern." Rachel wrenched the handle from him.

The man's attention veered toward the flame-filled window. He released her and started forward.

Kyle careened around the corner. "Get that woman!"

Rachel spun away, but the sailor dove after her and caught her skirt. She whirled and swung the light at him.

He ducked, stumbling backward, freeing her.

In the circle of lamplight, she ran toward the stern as more of the ship slipped past the end of the pier.

"Get her!" Kyle yelled again, and she heard boots pounding after her.

Dodging around another stack of timber, wet skirts slapping against her legs, she reached a section of railing with the dock still alongside. She lifted her skirts and slung a leg over. But the ship had drifted several feet from the pier. She clambered atop to jump.

Someone snatched her back. "I've got you now, you flyblown bitch!"

Kyle. With all her strength, she swung the lantern up toward his head.

He ducked.

It soared free, like a glowing rainbow, and crashed into a yardarm. Flames shot into the billowing canvas. Incited by the breeze, fire licked out in every direction.

Kyle wound jerky fingers into her vulnerable tresses again, and yanked her to him, forcing her up on her toes to face him. His mouth twisted with rage. "You'll beg to die, before I'm through with you."

With a snarl, she raked his face.

He drew back a fist . . . and stopped. His eyes popped wide as he peered past her. His hand dropped from her hair.

She whirled around.

Swinging on a boom chain, Jake soared out of the night toward them.

((chapter 26))

JAKE hit the deck with the grace of a pouncing panther. His eyes, flashing cuts of emerald, stabbed Kyle with contempt.

"Jake!" Rachel's joy uncontainable, she sprang forward. She rushed toward that glorious face burnished gold by the light of the flame-swept sails.

In one fluid motion, Jake caught her and set her aside as he advanced toward his prey. "Stay behind me."

Kyle looked around with frantic eyes. "Sanders! Men!"

But, Rachel thought, congratulating herself, the crew was far too busy fighting the spreading fires to notice an intruder. Kyle's cries for help merely mingled with the cracks, snaps, and bumps punctuating the roaring blaze that raced along the rigging and down the mast.

He dodged backward. An agitated hand searched furiously, vainly, inside his coat. The dismayed twist of his brow announced that his derringer was missing.

A sundering clap resounded above Rachel's head. She darted a glance upward.

A ball of flame hurled toward her.

"Rachel!" Jake seized her and dove across the deck.

She landed beneath him, the wind knocked out of her.

He sprang to his feet, bringing her with him. "Are you all right?" he cried above the bedlam. Worry creased the sculpted planes of his brow.

Gasping for breath, she nodded and waved him off.

"Get to the stern!" He pushed her in that direction, then wheeled about.

Still struggling for air, Rachel backed away as she watched him leap over the blaze of a fallen spar.

He ran toward the bow. Dodging with agile prowess through a cascade of burning debris, he veered to starboard then back to portside, then . . . vanished into a wall of smoke.

Rachel sprinted forward. She couldn't lose him again.

Jake moved past the acrid smoke roiling out of a smoldering rag bin. He rubbed the tears from his eyes and searched for McLean among a half-dozen men desperately, uselessly, flailing at the fire-engulfed deck structures with wet blankets and buckets of water.

"Grab a pail!" yelled one, not questioning Jake's presence. He pointed toward a stack next to a rain barrel.

"Where's McLean?"

No one took the time to even glance his way.

With a screeching crack, the top of the forward mast crashed down onto the portside of the cabin.

The men dove out of the way.

"It's no use!" yelled one. "Abandon ship!"

Tossing buckets and blankets away, the men banged past Jake and jumped into the dinghy bobbing alongside.

Jake rushed to the rail and looked down into a sea reflecting the holocaust. He searched for McLean among the crew, then scanned the water fruitlessly for a lone swimmer. Swatting at falling embers, he charged to the other side and surveyed the area between the ship and floating logs.

Not a single head appeared in the glaring water.

"McLean!" Rachel screamed.

Jake spun toward the sound. Feeling a rush of air and hearing a splintering crash behind him, Jake spun back.

A mangled bucket came at him again with blurring speed.

Jake swerved too late. It caught the side of his head. He stumbled back, seeing nothing but an explosion of stars.

"Jake!" Rachel's shrill cry pierced the haze and jerked him alert. He locked onto the marauding determination in McLean's eyes as the bastard swung again.

"I'll teach you to mess with me! You stupid moose!" McLean slung the bucket with all his strength.

It glanced off Jake's forearm as he lunged for McLean.

The coward sprang backward. Escaping Jake's grasp, he shot to the portside and flung himself over.

Jake caught him by one boot.

Dangling down the side, McLean screamed and kicked as if he were caught in a bear trap.

Jake strengthened his hold with a second hand before turning to find his wife. Her face was scored with the embattled fear of a hunted animal, and her hair, tangled about her, only partially hid the tattered front of her dress. He ached to go to her, to comfort her, and would after he dealt with McLean.

The aft mast exploded into flames at its base. Eyeing the teetering pole, Rachel backed into the railing.

"Jump!" Jake yelled.

Her frantic gaze darted from him to the water below and back again. "I can't swim!"

With a deafening crack, the mast broke.

Jake looked up. His heart stopped.

The fiery rigging tipped in Rachel's direction.

Dropping the flailing McLean, he lunged for her and swept her overboard.

That instant, the huge beam crashed behind them.

She clung to him with strangling ferocity as he took her deep, below the carnage. He swam underwater with all his might, till he'd outdistanced the burning debris and Rachel began to struggle.

Surfacing, Jake sighted the pier with a group of men lining it. With his gasping wife in tow, he swam to them.

"Jake? Mountain Jake? Is that you?" called a silver-haired man.

"Yeah. That you, Captain Sanders?" Jake returned while pulling Rachel past the docked dinghy to a ladder.

The man's wiry brows spiked. "Where the hell did you come from?" He reached down. "Let me give you a hand."

Jake hoisted Rachel out of the water and onto a rung. "Thanks. Help my wife up."

The captain grabbed her wrist and hauled her to the top, looking from her to Jake. "What the hell you doing in the—Did you say wife?"

"Tha-that's r-right," Rachel sputtered through chattering teeth.

"McLean said you was one of his girls from Astoria." Disbelief rang in the hoarse voice of a bearded seaman as he stripped off his jacket and wrapped it around her shoulders.

"Th-thank you." Her attempt at a smile only made her look more pitiful. "K-Kyle McLean was tr-trying to k-kidnap me."

"McLean did what?" boomed the captain.

Jake turned to search the ever-widening space between the pier and the drifting inferno. "Anyone seen him?"

A rumble of no's and wagging heads answered him.

Captain Sanders turned and pointed to a couple of men. "You and you. Get back in the dinghy. Find Mr. McLean while there's still light from the ship."

"I'm going, too," Jake said. "The bastard's also wanted for murder, among other things."

"Who'd he kill?" asked one man.

"When?" another asked.

"The land recorder and a no-account that worked for him, then he took my wife to make good his escape." Jake's gaze slipped from them to his shivering Rachel huddled in the sailor's jacket. "Take her to the foreman's shack and get her into something dry. She's had a real rough time."

"But what about you?" she cried, reaching out to him.

"Get her inside," Jake yelled and clambered down to the small boat.

Hovering close to the potbellied stove in the privacy of the splintery little shack, Rachel began to thaw. Prickles from the scratchy wool blanket cocooning her bare skin replaced the numbness. And she felt alive, really alive. Her magnificent Oregon Viking had rescued her.

Smiling, she closed her eyes and hugged the cover tighter, hoarding the exhilarating moment. What a sight he'd made, swinging aboard ship. Just like in her dream . . . no, better. Her very own live hero, swooping in to rescue her from the dastardly villain. She stretched out her hand and let his treasured gift, the blue-gemmed ring, shimmer in the lamplight.

And now her Jake was out there, bringing that lowlife reprobate to justice. A stab of fear shot through her. What if Kyle found him first? Bashed him in the head with a chunk of beam. Killed him.

No! She refused to let her thoughts take her in that direction. She couldn't bear to consider the possibility. Not now. Not after the suffering she'd endured before when she thought Jake had been killed.

The door burst open.

Kyle, her frayed mind screamed. She whirled around.

But it was Jake! Her big, handsome husband slammed the door behind him and rushed for her.

Joy danced through her as she stretched out to him.

But he swerved past her. To the stove Placing shaking hands over it, he mumbled something unintelligible through teeth that clattered as loud as a herd of horses racing down a cobbled street.

"My word, Jake. You're going to catch pneumonia." With flying fingers, Rachel unbuttoned his shirt and stripped the wet thing away, then unbuckled his belt.

"Having you undress me," he ventured in a jerky voice, "is getting to be a habit I could get used to real easy."

Unhooking a trouser button, she lifted her gaze to revel in his shivery attempt at a smile, before meeting green eyes that had turned quite scampish. "That could be arranged. But, first, did you get McLean?"

"Yeah."

"Sit on the bed so I can take your boots off." She pushed him toward the cot along the side wall. "Did he give you any trouble?"

Jake sat down and extended a foot, while watching her tuck the top of the blanket over her bosom. "Who?"

"McLean, of course." Turning her back to him, Rachel straddled his leg and pulled off the soggy boot.

Just having her cute little rear so close began to thaw him. Watching it wiggle, he almost forgot to answer. "No."

"He gave up without a struggle?" The soggy leather hit the floor with a thud.

He lifted his other foot and watched her move to it. "He's dead."

She turned hesitantly, her gaze not quite meeting his. "Did you kill him?"

"No." He waved his uplifted leg at her. "Get the other one."

She yanked it off and chucked it away as he continued.

"The mast must've come down on him. We found him caught in the rigging, floating facedown."

"Oh, dear." Only a short time ago she, herself, had tried to kill him. But that was before she knew Jake was alive.

"I wouldn't waste too much sympathy on him if I were you. If I hadn't arrived when I did, we'd be fishing you out instead of him." Standing up, he removed his britches, then pulled her with him to the little round stove. "Now, how about sharing some of your heat?"

Untucking the blanket, her gaze wandered to the golden curls sprinkling his immense chest before lifting to his eyes. Heart jolting in a sharp, sweet lurch, she opened the wrapping to him.

She noticed Jake's own perusal was far from shy as he stepped into her warming embrace, especially since she wore nothing save the ring he'd given her. He cupped her chin. Her breath caught as he outlined her cheek with his thumb. His autumn eyes grew darker, his face lost its amused expression as wonderfully practiced fingers roamed down her throat and over her collarbone to her shoulder.

Every nerve tingled. Her breathing returned in short gasps as she reached out and caressed the smoothly muscled arm that was sending signals of pleasure to every hollow in her body.

"I came so close to losing you." His husky whisper held more emotion than she had ever heard before. "If I hadn't turned back when I did—" He pulled her against him and wrapped them both within the folds of the blanket.

Rachel felt a tremor travel the length of his chilled body. She hugged him close. "It's all right. We're together now. That's all that matters."

He nestled her against his shoulder and kissed the top of her head. "I knew McLean would never go for the Cascades. He'd never give a mountain man that kind of an advantage. I told the others, but they wouldn't listen. They kept on going."

Rachel tilted back and looked up at him. "What are you talking about? Who went where?"

"Most everyone that was at the Jenningses' rode with me after you and McLean. Even with a torch, it's hard to read tracks at night, but before long I knew McLean was headed for Charley Bone's. I almost died when I heard that gunshot. I thought the bastard had killed you." Jake paused and took an uneven breath.

Rachel clung harder. The sound of that awful piercing crack had almost destroyed her, too.

"We were about a quarter-mile from Bone's place when we heard it. I thought I'd find you lying there in a pool of blood. But when we got there we found this wolf of a scalp hunter dead instead, and Cooter's woman was there alone, all beat up and blubbering. We couldn't get much out of her. Just her saying over and over that he had it coming."

Even with Jake standing there, alive, holding her, it was hard to believe that the vile Crow Dog Catlin, not her husband, had taken the lone bullet.

"Anyway," he continued, caressing her with a low, mellifluous voice, "the oldest Stockton boy found two sets of tracks heading east into the mountains. And we all jumped on our horses and started after 'em. But it wasn't more than five minutes before I knew they couldn't be yours. But no one else would listen. So I turned back alone. When I returned to Bone's place, I found your trail."

"You said Rose was there by herself? Most likely those other tracks belonged to Esther and her husband."

"Yeah, that's what I figured. They knew it was time to hightail it. Anyway, I made another torch and started after you. When I realized you were headed back to the road, I knew I was in real trouble. You two were mounted on the best horseflesh in Oregon. So, when I got to Sam's stable, I took a string of mounts. When one wore out, I left him and hopped on the next."

Rachel cozied her head into his shoulder. "And all the time I thought that gunshot had killed you. Words can't express what I went through."

He settled her closer against him, molding her softness to his strength. "So, you missed me a little, did you?" An irritating cockiness permeated his tone.

She stiffened and drew back far enough to view his face. "Might I remind you, dear one, of who it was chasing after whom."

A flaxen brow perked as his mouth fell into a slack grin. "Yeah, you're right. I was real worried. With someone green as you riding Prince, you could've taken him into a hole, broken his leg or something."

Rachel gasped and pushed him away.

But the cool air rushing between them scarcely had time to wash her body before he pressed her to him again, his hands roaming the curve of her hips.

She felt herself melting, then remembered the horse. She pulled back slightly. "I heard the men talking earlier. They said Prince and the other horse ran away."

He hugged her close again. "It's all right. I ran across 'em. I tied 'em up at the top of the bluff."

"That's good." The rhythm of her heart increased as his thumbs wove circles closer and closer to the hithermost region of her desire. "They deserve a good rest." Rachel slid her hands past his waist and traveled up the smooth hardness of his back, wantonly warm, now, beneath her touch. "They've certainly been put through their paces lately."

This time Jake pulled away from her. "Speaking of paces, you've sure been putting me through mine lately, with all these beaus of yours. Just how many more do you have stashed out there waiting for me?"

He watched a delicious smile curve those lush lips of hers. "You're safe. I haven't had time to woo any more."

His hunger for her gaining, he edged her toward the cot along the wall. "That's a relief," he whispered in exaggerated tones as he eased down on the bed, pulling her with him. "There's something about you that makes a man take leave of his senses. Even a lily-livered dandy like Harvey Best was willing to go up against a Hawken for you."

Rachel stretched the length of her body against his. Her leg pressed tauntingly against the hardness of his arousal. "Oh, I think both Harvey and Kyle were far more attracted to all my money than to me."

"Money?" Jake rose up on an elbow and stared down at her. How many more secrets did she have? "What money?"

"It's really nothing. Just my father's bank account Harvey was transferring here for me." She tried to pull him down.

He refused to yield. "How come you never mentioned it before? Just how much do you have?"

Rachel eased away from him and sat up, her gaze wandering off. "Something over twenty-seven thousand."

A mule's kick would have stunned him less. "What else haven't you told me? That you plan to run away from this fool of a mountain man as soon it comes?"

Her gaze returned abruptly to his, and she grabbed his shoulders. "No, Jake, that's not how it is. As a matter of fact," she said, her voice softening, her grip easing, "the money's no longer even mine. The day I married you, it became yours."

"The money isn't important. But the fact you didn't tell me about it is. I needed your trust. Your love."

"But you have that."

She loved him! Her confession sent his anger on the wing. Her fingers toyed with the fringe of his hair, further weakening his resolve. But he *would* have an answer. "If that's so, why didn't you tell me of my great windfall before now?"

Her gorgeous smile drooped into a mocking pout, and she leaned closer, the tips of her breasts bedeviling him. "As a wealthy man, you might have been tempted to leave your prison-tainted wife. Maybe even go back to St. Louis to find the kind of bride you sent for in the first place."

Jake sat up, his eyes narrowed. He frowned. Then, gradually, it faded, and his gaze sparked with mischief. "Did you really think I could ever leave my *'jailhouse rose?'*"

His surprising description of her stopped her for no more than a second. "Prove it." Wrapping an arm around his neck, she pulled him down beside her again.

A grin split his face as she dared him with her eyes. "I don't know. You're turning into such a lusty lady, I don't think this little bed will hold up."

Her expression changed to smug bemusement as she moved against the bold evidence of his desire. "Well, this 'lusty lady' is not above a little blackmail." He gave no resistance as she drew him over her. "If I don't leave this room thoroughly—and I mean thoroughly—bedded, I'm going to introduce you to the whole territory as the honorable Mr. Jacob Obadiah *Cherubim* Stone."

Jake's head jerked up. "You little minx." Then slowly his expression relaxed into a rakish smirk. His eyes turned to a dark smolder as his hand careened over her thigh, down to her velvety haven. "You leave me no choice."

A ragged sigh escaped at the mere thought of her Viking lover piercing the heart of her need. Overtaken with eagerness, she grasped his ready weapon and hurried it home.

Every nerve throbbed with the teasing leisureliness of his entry, his slow glide into her hot silken sheath.

She moaned and arched upward in her own impatient pursuit, taking him all the way to the hilt.

Jake felt her whole body clamoring for him, recklessly urging him to match her frenzy. He drove into her, deeper, deeper. She moaned and his mouth found hers in a dizzying, breath-stopping kiss. When there was no more air left in him, he relinquished her lips and looked down at his golden-haired beauty. At the sight, a profound peace washed over him. He stilled himself to savor the moment.

Her feathery lashes rose, and her eyes, a dusky invitation, held him.

The look sent him dangerously close to bursting too soon. He checked himself by remembering the words that had spurred them into such fiery lovemaking. "You seem to have me where you want me, my blackmailing little vixen. Satisfied?"

"I'm sure I will be," she whispered. Her breath tickled his ear. "Soon."

He thrust into her.

With pulsating waves so exquisite they bordered on pain, he felt her whole being pour through his with such love and purity that no doubt remained. The sound of her panting breaths, the hurried caress of her hands roaming his back, sated him to his very soul. This beautiful lady truly loved her backwoods homesteader.

In the afterglow, those glorious sky-filled eyes fluttered open and found his, and she gifted him with an incredibly innocent smile. "Well, I suppose your secret's safe, *Cherubim*." Her mouth then tilted into an impish grin. "At least . . . for the moment."

"That's my little jailhouse rose. God a'mighty, how I do love you."

FREE
Romance
(a $4.50 value)

Send in the Coupon Below

To get your FREE historical romance and start saving, fill out the coupon below and mail it today. As soon as we receive it we'll send you your FREE Book along with your first month's selections.

Mail To: **True Value Home Subscription Services, Inc. P.O. Box 5235**
120 Brighton Road, Clifton, New Jersey 07015-5235

YES! I want to start previewing the very best historical romances being published today. Send me my FREE book along with the first month's selections. I understand that I may look them over FREE for 10 days. If I'm not absolutely delighted I may return them and owe nothing. Otherwise I will pay the low price of just $4.00 each: a total $16.00 (at *least* an $18.00 value) and save at least $2.00. Then each month I will receive four brand new novels to preview as soon as they are published for the same low price. I can always return a shipment and I may cancel this subscription at any time with no obligation to buy even a single book. In any event the FREE book is mine to keep regardless.

Name _____

Street Address _____ Apt. No. _____

City _____ State _____ Zip Code _____

Telephone _____

Signature _____
(if under 18 parent or guardian must sign)

766-5

Terms and prices subject to change. Orders subject to acceptance by True Value Home Subscription Services, Inc.